Shiver

GIULIANA VICTORIA

Editing by Steph White (Kat's Literary Services)

Proofreading by Louise Murphy (Kat's Literary Services)

Jamaican Patois Translation confirmation by Kai (_robyn.reads on Instagram) and Savannah with the help of her amazing mom <3

Illustrated cover by Sonia (artbysoniagx on Instagram)

Typography and hardcover design by Disturbed Valkyrie Designs

Internal formatting and chapter headers designed and drawn by me

Contents

Also by

Philia Players Series

Quiver

Tremble

Quake

Shiver

Book #0: The Prequel (Out May 10, 2026)

Ps. Did you find the title hidden in Shiver? (The title as well as an excerpt from the first book in the rugby series is hidden in Shiver as well!)

Secret Trials Series

Out June 2025!

Rosa Ranch Series

Out August 2025!

Standalones & Novellas

Mistletoe Misconduct

Stripped Away (Patreon Exclusive)

Content Warning

There are mentions of domestic violence resulting in the homicide of a mother and child with resulting murder-suicide (extremely brief mention), graphic on-page depiction of a failed round of IVF (prologue), survivors of domestic violence, parental abandonment (not of or by the MCs), postpartum depression (not of the FMC), anxiety, imposter syndrome, infertility, mentions of a voluntary abortion (not of the FMC), judgment from family members, and mention of past suicidal ideation (not by the MCs), as well as explicit language.

Chronic illness and mental health representation are a few main themes in ***Shiver*** and will be in each of my books.

This is an open-door romance with lots of consensual spice. If you aren't a fan, this book may not be for you, or you're welcome to refer to the "Table of Cocktents" on the following page so you know which chapters to avoid.

For a detailed list of events, please feel free to contact the author via Instagram DMs or email at Giuliana.Victoria.Author@gmail.com with any specific questions you may have about the contents of this book. While ***Shiver*** is filled with lots of light and laughter, some themes may be triggering for people. Your mental health is *always* a priority. Never be afraid to ask for specific chapters to avoid or to just avoid reading the book entirely. Please take care of your mental health <3

Table of Cocktents

Foreword

If you've read any of my books prior to this, you know that I put pieces of myself into every story, and Shiver is no exception. If you're someone who often skips content warnings, I'm begging you to read this note before you read any further.

I have my own experience with domestic violence/intimate partner violence, sexual assault, and several of the other themes littered throughout these pages. While they're not necessarily a focal point of this book, they still take up space in my head and in my heart, and you'll see that throughout this story. As with many of my books, the experiences of the MCs are both similar and very different from my own. I, like Samara, have had a personal battle with infertility (one that is still ongoing). Parts of this story may be very difficult to read for many of you, as infertility is not at all uncommon and is an unfortunate reality for many, including myself. I just want to prepare you for this ahead of time, much like I have with Quake.

When Vea, Samara's sister, said there is more than one way to have a family, those words were what I've not only told my patients, but been told myself. Words cannot express how deeply frustrating it is to be someone who has dedicated nine years of my life to my education with the hopes of helping others have a safe pregnancy and delivery (and so much more), helping these wonderful mommas bring their tiny humans into the world each and every day, only to go home knowing that I will never experience that for myself.

I have felt pretty much every emotion surrounding this, the largest of which being a tremendous amount of guilt. I feel so *goddamn* guilty for being upset about this. My career isn't just a way to pay my bills. I really, truly love every second of it, and I wouldn't change a thing.

I am ALLOWED to be upset. I am ALLOWED to be frustrated, and so are you.

Throughout the Philia Players series I have depicted several ways in which people become families. Kat & Ale have adopted, Rose & Charlie are a lesbian couple who have both adopted and undergone IUI, Arielle & Dante have conceived all three of their own children. Aiyana and Kas had no desire to have children, so they never did. Gianni and Lark conceived their own children as well. And Luca and Samara experienced an unexpected child, blended family, failed IVF, and something special you'll find out in the end.

So when I say THERE IS MORE THAN ONE WAY TO HAVE A FAMILY, that is exactly what I mean.

You don't have to have children to have an incredible family. Your friends are the family you've chosen, and that's an unbelievable gift in itself.

And one day, my husband and I will have an even bigger family, whether that's with children or without. I hope the same for each of you.

I did my very best to handle these sensitive topics with care, but they are still raw and painful at their core. Please protect your mental health and wellbeing as you read and reach out to me if you need some help navigating which chapters may or may not be safe for you to read.

It's always incredibly important for me to accurately represent chronic and mental illnesses, but I want to be very clear that no two people are alike in their experience. Please be mindful of that as you read Luca and Samara's story.

I also want to point out a few other things. I recognize that the beginning of this story is fast-paced and that in real life, these court cases don't necessarily go this way. For Gia's sake and the sake of romantic interest in this book, I've blurred the lines of reality.

This is fiction, after all.

Lastly, Samara is Jamaican and Dominican. Her father grew up and spent most of his life in Jamaica. He has a Jamaican accent as a result and speaks in Jamaican Patois.

What is Jamaican Patois? It's an English-based Creole spoken in and around Jamaica. I'll be adding translations for anything I think may be difficult to understand in italics after the sentence, and for parts where it doesn't make sense to do so, these will be written in the footnotes.

I never want to write my BIPOC characters in a way that is a disservice to them or their culture. I always work to be mindful of these things, as I think all authors have a responsibility to. But even more so, I do not wish to profit off BIPOC stories without ensuring accuracy and paying the respect that they deserve. I'll be clear that I'm fully aware that I *am* profiting off these stories, and because of that, I've done my best to represent them with respect and care.

So, for this reason, there are going to be sentences that should still make sense, but they may not look "correct" based on US English guidelines. That does not mean they are wrong or contain typos; it just means that the dialect and tone are different from that of a native English speaker born in the US when compared to a Jamaican man from Jamaica. Please keep that in mind as you read, and remember that code-switching exists as a result of racism and being repeatedly told that African American Vernacular English (AAVE) is not a language and is "inappropriate," "unprofessional," and "distasteful." None of which is even remotely true, but it's an unfortunate belief that many hold until we make the change we wish to see. So, just because Samara, a Black woman, speaks in a way that is comfortable and casual for her around her family and close friends does not mean that she will speak the same way around Luca and his white family. Why? Because, like many of my friends and readers, she's been raised in a world where racism very much exists today, and code-switching is one of many ways in which she has adapted to make succeeding in a white male predominant field a slightly less tumultuous task.

As I've said, this story is a work of fiction, so lines of reality are blurred, but the lived experiences of many of my readers are incorporated throughout this story. I ask that you keep that in mind as you read and are respectful of the incredible people who've spent hours of their time reading and commenting throughout this book to ensure their voices and the voices of people similar to them are heard and written in a way that is true to them.

Playlist

Everywhere I Go – Hollywood Undead

Porn Star Dancing – My Darkest Days

Bad Girlfriend – Theory of a Deadman

Fake It – Seether

Cut the Cord – Shinedown

Paralyzer – Finger Eleven

All The Stars – Kendrick Lamar & SZA

Bed Peace – Jhené Aiko (ft. Childish Gambino)

Pretty Little Birds – SZA (ft. Isaiah Rashad)

Nights – Frank Ocean

Caroline – Aminé

Feeling Myself – Nicki Minaj (ft. Beyoncé)

Wonder Woman – John Legend

Keep A Place – Shenseea

Intro – Kehlani

20 Something – SZA

Who Is She 2 U (Recall Version) – Brandy

Electric Lady – Janelle Monáe (ft. Solange)
Pray For You – Jhené Aiko
Every Kind Of Way – H.E.R.
Yo No Sé Mañana – Luis Enrique
Mi Corazoncito – Aventura
Tengo Un Amor – Toby Love
Corazón Sin Cara – Prince Royce
None Of Your Concern – Jhené Aiko (ft. Big Sean)
After Hours – Kehlani
Truth or Dare – Tyla
Petty – Gemaine, MadeinTYO
Hooked – Zeina
In The Night – Childish Gambino, Jorja Smith, Amaarae
HEATED – Beyonce
Next 2 U – Kehlani
We Might Even Be Falling In Love – Victoria Monét
You Are The Reason — Calum Scott
Conversations In The Dark — John Legend

De Laurentiis Family Tree

Gloria: Mother

Angelo: Father

Alessandro (Ale, pronounced "Ah-Lay"): Oldest Brother

Luca: Second Oldest

Giavanna (Gia): Luca's Daughter

Dante: Oldest Adopted Brother

Arielle: Dante's Wife

Sammy, Benny, & Lily: Dante & Arielle's Children

Gianni (Gi): Youngest Adopted Brother

Lark: Gianni's Wife

Jeremy (Jer): Gianni & Lark's Son

Charlene (Charlie): Youngest & Only Adopted Sister

Rose: Charlie's Wife

Arlo & Sofia: Charlie & Rose's Daughters

Signature Fragrances

Samara Perez-Allen:
Burberry Goddess Eau de Parfum by Burberry
&
Angels' Share Eau de Parfum by Kilian
Luca De Laurentiis:
1 Million Eau de Toilette by Paco Rabanne

To all the women who've worked their asses off to get to where they are and still receive such little recognition.

You're worthy of good things. Don't ever let anyone convince you otherwise.

This one's for you. <3

Prologue - Samara

My body shakes as I *shiver* against the cold tile floors of my bathroom.

I knew this would happen again, but somehow, I kept hoping it would be different this time.

"When am I going to quit putting myself through this?" I mumble to myself between sobs. "If it hasn't happened by now," I choke out, "it's probably not going to."

More tears fall, leaving hot streaks down my cheeks. I struggle to get air into my lungs, and thick saliva clogs my throat. The salty liquid burns my eyes and chapped lips.

I clutch the piece of plastic like a lifeline, knowing that it won't change anything but also hoping and *praying* that it will. That it just needs *one more minute.*

When I look down at it, nothing's changed.

I feel the fissure, ever present in my heart, crack wider with every passing second as denial starts to clear and realization settles in.

The single line hasn't magically been joined by a second one, which can only mean one thing.

I'm *still* not pregnant.

"Maybe I'm not cut out to be a mother," I whisper, my voice shaking.

"Don't you dare say that!" Vea's voice booms behind me as she slams the door shut before sliding to join me on the ground.

Her warm arms wrap tightly around my upper torso as she rests her head on my shoulder. "This has nothing to do with how you'll be as a mother and everything to do with a hormonal imbalance that *you have no control over.* So stop blaming yourself. *Please,*" she pleads quietly.

Her warmth seeps into my frozen body, but I'm not sure that anything could truly defrost the ice-cold block that's taken root in my chest as I stare at the pile of negative pregnancy tests littering my bathroom floor.

Chapter One

Luca

Wednesday, July 1, 2026

"Oh fuck, Luca," Veronica shouts, her perky tits bouncing as she rides my cock.

I smirk up at her, reaching up to toy with her nipples. "You look so hot riding me like such a good girl."

"You know what they say," she pants out. "Save a horse, ride a goalie."

I chuckle, tweaking her nipples and tugging on the sensitive buds as I pump my hips upward into her. Trailing one hand down her abdomen, I slip my thumb through her slick heat, watching as our bodies join repeatedly. I apply pressure to her clit, and her back arches. She clamps down around me, and a tingle travels up the base of my spine, though it's unfulfilling in the way many of these encounters have been for me recently. *Or maybe it's been longer, and I just haven't allowed myself to realize it yet.*

She throws her head back, letting out a choked moan. "Oh my god!"

"I've been called that a time or two."

She leans forward, giggling slightly, but as she moves her body to slap my chest playfully, my cock shifts angles inside of her and hits her exactly where she wants me. I can tell by the way she throws her head back, eyes wide and lips parted on a low moan.

I grip her hips, helping guide her up and down my shaft. She's milking my cock, the walls of her pussy spasming around my length. Just as I'm about to blow my load into her, I hear the doorbell ring, followed by a loud banging.

My head snaps in the direction of the noise. "What the fuck?" I grumble, guiding Veronica off my lap. She lies back against my pillows, her hand slipping between her pussy lips, fingers circling her clit.

Her eyes are hooded, and she's clearly more turned on than I seem to be. *What the hell happened to the guy who was totally fulfilled by just getting his dick wet?* "Come back and fuck me, baby. You can get whatever's at the door later." Her face is flushed, dark curls sticking to her sweat-covered skin.

I'm working to pull on a pair of gray sweats. Looking over at her, I grin, ready to follow through with her suggestion, but whoever's at the door rings the bell three more times in succession.

I call over my shoulder to Veronica as I head out of the room, "I'll be right back."

Padding across the hardwood floors, I unlock the front door. Standing on my porch is a well-dressed businessman, likely in his late forties.

"Mr. De Laurentiis?" he asks, his eyes squinting in the bright summer sun.

"Shouldn't you know for certain who lives here before you go banging on their door like the police?" I ask, annoyed that he prevented what was going on moments ago.

"Are you *not* Luca De Laurentiis then?" he questions, a graying brow raised at me in annoyance.

I step out onto the porch, closing the door behind me. "I am, and who are you?" I ask, the inflection in my tone making it clear that I don't appreciate the interruption.

"I'm Ted Murphy, a social worker for the Philadelphia County Child Protective Services."

My head rears back, eyes wide in confusion. "What is this about?" I ask, my voice sounding shaky to my own ears.

"Your daughter."

My what? My heart is suddenly hammering against my ribs and a lightheaded feeling threatens to drag me under.

"She's been dropped off by the mother at a local hospital. She left her with a birth certificate that states that *you* are the father." He tells me this with a straight face as if this isn't news to anyone. *It's certainly news to me, fucker.*

"I'm sorry. Who exactly is this mother who left a child, claiming it's mine?" My tone is indignant. *Is someone setting me up now that I'm playing for a top team in the NHL and making solid cash?*

"*She* was left by a Ms. Cecily St. James."

My eyes must be the size of saucers. Cici? We broke up a *year* ago.

"How old is the child?" I rush out.

"Three months." His tone sounds bored, but I'm anything but.

Fuck.

"You have a couple of options here. You can petition for temporary custody of the child at court tomorrow morning as this specific type of court case is only held on Thursdays, and we'd really like to place her sooner rather than later, or—"

I cut him off. "How do we find out if she's really mine?"

His brows are pinched, assessing me for a moment before he says, "You'd do a paternity test to be sure she's yours. Once the results are confirmed, you'll appear in court for the judge to sign off on the temporary placement after I inspect the home to ensure it's safe and you have everything necessary to properly care for her. If you move quickly, we can have this done by Friday."

Friday! That's two days away.

"What happens after that? You're saying the placement is temporary. What does that mean?" My mind is reeling as I fight to keep up with his words and their implications.

"What the mother did was drop the child off at one of our compassionate care drops. What that means is that if a parent is feeling overwhelmed and unable to care for a child under the age of six months, they can drop them off and be able to petition for their parental rights back, so long as they come forward within three months. You will need to get an attorney and take the mother to court for full parental rights, but if she really didn't want the child, then this should hopefully only entail a lot of paperwork on your lawyer's end."

I nod in a daze. "I'll do it. When can I do the paternity test?"

"As soon as possible. I'll get you set with all the information. Mind if I come in?"

Chapter Two

Luca

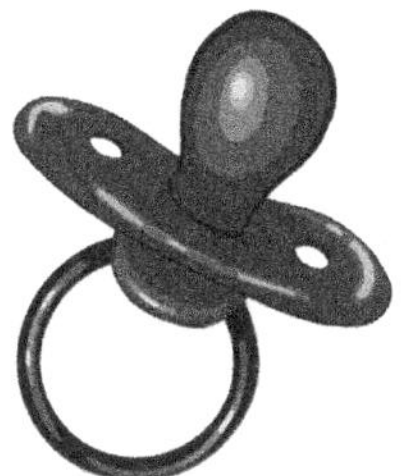

"Will your partner be willing to care for the child as well? We need to ensure a stable living environment for her." The moment the words leave Ted's mouth, Veronica comes traipsing by.

"Oh, don't worry about me. I won't be involved. *Ever.* We're officially over," she says, her voice dripping in venom as if this is somehow *my* fault. Veronica storms out of the house, her arms full of the clothing she had tossed around my room.

Well, I guess that answers that question. As they say, she wasn't here for a long time, just a *good* time.

***

My head is pounding as I kick off my shoes at the door, pushing it closed behind me before stumbling through the house to collapse onto the couch.

A baby.

I have a fucking baby. Or I might? God, *this is fucked.*

Groaning, I reach under my ass for my cell and dial the one person I know will answer.

On the second ring, Dante's low, grumbly voice comes across the line. His tone is clipped, and all he says is, "Luca," waiting for me to speak.

"Hey, you remember that model I dated last year?" I ask hesitantly. He's really not going to like what I have to say this time.

"Yeah, the tall blonde. What about her? You guys back together or something?" he asks, but I hear him whispering, probably speaking to his wife, Arielle.

"Not exactly. A social worker from the state showed up, informing me that she was at the hospital today *with our child.*" I let my words hang in the air, waiting for his response. I called him because he's a child psychologist, and I figure he'll be the biggest help as far as what resources are best to deal with the situation.

Situation? Jesus Christ, I really sound like a jackass. A child isn't a situation, and this isn't her fault, *but fuck*, I have no idea how the hell to navigate any part of this, and *that* is a fact.

He hums across the line before answering. "I'm sorry, you'll need to repeat that last bit for me. I think the line may have broken up."

I release a long, frustrated sigh. Now really isn't the time for him to be making fun of me or developing a newfound sense of humor. "She dropped the baby off at the hospital with paperwork, stating she doesn't want her, and now I'm being asked to appear in court tomorrow to accept responsibility for her if it turns out she's mine."

"You have a child." He says it as a statement, not a question.

"I'm pretty sure I've said that multiple times now. Could we move the fuck on?" I practically beg for this one small mercy as my temples continue to pulse.

He remains silent, waiting for me to tell him why I called. He's one of the kindest people I know, but he's also very "no-nonsense." And unfortunately for him, I've led a lot of nonsense to our family's doors over the years.

I know he won't ask me what everyone else would be thinking. It's another reason I called him. So I answer the unspoken question lacing his words. "The social worker seemed pretty certain she was mine for some reason, and I just got back from getting lab work. They put it in as a rush and said they should call with the results either tonight or early tomorrow morning." I hear a sharp intake of breath from his side of the line before he finally answers.

"Okay. And what's the plan if she is yours?" he asks me, slipping into his professional tone.

"I'll do what needs to be done. I'll talk to Coach and Ale about taking a leave once the season starts back up again, assuming she needs more time to adjust. I'll find a nanny for when I go back to work, and I guess we'll take it one day at a time." I'm shaking my head in disbelief at the entire situation, but I somehow manage to keep my tone steady, and internally, *I'm freaking the fuck out*.

"Fucking hell, Luca. I can't believe she didn't tell you about her." He's raising his voice and cussing, two things he almost never does. While he's a hulk of a man, covered neck to ankle in dark tattoos, he's generally a calm, peaceful presence to most people, which makes him great at his job.

"Honestly? I thought we ended things amicably. Besides, she's the one who decided to split up. Not that I was particularly devastated about it, but it wasn't my suggestion."

He grunts, acknowledging his understanding. "Well, whatever her reasoning, we'll have to figure it out later. I'll get some things together for you and drop by with Arielle in an hour, less if I can make it happen." A long silence echoes across the line, anxiety threatening to take hold of me. "You're going to get through this, brother," he tells me with such solid certainty before he hangs up that I actually find myself believing it for a split second and then it vanishes.

Chapter Three

Luca

I hear the chirp of my cell—a text from Dante letting me know he's here. I slip on the flip-flops I keep by the door and head outside. In the small driveway is an army of people, all holding shit for my kid. My chest clenches, but I push the emotion down, much like I do with everything else. *I'm supposed to be the fun brother, the one that doesn't cause too much stress, just good times and fun vibes.*

"So much for only bringing your wife, huh, bud?" I call over to him, my smile strained.

He smiles back, shaking his head as his wife piles items into his arms.

I call over to Kat, "Hey, gorgeous girl, you get out of work early today?"

Kat gives me a knowing smile, always able to read my emotions, but never calls me out on them. She heads toward me, arms full of diapers, and knocks into me purposefully. She transitions some of the items into my hold as she gives me a small smirk. "Anything for you, *stronzetto.*" She chuckles as she passes by me into the house.

I roll my eyes. Clearly, after years of tormenting her fiancé—my oldest brother—about our mother's nickname for him, "rattino," or little rat, she decided to give me one of her own. One that the entire family followed suit on: "you little shit."

I see my mother wheel herself to the door, formula and bottles in her lap as she makes her way up the ramp I had installed as soon as I moved in. She looks up at me, blue eyes gleaming brightly as she chortles. "You've really done it now," she tells me as she makes her way into the house. *Don't I know it?*

"Sure have," I groan, and head down the steps, helping to unload everything else from the car. Ale, Dante, and Arielle all work to unload the vehicle, each of them smiling ear to ear. I look over at Lark as Dante grabs the box of wipes out of her arms, replacing them with a single roll of paper towels. She rolls her eyes at him but doesn't argue. She recently gave birth to my newest nephew, Jeremy, who decided to make his big entry into the world a day after his parents' small garden wedding.

"Gi couldn't make it to this little pity party?" I ask her, my tone teasing.

Her cheeks still flame at the mention of my brother. Those two must do some seriously kinky shit with the way she's always blushing.

"He's coaching the kids' soccer team, but he said to let you know he'll give you a call in the morning to check in." She looks at me sympathetically.

I give her a nod, slam the trunk of the Tahoe closed, and follow everyone into my little blue house.

Everyone piles the items at the entryway or on the kitchen counter before getting to work. Each one of them busies themselves with a task. Lark starts by cleaning up the couple of dishes I have in the sink, then moves to cleaning all the baby bottles and on to reorganize my kitchen cabinets, making space for the baby items to all be in one place.

Dante is in my room with Arielle, setting up the bedside bassinet and what I think is some sort of dresser and changing station on wheels.

Luckily, having such a big family with nieces and nephews around means I'm at least familiar with what each of these things is used for. I can't imagine doing any of this if that weren't the case. I'd be totally lost. *Hell, I'm sure I will be soon enough.*

Ale is seated on the gray wooden floor, surrounded by plastic baskets in shades of gray and navy, labeling each one and filling them with clothes, diapers, diaper rash creams, binkies, and all sorts of other items I guess I'll be needing to have in my home now.

"You guys don't think this is all a bit much? We don't even know what the test says yet." I shift uncomfortably as they all watch me.

Ale pushes himself up off the floor to come stand beside me. He places a hand on my shoulder, squeezing it tightly. "If she's not yours, we'll donate everything, return it all, or use it on the kids. Whatever you want. But if she is yours, at least you'll be ready. Okay?"

As usual, Ale is the leader of the group. When he says we'll make this work, he means it with his whole heart.

I nod, hoping that his confidence will make its way into me as I head to my room to grab laundry and make myself useful.

***

Some of the weight has lifted off my chest over the last few hours. My blood still feels like it's buzzing, but at least I can take a full breath.

"You guys really don't have to wait around with me, you know. Gi shouldn't have to wrangle the kids all by himself, and we don't even know if they'll call tonight." I say this, but in reality, I don't want them to go. I'm afraid that the moment they leave, everything will come crashing down around me, and I won't be able to hold myself up without them.

I've never truly had to do anything alone. My family has *always* been here for me.

"Kat, Lark, and I will go help Gi with the kids, and someone will call us when you find out," Ale tells me. He takes on his role as "big brother" even at thirty-five years old. He still can't seem to leave that particular personality trait behind.

Rather than argue, I just agree, closing the door behind them.

Mom smiles at me from her seat beside the couch and pats the armrest. "Come sit down."

I know she's trying to help, but I'm not sure anything could work right now.

Reluctantly, I take a seat beside her, but it makes me feel even more restless.

***

Mom laughs beside me as she keeps her eyes trained on the reality TV show she put on in an attempt to distract me from my racing thoughts. Unfortunately, it hasn't helped.

Sitting down is only adding to my anxiety. I'm itching to get up and work on something, eager to do anything to keep my mind busy until I know for sure what my future holds. Never in a million years would I have imagined this day going the way it has. So much about my life has changed in mere hours.

My heart is racing so fast, I'm fighting to sit still. My leg is bouncing a mile a minute as every second ticks on.

This wait is killing me.

I practically jump out of my skin when I feel the familiar buzz of my cell pressing against my leg. My ringtone blares with one of my favorite songs.[1]

Mom's fingers snap in front of my face, pulling me from my daze. "Pick it up already!"

I grapple for the phone, sliding it unlocked and bringing the speaker to my ear. "This is Luca."

"Mr. De Laurentiis, this is Stacey from Philadelphia Regional Hospital. I apologize for the late hour. I wanted to get this message to you as quickly as possible, given the circumstances. Are you available to speak?" she asks.

---

1. **Fake It — Seether**

"Yeah, now would be great. Thanks for calling," I tell her, eager to find out my fate.

"Before I provide the results, would you mind confirming your date of birth and address as well? I need to be sure I'm speaking to the correct person."

I give her my details, and once I'm done, she says, "You *are* the father. Your paternity test came back with a confirmatory result with matching alleles."

My breath catches in my lungs. *I'm the father.*

Just like that. My entire world has been flipped upside down, and I don't have a single fucking clue what I'm going to do about it. My jaw aches, I hadn't even realized I was clenching it so tightly.

"Mr. De Laurentiis, did you hear me?" Stacey asks.

Clearing my throat, I take in the watchful eyes surrounding me, silent as they take in my expression. "Yes, yes. I heard you. Thank you for the information."

"You're welcome, Mr. De Laurentiis. I hope things work themselves out okay. Have a good rest of your evening."

"Thanks, you too," I grunt, hanging up.

I hang my head between my shoulders, releasing a long, calming breath. When I finally look up, it's my father's empathetic green eyes that I focus on as I speak my next words.

"*I'm the father*," I tell my family. My heart is starting to race again, and while I know this is the information I've been waiting for, *I'm fucking scared.*

I'm not cut out to be a father. I can barely take care of myself.

Hell, I beat myself up every time a puck slips past me and blame every loss on myself. And I've been playing hockey my whole life.

This is all so new to me, and there are a seemingly endless number of ways in which I could mess this up.

"Alright, what next then?" my mom asks, appraising me warily.

Taking another steadying breath, I tell her, "I guess I contact the social worker and go to court tomorrow. We'll see what happens. If the judge doesn't grant me temporary custody, it's all kind of a moot point for now."

They each nod slowly, afraid to say anything. "Can you call him now?" Dad asks.

"That's probably a good idea," I agree, heading to my room to give him a call and see where we go from here.

Chapter Four

Luca

Thursday, July 2, 2026

My hands are shaking as we leave the courtroom.

The moment we make it outside into the warm sun, my shoulders relax negligibly. My hands are still clammy, and my mind is a frazzled mess, but at least it's over with, and we have our answer.

"Mind if I head back to your house to complete the home assessment? I don't want any delays for tomorrow."

I nod, turning on my heel and jogging down the steps of the courthouse. As I get to my car, I realize I have no idea how to put a car seat in. I know how to securely put the baby *in* the car seat, but not how to properly install one.

Fuck.

It seems there'll be a lot more of a learning curve than I had initially hoped, but at least I have the time to do it. I have a few months until the season starts, and Ale already arranged for me to train with him in the offseason so I don't have to leave Gia at home with a nanny or burden our family so much.

Gia. She named her Giavanna, and I couldn't be more thankful for that, given the meaning of the name. *Greatest gift.* Though there's also irony at play here. How could she pick a name like that and not want her?

A chill wracks through me, and my stomach churns at the thought. Something doesn't add up here, but I can't figure out what without speaking to her.

***

I hold my breath as Ted surveys my home, marking things down on a list, mumbling notes to himself as he goes.

Once he's inspected the whole house, he slides his pen back into his breast pocket and drops the arm holding the clipboard to his side.

"Everything seems to be in order. I'll call you tomorrow when I'm on my way, and please make sure to have that car seat set up before I arrive. I'll need to check that as well."

"Sure thing. Thanks, Mr. Murphy," I say as I walk him out.

"Call me Ted." He starts to leave but stops just short of my porch steps before turning back around to face me. What he says next surprises me. "You're doing a good thing here, Mr. De Laurentiis. Not everyone in your position would have made the same decision, but I think you'll find that it was the best thing *for both of you.*"

My brows pinch at that, unsure of who he's referring to as "both" of us. Me and Gia or Me and Cici?

I work to smooth my expression before giving him a wave. "Thanks, *Ted*. I'll see you tomorrow."

I watch as he climbs into his blue sedan.

"Now to install that damn car seat."

I sit on the couch, my legs sprawled out in front of me as I search for videos explaining how to set it up, and once I think I've got the idea, I drag the hunk of plastic out to my SUV.

***

Sweat drips down my brow as I stand back with my hands on my hips, taking in my handiwork.

It took me damn near an hour to install the fucking thing, but I did it *without* having to call my brothers for help.

Maybe I really can do this? Unlikely.

Chapter Five

Luca

Friday, July 3, 2026

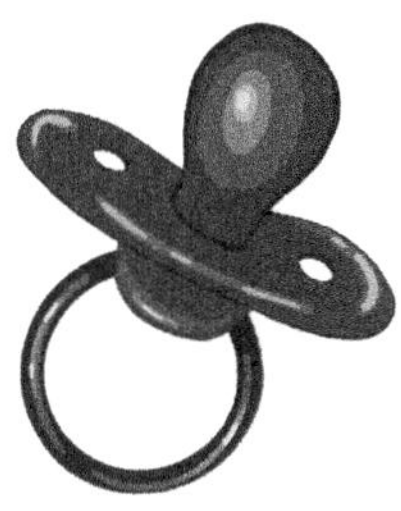

I hear a knock at my door, and the nerves coursing through me leave me feeling unsteady. My heart feels like it's banging against my ribs, trying to fight its way free of my chest. *I never feel like this.* I'm usually so confident, but not right now. *This* I know nothing about.

Maybe my so called "confidence" is merely a mask, and I'm finally being forced to let it fall.

I rush to answer the door, eager to get this moment over with. As I unlock it, turning the knob and yanking the door open, my mouth is agape at the sight in front of me.

Ted is standing at my door, holding *my daughter.*

She's beautiful.

Her tan skin and dark, fluffy curls are in complete contrast to her light eyes.

My eyes.

I suck in a breath, unable to speak yet as the small child flutters her lashes groggily at me, taking me in and attempting to sort through the new information her little mind is being forced to process.

That thought alone leaves me with a bitter taste in my mouth. If Cecily had been honest about this, we'd all have been saved from so much frustration. I can't fathom that this is really what she wanted.

"Now you see why I was so sure, huh?" He chuckles, adjusting Gia's swaddled body in his arms.

I nod my head slowly, in a daze, but have the frame of mind necessary to reach for her. I want to hold her, comfort her, and show her all the love she's had withheld the last few days. Maybe even *months* if Cecily had really not wanted her at all.

Ted gathers her up and places her in my arms. I clutch her tiny body to my chest, the yellow blanket with little white giraffes holding her snugly.

She peers up at me, meeting my gaze. *Those eyes.* One ice blue and the other sage green. She's all mine. This I know for sure.

It's as if something changed in me at a cellular level the moment she was placed in my arms. Some fatherly instinct fighting to be let free. *I love her already.*

If I'd seen her before the paternity test, I'd have had no doubt in my mind she was mine.

Somehow, seeing the immediate resemblance between us has me choking back a sob. My throat constricts, and my face flushes with heat as I purse my lips, holding back the tears. She's only three months old, and I've already missed out on so much.

Ted reaches out, gripping my shoulder firmly. "You're going to do great. I'm confident in this," he says, and the way his eyes bore into mine with absolute certainty gives me the ounce of faith I need to get through this first day. "Now let me check out the car seat, and I'll get out of your hair."

***

Once we're settled on the couch with a Boppy pillow on my lap, Gia coos softly, suckling on her binky.

I gently rock us back and forth, making a mental note to buy a rocking chair soon. I'm sure I'll be needing it.

Her eyelids look heavy as she wrestles her need to sleep, doing her best to keep them trained on me, but eventually, she loses the battle between her willpower and her exhaustion.

I clench my eyes tightly shut, blowing out a breath of relief.

I should update my family.

Doing my best to avoid as much movement as possible, I wiggle my phone out of my back pocket and unlock it, searching for my family group chat.

She's sleeping. I'll try to update you guys later.

I snap a photo of her, making sure I have the flash turned off before I do, and send it along with my message.

Mom

Oh my gosh, look at that sweet face! When can we come over?

Arielle

Just give me a few minutes to get the kids ready, and we'll be right there!

The messages flood in from every direction, my anxiety climbing as they do.

Please don't take this the wrong way, but I just want the weekend to adjust. I'll let you all know if I need help, but for now, I plan to bring her to dinner on Sunday. You'll meet her soon, I swear.

Mom

We understand. See you soon, honey.

Thank god, that was easier than I had anticipated.

Chapter Six

Luca

Saturday, July 4, 2026

She's finally stopped crying.

I've been up all night, miserable, as I try everything I can think of to calm her. *I don't know what I'm doing and now she knows it too.* Everything that works on my nieces and nephews only makes her more aggravated. I even tried driving her around, but that riled her up further.

I scoured the internet, silently pleading for a solution as she screamed her head off. I came across an article about skin-to-skin contact.

And it worked.

When she finally settled down, I tried to get a hold of Cecily, but naturally, her line had been disconnected.

I know I need to nap before she wakes up again, but I'm sure I won't be able to sleep until I've spoken to the one person who might be capable of easing my mind right now.

The line rings and rings, and on the fifth ring, he answers. "Luca," he huffs out with a heavy breath.

I chuckle. "Did I catch you at a bad time?"

"Not at all, honey. What can this grump help you with?" Audrey's sultry tone filters across the line, her breathy pants a telltale sign of what was going on moments before he answered. *Looks like those days are gone for me.*

"I have every right to be upset," Rome groans across the line. "Seriously, the hell do you need? I'm a little busy if you couldn't tell."

"Well then, I'll get right to it," I tell him sarcastically.

At that moment, Gia wakes, a high-pitched wail releasing so loudly it could burst an eardrum.

I groan, getting up from the couch to head to her room. I tuck the phone between my ear and shoulder before leaning into her bassinet to lift her out.

"Luca, was that a fucking *child* screaming?" Rome demands.

"Sure was, which brings me to why I called."

He groans again. "How come everyone is always asking me to fix something when they call?" he complains.

"Don't be such a baby. You're a lawyer. It's your job," Audrey chides.

"Yeah, Rome, stop being a baby. It's your job," I taunt, bringing Gia into my arms and allowing her to relax onto my chest.

"Between the two of you—" Rome stops abruptly as Audrey cuts in.

"Finish that sentence and see what happens."

Another laugh slips past my lips. "Could we get to my dilemma now?" I ask.

"Alright, what is it?" Rome questions, annoyance evident in his tone, not that that's unusual for him.

"Cecily St. James broke up with me a year ago. And she was pregnant with our daughter. She decided she was done with the whole parenting thing and left her at the hospital after informing the staff that I was the father. Long story short, I am, and I have temporary custody of her, but I need a lawyer. I know you're in New York, but any chance you know any good attorneys in Philly who could help me out?" I do my best not to sound pleading.

He doesn't answer for a moment, humming as he thinks. "Actually, yeah, I do. My friend, Samara. We went to Columbia Law together. She's a child custody attorney in Center City. I'll text you her number and give her a call to let her know I sent you her way."

I exhale a relieved sigh. "Thanks, man, that would be super helpful."

He grunts. "Anytime. Now, if you don't mind, I'd like to get back to my fiancée." I don't get a chance to respond before he hangs up the phone.

A moment later, I receive a contact card from Rome that reads, "Samara Perez-Allen, Esq."

Chapter Seven

Luca

Sunday, July 5, 2026

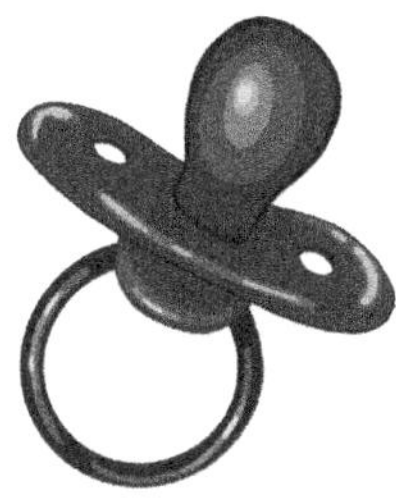

I've seriously underestimated the time it takes me to get both myself and my daughter ready to go absolutely anywhere, so I hope my mother will take that into account just this once. Normally, being late to Sunday dinner would result in my ass being reamed out... by the entire family.

That's never stopped me before, but I have a whole lot of extra reason not to disappoint them now.

I park in front of my parents' newly finished one-story home. It's so different from the three-story brownstone I grew up in, but with Mom's mobility limitations from her multiple sclerosis, it only made sense for them to eventually move. My oldest brother, Alessandro, had worked for years to make this dream a reality and put a lot of time into figuring out what could be done to the design to make it easy for her to maneuver and live a full life.

The home still has several of the same touches as the old one had, ensuring it met Mom's style and didn't make her feel out of place.

Once again, making him the better son. Not that I try very hard.

***

I unbuckle Gia from the car seat, thankful that she fell asleep quickly. I guess when you've been crying all night, it really tuckers you out.

Hell, *I would know*.

I'm fucking exhausted, and I had to watch some video online about reducing under eye swelling. Cold tea bags really did the trick.

Being as gentle as possible, I pull her to my chest and throw the massive diaper bag over my shoulder. She wiggles in my arms at the movement, and panic seizes my chest. I stand as still as a statue, holding my breath until she's settled.

This parenting business is *not* for the weak.

The door of my SUV stares back at me, taunting me as I debate how to close it without waking her. Shaking my head, I walk up the driveway. Someone else can go out there and close it for me.

The moment my foot makes it onto the porch ramp, the door creaks open. Charlie's head pokes out. "Need a hand?" she whisper-screams at me.

I nod, jutting my chin in the direction of my car door. She opens the door wider, slipping out and sprinting down the driveway to gently close it. When she returns, her dark curls create a haphazard halo around her face, and she's breathing heavily as she holds the door open for me to head inside.

Instead of seeing my family sitting around the dinner table that we had custom-made for the house to fit an excessive number of us, I see pastel yellow and green balloons all around the living room. My family, teammates, and their spouses all whisper, "Happy baby shower!" in unison.

My cheeks heat, but the smile that stretches my mouth is genuine, warmth seeping into my chest. "Give me a minute to set her down," I tell them all as I make my way down the hall. Ale gets up, following behind me.

"I set up a bassinet in this room before you got here," he tells me, his voice low but without the obnoxious whispering that everyone else seems to be doing.

I'm so damn grateful for my family. They've never let me fall on my ass, even when they probably should've.

Hell, maybe if they had, I'd have learned my lesson, but that's not on them. That's entirely *my* fault.

"Thanks, man, I appreciate you," I tell him earnestly, entering the dark room with rain sounds already playing in the background.

Gratitude fills my chest as I lower my daughter into the bassinet, a sleep sack already laid out for her. I set her down on it, quietly fixing the snaps together and holding down each of her arms to swaddle her. She wriggles momentarily before her body goes still, and I can back slowly out of the room.

When I make it back into the living room, my family and friends are all seated with decorations, gifts, and food all over the place.

There's a massive wicker chair covered in pink hockey balloons with faux flowers and streamers.

My mom points to the chair in the middle of the room. "That's your seat," she says with a bright laugh.

I take my rightful place on my makeshift throne and let the festivities begin.

My mom and sisters managed to set up a ton of baby shower games, including the one where you guess what's in the diapers, don't say the word "baby," and chug beer from baby bottles. Not that you can really call it chugging when it comes out one drop at a time.

By the end of the night, I'm even more exhausted, but having the support of all of the most important people in my life has managed to quiet the little voice in my head that's been yelling, "You can't fucking do this! You're a bad father, Luca!" While that voice is most definitely still present, at least the screaming has dulled to a steady hum.

I have the most incredible support system, and regardless of how unprepared and undeserving I feel, at least I have them to help me through it.

Chapter Eight

Samara

Monday, July 6, 2026

Wind whips past me, my curls tangling as my heels click across the pavement toward the doors of the courthouse.

Buzzing comes from inside my purse, and I halt my movement as I scrounge around for it. Finding my cell at the bottom of my brown NDG bag, I quickly answer the call. A smile lights my face when I realize who it is.

"*Roman Wilde*, as I live and breathe," I say with a chuckle, a small smile stretching my lips.

"Samara, how've you been? Crushing the souls of other, lesser attorneys and leaving no prisoners?" Rome asks, a joking lilt to his deep baritone.

"Of course. What else would I be doing in my free time?" I retort sarcastically.

"About that..." He trails off.

I roll my eyes. *He needs something.* "Spit it out, pretty boy. I have court in three minutes."

He huffs out a nervous laugh. "I've got a friend living in Philly who needs a child custody lawyer. I gave him your number and just wanted to give you a heads-up."

"You sound nervous about that. What are you not telling me?" I question, knowing this isn't a man who gets nervous, *ever.* It would sort of dull the effect he has in the courtroom as a criminal defense attorney.

He blows out a heavy breath that's audible even over the line, and I feel a fluttering in my gut as I wait for whatever it is he's about to say to make my life more complicated. "Yeah, he's known as a bit of a player, but I swear, he's not like that. Just give him a chance; you'll see. He's in a real messed-up situation, and you're the most capable attorney I know," he finishes.

"Ah, there he is. Mr. Congeniality trying to butter me up with praise," I quip, the smile returning to my face.

"Is it working?" he asks, hopeful.

I laugh. "Of course it is. Send me his details so I don't mark his number as spam. I'll see what I can do."

He lets out a breath he must've been holding while awaiting my answer. "Appreciate you, Mara. You a real one."

"Don't I know it? Have a good day, Rome. We'll link up soon. Give Audrey a good smack on the ass for me," I tell him.

"Will do, but can't say it'll be from you." He laughs. "Good luck in court. Talk later."

I end the call, shoving my phone back in my bag and hauling ass into that courtroom.

***

I kick my feet up on the couch, turning the TV on for some ambient noise before doing a deep dive into Luca De Laurentiis.

If I'm going to represent him, I need to know everything that could be dredged up and used against him. Which means ensuring I find the things he might not be willing to tell me himself.

As I type in his name, the search populates with hundreds of articles. "Shit." I groan, sinking farther into the couch cushions. *This is going to be a long-ass night, but at least I've got wine.*

I take a sip of my pinot, a tingly sensation slithering down my throat as I swallow before diving into these articles. Alcohol makes me bloat even more than usual, but I like to enjoy a glass of wine here and there. I have no desire to live my life based solely on the whims of my hormones.

I can already feel my limbs getting heavier, and my ankles are swelling. I set my phone down for a moment to massage my tired feet before taking a closer look. The vast majority of the articles I find surround my new client's sexual prowess, and while it's inconvenient to have to represent someone with such an open sex life, especially in child custody cases, it isn't a make or break. I continue scrolling, truly shocked by the time I'm an hour in, and I've seen photos of this man leaving bars and clubs seemingly every night of the week with a new woman.

I've seen a lot over my career, and while it doesn't stun me that these articles exist, it is a little startling to see just how many women have fallen for whatever lies he tells them to get them to sleep with him. Though I suppose there's always the possibility that they know his intentions and simply don't care. *Or that he's got a golden dick, who knows?* I guess I might not either if I was looking for a night of fun and had the opportunity with a man who looked like *that.*

I slip farther into the cushions, continuing to scroll until I land on a smattering of several articles from a few years ago, referencing his older brother's diagnosis of multiple sclerosis.

I skim through the articles briefly but realize pretty quickly they have little to do with my new client, so I move on.

Another hour passes, and my eyes are starting to feel heavy until they land on something that jolts me out of my sleepiness.

Nearly a decade ago, Luca De Laurentiis was photographed bringing his girlfriend to a non-profit clinic that provides reproductive services. A reporter did some digging, as this was his first year playing in the NHL, and found that he had transferred a large sum of money to her, presumably paying her to have an abortion and to keep quiet.

My stomach begins to churn with unease. *I don't like where this is going.*

Luca never denied the claims, and it was discovered that the two had broken up the next day, but the identity of the woman in the photo had been concealed.

Based on how well he's keeping her face covered as he hides her under his sweatshirt, the reporters likely couldn't figure out who the hell she was. It's highly improbable that they'd have had the decency to protect her identity had they actually known.

That's good news for his case, but it doesn't stop the way my blood boils at the thought. *He paid a young woman to abort her child so he wouldn't tarnish his little hockey career?*

"How privileged of him," I scoff to myself.

If it were Luca himself who'd asked me to take his case, I'd fire him as my client. He doesn't deserve that child.

But it isn't, I remind myself. It's Rome who asked me, and for that reason alone, I'll do my best to keep the anger brewing inside me from bubbling to the surface.

Chapter Nine

Luca

Tuesday, July 7, 2026

My phone rings from the next room, and I rush to answer it before Gia wakes. There's nothing quite like the panic that rushes through a new parent when they've finally gotten their kid to sleep and something tries to disrupt that. I snatch it off the counter, swiping to answer before bringing it to my ear. "This is Luca," I say in a rush.

A smooth, feminine voice curls over the line. "Luca, this is Samara. Could we meet today? I'm sure you'd like to get this process started, and I have a free hour at three."

I rub at the skin of my throat, my eyes swinging to the stove clock that reads, "2:37 p.m." "Fuck," I groan out, not meaning for the word to slip past my lips.

My heart stops in my chest at the realization of what I'd done. "What was that?" Samara's even tone holds a rigid quality to it, and I know, without a doubt, I'm *already* fucking this up.

I release a long breath, steeling my nerves before apologizing. "Sorry," I say, my voice wavering as I stare at my bedroom door where Gia's tucked safely away. "I just got Gia down for a nap, but if you could do three thirty, I could probably get one of my siblings to come over and watch her."

I shouldn't feel so damn guilty for having *my own* schedule to work around, but something about this first verbal interaction with Samara has me feeling even more inadequate as a father than I already had. *If this woman, who doesn't even know me, already thinks I'm unworthy of Gia, maybe she's right.*

"Fine," she huffs out. "I'll move some things around. Three thirty p.m. at Ice Blue. Don't be late." With her last words, she hangs up the phone, leaving me scrambling to get dressed and figure out which of my siblings can look after Gia on such short notice.

***

"And you're *sure* you don't mind?" I triple-check with Gianni, hesitant to add yet another thing to his plate with a newborn at home, and I'm even more reluctant to leave my daughter.

"You appear to forget that I have a newborn, who I seem to be keeping alive just fine," he jokes. "We'll be okay without you for a couple of hours. Go, and don't mess it up." He waves me out the door, all but slamming it in my face.

***

My tires squeal across the pavement as I pull into a parking spot in front of Ice Blue, the swanky lounge that opened a few months ago.

I used to frequent this place, getting free bottle service when I arrived. That fact alone sends apprehension trickling down my spine.

Hopefully, no one here recognizes me, and I can avoid making a scene in front of my lawyer. A lawyer who, it seems, already can't stand me.

I look down at my tan leather loafers, staring at my feet as I make the trek across the parking lot and into the restaurant. As soon as I'm inside, I lift the sleeve of my navy suit jacket, my watch indicating I've got three minutes to spare.

Thank fuck. Samara doesn't seem like the kind of woman who bluffs. She'd probably leave my ass here had I been a single second late.

I scan the restaurant, and I quickly realize my mistake. I have no idea what this woman looks like. Fucking hell, I should've at least googled her. I fight the groan threatening its way up my throat and take a calming breath, closing my eyes for a quick beat.

When I open them, they snag on a woman wearing an electric-blue dress that hugs her every curve. Her warm-brown skin looks dewy. It's a beautiful contrast to the bright shade caressing her figure.

Her eyes meet mine, narrowing on me, and I swear I see them roll from all the way across the restaurant.

That must be her, then.

She stands abruptly, heading straight toward me.

When she's less than two feet in front of me, she sticks her hand out for me to shake. "Samara Perez-Allen. Nice to meet you, Mr. De Laurentiis," she says, but judging by her tone, she doesn't think there's anything "nice" about it.

I take her palm in mine, giving it a gentle shake, which she returns much more firmly, nearly crushing my fingers.

Okay, that definitely confirms my suspicions. She absolutely is *not* a fan of me, but why?

Releasing my hand, she turns back toward the booth she was seated at and saunters ahead of me. I guess I'm expected to follow her? It's not much of a hardship, not with that magnificent ass swaying as she walks.

Shut the fuck up, you absolute goddamn pig, I internally scold myself, shaking my head.

I take a seat across from her, and the moment she opens her mouth to speak, the waitress approaches eagerly.

"Luca De Laurentiis." She beams at me, entirely ignoring Samara.

My stomach drops to my toes. "Lacey, hi." I nod at the petite blonde staring down at me seductively. Her eyes are hooded as she twirls a lock of hair around her finger. What she doesn't appear to realize is that when I turned her down and gave her a ride home the last time I saw her here, I had *really* meant that I wasn't interested. I didn't want her driving home drunk, though she had been working at the time, so I'm not even sure if that was the truth or if she had been hoping she could get me to change my mind. In either case, it makes me extremely uncomfortable that she's ignoring Samara. What if we had been here on a date?

Internally, I scoff at the thought. There's not a single soul in sight who would misinterpret our meeting for a date, not with the daggers Samara's shooting my way.

"What can I get you to drink?" Lacey rushes to ask—again, keeping her eyes plastered on me.

I turn my attention to Samara, who's scowling at us, with a neatly trimmed, dark brow arched in my direction. "What would you like, Samara?" I ask her, hoping to break some of the tension and remind Lacey that I'm not alone.

"Pinot grigio," she tells her, shifting in her seat to cross one leg over the other as she glares at me.

I glance back over at Lacey, whose eyes are still trained on me, not paying Samara any mind as if she weren't here at all. I tap my foot against the dark vinyl flooring, and my stomach twists in knots. "Just water for me, thank you."

A relieved sigh passes my lips when she takes my dismissal for what it is and heads back for the drinks.

"Let's get to business. I only have till four thirty."

I work on a swallow, sinking back into the leather seat. *Straight to the point, I see.*

Over the next hour, she outlines what the process will look like, alternative options for what may happen when we get to court, and timelines for how quickly this kind of stuff can get put together.

I can't say I'm not overwhelmed. Because I most definitely am, but at least Samara has a game plan, so while she clearly isn't my biggest fan, she knows what she's doing. I've got to trust the process... *and her.*

Chapter Ten

Samara

As we walk out of the restaurant, I turn to look at my new client, taking in his bad-boy demeanor. His dark waves give off the impression that he wakes up looking like this even though he likely uses product to style it that way. Those perfectly muscled arms bulge under his suit jacket, and the tattoo on his chest peers out from beneath his unbuttoned white shirt, practically screaming "bad decisions."

He thanks the middle-aged man standing beside him, giving him a clap on the shoulder after having agreed to take a selfie. For some reason, it disappoints me. I'd been hoping that the rumors were just that, and that *maybe* he'd grown up since many of the remarks made about him were written online, but that clearly isn't the case.

He turns back to face me, his smile falling when he sees my grimace. "Sorry about that," he apologizes.

"You have to work with me here, Luca," I tell him, shaking my head in disbelief. "If you want to be taken seriously, you have to at least *pretend* to be serious. I've seen endless photos of you online, always leaving the bars with someone new. That stops now. As long as you're my client, you play by *my* rules. I won't have you making a mockery of me in a courtroom." I huff.

He rears back as if I've slapped him, his dark brows pulling together over those multicolored eyes of his. If he weren't such a player, I might even find him attractive.

"In case you hadn't noticed," Luca says, his tone flat and nostrils flaring slightly, "that man was a *fan*, not some woman I'm taking home for a *consensual* night of fun. Wouldn't it be *more embarrassing* for you had I ignored him?" he asks, tossing his hands up. "I'm confident you, like the press, have misjudged me. I'm not doing anything to mess with my chances of keeping my daughter." He speaks confidently, keeping his head held high. "Have a good evening, Samara. I look forward to hearing from you," he says before heading to his SUV without another look in my direction.

Unease churns in my gut, but I don't think I've misjudged him at all. He's a playboy. Simple as that, and I wouldn't be taking this case if it weren't as a favor to a good friend of mine. If *anyone* else were asking, I'd have told them *no* to taking on one of the most infamous goalies in the league right now.

It sounds like a recipe for disaster, and much like in my personal life, I prefer to only play games that I can win. That most definitely extends to the courtroom, though I'm not entirely sure I *want* him to win based on what I've seen so far.

I don't need the extra stress, but I trust Rome's opinions, and unfortunately, that little girl is probably better off with Luca De Laurentiis than she is in the system. The younger they are, the better their chances of finding a home, but there are no guarantees.

Hoisting my bag over my shoulder, I turn in the opposite direction to him. Anger simmers below the surface of my skin as I retrieve my cell, opening it up to a message thread with Rome.

I unlock my car door, place my bag on the passenger's side, and hoist myself into the leather seats of my Range Rover.

Typing out a quick message to Rome, I let him know how I'm *really* feeling about this little situation he's gotten me into.

You're officially on my shit list, Roman Wilde.

Three little bubbles play across my screen, but I don't wait for his response before tossing my phone in my bag and pulling out of my parking space.

I need another glass of wine, like yesterday.

Chapter Eleven

Luca

My shoulders feel heavy with the weight of all the changes in my life. I feel fucking terrible that I suddenly have to add so much more to my family's plate, and all because an ex of mine didn't trust me enough to tell me she was pregnant.

What kind of fucked-up person must I be that she didn't think she could tell me?

It only further adds to my frustrations.

Clenching my eyes tightly shut, with my hands balled into fists at my sides, I release a long sigh before shaking myself out and trudging into the house.

Ale's lying across the couch with Gia resting on his chest, and the TV is set to his favorite rom-com. *Mom calls these rom-cums*, that thought the first to shake this feeling of dread.

I shake my head at the sight, a small smile tugging at my lips as I slip out of my shoes and head over to them.

"Ale, wakey, wakey," I whisper behind him.

He opens his eyes to glare up at me. "I wasn't sleeping. I was just resting my eyes," he explains, slapping his hand over his mouth to muffle a yawn.

I roll my eyes at him. "Yeah, okay…" I draw out the word. "You swap out with Gi?" I ask, confused as to why Ale's here in his place.

"Yeah, he left a few minutes ago. I was dropping by to check on you guys and figured I'd relieve him," he says with a low laugh.

I nod, grateful for the way they've all jumped right in to help me, not that I'd expect anything else from my family. "How come you're so tired? The sun hasn't even set yet." I chuckle, rounding the couch to sit beside him and take Gia.

She wiggles in my grasp, groggily blinking her eyes at me before finding a comfortable position in the crook of my arm and falling back into a milk-drunk haze.

She really is the cutest kid. *My kid.*

"The wedding planning is taking more energy than either of us had imagined, and—" He looks down at his empty lap before peering up at me with an expression that makes my stomach churn.

"You're wearing that guilty look on your face you used to give me when we were kids. Just because I haven't seen it in a long time doesn't mean I don't recognize it," I tell him warily, my brow quirked in question.

He sighs, leaning forward with his elbows pressed to his thighs. "You can't say anything to anyone about this yet. I don't wanna jinx it."

"Fine, just tell me," I practically beg.

He shakes his head, a slow smile spreading across his face. "Dante's been helping us set up an adoption for a little boy named Oliver. We're already in love," he says, his green eyes glossy, "but it's been such a process to get it together with everything else going on, and the fact that we aren't married yet has complicated things a little. We have an advantage since Dante's helping facilitate the adoption, but there's still a lot of legal shit to trudge through."

The hand not supporting Gia shoots out almost of its own will, smacking Ale in the back of the head. He bolts upright, gripping the spot before his bright eyes meet mine. "What the hell was that for?" he grunts out.

"For making me worry! You made it sound like something bad was happening, and honestly," I tell him, peering down at my daughter, "I can't take a whole lot more right now." The moment the words leave my mouth, I realize how selfish they are. He and Kat will make incredible parents, and yet they're struggling to adopt a child in need of a family. And here I am, feeling like I have the weight of the world on me because I've suddenly become a father.

Ale doesn't seem to clock my shift in emotions though. He chuckles, dropping his hand back to his lap. "I know we may not have anticipated *you* becoming a father before me, but I promise, Luca, this is going to be good for you. I can feel it. And you're already turning out to be an incredible dad."

We both look down at Gia, soaking up these quiet moments before the madness begins again. "What's meant for you will come; this is just a changing of the tides."

"Alright." I grab the remote control lying between us, flipping the channel to a sports station. "Enough of this romantic shit for you, buddy. You're starting to sound like a poetic fortune cookie. Now get out of my house and back to your fiancée."

Gia decides at that moment to have the burp of a lifetime, up-chucking the contents of her stomach all over my dress shirt.

Ale tosses a cloth at me as he gets up from the couch, laughing at my misfortune. "And that's my cue to leave," he says as he makes his way to the front door.

I gently wipe the milk from Gia's quickly reddening face, then readjust her onto a towel over my shoulder to burp her in case she's got anything else brewing in there.

My gaze shifts to Ale's as he watches me from the open door. "You're going to be fine, Luca," he tells me in an assured tone.

"Thanks, and thank you for watching her on such short notice. I really appreciate it."

"Anytime." He grins and heads out the door.

***

"Shhh, Gia, please, *mia bambina*, stop crying," I plead with her for what feels like the hundredth time tonight.

Her face is beet red, tears streaming down her cheeks as she wails so loudly I think my eardrums must be permanently damaged from it. My heart feels like it's shattering as she cries.

I don't know what the hell to do.

I've tried everything, and *nothing* is working.

My pulse speeds up as I dial Dante's number, continuing to bounce on the balls of my feet as I wait for him to *hopefully answer* my call.

On the eighth ring, he finally picks up. "What is it?" he grunts into the phone. Before I can answer, a new voice comes over the line.

"*What he means* is, good morning, Luca. How can we help you and that screaming baby?" Arielle's chipper voice singsongs.

"Thank god." I sigh. "She won't stop crying, and I've tried all the usual things, and nothing has put her to sleep."

"Have you tried skin-to-skin?"

"Yes, she's currently wearing nothing but a diaper while I hope to god she doesn't vomit on my bare chest." I groan.

Her light laughter trickles over the line. "Okay, well, if nothing else is working, she may be teething."

"Teething? *Already*?"

"Yep, maybe try one of the frozen teething rings I put in your freezer the other day," she suggests.

"You mean to tell me that some people breastfeed for over a fucking *year,* and these little gremlins can have *teeth* at three months old!"

"Having a baby with razor sharp teeth latch onto your nipple isn't all it's cracked up to be, unless we're talking about literal cracked nipples. This is why I'd knee you in the balls if you ever judge someone for formula feeding their kid. Now go get the teething ring so your *gremlin* stops screaming," she teases.

I walk her over to the freezer and grab a dark-blue ring, offering it to Gia. She tries gripping it loosely in her fist, but I hold onto it for her as she mushes her gums over the cold silicone.

She continues suckling on it, and like magic, the screaming stops a few moments later.

"I don't hear any crying. Does that mean I can go back to bed?" Arielle asks.

"Yes, thank you." I blow out a relieved breath. "Sorry to wake you." I look at the clock over the oven. "*Shit*, at nearly four in the morning."

"It's okay, Luca. Call anytime. Goodnight," she tells me, ending the call.

Gia's eyes are puffy and red as she peers up at me. Her fine dark curls are a wild mess, not long enough to comb into a Pebbles-style ponytail.

My chest clenches. I barely even know her, and I'm already in love with this tiny girl in my arms.

I missed out on so much of her life; I'll be damned if I miss out on any more.

Chapter Twelve

Samara

Friday, July 10, 2026

I tap my foot, impatience coiling through me as I wait for Luca to grace me with his presence. He isn't late, but he's also not early, and that rubs me the wrong way. Though *everything* about him rubs me the wrong way, so I shouldn't be surprised.

When I finally see him flying through the parking lot toward the doors of my law firm, I square my shoulders, ready to get this over with.

"Good morning, Samara," he tells me, wiping his palms down his shirt to smooth them over his muscled chest.

"Luca." I nod, turning to head inside. He hastens his pace to get ahead of me, reaching for the door and holding it open.

My brows pinch together. "Thank you," I say with a curt nod.

What the hell?

"Follow me. We have a few things to discuss prior to meeting with your ex and her attorney."

We head into my office, my cobalt blue heels clicking against the marble floors, taking a seat at my desk.

"I thought we had pretty much covered everything the other day," he says.

I nod. "We had, but I reviewed the case more thoroughly now that I have all the details from you, and I wanted to discuss a few more things. The most important one being that I need you to level your expectations."

"In what way?" he asks, cocking his head to the side.

"Cecily has made it clear up to this point that she'd like to sign over custody to you, but between now and the official court hearing, she *could* change her mind. I'm not saying that to disappoint or upset you. I'm not even saying she'd win, but I want you to know that there's a lot that goes into custody battles. Unfortunately, a jury is more inclined to award the mother full custody than they are the father, especially since you haven't been present for the majority of her life."

He leans back in his chair, crossing his ankle over his thigh as he stares me down. "I wasn't *present* because she didn't tell me Gia even existed. It wasn't as if I had a choice in the matter," he grits out.

He's right, and for once, I'm not judging him, but it's an unfortunate truth. "I understand that, but the court may not. Regardless, this is a moot point because as of right now, she's planning to sign over parental rights. I only wanted you to be cognizant of the possible challenges we could face in the coming weeks or even months. Okay?" I ask, hoping to get this show on the road.

"Okay," he says, nothing else.

Well, alrighty then.

"Any questions?" I ask, already pushing away from my desk to stand.

"Just one." He squeezes the back of his neck as he peers up at me. "Am I really such a shitty person that you can't be bothered to treat me like a human being?"

His question nearly knocks me out.

I've been nothing but nasty to him since our first conversation; I've given him no grace. As a Black woman who's had more than my fair share of people treating me less than, his statement pulls at my heartstrings and makes me more uncomfortable than I'd already felt. My chest squeezes, throat suddenly dry. If I weren't so distraught, maybe I'd have a better, kinder response for him, but as it stands, I don't.

Not yet.

I have to work to cool my expression. "What I think of you doesn't matter. It's what the judge and jury think of you. Focus on being a good father to that little girl, and we shouldn't have any issues."

I hightail it out of that office, hoping he'll follow me because I can't bring myself to look him in the face right now.

He's right. He's given me no reason to dislike him as much as I do. So far, all I've seen is a sort of cocky guy who leans on his family for help and is dealing with an impossible situation. And still, I prejudged him based on tabloids alone.

That thought makes my skin crawl, but then I'm quickly reminded of the way he paid to have his problems solved for him. And not just *his* problems, but another woman's chance at being a mother if she had wanted it.

Chapter Thirteen

Luca

I have to fight to keep my composure. My hands remain in fists under the wooden conference table as Cecily and her attorney quietly discuss their terms. She agrees to sign over parental rights but refuses to pay child support, which is fine by me as I never even asked her to.

I don't want her money.

I don't even want her involved after this. She wants to wash her hands of Gia so badly, let her do just that.

Because she is *my* kid, and even if Cici doesn't want her, *I sure as fuck do.*

I plan to make sure she grows up knowing that. Every. Damn. Day.

Samara clears her throat beside me, drawing my attention back to the conversation. "As I was saying, Cecily St. James will sign the agreement in front of the judge. As soon as we've heard back about a court date, I'll be in contact," her attorney, a middle-aged man named Hank, says with all the authority he can muster.

"If that's all, we're done here," Samara says, standing and effectively ending the meeting without another word. We each reach across the table to shake hands as Cecily's big blue eyes stay cast downward, never once meeting mine.

This just feels so... off.

***

"Thank you, Samara," I tell her as she walks me down to the lobby.

She nods. "You're welcome, Luca." She continues ahead of me until we're at the front doors. "I'll call you with updates. Have a good rest of your day," she says before strutting off in the direction of her office.

I wouldn't exactly call her shift in attitude warm and fuzzy, but it's a positive improvement from the way she's been speaking to me since we first met. Rome had warned me that Samara would see through all of my "pretty boy charm," as he calls it, and considering at one point *he* had been the biggest player of the two of us, I can imagine he's speaking from experience.

My eyes snag on her hips as they sway with her, that snug pencil skirt hugging against every one of her perfect curves.

If she weren't my attorney and *didn't want to punch my lights out,* I'd love nothing more than for her to come all over my tongue while she rides my face with those thick thighs.

Jesus Christ, I need a cold shower.

I haven't gone this long without an orgasm since I was a fucking teenager.

I shake the thoughts out of my head, and instead, I revel in the relief of knowing that Gia, *my kid,* is going to really be mine soon.

Now, it's just a waiting game.

Chapter Fourteen

Samara

Sunday, July 12, 2026

"Alright, sis, it's time to tell me why you polished off three glasses of wine already tonight." Vea eyes me speculatively. Before I can respond, she puts both of her palms up in surrender. "I'm not judging you, but this isn't like you." She leans forward to grab her own wineglass. "So spill."

I groan, leaning back into the royal-blue couch cushions.

Nosy pain in my ass... always knows when something's bothering me.

"Aren't we supposed to be planning your wedding anniversary?" I question, trying to change the subject, but I know it's futile. Once she's gotten her claws in something, she doesn't let go. *Maybe she should've been the lawyer.*

"Yeah, don't give me that. Tell me what's really on your mind 'cause I know you don't wanna hear about your older sister getting some 'cause *that's* how I'm celebrating my anniversary."

"Lord Jesus, woman! Can you chill?" I yell, snatching the pillow beside me as I try and fail to suffocate myself out of this conversation.

"Damn pillow is too breathable," I grumble before tossing it at her instead.

She dodges it and cuts right to the chase. "Is it the IVF? Have you decided to try another round or something?"

I blow out a breath, already wishing I could crawl into bed and hide from this conversation. "No, Vea, I'm not doing it again. I just *can't.*" *It nearly killed me the first five times.*

"Well, why not? I know it ain't the money, so what is it?"

"You know, for someone who carries on about being so damn sensitive to other's feelings, you don't seem to be doing a great job," I snap, feeling bad about it the moment the words leave my mouth. I've always been a little impulsive with my words when I feel personally attacked. It's as if I'm being backed into a corner, and the feeling makes my mouth move faster than my brain can seem to. Luckily that doesn't extend to the courtroom when it's my clients under attack.

Her expression softens, and she places a hand on my thigh, squeezing gently. "All I'm saying is that there *are* other options. You don't have to give up entirely. Even if it isn't IVF."

I nod slowly. "I know there are other options, but I'm a single Black woman. Please tell me where the adoption agencies are that are jumping for joy for applicants like me. I'd *love* to know."

She gives me an incredulous look. "Exactly." I shake my head.

"Your feelings are valid, as are your concerns, but why not surrogacy or one more round of IVF? There's more than one way to start a family, Mara," she says, hope lacing her words.

"Because it fucking hurts. Emotionally, every time I have another negative test, physically, as I jab myself with needles senselessly, hoping for a different outcome, and financially, it's a huge burden. Even if I have the money, it's too much of everything. IVF usually has a very good success rate at nearly seventy percent. So I have to think that when I've done five rounds of this shit with no results, it's just not going to happen for me," I explain, rubbing at the ache in my chest.

"*A dat wid yuh now.*" She rolls her eyes, crossing her arms over her chest.

"Oh, you can't stand me? *I'm sorry,* but you asked! I'm giving you the only answer I know how. Or did you want me to lie?" My voice is becoming louder the more defensive I feel.

"Stop with that." She waves her hand in front of my face. "You always find the negative."

"Vea, please." I plead with her to understand. "My body is so tired. *I* am *so* tired. I have to shave my face daily to keep my lady beard in check because most laser hair removal systems aren't safe for our complexion. I work my ass off to stay in shape so I don't have to sport something so *lovingly* referred to as an 'apron belly.'" I say the phrase with every ounce of disgust I feel toward it.

The fact that so many people with ovaries and a uterus have to suffer from polycystic ovarian syndrome is fucked. You'd think with how prevalent it is that there'd be real treatments for it, but there aren't, and I think it's largely to do with it being something that doesn't impact people with a dick and balls. *As if either of those are so damn useful.*

"You and your body are beautiful, sis. You do hard things with that body every day! You should be proud of it!" It's moments like this that remind me how much of a disconnect we sometimes have between us.

My body sags. "I know my body does hard things, but it's also difficult on my mind. Now, can we *please* stop talking about this?"

"Fine," she huffs out. "Tell me about work."

This is safer territory, and *maybe* she can help me work something out. I share limited details with Vea, maintaining attorney-client privilege, and I mention how off-putting I find Luca, and throughout the entirety of it, several things become more and more clear to me.

She clucks her tongue. "Uh-huh, and you don't think that this man having a baby dropped into his hands with not one effort could be playing a factor in your *feelings* toward him?" she asks, suspicion clear as day in her words.

My shoulders sag. "It's *possible*." I groan.

She rolls her eyes again, not even bothering to justify what I've said with a response. "Okay, *fine. Maybe* I have been putting some of my trauma on him, but it doesn't change the fact that he's a playboy, and based on how easily he dumped that poor woman after her abortion, he probably had no plans of becoming a father. Who's to say he really even wants this child? Besides, he has all this money and walks around getting recognized left and right, always being seen with a new woman. *That* definitely plays a part in why I don't fuck with him like that."

"Mhmm," she says. "I'm sure it does." Her big brown eyes glimmer as a smile tugs across her lips. "Maybe if he's so fertile, he could help you with your pum-pum problem."

Wine dribbles out of my mouth as I fight to stop myself from spraying it across the room. "I *do not* have a pum-pum problem! My vagina is *fine.* It's my fucking ovaries that are useless."

"Ohh, you don't have a pum-pum problem, huh? When was the last time you had an orgasm with a *person* and not your hand?" she asks, already knowing the answer.

"Four years," I grumble somewhat incoherently.

"Sorry, what was that?" she asks, her hands cupped behind her ears as she leans into me dramatically. "I couldn't hear you, sis. You couldn't possibly have said *four years.*"

"You suck," I deadpan.

She cracks another grin. "And sadly, it seems you don't. Maybe if you did, you'd be having more orgasms." She stands abruptly, downing the rest of the wine in her glass before heading in the direction of my guest room.

"*Mi gaan,*" she calls over her shoulder, disappearing down the hall.

I let my body slide down into the cushions. I love my sister, but she has a way of dredging up every uncomfortable topic on the planet, and it isn't what I needed tonight.

My mind wanders as I scroll mindlessly online, reading article after article about Luca De Laurentiis and his most recent "conquests," as the media so disgustingly calls these women he's seen with.

They're *human beings,* not quests to be conquered.

I place my phone down on the coffee table before turning the TV on. Clearly, I can't be trusted with social media tonight. Nothing good can come from my doomscroll.

My body finally starts to relax, and with it, my mind, but the harsh screech of my phone ringing startles me.

As I grab for it and see a newly familiar name across the screen, annoyance ramps up inside me.

"This is Samara," I answer.

"Ms. Perez-Allen, this is Hank. I'm calling about Ms. Cecily St. James. There's been a change of plans for our court hearing tomorrow."

My stomach drops to my toes. *I knew that woman was wifty.*[1]

"What kind of change?" I ask through gritted teeth.

"She no longer wishes to sign over her parental rights. She wants full custody." And with that, he hangs up.

"Fuck, fuck, fuck." I try not to scream.

I can't help but feel somewhat responsible for this.

I *know* that I'm not *actually* the cause, but somehow, I feel guilty for even putting this kind of bad energy into the universe for my client.

My hands shake as I dial his number. On the second ring, he answers.

"Samara?" he asks, and I can hear Gia crying in the background.

"Shh, shh, it's okay, Gia, *mia bambina.* Daddy's got you," he coos to the little girl, and her cries quiet almost instantly.

My chest tightens with the blow I'm about to deliver.

---

1. "Wifty" is a term used in Philadelphia to describe something as not being concrete or solid.

"Luca, I'm very sorry to call at this late hour, but there's been a change to tomorrow's agenda." I do my best to keep my voice from wavering as a crushing feeling settles over my chest.

"Oh, okay. Well, that shouldn't be a big deal. Let me know what time it's been moved to, and I'll arrange for someone to watch Gia," he tells me, clearly having no idea what I'm really getting at.

"It's not that kind of change, unfortunately. Cecily St. James has decided that she wants full custody now," I explain.

"Why?" His voice comes out so soft, like a defeated little puff of smoke, and a fissure slices through my heart.

"I'm not sure, Luca, but we'll get it figured out tomorrow. For now, try to get some sleep, and we'll talk in the morning." I try to sound as comforting as I can manage. After the way our conversation with Cecily and Hank had gone, there was no indication she'd change her mind so abruptly.

He doesn't respond at first, but when he does, it nearly breaks my heart in two. "Thank you, Samara, for"—he clears his throat—"for letting me know. See you tomorrow."

My job isn't always full of wins, but it's moments like these that remind me just how difficult certain parts can be.

This is going to be harder than I thought.

Chapter Fifteen

Luca

Monday, July 13, 2026

I'm exhausted, and this time, it isn't because of Gia's late-night cries. Ever since I moved her bassinet to be at my bedside, she sleeps pretty soundly once I can get her to sleep.

No, this bone-deep exhaustion is from worry.

I was up the whole night pondering every decision I've ever made, wondering what I could've done differently and if any of it would have changed anything.

I wish I had heeded my family's warnings more and avoided being seen out with so many women. And if Cici's attorney decides to use this against me, it'll be up to the judge as to whether or not she thinks I'm fit to be a father. Unfortunately, I'm afraid I already know the answer to that.

All I'm guilty of is consensual, be it frequent sex, and still, something so simple could cost me my *daughter.*

If it does, I don't think I'll ever forgive myself.

Samara asked me to keep quiet unless she says otherwise, so I'm doing exactly that.

I've had more than enough experience with my mouth getting me into trouble, and I'm not willing to risk Gia for my chance to put my two cents in.

But that becomes increasingly more difficult as I sit here, shifting uncomfortably in my seat as Cecily's lawyer outlines all of my shortcomings for the judge to hear. *As if I'm not already fully aware of every mistake I've ever made leading up to this point.* I'm sure this will be great for my nightly inner monologue, hell bent on humbling me. If it comes down to it, we'll have to pick a jury, and then I'll have the *lovely* experience of doing this all over again.

I'm trying my best not to pay attention to what's being said since there's little I can do about it now. Instead, I focus on the handrails against the far wall with a hanging sign that says, "Wet paint." The smell of the fresh lacquer has been burning my nose since we sat down.

When Cecily takes her turn, making little jabs at me, acid settles in my gut. While most of the things she's saying would usually bounce off me, today, they stick.

The problem is that a lot of what they're saying *is* true. I wouldn't exactly consider myself someone who's fit to be a father either, but the way Cici's acting doesn't add up to me. The mood swings, and the way she's suddenly nit-picking my every action make me realize something I might've missed or not considered before.

Yes, she's absolutely lived her life with a silver spoon in her mouth, but she's never been someone I'd considered mean-spirited. She was always kind and generous, and frankly, I think we could've been together for a while if she hadn't broken things off.

I don't have any residual feelings for her, and I certainly wouldn't say I was ever *in love* with her, but we got along fairly well. I'm so confused as to how we ended up *here*.

Pregnancy is fucking incredible. The fact that a human being can take something practically microscopic and turn it into *another* living, breathing *person* is miraculous, but it can also wreak havoc on a person's body. There are so many hormonal changes that mess with your brain chemistry, and it can take months to feel some semblance of normalcy.

I've seen it time and time again with each of my sisters-in-law during their pregnancies. As much as there's a part of me that almost *wants* to just hate Cecily for the time I've missed out on with Gia and the stress that she's put me through, I *can't*.

I don't have the energy to hold that kind of hate right now, especially not when it isn't what's best for my daughter.

I've had to fall into a new role very quickly, and I recognize that there is so much that I'm still learning, but what I know for sure is that Gia having her mother in her life *is* what's best for her. But that doesn't mean that I shouldn't *also* be a part of it.

Without another thought, I push out of my seat, standing abruptly as I turn my attention to Cici.

"Luca, *sit down*," Samara grits out at me.

I bend to whisper to her as everyone watches me silently. "I need to speak to her," I say, straightening and heading toward Cici and her attorney, Hank.

He eyes me warily, and I can practically *feel* Samara's dark eyes burning holes into my back.

I hover over Cici for a moment, and when she keeps her eyes cast downward, I crouch beside her to meet her where she's at.

Her blue eyes are filled with sadness, and the red rimming her lashes nearly confirms all of my suspicions.

"Cici," I say quietly, hoping only she can hear me. I place a hand over her knee, squeezing gently. When she doesn't flinch or pull away, I maintain the point of contact, trying to physically ground her. "Tell me what you need," I whisper.

A sob wracks her body as she hunches forward, nearly collapsing into my arms.

I wind them around her, holding her securely to me as I continue speaking while she lets her emotions ebb and flow for everyone to see. "Cici, this isn't you, and I know it isn't. I want what's best for Gia, okay? And what's best for *her* is for *us* to work together. She needs us *both*," I tell her as she sobs into my chest. "I don't want to take her from you, but you've got to give me something here, Cici. I need to know what's going on so I can help."

She continues crying, her tears soaking through my suit jacket as she trembles against me.

Chapter Sixteen

Samara

Out of the hundreds, if not *thousands*, of times I've been in court, I've never seen anything like *this* before.

Instead of getting aggressive when Cecily and her attorney were trying to tarnish his reputation and make him out to be a villain, he consoles her.

He actually left me here to go hold the woman who's trying to take his child away as she sobs into his ten-thousand-dollar suit.

What kind of backward-ass universe am I living in?

And if *Hank* thinks he's getting away with badmouthing my client the way he did, he's got another thing coming. I'm gonna tell him about himself because he was outta pocket with that bullshit.

Chapter Seventeen

Luca

"I can't, Luca, I really can't," she sobs.

"You can't *what*, Cici? You've got to tell me what's going on here," I beg.

"Everything is too hard," she cries. "It all hurts. My body aches, and I want to be with her, but every time she cries, I just want to *strangle* her, and it's not right, Luca! This isn't how this was supposed to be. I was supposed to have her and love her unconditionally and give her anything she needs, but I'm just not good enough."

Believe me, I feel similarly.

My heart thuds violently against my ribs. My mind is catching on to a few specific words that send a chill of fear racing through me. "Cici," I whisper, my voice cracking. "Have you ever thought of ending your life?"

She freezes in my arms before the floodgates open even wider. She shakes against me as I fight to hold her still.

"Yes," she whispers when several minutes have passed, and her body lies limply against mine.

I run my hand over the crown of her head, stroking her silky strands in an attempt to comfort her. "I need you to get help," I whisper, my throat raw from repressed tears. "*Gia* needs you to get help, okay? I'll take care of her full-time while you get what you need, and you can see her as often as you want until you're cleared by a psychiatrist, and then we can co-parent." I hope the confidence in my words can somehow give *her* the strength she needs to seek help, but I pulled that plan out of my ass and have no idea what I'm doing either. "We can *both* be the parents that she needs us to be, but I need you to work with me here."

"Okay," she answers quietly a moment later, finally pulling away from my chest to look me in the eyes. "Thank you, Luca," she adds, and it cracks my heart wide open.

Chapter Eighteen

Samara

Tuesday, July 14, 2026

It's late by the time I get home.

My feet ache as I kick my heels off at the door, wiggling my cramped, swollen toes on the hard floors.

I roll my head from side to side, stretching out the tension gathered in my neck and shoulders from the first day of what's turning into a long string of days spent supporting Sierra, a client I've been meeting with for two months now.

She's worked so damn hard to get her shit together for her son, but her ex has found an attorney who's more than happy to stereotype my client, using harmful insinuations about her character to back up his claims.

There are very few things in this world that piss me off more than people with inherent privilege from the color of their skin and the dick and balls swinging between their legs to get further in life.

My muscles feel rigid, and my jaw has seemingly ceased to unclench since we finished up today.

I set my purse on the entryway table, grabbing my phone from the inside pocket and sorting through messages as I make my way to my room for a nice, hot bath.

My eyes land on a text from Luca, and my lips pinch together as I read the message.

Luca

Hey Samara, I just wanted to thank you again for everything you've done for Gia and me. I know we may have gotten off on the wrong foot, but I couldn't have done this without you guiding me through the process. My little girl and I get to have many more nights like this one because of you, and I can't thank you enough for that. Have a great rest of your night.

It doesn't really feel like I did much of anything.

Frustrated tears well in my eyes as I click on the attached image. Luca and Gia are cuddled up on a couch with a fluffy pink blanket wrapped around them. Gia's lids are barely open, but there's no hiding those stunning eyes that mirror her father's. *One green and one blue.*

For the rest of the night, I will myself to stop thinking about Luca. He's done nothing but add stress to my already hectic life, and somehow, he's an anomaly. I find myself repeatedly thinking about every way in which this man has surprised me since knowing him, and it frustrates me to no end that I'm starting to think far more of the good than I am the bad.

Chapter Nineteen

Samara

Thursday, July 16, 2026

My heart feels heavy after my final day in court with Sierra.

The judge afforded her custody two days out of each week, with the possibility for additional time spent with her son after she can supply proof of a stable and sufficient income and a home to match.

Every time I have an outcome like this, it brings up the errant feelings I still struggle with surrounding Cora. I don't love the idea of my clients having to be around their abusers, even if they weren't physically abused. Emotional abuse is just as bad, if not worse, to some because, without the physical evidence, it can be extremely difficult for victims to realize they're being abused and have the strength to seek help.

The emotions swarming inside me from Sierra's case are so different from how I felt earlier this week after Luca's hearing.

After we left the courthouse on Monday, I was dazed and confused, to say the least.

I've spoken to Luca a handful of times since then, getting paperwork together and finalizing his agreement with the mother of his child. It'll be a few weeks before everything is completely settled from a legal perspective, but she's already started at an inpatient psychiatric hospital, where she'll have access to medication, group therapy, and one-on-one counseling until she feels ready to transition to an outpatient setting.

I should be happy that this went so well for my client, but mostly, I'm confused.

And while confusion is definitely at the top of the list of emotions I've been battling with in regard to Luca and Gia, it certainly isn't the only one.

I'm in disbelief that Luca was even able to recognize what Cecily was going through, let alone act on his intuition in front of a room full of people actively making judgments about him.

And I was one of them.

I'm annoyed that he's somehow managed to weasel his way into my mind in every spare moment I have.

There's also a sense of unease filling my gut that makes me worry I might be losing my touch. *Maybe I'm not as good at reading people as I used to be? Maybe I've become cynical after so many terrible experiences for myself, my friends, and my clients?*

And then there's the anguish I felt for Cecily, and frankly, still do. I feel crushed for her and every other woman who has to battle it out with so many changes and the stress that comes with pregnancy only to be thrown for another loop after delivery.

Postpartum depression is a hell of a thing to go through for anyone, but especially when the pregnancy was a surprise. I'm frustrated that she didn't tell Luca that she was pregnant, but I can also sympathize with the fact that she was likely overwhelmed and probably thinking a lot of what I was when I first met him.

That there was no way he would change his ways for that child.

And then there's the unsteady feeling surrounding why I can't seem to stop thinking about him in the first place.

It's clear that there's more than meets the eye with Luca, and even that irritates me.

"Ah, come on," I grumble, making the decision I've been dwelling on for hours now.

I'll just drive over there, make sure he's adjusting fine, and then I'll leave. It's nothing more than a professional visit from his lawyer to ensure everything is going well for my client.

That is all this is.

Christ, I *hope* that's all this is.

Hopping in the Range Rover, I set up my Bluetooth and start up my favorite playlist for when I'm feeling out of it.[1]

I pull out onto the road and head toward the last person on the planet who I thought I'd be willingly seeking out.

***

My hands are practically shaking as I head toward his front door. *Why the fuck am I here again?*

---

1. **Wonder Woman — John Legend**

I banish the thought as soon as it pops into my head. *I probably won't like the answer to that question.*

Knocking gently, I stand here unmoving, staring at the dark-blue door before me as I contemplate all of my life decisions up to this point.

Why am I here?

I should leave. Besides, I probably didn't knock hard enough for anyone to hear me.

Yep, no one would've heard me. I'll turn around, get in my car, and save myself from this awkward-ass conversation.

Just as I'm finally ungluing my feet from the ground, his door bursts open.

A cloud of cool air rushes out of his house, and a woman who I recognize to be Luca's mother smiles up at me from the doorway. She's seated in a purple electric wheelchair with rhinestone flames emblazoned on the sides.

Well, you can't say she isn't making the most of her condition.

"Hello, can I help you?" she asks politely, her lips turned up in a small grin.

That's when I realize I've been staring at her, unblinking, unmoving, and unspeaking. *This was a horrendous idea.*

"Oh, sorry, I'm Samara. I'm Luca's attorney. I wanted to stop by and check in on him and Gia," I stammer, trying to explain my presence, but as the words leave my mouth, I'm nearly certain they do nothing to make her believe this would be considered typical behavior for an attorney.

One light brow quirks as she appraises me. The breath finally leaves my lungs as she wheels herself backward, opening the door wide for me to enter.

"Come on in, Samara. Luca should be out of the shower soon."

I nod, following after her and closing the door behind me. It takes some time to get my bearings because, like every other time I've been near him, *Luca De Laurentiis surprises me at every turn.*

I expected a bachelor pad with a few children's items lying around, but that's not what I see inside the single-story home I'm currently standing in.

His home has a very masculine quality, but it's tastefully decorated and *cozy.*

There's a mix of light and dark-blue accents that bring a certain calm to the space, and it's exceptionally clean. Like, impeccably so.

The smell of freshly baked cookies wafts up my nose, and damn, I could go for a chocolate chip cookie right now.

The kitchen counter is lined with baby bottles, and there's a myriad of toys, blankets, and other children's items, but everything seems to have its place.

"I'm Gloria, by the way. Go ahead and take a seat." She waves at the large gray sectional couch positioned in the living room.

"Thank you. I didn't mean to intrude," I say, now that some of my nerves have settled. "Things hadn't gone according to plan, so I figured I should make sure my client is doing well." I pray she doesn't hear the lie.

She chuckles, bringing her hand up to cover her mouth in an effort to muffle the sound as she peers up at me. "Mhmm, I'm sure you make house calls like this for *all* of your clients," she says suggestively. "Don't worry, your secret's safe with me."

I don't bother responding to her because it's clear that she's aware this *isn't* typical, and saying anything else is likely to dig the hole deeper.

So, instead, I take a seat, positioning myself toward the television. She turns it on, and of course, a pre-recorded hockey game is playing.

But it's not just any game; it's an old Philly Scarlets game.

Luca's face comes into view, and the camera zooms in on it. Even with his headgear and mouthguard, you can tell he's gorgeous.

His eyes glimmer as he waves to his fans from the ice, and it takes everything in me to peel my gaze away from the screen and turn my attention to Gloria.

She smirks at me and asks, "Do you read?"

My cheeks heat at that, and not for the first time, I'm glad my brown skin doesn't give away my blush as easily as it would for someone more fair-skinned.

"I do," I tell her, not wanting to provide any additional detail.

"What kind of books do you read?" she asks, and I shift in my seat as nerves dance in my belly.

I clear my throat. "Oh, you know, romance."

Her smirk grows wider. "Any chance you read smut?"

My eyes widen as I choke on my own saliva, sputtering as she claps me firmly on the back from her seat beside the couch, making the coughing even worse as she does.

"You okay, dear? I didn't mean to choke you," she chortles.

"I'm fine," I say with a half-hearted laugh.

"I take it you *do* read smut," she says with glee. "I have a book club I've lovingly named 'Always Smutty In Philadelphia.' We even have our own T-shirts, personalized wine glasses, and a whole line of merch!" Her tone becomes higher with every word as excitement flows through her.

My brows pinch in confusion for a moment as I take that in. "That's"—I pause—"well, hell." I chuckle. "That's actually pretty cool." A smile tugs at the corners of my lips.

It appears Luca isn't the only one in this family whose personality holds more than meets the eye.

"You should come! We usually have it the last Saturday of each month, but with everything going on last month, we pushed it to this weekend. I'll have Luca text you the address," she tells me, making it clear there was not a single question in her comment. She wasn't *asking* me to come; she was making a request.

Before I can argue, Luca walks out of the room adjacent to the living area wearing nothing but a pair of gray sweats as he holds Gia tightly to his bare chest.

My ovaries do a little dance that causes me to shift in my seat again, and I can't help but suck in a breath.

For the love of god.

"Samara?" he asks, his dark brows drawn tightly together as he takes me in. "What are you doing here?" He doesn't sound upset, more like concerned.

I guess if I were in his position, my lawyer's presence would cause some unease for me too.

"I was in the area and figured I'd stop by to check on you and Gia. It isn't often..." I chuckle. "Or ever, actually, that a custody battle ends the way it did with you, so I thought it'd be good to stop by and check in." I stand abruptly, doing my best to ignore the expression on Gloria's face. I have a sneaking suspicion her kids never got away with a single thing in their lives, at least without her intentionally allowing it to happen. "And now that I have, it seems you're doing just fine, so I'll get out of your hair," I say, clapping my clammy hands against my thighs.

I do my best to rush to the door but trip on something in front of Gloria.

Did she just trip me?

"Oh dear, I'm so sorry! Are you alright?" she asks me, not sounding the least bit concerned.

I don't miss the way Luca rolls his eyes at her as I pick myself off the ground before he can try to help me up. Unfortunately for my pride, I'm too damn slow.

He reaches down, holding Gia firmly to his chest with one arm as he leans and winds his free arm around me, hoisting me up off the floor.

Luca doesn't let go of me until I'm firmly situated in front of him. "Thanks," I grumble.

He grins, shaking his head lightly at my response.

"Anytime, Samara." His bright eyes roam over my body slowly, leaving a lick of heat in their wake. *I need to get the hell out of here.*

I nod, but there's an annoying swarm of butterflies flooding my stomach that does nothing but distract me. "Well, it was nice to see you again, Luca, and nice meeting you, Gloria," I tell them, keeping my eyes cast downward as I try for the second time to make my exit. Hoping for a more graceful and *successful* departure this time.

"It was nice meeting you too!" She waves at me. "I'm excited to see you Saturday; we start at six!"

Before I can even get a response out, Luca's eyes cut to mine. "Saturday?" he asks his mother but keeps his eyes trained on me.

"Samara will be joining us for book club," she explains as if I had already agreed.

His brows pinch together. "You will?" His next question has me plastering a cool expression on my face before leaving the house. "Who would've thought?" he clucks. "You read those *nasty* books too, huh?"

I huff, rolling my eyes at him as his smirk grows. "Goodbye, Luca," I say as I *finally* get out of this house.

Chapter Twenty

Luca

After Samara left earlier, I texted her my parents' address per my mom's request. *Who am I kidding?* Her demand.

I have no idea how the hell that conversation started or *why*, but I have a sneaking suspicion that it was entirely my mother's doing. As to why she would invite her, I'm not sure, and if Samara doesn't want to go, I desperately hope she doesn't. My mom means well, but I wouldn't want Samara, or anyone else for that matter, to feel obligated to humor her if they're uncomfortable.

But when Samara never responded to my text, I actually felt sort of… disappointed?

I'm not totally sure why. An address doesn't exactly warrant a response, but I was kind of hoping that she's warmed up to me. I mean, her explanation about checking in on me and Gia was total bullshit, and we all knew it. My mom made sure to hammer that home the moment Samara was out the door. Maybe my mom's whimsical thoughts of Samara and me having something managed to mess with my mind.

But if her explanation wasn't the real reason, then *why* would she have stopped by?

This woman is infuriating.

She leaves me with so many questions and no answers. I don't even know why I'm still thinking about her. Up to this point, she's made it extremely clear that she doesn't like me. Hell, she barely even tolerates me, yet she showed up at my home. And here I am, hoping that she's changed her mind about me.

Peering back at the TV, I do my best to focus on the play-by-play on the screen, wishful for anything to take my mind off Samara, but not even sports are working.

My dick stiffens in my sweats as I think about how maddeningly sexy it is that she doesn't put up with my bullshit.

I know very little about her, and that fact alone keeps drawing me right in. She's like a silk weaver. Beautiful and dangerous, just the same.

I'd love to get tangled in her web, but something tells me that if I did, *I'd never find my way out.*

Chapter Twenty-One

Samara

My skin feels sticky with sweat, and there's a pounding in the base of my skull that won't let up. I've been tossing and turning for over an hour, unable to sleep despite the unyielding exhaustion that's settled into my bones.

It was ungodly hot today, and every cell in my body feels swollen from the heat. My ankles are the size of cantaloupes, and I feel overheated and entirely too uncomfortable to sleep.

I've stripped down to nothing but my panties, and somehow, I am *still* hot.

Unfortunately, I'm not able to dissociate enough to even pretend I don't know what's really happening here.

Ever since Luca texted me, I can't stop thinking about how good he looked shirtless. Granted, he had a child on his chest, but that didn't keep me from noticing his corded arms and washboard abs.

Even his ass looked perky in those sweats, and I keep trying—*and failing*—to tell myself that the girthy length I saw in the front of his pants was his phone.

Sadly, my pussy doesn't seem to have gotten the memo that we're actively avoiding thoughts of this man.

My hand slips down my soft tummy, my fingers toying with the delicate lace of my panties.

Maybe if I just make myself come, I'll be able to sleep.

I'm sure it isn't really *Luca* who's causing my thoughts to be in such disarray. It's merely that he's the most attractive man I've seen *recently,* and my mind has snagged on that.

That absolutely *has* to be it.

I reach for the massive pump bottle of lube on my nightstand, and sigh against my pillows as my fingers slide under the soft fabric, making their way to my center.

Groaning, I press my middle finger over my aching clit, applying just the right amount of pressure as I close my eyes.

Chapter Twenty-Two

Luca

My dick springs free as I lower my sweats down my thighs. Gripping myself at the shaft, I give it a tight squeeze, and my eyes nearly roll in the back of my head from the pressure.

"Fuck," I mutter.

I stroke myself from base to tip, switching up my pace as I close my eyes. I haven't come in weeks.

I need this.

As my balls start to tighten and my thighs clench from the pleasure building, I can't help but think of *her*.

How her dark eyes would look glazed over from the pleasure I'd make sure she'd had before she even thought about taking care of me. How her plump wet lips would look wrapped around my cock as she filled her throat with it.

I'd run my fingers through her thick coils, gripping her roots and making her take me all the way to the hilt.

But I wouldn't come like this.

No.

I'd have to be inside her. I'd love nothing more than to watch as she comes undone around me, riding my dick. Her thick brown thighs squeezing my sides as she lowers herself onto me.

My hand pumps faster, seeking the friction I wish *she* were giving me.

My breath comes out in pants, tension coiling throughout me as I picture her smart mouth open wide. Her gorgeous head thrown back as I fuck myself into her, watching as she takes every ounce of her pleasure from me.

Chapter Twenty-Three

Samara

My fingers work frantically, transitioning from pumping in and out of my core to circling my swollen clit.

My mind wanders to *him.* I do my best to picture literally *anyone* else.

I think back to the men I've dated in the past, and when that doesn't work, I try to picture celebrities, but that doesn't cut it either.

Time and time again, the man I see pleasuring me is *Luca.*

I imagine him eating me out from behind, smacking my ass just the way I like. When I'm nearing the edge, he buries his tongue deep inside me before flipping me over and pulling me to the edge of the bed.

Without a word, he grips the base of his dick, rubbing his engorged tip between my pussy lips, pressing it against my clit before sliding into me.

He tosses my ankles over his shoulders, gaining better access as he thrusts so deeply I feel it *everywhere*.

Chapter Twenty-Four

Luca

Fire spreads through me as I picture her finally meeting her release. She comes around my cock, spasming and gripping me like a vice.

I can practically feel the ache between her legs and the pinch in my sides as she squeezes her thighs around my hips. My mind paints a pretty picture and an even prettier symphony of the sounds she'd make as she cries out for me to fill her sweet cunt.

My ass clenches, and hot cum spurts out onto my stomach as I ride the wave of my release, wishing it were Samara I was coming inside of and not the palm of my calloused hand.

I haven't even had her, and I might already be obsessed.

Chapter Twenty-Five

Samara

"Oh god," I moan, my core clenching and spasming as I fight to keep up the pace, slipping my other hand in to work my clit.

Except, it isn't *my* hand I'm imagining right now.

It's still Luca as he brings me over the edge.

My pussy walls clamp around my fingers, and my lace panties rub against my knuckles as I come apart thinking about Luca De Laurentiis and his goddamn monster dick fucking me into the next century.

This is so messed up.

Chapter Twenty-Six

Samara

Saturday, July 18, 2026

A small smile spreads across my lips as my foot halts on the pedal, taking in the green onesie with rainbow dinosaurs. "Just a couple more stitches and I'll be all done," I say to myself with a little nod.

I really should get a new sewing machine because this one is, frankly, ancient, but I can't bring myself to part with it yet.

It's the first my dad was ever able to buy my mom after he worked tirelessly to open the restaurant of his dreams, all while somehow managing to keep food on the table for us.

This old-ass machine is the same one my mom taught me how to sew on when I was five years old, and it still works. It doesn't have all the fancy attachments that the new ones do, and if I'm being honest, it would probably take me a quarter of the time to finish a piece of clothing with any other machine.

Maybe I'll keep this one as a sort of art piece and upgrade to something more practical soon.

My foot lifts off the pedal as soon as I get to the end of the garment, and I snip the last bit of thread off.

I fold the onesie and place it in the bag at my feet with the rest of them before scooching out of my chair to get ready to go.

***

As I enter the shelter, I see Brandi standing at the counter, speaking with one of my clients. "Hey ladies," I greet them.

"What are you doing here on a Saturday at this time? Shouldn't you have a hot date or something?" Brandi jokes, knowing damn well I *never* have a hot date.

"Ha ha ha, very funny." I roll my eyes playfully at her. "Hey, Charice, you're just the woman I was looking for." I wink at her from behind the counter.

Brandi buzzes me in, so I head on back. "Is now an okay time to go over the details for next week?"

"Of course it is," she tells me, making her way around the counter to follow me back to one of the private meeting rooms reserved for counselors and lawyers like me working pro bono cases.

I hold the door to an empty room open for her and close it once she's passed me. We take a seat on opposite sides of the plastic folding table.

I set the bag of clothing on the floor beside me and lay the file containing all of her court documents in the center of the table.

I slide my hands palms up across the table for her to take. She squeezes them gently and gives me a hopeful smile that wreaks havoc on my emotions.

I feel a lump forming in my throat and hot tears threatening to well behind my eyes but push them away before they can make an appearance. *This isn't about me.* It's about Charice and her gorgeous children getting the opportunity they should've been afforded so long ago.

"We're going to get those babies back to you. Do you understand me, Char?" I ask, pushing every ounce of confidence I can muster into my voice.

She nods her head, but I don't miss the way her lips purse together in a slight grimace. "We are," she says, her voice cracking.

We spend the next half hour sorting out the final details of her case. It's been months of compiling this information, all while ensuring the safety of my client remains intact as she fights for her future inside the walls of this shelter.

Offering pro bono services at a place like this comes with its unique challenges. I have to be extremely strategic as to what I'm willing to divulge about my clients and their circumstances during court hearings, even if giving more detail would increase their chances of actually winning.

The thing is, these people have been dealt an unfair hand in life, and while I know I'm playing the absolute smallest role in helping them get their lives back on track, it's something I take very seriously. It's easily the most important thing I'll ever do in this lifetime.

Sure, I help a lot of people settle custody cases, but the truth is, I only take the paid cases in order to fund the ones like these.

"Alright," she says with a small smile. "I guess we're all set then."

She moves to stand, but I stop her. "Wait, one more thing." I grab the bag from beside me and set it on the table. I push it toward her, and her brows climb her smooth, tan forehead as she eyes it in shock.

"For me?" she asks, hesitantly pulling it toward her when I dip my chin.

She takes out the items, her eyes glistening with unshed tears, and as she makes her way to the bottom of the bag, pulling out the cross-stitched blanket, they fall down her cheeks.

"Let's get those babies back to their momma, okay?" I ask, and she nods, squeezing her eyes tightly shut to stop the tears from falling.

***

I pull out of the shelter parking lot and follow the GPS to Gloria's house.

My heart feels heavy as I make the drive, my mind wandering.

I'm at the shelter most weekends and on the rare occasion that I don't have a client during the week. It always manages to make me think of Cora.

God, *I miss her.*

My best friend was the strongest, most outgoing, and hilarious person I've ever known. She was an incredible mother, *and then he used that against her.*

My eyes brim with tears as I imagine the future she could've had before it was all stolen from her.

***

I can't believe I actually showed up to this.

I never even asked what the name of the book was, so chances are, I haven't read it.

Why am I here?

I seem to be asking myself that question a whole lot since having met Luca De Laurentiis, though I find solace in knowing that this night isn't about him. It's about *hopefully* making some new girlfriends. I haven't really done much socializing since moving back to Philly after law school, and it would be nice to get to know some new people.

Upon entering the huge one-story home, I'm ushered to the living room by one of Luca's family members. She introduced herself as Charlie, and from my internet stalking, I believe that means she's Luca's only sister.

Apprehension fills my gut, and my chest feels tight as I make my way into the room, which is filled with a cacophony of women. This isn't some small book club like I'd hoped.

While none of these women look even remotely similar to one another, they all have one thing in common. They're all wearing T-shirts and crop tops that look like band tees which read, "Always Smutty In Philadelphia."

I hate to admit it, but they're adorable.

"Samara! I'm so glad you could make it," Gloria tells me, wheeling over to take my hand in hers. "Follow me. You can pick out your own shirt."

I like a woman who knows what she wants and has no qualms about getting it. And for some reason, Gloria De Laurentiis has her sights set on me. In what capacity? I have no idea.

Before following her, I look over my shoulder to see that all the women are no longer paying attention to me. It calms some of my earlier worries.

I hate being stared at.

She leads me into a small room with shelves lining the walls and organizers filled with all sorts of stickers, bookmarks, keychains, and stacks of T-shirts.

"Pick whatever color you want. You can change in here or use the bathroom down the hall." She smiles brightly up at me before leaving the room.

Dread fills me as I approach the stacks of shirts. I'm going to be humiliated if none of these fit. If they don't, what will I even do? Leave the room and tell them I'm allergic to jersey knit?

My lungs seize with relief so potent I almost want to cry as I scan the shelves, which are labeled with sizes ranging from extra-extra-small to a five-XL.

I grab a black full-length XXL T-shirt off the shelf and hold it up, ensuring it'll be roomy enough to be comfortable. The material is soft and stretchy, so I shouldn't have any problems.

Tugging my top off over my head, I set it down beside me before putting the new one on.

It's baggy enough to give me room for the inevitable bloat I'll be experiencing after a glass of wine or two.

After folding my other shirt, I slip out of the room and make my way back down the hall, tossing it in my purse and rejoining the women in the living room.

A petite woman with long, dark hair scooches over on one of the couches and pats the seat beside her. "You can sit next to me. I promise I only bite if you ask me to," she says with a wink.

I can't help but laugh at that and take a seat beside her. She gives me a reassuring smile. "I'm Aiyana," she says, introducing herself.

"Samara," I tell her. "Nice to meet you."

She smirks, her dark brows rising. "Oh, I know who you are. Gloria couldn't wait to tell us all about the gorgeous lawyer who saved our little Luca's ass *and* even came over for a house call."

My eyes widen an iota, but I suppress my initial reaction to that. *Of course Gloria would tell everyone about the lapse in judgment that ended me up here in the first place.*

"Aiyana," another woman whines. "Stop picking on her."

She rolls her eyes, leaning farther into the couch cushions. "I'm not picking on her; I'm making conversation," she says with a pout.

"You're an asshole, and you're patronizing her," another woman with bubblegum-pink hair calls from across the room, but her tone holds no bite, and it makes me smile. The way these women banter reminds me a lot of how things used to be between my sister, Cora, and me.

"Okay, ladies, I think it's time we play a little introductory game, don't ya think?" Gloria asks with a wide grin that sends a chill down my spine. I've already caught onto the fact that everything she does is with purpose and sheer mischief.

Everyone around me groans.

"Nothing good ever comes of this game," I hear someone whisper quietly.

She waves a hand in the air, dismissing the loud groans and protests as if they never happened at all. "Let's play truth or dare, but with a twist," Gloria says, her face beaming. *I'm beginning to realize this woman is a menace to society, and I think I may be her next victim.*

"Oh, here we go," Aiyana says, chuckling under her breath. "What the hell could be the twist this time? Don't you think you've run out of those by now?"

"Not a chance. The woman has the brain of a genius, but she uses it for evil," one of the women says with a groan.

"Yeah, yeah, yeah. Stop complaining," Gloria says cheerily, slapping her hands to her thighs. "This is how the game will go. We'll each go around the room and introduce ourselves. You'll say your name and one fun fact about you. The twist is that you get to choose whether or not this 'fact'"—she says the word with air quotes—"is actually true or not. If someone calls you out on your lie and it actually *is* a lie, you have to play truth or dare."

"Okay, so to clarify, we're basically just saying our name and something about us, and we can choose to fuck with each other?" Aiyana asks.

"Yep," Gloria confirms.

"Alright, I'll start," the curly-haired brunette who greeted me at the front door says. "I'm Charlie, Gloria's youngest daughter, and one fun fact about me is that my mother has been tormenting me since the day I arrived as a wee lil' babe."

"I won't deny any part of that statement," Gloria says proudly.

Charlie rolls her eyes and nods her head toward the pink-haired woman beside her. "Okay, I'm Rose, and Charlie's my wife."

"Well, that's not a fun fact, but it's true," Gloria grumbles, clearly disappointed by Rose's mundane response, though I sort of love how cut-and-dry she is.

Charlie laughs, planting a kiss on top of her wife's head as she says softly, "I think it's the most fun fact there is." It damn near makes me *swoon.* If I were reading that line in a book, I'd be giggling and kicking my feet.

"Alright, lovebirds, onto our little bird, Lark." Gloria tips her chin toward one of the two redheads in the room.

We continue like this for the next hour. Some of the women finally decide to tell a lie, each of which is easily caught because they know each other so well.

And much to my surprise, I'm actually having *fun.*

When they get to me, my stomach starts to twist. I was enjoying myself to the point that I forgot to formulate a response, and now I feel stuck. *What should I say?*

"Hi, I'm Samara." I try to think quickly on my feet. "And I graduated from Harvard Law before moving back to Philadelphia to practice family law."

"Hah." Aiyana snorts, pointing a finger at me. "That's a fucking lie; you went to Columbia with Rome."

My eyes widen. "How do *you* know Rome too?" *Good lord. For a homebody, that man certainly gets around.*

"Audrey was my wedding planner, thanks to Luca's suggestion," she says, smiling brightly.

Before I'm even able to form a response, Gloria's already back on her bullshit.

"Truth or dare, Samara?"

I repress the groan building in my throat as I consider the possible consequences of either option. Truth is probably safer because, from what I've seen of Gloria so far, she's likely to dare me to streak down the road, and I have zero interest in getting arrested.

"Truth," I grumble halfheartedly.

Her eyes light up, and a wide smile spreads across her face. "Why did you *really* come to see Luca the other day?"

I roll my eyes, doing my best not to come across as flustered as I am. Considering that's literally half of what makes me so good at my job, it shouldn't be as difficult to pull off as it feels at this moment. Namely, because *I'm* not even sure why I went over there. "As I said, I was only checking on my client. Nothing unusual. That was such a waste of a question," I say, keeping my tone even.

"I don't buy it," Charlie says.

"Me neither," a few others respond, and I know they aren't going to let this go.

"Majority rules. If your 'truth' is deemed a lie by most of us, you have to do a dare."

"You know, this feels a lot like hazing," I joke, a lighthearted laugh slipping past my lips. I don't actually feel threatened in any way, but I am a little miffed that they're not letting this go.

Gloria's eyes widen before her whole face softens. She places her hand on my thigh, giving it a gentle squeeze before quietly saying, "I never want you to feel that way, Samara. I'm truly sorry if we've pushed you too far. I'm a bit of a jokester, but everyone has their limits, and I sincerely apologize if I've overstepped."

I'm taken aback by this. She seems like someone who's usually unapologetic for her actions, but evidently, that's a poor assessment too.

"I won't lie and say I'm used to this kind of banter because I'm not." At least, I haven't been in a few years. I haven't really had many friends since Cora, and I've poured myself into my work as a result. "But I don't really feel like I'm being hazed. Don't worry. I'll do your dare; just make sure it isn't anything too wild."

"I have a dare," Kat says excitedly. Something about her soothes me. She's the type of person you can *tell* doesn't have a single malicious bone in her body. My shoulders relax at the thought of her being the one to make a suggestion.

"Okay, go for it," I urge.

"I dare you to come to my wedding," she says.

The thought makes me smile. I love weddings. "That's really sweet, but I'm not sure that's much of a dare." I chuckle.

Her eyes crinkle at the sides. "You see, the thing is..." She trails off, and my stomach twists before she finally continues, wringing her hands nervously. "The wedding is only a few months away, and we don't have any extra space. We've been trying to keep it relatively small so the venue doesn't accommodate any extra people."

My brows pull together in confusion. *Where the hell is this going?*

"There's one seat available..." She looks down at her feet, cheeks glowing pink. "As Luca's plus one."

I have to fight the urge to smack a hand over my face. Even *she's* a little deviant. "This whole family is full of troublemakers." I groan, but there's a part of me that enjoys it. I *like* that they've taken me in as one of their own immediately, not knowing me at all, and yet they feel comfortable enough to treat me the same as they would anyone else in this room.

"I'm not setting you up!" she exclaims. "I'm simply looking out for my wedding party. Luca's one of our groomsmen, obviously, and he needs someone to walk down the aisle with him. Otherwise, our photos will be ruined, and frankly, he probably won't have a lot of time for dating now that he's got Gia." She flutters her lashes at me. "Please, help me out?"

"Trouble, every single one of you," I say, shaking my head. "Fine, but only for the sake of your pictures. *And* I won't wear pastels," I say with a pointed glare.

"You can wear a tutu for all I care, but the bridesmaids' dresses are cabernet satin, so I'd suggest one of those," she says with a chuckle.

"Alright, send me the details, and I'll do my best to be there."

"Ah, really? Oh my gosh, this is so exciting!" she says before snatching a handful of salt-and-vinegar chips from the coffee table and settling back into her seat. As I peer around the room, everyone looks incredibly pleased with this turn of events, and the idea that I sort of am, too, has my ears burning.

It's just one night. One single night with Luca De Laurentiis.

Chapter Twenty-Seven

Samara

Sunday, July 19, 2026

Kat sent me the link to the website her other bridesmaids used for their dresses. Luckily, she wasn't picky about the style. She said I could choose whatever I wanted so long as it was satin and in the correct color.

I appreciate that more than she knows. I've been in more weddings than I can keep track of, and every time, the bride made me wear a dress that fit everyone *other than me.* I always felt so uncomfortable. My breasts were either pooling out of the top, my back fat was being strangled, my belly pooched out, or my hips were so constricted that I could hardly move, let alone dance.

It definitely eased my mind to know that I get to choose my own dress so it fits me properly.

But that doesn't calm the warring emotions I'm feeling about having to go with Luca.

This feels wholly inappropriate.

Hell, *I know* it's inappropriate, but hopefully, in the next week, the last of the paperwork will be filed, and I won't really be his lawyer anyway.

It'll all be fine.

I hear a knock on my door, and excitement suddenly rushes through me.

"Thank god for overnight shipping."

A middle-aged man stands on my porch, holding my package.

"Hey, thanks so much."

"No problem. Have a great day," he tells me, handing me the package before heading back to his van.

I tear into the package the moment I've closed my door, and a little squeal of delight leaves my lungs at seeing the gorgeous illustrated cover in my hands. I'm so glad this is the book they selected for this month's book club. I've had it on my TBR since before it was even released.

Relaxing back into my couch cushions and tossing my legs up, I settle in to read *Resilient Love.*

From the get-go, I'm dragged right into the prologue.

I tear through the locker room, fists balled as I make my way to Coach's office. Yanking the door open, it slams against the wall at my entrance. Coach leans back in his chair, his head supported by his forearms as he eyes me with a smug smirk stretched across his lips.

"What the fuck is this about?" I challenge.

"What ever are you talking about?" he asks, his tone dripping in sarcasm.

"You know good and well what I'm referring to."

At that, he sits up in his chair, wiping the smirk clean from his face. He levels me with a flat expression before saying, "You want my job when I retire. Do this for me, and it's yours."

The wind is knocked from my lungs, a rebuttal on the tip of my tongue but it never makes its way out of my mouth.

Coach Auclair relaxes back into his seat, crossing his arms over his chest. "I don't do ultimatums, so the job is yours regardless of whether you accept the position or not, but I really hope you will. I plan to retire in the next two years and I don't want to have to worry about what I plan to do with this team."

I can barely think past the throb of my heartbeat against all of my pulse points as my mind works to figure out what his intentions are. "What's so special about this women's football team that I, of all people, am being requested as their interim coach? And why would you suggest me in the first place? I haven't competed in a football match in years."

Coach Auclair knows all about my painful past with football, and if that weren't reason enough not to include me in whatever plan he has, I'm not sure what is. This isn't adding up.

He lets out a sigh, placing his hands on the desk in front of him. He squeezes his eyes shut, and pinches the bridge of his nose, steadying himself.

"It's my daughter's team."

My brows scrunch together. "I'm still not understanding," I answer plainly.

His eyes finally open, and the pained expression chiselled into his features has my heart clenching in my chest. I know desperation when I see it, it's an emotion I've grown entirely too familiar with.

"My daughter's team has won the National Championship the last two years. Elise plans to make it onto the Olympic team, and that can't happen without a coach. Her previous one was caught in a scandal and no one wants to take the team on right now because they don't want their name involved."

Shaking my head, I ask, "What kind of scandal would deter potentially hundreds of available coaches, especially if the team is as good as you're suggesting?"

"It was with the players," he reluctantly admits, rubbing the space between his brows where the skin is wrinkled, his lips pulling taut. "The coach was sleeping with the players."

A chill runs down my spine as his words sink in. I blink, the weight of them pressing against my chest, and slowly nod, my mind racing as I trace the quiet tension in the air. My fingers curl into a fist at my side, but I don't move, standing here, assessing the shift in the space between us. "And you think it's a good idea to send one of your players, who hasn't played football in years and has definitely never coached, to act as interim coach, in the middle of the season? I'm genuinely curious where the hell this idea came from."

"I can't say I trust you to keep it in your pants, okay?" He rolls his eyes. "But at least you aren't old enough to be one of these girls' fathers. That said, I'd really prefer it if you kept your dick to yourself."

"Okay," I answer slowly, "let's say I agree to this, how do we plan to make this work with my practice and game schedule?"

"I'll rework practice times to be immediately before or after the Blaze's practices and I've already arranged to have all of ours on their campus so you don't have to travel between locations. They're a sport oriented school with a lot of money. Their facility is as nice, if not nicer, than ours. It won't be a downgrade. Besides, their season is nearly halfway through."

Shaking my head, I release a grunt. "Fine," I tell him, turning to leave.

"Wait! 'Fine'? You're saying yes?" he asks, dumbstruck as his hands grip the armrests of his wooden desk chair, his ass halfway out of the seat as he stares at me with wide eyes.

"Sounds like it," I say, calling over my shoulder as I stride out the door.

This is a terrible idea.

Blowing out a breath, I lean back in my seat. "Damn, talk about a lot riding on a single decision."

I dive back into the book, having no obligations for the night and no desire to stop here. The book is dual point-of-view, so the next chapter is from the female main character's perspective.

"Elise," the massive Brit purrs as he swipes the head of his engorged cock through my slick heat, "will you be a good girl and accommodate us both at the same time?"

"Yes," I moan.

Leo chuckles, lining his swollen tip up with my mouth. "It's really poetic, isn't it mate?" He pauses, laughing again. "The good little French girl is about to do her first Eiffel Tower."

A laugh squawks out of me, hiding my disdain for the ignorant comment. Leo is often brash, leaning into certain stereotypes about Australians, never one to hold his thoughts in which is something I usually enjoy about him, so I brush the comment off. "When did I say it was my first?" I challenge.

Noah smacks my ass from his position behind me. "He should've known better."

The sting sends a zap of electricity down my spine, and a moan slips past my lips. "Shut up and fuck me already," I instruct, letting the sass seep into my voice.

"Don't have to tell me twice," Leo responds before plunging his cock into my mouth.

"Oh, we've already started, huh?" Noah comments from behind, pushing into me, causing my mouth to drive forward meeting Leo's hips.

Noah's pounding thrusts and the slap of his pelvis against my ass causes heat to pool in my core. My eyes are watering with the effort to remain on all fours with Leo's length threatening to suffocate me.

Noah's hand snakes around my bare abdomen, his thumb stroking over my clit. Another moan escapes me, and my thighs clench together as the firm pressure starts to coax my orgasm out of me.

Leo's position changes, his hips angling himself even further, burrowing into my throat.

I look up at him through my lashes, and see that he's extending his arm over my head, presumably reaching for Leo's behind me. A real Eiffel Tower, well, I'll be damned.

It takes everything in me not to laugh with his cock impaling my throat. If I did, he'd likely wind up with teeth marks.

Drawing in a deep breath through my nose, I focus on two things. Not choking and having an orgasm before I have to make it to practise.

Leo's callused hand grips my chin, then drags across my cheek. His fingers dig into my scalp, his groans of approval growing louder.

"Fuck Frenchy, your mouth is fucking delicious," he moans.

"She's gagging for it," Noah murmurs, his thick British accent sending another jolt of pleasure through me.

My walls are clenching around his length, the methodical rhythm of his thumb driving me wild. Tension builds throughout me, my muscles aching for release.

Leo's body goes rigid. "I'm about to come."

The hot, salty taste of his release fills my mouth, sliding down my throat. A satisfying moan escapes me as Noah pulls himself out entirely before plunging back in. I bounce my ass back into his hips, taking him to the hilt as I come undone around him. My body writhes against him as he fills me, tendrils of pleasure licking up my spine.

Once they've both pulled out, I collapse on the bed.

"Fucking hell," Leo groans.

Noah's arousal trickles out of me and down my thighs. I'm spent.

Noah slumps beside me, angling his face to peer over at me. He's wearing a contented smile as he says, "Sorry 'bout that love." He nods his chin towards my coated thighs.

A laugh escapes me as I roll over, smacking a hand to his chest and using it to push myself up. "Alrighty boys, stay as long as you'd like, but I've got to get going."

"Your new coach starts today, right?"

I nod, heading to the bathroom to clean up.

Neither of them move to stand, but I leave the door open so we can continue talking while I freshen up.

"Know who it is yet?"

I shake my head before realising that they can't see my response. "Not yet."

"Hopefully they're not a wanker like the last one," Noah drawls.

"He wasn't a wanker," I chuckle. "He was a slut. But so are we and I'm not judging either of you."

"The man was old enough to be our father," Leo groans.

Grabbing a pair of shorts, I work them up my thighs. "Different strokes for different folks," I shrug. "Not my cup of tea, but I can't fault the man too much. If I looked like him at nearly fifty, I'd be sleeping with whoever I wanted too."

"You already do that," Noah jokes.

"Yep, and I've no plans to stop anytime soon."

"And why is that exactly, Elise?" Noah asks, a light brow raised at me.

Oh, here we go again. Why can't he leave well enough alone? I don't have the time, nor the desire, for more than what we're already doing and with Noah's incessant questioning, I'd never be open to anything serious with him, anyway. Of course, I don't say any of that and opt for a kinder, more rehearsed version of the same sentiment.

"I don't have time for a relationship right now, and I have no reason to settle for just one cock. Maybe one day when I find one that satisfies me I will, but lucky for you," I wink, "today is not that day."

Noah chuckles, but the sound is tense. He sits up to get dressed and my shoulders sag with relief. "Fair enough, but I'm not sure there's any human cock that could satisfy you. Hell, this bloke and I have been trying for months now."

I roll my eyes at that. "Don't act as if it's some hardship." Sex is the only time I can afford to feel anything

besides the constant weight of loss. Sure, I might've let go of the resentment I used to carry around, but it doesn't mean it's not impossible to miss the two people I once counted on most. Without them here, focusing solely on my career is a necessary evil to ensure my success.

Bending forward, I double-knot my trainers. "Alright, let yourselves out, I'm gonna be late." I catch sight of the alarm clock on my nightstand. "Again," I groan, heading out with a noncommittal wave in their direction.

Over the next several hours, I get sucked into the story, unaware of the time passing until it becomes so dark in my living room that I'm forced to put the book down to switch on a lamp.

Well, shit, there's a reason this author is an auto-buy for me. I've spent my entire day reading, and I couldn't think of a better way to spend a well-deserved Sunday off from the madness of work.

As much as I love reading, and I seriously value my alone time, sometimes it gets lonely. I haven't been in a serious relationship in what feels like forever, and while I love my career, I've always wanted a family.

I just never thought that I'd have to choose between being a lawyer and having a fulfilling home life.

Chapter Twenty-Eight

Luca

Tuesday, July 21, 2026

Gia and I are in the garage, finishing my final set of squats as I use her like a weight, hoisting her up over my head and back down to my chest with each squat, my fingers remaining at the base of her skull to protect her neck.

She smiles widely, her top and bottom gums showing.

"Alright, Gia, it's tummy time!" I say excitedly.

She gives me a goofy grin that sends my heart fucking soaring. She's just so damn cute, and I love her more than words can even describe.

It's truly unbelievable how quickly she's come into my life and changed *everything* in the best way possible. *And I couldn't be happier.* Or more terrified that I'm going to fuck it all up.

We make our way into the living room, where I've got her play mat set up on the ground. I take a seat beside it, laying her on her stomach, and I watch in awe as she grips the dangling toys and stares at her reflection in the tiny mirror.

She starts rocking back and forth, and before I know it, she's trying to roll over onto her back!

"That's amazing, Gia, *mia bambina*!" I practically yell with excitement as I grapple to stand, running to the kitchen for my phone.

"Okay, now do that again, just one more time for Daddy," I coo, hoping I'll catch it on camera when she actually makes the final roll.

My family's gonna lose it, and hell, maybe this'll bring a little joy to Cici too.

Gia tries and fails to roll over a few more times, but the spit running out of the side of her mouth as she babbles happily tells me she isn't the least bit frustrated.

She'll roll when she wants to.

"You've got it, baby girl, don't worry. No pressure from Daddy, okay? You do everything in your *own* time," I say, hoping to start early on with the affirmations.

And just like that, she hoists herself up on her chubby little arms and makes the final push. *She rolls over.*

I clap my hands quickly, causing my palms to burn. My chest tightens, and warmth radiates throughout my body. "You did it! You did it, Gia!" I'm fucking elated as I take in the sight of this precious gift, accomplishing some of her first major milestones with me. It's moments like these that ease the sting of missing out on the first three months of her life.

I quickly send the video to my family group chat and open up the message thread between Cici and me. Thankfully, she remembered to give me her new contact information the other day.

I hit send, and a moment later, a call comes through.

It's Cici.

"Hey, you doing okay?" I ask her hesitantly, not bothering to make pleasantries.

"Yeah, I'm, uh, actually doing a lot better," she says, sounding nervous. "I've been talking to my therapist, and I know it hasn't been long since I started, but we agree that it's a good idea for me to see Giavanna soon. If that's okay with you?"

"Yeah, Cici, of course it's okay with me. I meant what I said. You can see her anytime. Just take care of yourself, and I'll take care of Gia. She needs her mother too; nothing's going to change that," I say, doing my best to reassure her.

She blows out a long breath before responding. "Thanks, Luca. Could we meet somewhere this week? My therapist suggested it be on neutral ground and said we may want to have a chaperone."

"A chaperone?" I ask, not entirely sure what that means.

"Yeah, she says it can be useful to have a third party there to make things feel less personal, and..." she stutters, "she says that with someone else there, it's less likely for me to just spend the whole time apologizing. So, would you mind finding someone? Just, um..." She continues to stammer. "Just not your family. They're really great, but I can only handle so much pressure right now."

My brows pinch, but I mull it over for a second before responding. "I'm not sure who to ask, but I'll figure it out. It's going to be okay, Cici. What day works best for you?"

"How is Thursday? I get discharged tomorrow, and then I start an outpatient program that I can do from home over video call. So anytime on Thursday should be fine," she says, her tone more confident this time.

A small, sad smile curves the corners of my lips. Hearing that is bittersweet. "I'm glad you're getting discharged tomorrow." I take a breath. "I'm really proud of you," I tell her honestly.

"Thank you, Luca, for everything. See you Thursday," she says before hanging up.

I let out a repressed sigh, shaking my head in disbelief as I look over at Gia. "You're gonna see your momma sooner than I'd anticipated," I tell her. My stomach flutters with nervous energy at the thought.

Now who the fuck would I call about chaperoning the mother of my child and me?

Chapter Twenty-Nine

Samara

Thank god this day is over.

I groan, stretching my limbs out as I get comfortable in bed. I'm exhausted. It's been one of those days that are full of surprises and not the kind I like. I won the case I went to trial for today, though, and finalized Luca's paperwork too. I'll just have to mail it to him, and then I can really close that chapter of my life.

Until the wedding, that is.

My phone rattles beside me on the nightstand. "Who the hell is calling me at nearly ten at night?"

I pick it up, expecting to decline the call, but I'm a little awestruck when I see whose name flickers across the screen. "Speak of the devil." I sigh before swiping the call button to answer.

"Luca, to what do I owe this immense pleasure?" I ask sarcastically.

"The pleasure is *all* mine," he drawls.

"You can say that again," I joke. "It is *all yours.*"

He chuckles. "You know what I think?"

I feel a fluttering in my chest at hearing his low voice over the phone, even if he *is* tormenting me. "In general? About very little," I quip, doing my best to hide the laughter that almost slips past my lips. That drags a deep-bellied laugh out of him that travels all the way from my ear to my toes.

Goddamn him. Even his laugh is sexy as sin.

"Actually, I think about a whole lot, and I'm *really* starting to think you might actually like me because something tells me if you didn't, at least a tiny bit, you wouldn't be answering my calls at all."

"Hah," I scoff. "Not a chance." *That may be a lie, and the realization does strange things to my tummy.* "Now, tell me why you called because I know it wasn't for this *charming* conversation."

I hear him clear his throat. "About that..."

"Do I have to remind you it's after ten at night?" I ask, doing my best to sound put out by his call, but truthfully, I'm not sure I mind.

"I'm sorry, Samara, this is going to be a really weird ask, and obviously, feel free to say no." He pauses, silence stretching over the line as I wait for the rest. "Cecily called tonight. She asked to see Gia on Thursday, but she said her therapist suggested having a chaperone for the visit, and she also mentioned it shouldn't be a family member. You're the only person I could think of who would be sort of middle ground and I wouldn't have to explain all the sordid details to. I'd pay you for your time, of course," he tells me, pleading.

My mind skitters to a halt. *He wants me to chaperone him on a playdate?*

"Um," I say, stalling while I find my words.

"Please, Samara, it would only be for an hour. I know you aren't my biggest fan, but I'll pay you whatever you want. Name your price."

The fact that he still thinks I can't stand him tugs at my earlier guilt, just enough for the next words I speak to come out of my mouth. *Words I know I'll live to regret.*

"Okay, fine. I'll do it."

"Really?" he asks, clear disbelief lacing his words.

"That's what I said, isn't it?"

"Fuck." He blows out a long breath. "Thank you so much. Let me know when you're available on Thursday, and I'll make it work."

Apprehension takes hold again. "But, Luca, I'm not really middle ground, am I? I was *your* attorney, not hers. To her, I was never in the middle. Before Thursday, could you please run it by her first?"

"I already asked her if it would be okay before calling. I didn't want to bother you if she wasn't going to be comfortable. Cici said that she recognizes you're on the child's side, and if you're willing, she'd be incredibly grateful," he says. *Well, that was thoughtful of him.*

"Okay, then. I'm waiting on a timeline for court that day, so I'll text you."

"Sounds good. Thank you again, Samara," he says, sounding every bit as genuine as I'd hope.

"Goodnight, Luca," I tell him, not waiting for his response before hanging up. The last thing I need on my mind before bed is Luca De Laurentiis wishing me a good night.

As I lie here, unable to sleep *again,* I do my best to convince myself of a different reality than the one I know but won't yet admit to myself.

This works fine. I needed to send Luca the finalized papers anyway. I can bring them on Thursday now. *At least, that's what I'll tell myself.*

Chapter Thirty

Luca

Thursday, July 23, 2026

Even as I buckle Gia into her car seat, just minutes from getting to see her mother for the first time in weeks, I'm *still* in shock that Samara agreed to this. I'm even more shocked that she agreed to let me drive.

With that thought, I see her pull into my driveway.

I finish clicking Gia in, pressing a kiss to the top of her head before closing her door and heading to the driver's side.

Samara heads toward me wearing the most casual outfit I've seen her in to date, and she's still fucking stunning.

She's wearing light-wash jeans that hug every delicious curve, paired with a sunny yellow crop top that shows off a sliver of the glowing mahogany skin between the waist of her jeans and the bottom of the top. I suppress a groan but don't manage to keep my thoughts at bay. *I'd like to take a bite out of her.*

I clear my throat and call over to her. "Hey," I say as she gets closer.

"Luca," she says, dipping her chin and all but ignoring me as she gets into the passenger seat.

Still not a fan, I see.

The thought almost makes me laugh. Or it *would* if it weren't for the fact that I, not so secretly, want her to like me. Although I'm done pretending, I don't know why. I find it unbelievably attractive that she doesn't humor me when I say something that annoys her. I also love making her squirm, and frankly, I have a fear of being unlikable. As someone with seemingly perfect siblings who everyone adores, it's been more difficult than I care to admit growing up as the resident fuckup. For the longest time, I found myself taking on the role of a people pleaser, but in recent years, I've gotten a kick out of people underestimating me, but with Samara, I don't feel that same thrill.

I climb in, fastening my seatbelt and turning to make sure Gia's where I left her.

I know she's a baby and can't go anywhere, but I'm maybe just a little paranoid.

We drive in mostly silence for the seven minutes it takes for us to get to the public park I chose for this reunion. It feels dumb picking a park when Gia can't do much of anything right now, but it's neutral, and there will be other children around, so hopefully, that'll make it less awkward.

Once we're parked, I look over to see Samara stuck in her thoughts and unaware that we've arrived. She's staring out the window, resting her chin on her hand. I take a moment to just breathe her in.

She comes across as such a badass, unfazed by everyone and everything, but I get the feeling that there's more than meets the eye with her. Coming from such a big family and grappling with so many personalities, I'm usually able to get a decent read on people. And Samara? This woman is definitely hiding a soft side that I'd be lying if I said I didn't want to dig down and find.

I unbuckle myself as quietly as I can, getting out and walking along the back, over to Samara's side. Pulling the door open, she falls forward from the loss of contact with the door. A small screech leaves her lips, and it takes everything in me not to laugh when she finally loses her composure as her hands grapple for my chest so she can steady herself.

"Luca, what the ever-loving fuck was that about?" she shouts at me, her glossy lips pinching.

I give her a cheesy grin. "Hey now, don't cuss around my daughter," I say jokingly.

She rolls her eyes at me, turning to unfasten her seatbelt, but I stop her, grabbing her hand and placing it back in her lap as I lean into her.

I slide my hand along her thigh, then her hip, and as I bring my lips so close to hers, I can almost taste them. "Thank you for coming," I tell her, keeping my voice low despite the way my breath seizes in my lungs as I draw in her heady, warm fragrance.

Satisfaction rolls through me as I watch her pupils dilate and hear her breath catch in her throat. She doesn't speak as I angle myself even more closely, taking in the way her rapid breathing makes her chest heave against the thin yellow fabric of her top. Her eyes flicker to my lips before finding their way back to my eyes.

I glide my hand farther over her hip, landing on the buckle. I click the button, successfully unclipping her. Pulling back and opening the door wide for her, I straighten as a crease pulls between her brows. She practically throws herself out of the vehicle, and it solidifies what I already know.

Samara may not *like* me, but she *definitely* wants me to fuck her.

I try not to focus on the fact that she also seems incredibly embarrassed and repulsed by her own response to me. Instead, I let the satisfaction that this stubborn-as-hell woman may be starting to change her mind about *parts* of me spur me on.

Chapter Thirty-One

Samara

"When did she say she'd be here?" I ask Luca as he sits beside me on this hard-ass bench, waiting for Cecily to arrive.

"She said five," he answers quietly. I look down at the screen of my cell phone, and just as I'd thought, *she's late.*

"It's ten after five. Are you sure she's coming?" I ask, annoyance slipping free. Though, for once, it's not aimed at Luca. It's Cecily who's been putting this man through the wringer, and *I don't like it.*

"I don't know," he whispers, sounding upset. It finally hits me that this is a monumental step for him *and* Gia.

Of course he wants things to go well with Cecily. She's the mother of his child, and as he's mentioned before, he fully believes that Gia having both of her parents involved in her life is what's best for her, and I can't help but agree.

It helps that Luca's slowly proven to not be the asshole I'd pegged him for, so for his benefit, I work to cool my rising temper.

Moments pass as we wait, but his dark brows shoot up his forehead when he sees her. She's wearing a light-blue, floral-printed sundress, making her way toward us from the parking lot. Her golden-blonde hair hangs like a curtain over her smooth, tanned shoulders. She's gorgeous, and it twists my stomach into knots. [1]

Luca stands with Gia tightly bundled in his arms. He greets her politely, placing a kiss on either cheek, the same way his family greets everyone.

Despite her put-together appearance, I can tell she's not holding herself together as well as her outfit might suggest. Her eyes are a bright blue, even brighter, with the red rim of her swollen lids surrounding them and the dark circles fighting their way through her concealer.

I can't imagine how difficult this is, and my heart aches for her.

"Ms. Perez." Her sad eyes meet mine. "Thank you so much for doing this," she says, hesitating as her eyes bounce between me and Luca. "I know this isn't something you usually do for your clients, but"—her voice cracks—"I'm so thankful."

A fissure runs through the center of my heart, and all of my earlier frustrations flow out with the blood inside.

I give her a small smile, doing my best to stay out of their way. I've never acted as a chaperone to a couple of grown adults before, but I'd imagine I'm supposed to stay quiet and out of the way.

---

1. **Who Is She 2 U (Recall Version) — Brandy**

Her big doe eyes look up at Luca. "I'm sorry I was late. Truthfully, I debated not coming at all. Probably a hundred times, but I'm glad I finally made it," she tells him as she averts her gaze to Gia.

A tear slips down her cheek, and discomfort ripples through me at being here and watching this display of raw emotion. I can't help but feel like I have no business being here, but I'll stay unless they tell me to leave.

I remind myself that I'm here for Gia and for *my client.*

"I'm glad you did too. You want to hold her?" he asks with a hopeful lilt to his voice.

She shakes her head, and surprise jolts through me that she wouldn't want to hold Gia, but I have to remind myself that she's figuring out how to trust herself with her again.

"I'm sorry, I'm just..." she stutters, chewing on the raw skin of her bottom lip for a moment before finishing what she had been trying to say. "I'm not ready for that yet. Can I just, um..."—she rubs the back of her neck—"sit next to you while you play with her?"

His voice is soft and comforting as he answers her. "Of course, Cici. How about I set up a blanket in the grass, and she can do some tummy time?"

She nods, and his eyes meet mine. "Would you mind holding her while I grab a blanket from the car?"

The question startles me, but I don't hesitate, nodding my head in response.

A grin pulls at his lips as he brings her to me, placing her in my arms. She yawns, waking from her car-ride-induced nap. As she looks up at me, her face begins turning red, and I know the waterworks are coming. "Shh," I tell her. "It's okay. Your daddy is just getting a blanket. He'll be right back."

Thankfully, this works to soothe her, and she calms down, sticking her fist in her mouth and sucking. A laugh escapes me as I gaze down at her, and when she pulls her slobbery hand from her mouth, Luca's beside me, ready and waiting with a wet wipe.

"You've got a little drool there, Gia," he says with a lopsided smirk as his eyes flit between his daughter and me. "Don't worry, I understand. Samara is *definitely* something to drool over." He winks at me.

And that wink settles straight in my core.

Jesus Christ.

After wiping her hand and face, he lays out the blanket and pulls Gia into his arms, swapping with me before setting her gently on the blanket. He helps Cecily sit and looks over at me in question. I shake my head, having very little desire to join this family reunion any more than I already am.

Over the next hour, I sit several feet away, *trying* and *failing* to pay attention to the words on my screen. I'm doing my best to not appear as if I'm eavesdropping, but it's hard not to when the most gorgeous man in the world is lying beside a literal supermodel with their perfect kid, just feet from you.

Cecily gets more comfortable with Luca and Gia, and by the end of the visit, she's managed to hold Gia for a couple of minutes before depositing her back into Luca's waiting arms.

They look like the picture-perfect family, living the American dream. I'm sure if you give them a few years, they'll have two and a half kids and be living in a ranch-style home in the suburbs.

I don't know why that thought bothers me so much; besides, Luca's given absolutely no indication that he even wants a relationship with Cecily. I barely even tolerate Luca, and as soon as Kat's wedding is over and I've completed my end of the dare, he'll be nothing but a distant memory.

Chapter Thirty-Two

Luca

I sink back against the leather seats, squeezing my eyes closed as the air-conditioning cools the car and my subsequent nerves.

That went better than I'd expected, but it brought on a lot of emotions I hadn't anticipated. As much as I want Gia to have her mom in her life, I also want her to have a happy home with two loving parents who she can count on. I'm not thrilled with the idea of her traveling between homes or having a nanny when neither of us can be there for her because of work.

But I know I don't want a relationship with Cici. I'm glad we've worked things out and will continue to do so, but I'm extremely certain that I have no romantic feelings for her anymore. I just want to co-parent and give Gia everything she deserves in this life.

I want her to have the happiest fucking childhood, just like my parents gave me and all of my siblings. And I want her to live the most incredible life.

I'm not sure how I'll accomplish any of that, but I'll be damned if I'm not working toward it every day.

"Luca." Samara's soft voice drags me from my thoughts. "You ready to get going?"

"Yeah, sorry, that was just a lot. Let me get you back so you can get home," I tell her, ensuring everyone's buckled in before I back out.

Unable to stand the silence for a second longer, I turn the radio on at the first red light, allowing the sultry lyrics to pour through the car.[1]

Samara's leaning against the window, staring out of it, and paying me no mind as we make the short trip back to my house.

My lips twitch with a smile as her soft but beautiful voice filters through the car. I'm not sure if she even realizes she's doing it or not, but she's singing along, and the idea that she might be feeling more comfortable around me does funny things to my gut.

Once we finally pull into my driveway, I turn to her and ask, "Can I make you dinner? As a thank you for today. You know, since you refuse to let me pay you."

She rolls her eyes at me. "I was just doing my client a favor," she says, but her words aren't the least bit convincing.

"A client? Is that what I am, Samara?" I lean into her over the center console, invading her personal space as I bring my lips a few inches from her ear. "Last I checked, all the paperwork had been finalized."

---

1. **Every Kind Of Way — H.E.R.**

"I'm unsure of what delusions you may be fighting, Luca, but yes, you are a *client.* And as you said, the paperwork is done, so I'll be heading home now."

She straightens in her seat, and I can tell she's ready to bolt, so I rush to say, "Come on, Samara. Let me feed you."

Fuck, that was probably the wrong choice of words too.

And just as I'd expected, she fires back a snarky retort. "I'll feed my damn self, Luca. Go worry about feeding your child, and refrain from contacting me about your personal problems."

Well, shit, that was a low blow. She doesn't wait for my response as she unbuckles herself and nearly tosses her body out of the car door.

***

It's nearly midnight when my phone vibrates on my nightstand.

Samara

I'm sorry for snapping at you today. I know you were just being nice, but I generally try to keep my private and professional life separate. Lately, you and your family have made that extremely difficult to do though.

My pulse starts to speed up, and my cheeks burn with the effort it takes to hold the massive grin her admission brings to my face.

Don't worry, princess. I've been known to have that effect on people ;)

And as for my family… Well… No one says no to Gloria De Laurentiis. It's her superpower and absolutely no fault of your own that you've fallen victim to her torment.

Samara

Thank you for that incredibly insightful and understanding explanation, Luca. I'll carry it with me forever.

I'm sure you will. Sleep tight, princess.

I put my phone face down beside me and rest my head on my forearms, closing my eyes. I fall asleep with a smile on my lips and enjoy a night of Samara-filled dreams.

Chapter Thirty-Three

Luca

Saturday, July 25, 2026

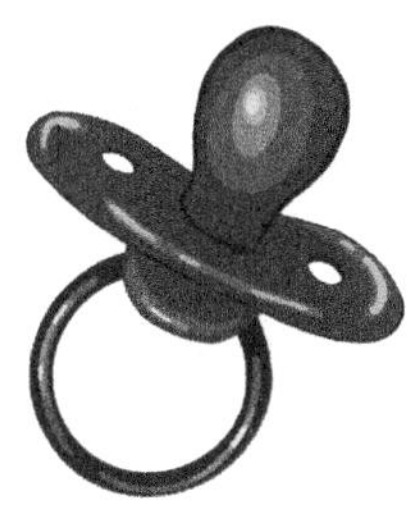

When I'm stressed, I bake. And today? I'm really fucking stressed.

My offseason workouts with Ale have been kicking my ass because I can't seem to get enough sleep with Gia waking up at all hours of the night.

Plus, there's the constant thought that I'm not only letting my team down but my family too. The season hasn't even started back up yet, and I'm already not balancing both aspects of my life well. What if I'm not meant to do both? What if I end up compromising on one to make up for the other and just wind up sucking at everything?

These are the thoughts spiraling through my head as I stand in the kitchen surrounded. There are loaf pans with chocolate chip banana bread, a seemingly endless number of cookies, and this terribly ugly Bundt cake from hell that has arguably caused me even *more* stress than it's relieved.

One massive blessing is that Gia's been napping long enough for me to have this fun little carby spiral, and thank fuck, I have the perfect place to unload it all.

***

"Alright, ladies, next we're going to practice with the dummies. I want you to put all of your energy into this drill because it'll be our last one for the week, okay?" I ask the group of women standing in the open rec room with the games and tables pushed up against the walls.

They all agree, looking even more excited to keep going now that they've started getting the hang of things.

I show them a combination of punches and kicks I want them to repeat, and when they've all confirmed that they've got it, they let loose and show those dummies who's boss.

I watch as they take turns pummeling the humanoid silicone blobs, some of them knocking them over entirely. My heart fills with pride each and every time a group of these incredible women makes it to this stage. When they've learned to trust their bodies and can feel confident in their ability to protect themselves, it lights them up, and I can see it practically illuminating them on the outside too.

I clap my hands when they've all completed the exercise. "Fuck yeah, you guys! You're all incredible!" I shout. "Now, make sure to grab yourself some cookies from the table before you head out." I go in for a high five from each of the women as they thank me and make their way back to their rooms.

Brandi enters the rec hall, smiling as she heads toward me and gets started wiping down the dummies. I do the same before dragging them into the storage closet for next week. “Thanks for letting me swap to weekends. I know you guys have a lot scheduled for these days, but now that I’ve got Gia, it’s just so much easier to have one of my family members watch her on the weekend, at least until hockey starts up again.”

She waves me off. “No need to apologize, Luca. You’ve been teaching these classes religiously during the week for years; it was time for a change. And frankly, these ladies enjoy your classes more than any of the other shit we’ve got planned for them on Saturdays. It’s really not a problem, and it’s nice having you back here in person.” She takes one end of a table, helping me maneuver it into its place in the center of the room. “I’d missed you while you were playing for the Monsters in New York. These classes just aren’t the same over video call,” she tells me.

I give her a small smile. “Thanks, Brandi. It’s good to be back.” And I mean it. I’ve missed this place more than I’d thought possible, and of course, my dream was always to play for the Scarlets and live close to my family. Now, I get to do that. I’m overwhelmed, but so damn grateful.

We finish getting the room back together before heading back out, but a familiar head of dark curls passing into a room at the end of the hall has me stopping in my tracks. Brandi skitters to a stop behind me, almost knocking into me at the suddenness of my movements.

“Woah there, what’s going on?” she asks, moving to stand beside me as her gaze follows mine to where Samara disappeared behind the door.

“What is Samara doing here?” I ask, mostly to myself, and I’m surprised when Brandi answers, making me realize I’d spoken the words aloud.

“She does her pro bono cases for the women trying to gain custody of their children, but with her work schedule, she can only get here on weekends most of the time.”

I’m stunned.

This woman, who seems like a hard-ass all the time, is really just a big softy. Something about that has my lips pulling up into a grin. *I know something about Samara that I’m sure very few people do, and that feels like a damn honor.*

Chapter Thirty-Four

Samara

"No, Mom, I don't have time to go on vacation right now. I have a *job*," I tell her for the third time tonight. What I don't bother saying is that I've blown through absolutely any funds I had set aside for vacation while helping Charice get back on her feet after we won her case last week, and I don't regret it one bit.

"You work too much," she tells me. "You need to let loose once in a while, and a vacation with your family is the best way!" She tries to convince me, but unfortunately, I disagree. A family vacation spent watching my nieces and nephews as my married cousins and my sister all go off to spend quality time together sounds like the *opposite* of a good time for me.

I groan. "Mom, seriously. I don't have the time."

"Chile, tap ih. Yuh mada jus waah yuh tuh tink bout sinting oddah dan wuk," Dad tries to remind me as if I don't already know her true intentions.

"Yuh work too much, sis. Yuh need to live a little. Let some a da island spirit and salt wata heal yuh," she tells me. *Heal me?* Do I seem broken to her?

"Can we please talk about this later?" The three sets of narrowed eyes that have settled on me make it clear that, no, we can't talk about it later. So I add, "I'll think about it. When is this vacation?" I ask, hoping that by sounding interested, I'll at least get them off my ass for another couple of weeks.

"The last weekend in August. The weather is usually better in the fall months, but since it's the end of the summer, it shouldn't be too hot, and our travel miles expire the first week of September, so I want to use them up," Mom answers, sounding cheerful.

I nod slowly. "Okay, I'll take a look at my work schedule and see what I can do." But I meet my mom's light-brown eyes as I say, "No promises though, okay? If it doesn't work out, I don't want you to be disappointed."

She scoffs, crossing her arms over her chest and leaning back in her seat. "I'm not getting any younger; this could be one of the last times we have this opportunity," she tells me, her light accent coming out.

"Oh, here we go," I say, standing to take my plate to the sink. I don't bother to look at any of them as I rinse the dish. "You're only fifty-five. Please stop acting like you had me in your forties. You aren't that old, and you aren't dying. *Please* just let me live my life how I want to and stop meddling at every turn," I tell her, feeling regret the moment I finish. *What makes this vacation any different? Why is she pushing so hard for it this time?*

My family gets on my nerves, but they've worked hard to help me achieve my goals, even if my dreams have been so vastly different from theirs. Though my words weren't a lie. I'm *so* tired of having similar conversations each time I'm with them.

Even though they've always supported me, they've never done a good job of hiding their disappointment that I chose to put my career ahead of finding a partner.

"Mi tink a time fi go yuh bed,"[1] my dad says, standing to usher my mom out of the kitchen.

Vea looks over at me, disdain clearly written across her face. She shakes her head and storms out into the living room.

I clench my eyes shut, trying to remind myself that I deserve to live the life I've worked so hard for, and I shouldn't be so bothered when they react poorly to me speaking my mind. Sure, I could've been less rude about it, but sometimes, it's just so overwhelming to have to deal with them getting on me about not having a family yet. They make it seem like I have no desire to be a part of this family or that I don't *want* a family of my own when that isn't even remotely true! I'm just not willing to drop everything for these vacations because they always shove my lack of a love life and my difficulty getting pregnant back in my face.

I grab my purse off the counter and slip my shoes on before locking up and heading out to my car.

Once inside, I slam the door, resting my forehead against the steering wheel. I release a long exhale before starting the engine and backing out.

***

I've had my face buried in these client files for hours since I got home. It's probably time I get ready for bed because I know the case like the back of my hand, and frankly, it should be an easy win.

I finish wrapping my hair up, toss on my bonnet, and crawl into bed, putting my phone on the charger. I've got tons of texts, most of them I've been avoiding because I know they're from my family after I left without saying anything. *Did they really expect me to let them walk all over me?* When have I *ever* let that happen?

Sure enough, there are tons of messages from my dad and Vea, and as expected, none from Mom.

Under their messages are a couple from clients, who I'll respond to tomorrow, and one from Kat.

Kat Narvaez

Hey Samara! I know it's a big ask, but any chance you'd be willing to come to our wedding party dance lessons on Sunday nights?

I *love* to dance, and while the idea of doing so with Luca doesn't exactly excite me, I really like his family so far, and I've been wanting to make time for friends, so maybe it wouldn't be a terrible idea. Plus, maybe I'd actually meet someone if I get out a little more or "loosen up," as my mom always tells me.

Sure, send me the details and I'll do my best to make it.

Kat Narvaez

Really? Oh my gosh, you're the best!

Lol I said I'll do my best. Don't get too excited just yet.

Kat Narvaez

Understood haha, see you soon!

A minute later, she sends a text with the time and location to meet. I don't see why I wouldn't be able to make it, but I don't want to disappoint her if I'm not up for it. Hopefully, it'll turn out to be a good time.

Chapter Thirty-Five

Luca

Sunday, July 26, 2026

"Seriously, thank you so much for watching her tonight. I know it's a big ask." Mateo puts his palm up to stop me mid-sentence.

"Dude, it isn't a big ask at all. You've watched Mya for me countless times. It's my turn I repay the favor. Besides, it's just for a few hours, and Mya's excited to get to hang out with Gia," he tells me, his broad smile calming some of the anxiety I have about leaving her with someone who isn't family.

Though honestly, Mateo kind of *is* my family. Just like all the guys on the team are, but he and I played together before we were on the Scarlets, so we're closer than I am with the other guys.

"I'm happy to watch Mya anytime; you know that." I smile down at the little girl latched onto her dad's calf. Her wide brown eyes shine up at me as I muss her hair.

"Can I hold the baby now?" she asks me.

I chuckle as her dad explains to her, "Not yet, Mya. I don't want you to accidentally drop her, okay? You can hold her on the couch, yeah?"

"Okay," she says shyly as her eyes cast downward.

"Ve y siéntate, mi niña.[1] I'll bring Gia over in a minute." She nods her head rapidly and runs inside, catapulting herself onto the couch in the far corner of the room.

I shake my head, a smile turning the corners of my lips. "Good luck, man." I laugh.

"Nah, I don't need luck." He winks at me, extending his arms for me to place Gia gently in them. I kiss the top of her head before transferring her over to his waiting arms.

"Thanks again. Just call if you need me."

"Will do," he tells me, shooing me away as he heads back inside.

By the time I'm buckled into my seat, he's already sent me three pictures and a message saying, "Proof of life."

I shoot him a quick reply and head over to the dance studio.

---

1. Spanish: "Go and sit down, baby girl."

Chapter Thirty-Six

Samara

I pull up to the dance studio at the far end of a small strip mall. It's got a vinyl art print on the front windows of a man and woman wearing red Latin dance attire.

As I take a deep breath to calm my nerves, it dawns on me that I've never been in a wedding party that required anything like this, especially not months in advance. I wonder if they're making the wedding party perform some cringy, choreographed dance together. In which case, I may be finding a way out of this entire arrangement because that sounds like my personal version of hell.

I like these people, but I don't know them all that well, so it's not like I'd consider any of them my friends yet. And as much as I'd love to make some, and frankly, I'm generally too stubborn to admit defeat, especially over something as trivial as a dare, I draw the line at this type of stuff.

I head inside anyway, sending up a silent prayer that this isn't as bad as I'm afraid it'll be.

Once inside, I see the entirety of the De Laurentiis family chatting among themselves. Kat sees me first, her face lighting up at my entrance. "Samara! You made it," she says as she jogs over to me, wrapping me up in a hug.

"Sorry." She laughs. "I've become a lot more of a hugger since dating Ale," she says with a smile, looking over her shoulder to meet her fiancé's googly eyes. *I want someone to look at me like that, and I won't settle for less.*

"It's alright," I assure her. "I do have a question though."

"Of course, anything," she tells me in earnest, her brows drawn together.

"Is this some sort of choreographed dance rehearsal for the wedding?"

Her eyes grow wide before she keels over in laughter, drawing everyone's attention to her. "Oh my gosh, no, definitely not," she squeaks out and continues laughing, a snort slipping free. "We're taking these lessons because everyone in the room can ballroom dance, but I have two left feet."

My racing pulse settles, and I feel so much better already. Kat's brother chuckles. "Choreographed? We aren't ready for that," he says, shaking his head. "We're just trying to get her through the first dance without *literally* falling on her face or tripping everyone on the dance floor when it opens up later in the night."

"Let's not forget the secondhand embarrassment it would cause me," Aiyana says from beside Kas, her arms snaking around his trim waist.

"Secondhand?" Kat asks.

"Yes, because there's not a chance in hell that I'd be participating in that shit," Aiyana says, rolling her eyes.

"You're an asshole," Kat tells her before turning her attention back to me. I'm listening to Kat speak, catching bits and pieces as she explains what kind of dance lessons these are, mentioning something about ballroom, but I can't seem to focus with the chill of awareness traveling down my spine. I feel like I'm being watched, and their eyes are burning a hole in my back. "Alright, so are you ready?" she finally asks.

"Yeah, of course." I smile at her just as the instructors enter from the side entrance.

"Hello, everyone. It's exciting to get to work with you all and make Kat and Ale's special day a beautiful night filled with lots of love and dancing," the dark-haired woman says, bringing both of her arms up and flicking her wrists for dramatic flair.

I can't shake the feeling that I'm being watched. I look over my shoulder, and sure enough, Luca is leaning against the wall behind me, his arms crossed over his chest and his feet crossed in front of him. He looks like a model on the cover of *GQ* magazine.

He quirks a brow at me, tipping his chin in the direction of the instructors speaking as if to tell me to pay attention to them. He's not wrong. I probably should be, but it's so damn hard to turn my attention away from him when I know he'll be watching me from behind the moment I do.

Reluctantly, I drag my attention back to them and listen as they explain the styles of ballroom dance we'll be learning over the next couple of months. *Well*, it isn't a choreographed dance, but ballroom isn't exactly my style either.

"Okay, everyone, split off into pairs, and we'll get started," the male instructor, Christian, tells us with a clap of his hands.

My eyes dart around the room, realization sinking in that I'll have to dance with Luca. And when he moves to join me, I feel the electricity from his touch pour into me as he trails his fingertips down my forearm, drawing my body into his.

"Have you ever done the slow waltz before, Samara?" he asks me; his slightly woody and bright citrus scent wraps around me, and my core clenches.

I shake my head. "No, I haven't. I dance, but this isn't my usual style."

"Follow my lead, and you'll be fine," he assures me, but his words do nothing but annoy me.

"Why do *you* think you'll be the one leading?" I ask, tilting my head. "You think because you've got a dick swinging between your legs that makes you the leader?" I roll my eyes at him.

He shakes his head, no humor in his eyes as he speaks. "Samara, I'm not sure if you've noticed or not, but I've been surrounded by the most incredible women my entire life." His eyes swing around the room as if to prove his point. "There's not a single ounce of me that lives under the guise that I'm somehow superior to any of them. I think you'll see soon enough *why* I'll be the one leading," he says, leaning into my space, his warm breath coasting over my ear. "And it'll have nothing to do with my massive cock." He chuckles deeply.

Another chill skates down my spine, but I stiffen, scoffing at him, not letting on to the way his words affect me. "Massive." I laugh. "Men who *actually* have it, don't flaunt it," I tell him, unconvinced by my own words. He's huge, and I have no doubt his dick is too.

Music starts to flood through the speakers around the room, bouncing off the slick wooden floors beneath our feet. "Alright, everyone, follow Cassandra and me. The lead will place their hands like this," Christian says, demonstrating.

"And the follower will place theirs like this." She shows us.

They nod their heads at us to give it a shot. I see Kat put her hands in the completely wrong place, and it's actually kind of adorable. Alessandro gently sets them where they belong before pulling her closer to his body. *They look so damn cute,* and it's hard not to long for something like that for myself.

Luca stands before me, clearing his throat to grab my attention back. "You ready?" he asks.

"Sure," I say, winding one hand around his back in the leader's position and the other in the air for him to grab hold of. His eyes glitter with mischief as he takes my hand in his, yanking my hand free of his back and depositing it onto his shoulder before snaking his arm around me and tugging me impossibly close to his chest. All the air is sucked out of my lungs as I'm forced to look up into his pretty eyes.

"I really don't think we need to be this close," I tell him, frustrated that he managed to make me the follower just as Christian makes his rounds over to us to check our stance.

"Perfect form, you two, brava." He claps before heading over to the rest of the group.

Luca says nothing, but he doesn't have to. His expression tells me just how goddamn smug he feels right now.

Once everyone is in position, they restart the music, showing us a few basic steps and telling us to practice on our own for a few beats as we get the hang of it. Luca and I fight for dominance the entire time, with me stepping on his toes, *mostly on purpose.*

I have to admit, it's fun to push his buttons as much as he does mine. This little game of cat and mouse we have going is starting to *almost* feel enjoyable.

He tsks at me when I stomp my foot down on his as he continues to try to take the lead. "What you seem to not realize," he says, pulling me abruptly into his chest before whispering, "*is that I like it rough.*"

My skin heats at his words, but I refuse to show that I'm affected in the slightest despite the wetness that's pooling in my core. "Cocky little boys like you always do," I tell him with a wink.

He laughs darkly, dragging me across the dance floor to the center of the room. Cassandra and Christian go into greater detail, and before I know it, we're on our own. "Okay, everyone, put those moves together, and let's see what you've got!" Cassandra tells us excitedly.

The De Laurentiis men and Charlie look around the room at one another, each giving the other a curious head nod that makes me apprehensive. *Nothing good can come of all these men being in silent agreement about anything.*

The moment the music starts, they all take off, grabbing their partners and pulling them in closely. I have no choice but to follow his lead as he expertly carries us across the floor in perfect sync with his family members.

Angelo and Gloria stand in the corner, dancing similarly, with her legs strapped against his and her feet on his shoes as he moves her body with his. For a snarky-ass woman, she and her husband truly have the most incredible kind of love. No wonder *most* of her sons seemed to turn out so well.

I wonder what the hell happened to Luca.

"Ignoring me, *principessa*?" he asks, dragging my attention back to his insanely gorgeous eyes. *Damn him and those pretty eyes of his.*

"Just looking for a better view," I tell him, clearly lying. I'm unsure that a better view even exists when Luca's in the room.

He smirks. "Let's go find you a mirror because there's no better view than the one I'm seeing." He winks at me, throwing me off kilter.

Who is this man? Does he just enjoy riling me up?

"Focus, Luca," I tell him. "I don't need to lose a toe because you weren't paying attention." Regretfully, I have a feeling this man could do this in his sleep. I'm doing very little work because Luca is, *unfortunately*, a good lead. Not that I'd ever tell him that.

"If I stub your toe, I promise to suck it and make it better," he says with a laugh, carrying me off in the opposite direction of where I was about to try and steer us.

"Yeah, somehow, I don't think that would fix anything," I say in defiance.

"Well, if it helps, I've been doing this all my life. The woman down the street from me growing up was a retired ballroom dance teacher. She gave us all lessons on the weekends until she passed when I was in high school," he tells me in a moment of vulnerability, calling a silent truce between us.

Well, that surprises me, but at least it clears some things up. That's for sure.

Before I can think of a response, he says, "Do you mind if I check my cell real quick? I left Gia with a friend and just want to check in."

"Oh, of course not," I tell him, not minding one bit, and I kind of need the breather. It's not fair for any person to smell as good as he does. It's intoxicating.

He smiles at me before heading over to the corner of the room and bringing his cell out. I stand here awkwardly, unsure of what to do in his absence, but a massive looming figure reaches out his hand for mine. His deep voice rakes over me. "Samara, it's nice to finally meet you. I'm Dante," he tells me. I recognize his name as Arielle spoke about him at book club.

"Likewise," I tell Mr. Tall, Dark, and Mouthwatering. *Do all De Laurentiis men look like this?* Really, though, this guy is kind of intimidating. He's covered head to toe in tattoos and black clothing. His eyes are as dark as his hair, with little difference between his pupils and irises.

I noticed him earlier, but it's a tad strange to imagine someone as sweet and fairy-like as Arielle to be with a man who looks this tough.

"Care to dance? Arielle's resting her feet," he tells me, his eyes swinging over to his wife with her feet up on a chair and her nose buried in our book of the month.

"Oh, sure." He grasps my hands in his, placing them where he'd like them to go, in a different spot than we were taught earlier. "We're not doing the waltz anymore?" I ask.

"Not exactly." He chuckles, the sound such a contrast to everything else about him. He whisks me away, whipping me around the dance floor, and I can't help the bubble of laughter climbing up my throat.

This is undeniably *so* much fun. I let Dante swing me around, my feet sliding easily across the slick wooden floors as he twirls me, and finally, he finishes the song by dipping me so low the ends of my hair graze the ground before he deposits me safely on my own two feet.

The massive grin shining across my face tells him everything he needs to know. "Thanks for the dance, Samara." He winks before releasing me to head back over to his wife.

I make eye contact with Luca, who's leaning against that damn wall again, his eyes trailing over me as he wears a knowing grin. He pushes off the wall, prowling over to me, and I find my pulse kicking up as he does.

Before he reaches me, the music stops, and Christian makes his way to the center of the room. He claps several times. "Incredible job, everyone!" he says, and my eyes swing over to Kat. She's standing limply, being held up by Alessandro. Her cheeks are bright red, and her hair is all over the place. The poor thing really *does* have two left feet. No wonder we're starting this shit months in advance.

"Keep on practicing, and we'll see you next week," he says, waving goodbye to us all.

I head to grab my things but see that Luca is already carrying them over to me. I hadn't even seen him step away.

I move toward him to take them from him, but he moves them to his other arm, sidestepping me. "Really, Luca?" I ask, rolling my eyes at how childish he's being.

"Just let me walk you to your car, Samara. I don't see why that's such a big deal," he says, heading toward the doors. I follow after him, too exhausted to care at this point. All I want is to go home, shower, and read until I fall asleep.

He holds the door open for me, and I wave goodbye to everyone before following him out. Luca hands me my bag and I search for my keys, unlocking the door. He opens it for me. I hoist myself inside, and he reaches across me, buckling me in, similarly to how he'd unbuckled me the other day.

I swear, this man is gonna be the death of me.

His hand lingers on my hip before he finally pulls it away, straightening as he says, "Goodnight, Samara." He turns back to the building and heads inside.

Strangely, I had fun tonight, but I'm not so sure I'll be able to handle more of this every Sunday for the next few months.

Chapter Thirty-Seven

Luca

As surprised as I was to see that Samara actually showed up, I can't say I'm not glad she did. I have fun messing with her.

I know she can handle it, and I fucking love that she can dish it right back to me.

But right now? I'm just excited to pick my little girl up and have some much-needed cuddle time. This is the longest I've been away from her since she arrived, and I've missed her all night.

Chapter Thirty-Eight

Samara

Sunday, August 9, 2026

It pains me to say this, but I've been looking forward to this class all week. Last Sunday was pretty fun, and the more I get to know everyone, the more I'm finding that I'm genuinely enjoying myself.

Plus, last week, we took turns swapping partners all night, so it wasn't as intimate as our first class. I even got to dance with Angelo, who I've come to realize is the perfect balance to Gloria's big personality. He's quiet and far more reserved than his wife, but when he does speak, he's hilarious.

Even Luca isn't all bad in small doses.

Before I can get out of the car, my cell rings from my purse. Normally, I'd ignore it, but the ringtone is the telltale sign that, unfortunately, it's my mom, whose calls I've been dodging all week.

I grab my phone out, swipe the answer button, and bring it to my ear.

"Finally," she huffs out. "I've been calling you all week, Mara!" she shouts in my ear.

"I've been busy, Mom," I tell her, knowing that won't cut it. It *never* does. Already, I feel twice as exhausted as I had before answering her call.

"Yeah, well, I gave birth to you, and I was *very busy* then, too, but I still did it, so the least you can do is answer my calls."

"You have me now, so what did you want to talk about?" I love my mom, but she isn't the easiest person to deal with when she's not getting what she wants. Though, I guess I can thank her for giving me all the necessary attributes to be a successful lawyer.

"Our family vacation. You need to go. I'm not getting any younger, and we've given you more than enough time to get your schedule together so you can go. There isn't any real reason you can't, so I don't wanna hear it," she says, making her demands loud and clear.

"I told you, I have to see what my work schedule is like," I try again.

"You said that weeks ago, Samara." She huffs.

"You guys go on family vacations without me all the time. Why is this one so important?" I finally ask the question that's been nagging at me since they first brought the idea up.

"Because this time, we're going back to my home, and one of my closest friends has a son I'd like you to meet."

Ah, and there it is. She wants to set me up.

I'm not sure why the next words leave my mouth, but they come flying out at a warped speed. "I'm actually seeing someone," I tell her in a rush.

The line goes silent for several moments, so long, in fact, I almost check to make sure the call hasn't dropped. "You're seeing someone," she breathes out over the line.

"Yeah, things are new, and I didn't want to say anything until we got more serious." *That's good, Samara, dig the hole a little deeper, why don't you?*

"Fine, then it's settled. You'll bring him with you," she says, her tone suddenly cheerful, and it sends unease ricocheting through me. "I'll tell your sister. She'll be happy to know."

"Okay, I've gotta go, Mom. We'll talk later," I tell her, desperate to get off the line.

"Goodnight, Mara," she says, her voice now bright and cheerful as she hangs up without any extra fuss. She got what she wanted, and regrettably, that means I need to figure out what the hell I'm going to do about it.

I silence my phone, not wanting any other reasons to lose my mind tonight, before heading into the studio feeling like I've been hit with a ton of bricks.

Chapter Thirty-Nine

Luca

Just when I'm starting to think she won't make it, Samara comes storming into the studio as Christian and Cassandra are going over what we'll be learning tonight.

I watch as she sets her things down and stomps over to my side. "You good?" I ask her, keeping my voice down, not wanting to interrupt or draw attention to her shit mood.

"I'm fine," she says, her voice strained as she speaks through gritted teeth. *Clearly*, she is *not* fine. Unease settles in my gut, and my mouth dries.

"Let's get to it then!" Cassandra says excitedly, everyone breaking off into pairs. Last weekend, we swapped partners the whole night to help familiarize Kat with dancing with someone other than Ale, but tonight, we're back to our pairs from the first week.

I try to place my hands around Samara, but she shrugs me off. "I thought we were past this." I groan, and my shoulders sag.

"If you have something to say, just say it, Luca," she tells me, annoyance lacing her words as she blows out a breath in an exaggerated huff.

I'm taken aback by this because recently I'd thought our banter was *mostly* kind of playful, but tonight she's out for blood, and I can't imagine why it would be mine.

I try to brush it off, but for the next twenty minutes, she continues to move my hands, stiffening each time they settle on her, and she steps out of my grasp constantly. It wears on me because as much as I'm aware that she isn't my biggest fan, I'd started to believe she was warming up to me.

But based on the way she's acting right now, I've seriously misjudged our interactions the last few weeks.

I let this go on for a few more minutes until I catch Kat looking at us with concern etched all over her face. She and Ale are whispering to each other, their eyes periodically looking over at us, and it not only embarrasses me, but it pisses me off.

"Alright, that's enough," I tell Samara, wrapping my arm around her waist and tugging her all the way against my body. Before she can make an even bigger scene and shove me off her, I bring my lips down to her ear. "I don't know what's going on, but we're about to talk about it because you can hate me *all you want*, but what you're not going to do is ruin any part of this wedding for my brother and future sister-in-law." My voice is clipped, and I don't leave any room for argument.

She goes rigid against me, and when I pull away, I expect to see fire in her eyes, but instead, those big, gorgeous brown eyes of hers are glossy and filled with what I can only imagine is regret.

And suddenly, *so am I.*

I don't get a chance to apologize. She pulls out of my grasp, nearly sprinting to the back of the studio. I follow after her, finding her standing in a smaller, empty room.

Her arms are wrapped tightly around her torso as I approach her slowly. "Samara, *please* tell me what's going on. If you don't want to come to the wedding, just tell me that. Honestly, Kat really won't mind, and if she did, we can just blame it on me." I try to reassure her, grasping at straws as I attempt to figure out what is happening.

"It's not about the wedding," she says, shaking that beautiful head of shiny curls.

"Then what's wrong? Because silly me," I say sarcastically, "I *actually* thought you might be starting to have some fun." I'm frustrated at how vague she's being.

I didn't grow up around people who kept things in. Sure, Gianni has always been kind of quiet, but as well as he thinks he hides shit, we all see the wheels spinning and can figure out what's on his mind without him having to say anything. And as for the rest of my family, you can't get any of us to shut the hell up if you wanted to, so I'm just not used to this kind of passive-aggressive behavior. I *want* her to tell me what's on her mind because, unfortunately for me and every woman I've ever dated, *I'm not a mind reader.*

She lets out a little sigh before finally turning to look at me. "I just got off the phone with my mom," she tells me.

"Okay...?" I say, dragging out the "O" sound. I'm possibly *more* confused now. "Is she alright?" I ask, and bile churns in my gut as anxiety washes over me.

She waves a hand around, rolling her eyes. "Yeah, *she's* fine. I, on the other hand, am not. She keeps hounding me about going on this family vacation, and in a moment of weakness, I not only *accidentally* agreed to go, but I also lied about something that's going to blow up in my face rather quickly." She presses her fingers into her temples, squeezing her eyes tightly shut.

"Princess, I've gotta be honest here," I tell her, gripping the back of my neck. "I have no idea what you're talking about, so I'm going to need you to spell it out for me."

Standing with her back against the wall, she drops her head back, looking up at the ceiling as she blows out a long breath. "I avoid these family vacations because I'm the only one who's single. All of my cousins and my sister are happily married with tons of children, and I'm the only one who's not. I prioritize my career, and according to my family, there's something *wrong* with that." She shakes her head, filling her lungs before continuing to explain. "So when we go on these vacations, I'm always the designated babysitter while all of the couples go out on dates and enjoy their child-free time. It's the way it's always been, and I'm tired of it. If I'm going to go on vacation, I want it to *feel* like a vacation. I don't want to act like everyone's au pair. Besides that, it only acts as a reminder that I don't have the family I'd imagined for myself by this age. I don't exactly have one foot in the grave, but I've always been a planner, and little Samara definitely had plans of being married with children by now."

She drops her chin to her chest, sliding down the wall, dragging her hands over her face as she shakes her head into them. I take a seat in front of her, fighting the urge to take her hands in mine to stop her from covering that gorgeous face of hers.

"So you said yes to this vacation, but what did you lie about?" I ask, trying to clarify because I am *still* confused.

"Well..." She pauses, hesitating. "I may have blown up on her a little and asked what made this specific vacation such a big deal, and it turns out that she's trying to set me up with one of her friend's sons."

Well, if my interest wasn't already piqued, it sure is now. And why the hell does the thought of Samara with another person bother me so much?

I straighten, my brow raised as she looks up at me. "Go on," I urge her.

"I may have..." She clears her throat. For the first time since I've met her, she's acting kind of... shy. "It's possible that I told her I've been seeing someone." She looks down at her feet quickly, refusing to make eye contact with me. "And agreed to bring him too," she says, her body nearly melting into the floor.

I try; I swear, I try really fucking hard not to let the laughter bubbling in my chest slip free at how dramatic she's being. But unfortunately for her, I fail miserably. She reaches over, smacking me on the shoulder, but for the first time tonight, she cracks a small smile, and laughter starts to pour out of her.

"What the fuck am I going to do?" she asks, the question clearly rhetorical.

I chuckle at that, and an idea that I'm bound to regret later pops into my head. *When will you learn, Luca?* You can't fix *everything* for *everyone* all the time.

I don't heed my own warning before answering her though. "Simple. I'll be your fake boyfriend. On one condition," I say as her eyes snap back up to mine. "It's gotta be somewhere sunny because I need a tan." I wink at her.

Chapter Forty

Samara

"You've lost your mind," I tell him, shaking my head. "Absolutely not," I add, trying to convince myself more than Luca.

"Why not? No offense, but you already lied. There's no coming back from that." He chuckles, not helping ease the guilt roaring inside me. "What's the big deal? We go on a little vacation, you get to enjoy your time away for once, get a massage or whatever you want to do, and then we say we broke up a little after we get back. Problem solved," he says, and he nearly has me convinced.

I shake my head. "You have Gia, and you're probably busy. It just wouldn't make sense." I try to convince us both, but the thought of getting away for a long weekend and not having to deal with my family's scrutiny over my lacking love life *is* appealing.

"Fine, when and where is it?" he asks, crossing his arms over his broad chest. *Goddamn Gloria and her ability to produce such gorgeous children.*

I scoff. "August twenty-eighth to the thirty-first in the Dominican Republic."

He hums. "Sounds great. My hockey season doesn't officially start until October, so I'll just hit up the gym at the hotel, and I'll leave Gia with Cici. She's been working up to time alone with her, so by then, she should be able to handle a weekend with her, and my family is nearby in case she needs anything." He says this with such finality that I nearly believe I've somehow agreed to yet another horrendous idea tonight.

"Luca, no." I move to stand, but he grabs my hands, pulling me down. I lose my balance and fall into his lap. "Oh!" I gasp at the contact, trying to shift off his lap, but he only draws me in closer, wrapping his arms around my waist.

"Come on, Samara. Just let me help you. I owe you one for being my date to Kat's wedding and for helping me keep my kid," he pleads.

"Firstly, you *paid* me to help you gain custody of Gia, and I'm pretty sure you did most of my work for me. And just to be clear, I'm not doing you any favors. I'm your date because of Kat, *not* you," I remind him.

This time, he rolls *his* eyes at *me*. "Stop being so difficult, princess." His words are soft, and that's likely the only reason my hackles don't immediately go up.

If I'm being honest with myself, this *would* solve a lot of my family issues. For now anyway. And it would be nice to have a vacation for once, which is why the next word slips past my lips. "Fine."

His dark brows shoot up his forehead. "Really?" he asks, clearly shocked.

"Yep, now let me up," I tell him, grappling to stand. My fingers dig into his shoulders, but he grips my hips and pulls me up with him before I can push myself up and off him.

He places a hand at the base of my spine, leading me out of the small room, but I step out of his grasp before pushing past the curtains hung in the doorframe. *I liked having his hand on me a bit too much, so it's better to cut that out now.*

Chapter Forty-One

Luca

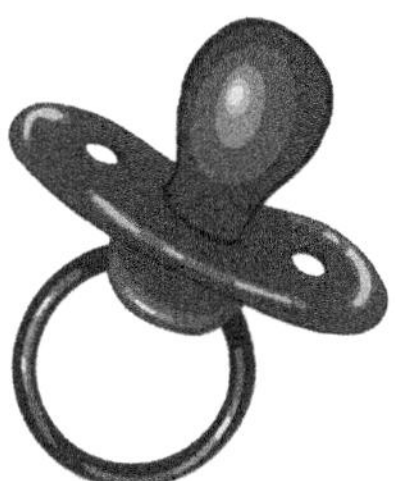

As we exit the room, I see the wide eyes of my family all huddled in the hallway, realizing they've been caught eavesdropping. Even our instructors, Cassandra and Christian, have joined them. They each shift their gazes, turning away from us.

Dante rubs at the back of his neck, looking up at the ceiling as if *that's* going to convince anyone he wasn't listening with the rest of them.

"You guys really are the nosiest people on the planet." I chuckle, walking past Kas as he whispers to me with a laugh.

"You are *so* fucked, my friend," he says, patting my shoulder.

As I look over at Samara, pushing her way back into the larger studio space with her curls framing her face, I realize *he isn't wrong.*

I can't be sure what possessed me to offer to go on a family vacation with her besides the fact that this strong woman just looked beaten to hell, and it crushed a piece of me.

I have no idea how we're going to make it through four days of being in each other's vicinity without her trying to kill me, but I'll have fun doing it and I'm determined to make it as enjoyable for the both of us as possible. I can't take the offer back now, and truthfully, *I don't think I want to.*

Chapter Forty-Two

Samara

Friday, August 14, 2026

Unfortunately for me, Luca's entire family is nothing but a bunch of troublemakers.

As much as I've been enjoying girls' nights, book club, and even Sunday dance lessons, I can't help but think they're trying to meddle in something that will literally *never* happen.

He's arrogant and laughs at his own jokes, and he's too damn *pretty* for his own good. *Or my good, for that matter.* Men like that aren't at all who I'd typically envision myself with, but when Aiyana invited me to the guys' offseason charity hockey game, I found myself saying *yes.*

Though that has nothing to do with Luca.

I wanted some friends in town, and now that I have them, I think having a beer or two at a hockey game could be fun.

Which is why I'm standing outside of this rowdy-ass hockey rink, waiting for everyone to arrive.

I see them heading toward me from the far end of the parking lot. They're hard to miss with how large the group is, and Rose's pink hair acts as a traffic cone under the streetlights.

"Samara!" Gloria shouts, waving as she wheels over to me.

I bend down to give her a kiss on either cheek as I've become accustomed to when greeting this whole family.

"I've got a gift for you." She beams up at me, but there's a glint in her eye that has the bile in my stomach churning immediately.

I groan quietly as she pulls out a black gift bag from where it rests on the handle behind her, extending it out for me to take. I arch a brow at her, still not trusting her intentions.

As I pull the black and red tissue paper out of the bag, taking out the folded jersey and letting it fall in front of me, I realize *why* my gut said she was up to no good. The back of the jersey reads "De Laurentiis" with a massive "69" beneath it.

As to why Luca chose that childish number, I can only imagine, but his mom is about to be the death of me.

"Gloria, I appreciate the gift, but you *do* know Luca and I aren't *actually* dating, right?"

She laughs. "Of course I know that." She rolls her eyes at me as if *I'm* the one being ridiculous. "I was front and center listening to that whole conversation, but *you* are the one who lied to your mother, so *I'm* just trying to make it believable." She smiles up at me. "C-Y-A, babycakes," she tells me. *Cover your ass.* A phrase I know all too well.

I roll my eyes at her, clearly not about to win *this* case, so I concede, slipping the oversized jersey over my red long-sleeved top.

We head inside, following behind Gloria, and Kat gives me a reassuring smile. The rest of the women, however, do not. They're all trying not to laugh, their cheeks filled with air, making them look like a bunch of squirrels with nuts packed in their mouths.

Aiyana is the first to school her expression, and she swings her arm over my shoulder playfully. It's a gesture I'm definitely not used to. "Gloria is kind of a wild card, but I promise, she's got your best interest at heart, and if you ever feel like she's genuinely overstepping, just tell her, okay? None of us want you to feel bullied," she assures me, and some of the stress melts from my tense shoulders.

We take our seats close to the ice after getting concessions, and I take a giant gulp of my beer and let the cool liquid ease some of my earlier anxiety.

Kat lifts her beer to mine, clanking it together when all the women say, "Cheers!"

"Kat, are you drinking a beer?" Arielle asks, leaning over my seat as she squints at the bottle in Kat's hand.

She snickers, passing it to her to read. "It's non-alcoholic." Her cheeks flush a rosy color, and she says, "Ale spoke with concessions and asked them to start stocking non-alcoholic versions for those like myself who prefer not to drink but enjoy the experience."

My heart squeezes tightly in my chest.

"That's so sweet," I say, practically swooning. I'm basically in love with every relationship these women have. It's ridiculous.

Over the next hour, I watch as Luca dances around the net, not letting any pucks past him. When he stops a puck, he makes a big show of it, blowing kisses, taking a bow, and at one point, he's literally *humping* the ice.

"I swear." Arielle giggles, cupping a hand over her mouth. "That just never gets old."

"He has a little *too* much fun out there if you ask me," Rose says in her very blasé way.

"Ale keeps trying to convince me that Luca's just stretching, but I sincerely hope I don't seem that freaking naive," Kat says with a snort.

"He doesn't think you're naive," Charlie says. "He's fucking praying you don't find the dumb shit Luca does attractive."

Kat nearly chokes on the slushie she swapped to about a half hour ago as Aiyana pats her back. "There, there, sweet child, Momma Aiyana's got you." That only makes Kat cough even harder.

"You're a terror." I chuckle at Aiyana, loving how freely she speaks her mind, even if what she says is entirely unhinged.

She smirks up at me. "Thank you," she says, and I think she honestly took it as a compliment. Not that I didn't mean it as one because I absolutely did.

"Kat, not to worry you further, but I have to say, I do find it just a tad concerning that you didn't deny what Charlie said."

Kat shakes her head, rubbing her thumb over the pendant of her gold necklace as she clenches her eyes shut. "There isn't much that Luca does that doesn't *mostly* repulse me. No offense, I love him with every piece of my soul, but I'm by no means looking to trade De Laurentiis brothers," she says with a laugh.

Thank god for that.

I finally turn my attention back to the ice, and just as Luca blocks another shot, his attention seems to snag over here. He drops his stick, takes off his helmet, and makes his way over to us as he pulls his gloves off. *What the hell is he doing? He's in the middle of a game!*

His coach is shouting at him from the bench, and beside him is Alessandro with his hands on his hips, shaking his head in disbelief, but I can see his wide smile from here.

Luca makes his way over to us, jabbing his finger at the glass and pointing straight at me.

"Looks like Luca wants to help you convince your parents that this is real too." Charlie laughs.

"My parents don't even watch hockey!" I tell them. I haven't even told them his name yet, and I definitely haven't told them what he does for a living or how we met. There's not a chance that would make our vacation go by more smoothly.

He pulls out his mouthguard and shouts, "Turn around, *princess*!"

I pretend I have no idea what he's saying. "What? I can't hear you!" I shout back, unable to keep the smile off my face. He shoots his gaze straight at his mom, who's chuckling beside me along with all the other women flanking me.

"Oh, come on, stand up and show off your new jersey," Gloria tells me, patting my thigh.

"Don't make me come over there and do it myself," he shouts at me.

And I can't quite tell if the chill that skates up my spine is from how much I actually like the thought of his hands on me or if it's the realization that everyone's eyes are on me.

"Fine," I groan, wanting to get this over with. I stand, turning around and moving my hair off my back to show him his name across my shoulder blades.

The crowd roars around us, clapping loudly and cheering their approval. When I turn to sit back down, his eyes are blazing with heat for just a moment before he brings his fingers to his lips, letting out a loud whistle. He shakes his head at me, and I see his lips move, but he doesn't speak loud enough for me to hear what he said.

It *looked* like he said, "Oh, fuck me," but that couldn't be right. This is Luca De Laurentiis. Everything he does is to get a rise out of me or someone else.

And when he starts to skate backward toward his goalpost, he puts his hands out in front of his chest, curving his fingers and thumbs into a heart. My heart thumps wildly behind my ribs as he turns, reaching down to grab his discarded gear.

Chapter Forty-Three

Luca

I've had hundreds, if not *thousands,* of women wear my jersey, but not a single one has looked as good in it as Samara does.

And that thought alone fucking terrifies me.

I'm not sure when I first realized it, but everything about Samara makes me want to ravish every inch of her.

So when I see her heading back to her car after I'm finished cleaning up, I can't help the fact that my legs literally drag me in her direction.

"Hey, princess, wait up!" I shout, jogging to catch up with her.

When her eyes catch on mine and she realizes who's shouting behind her, she shakes her head and continues in the direction of her car.

Too bad for her: *I like the chase.*

"Oh, come on!" I yell, speeding up as I sidle her.

"Go away, Luca." She groans as she makes it to the door of her Range Rover, pulling the door open. And before she can get in, I'm on her.

My hands rest on either side of her head, and I have to resist the urge to run my nose up the length of her neck. She smells so fucking good—intoxicating like cognac and something sweet like pralines.

God, why is this woman seemingly created just to test every ounce of my resolve?

"Luca, I want to go home," she huffs out, but there's no real annoyance in her words.

"Did you enjoy the game?" I ask, hoping she'll somehow forget she's not a fan of me.

"Yes, and now I want to go home and crawl into my bed, which I'm certain I'll enjoy just as much, if not more," she says, twisting her body to try and get into the car.

I don't want her to feel caged in, so I lean away from her reluctantly. She slides into her seat, clipping her seatbelt quickly, and looks as if she's about ready to pull away, whether I'm standing here or not.

"Have you eaten?" I ask her.

"I had a couple of beers and a pretzel," she tells me with a pinched expression.

"That's not a lot of food. Are you sure you're safe to drive home?" I ask, leaning into her slightly but stopping myself.

I've always been careful about those around me drinking and driving, but ever since Gianni's best friend passed away in that accident, I've arguably become even more paranoid about it.

"I assure you, I'm fine." But the way her brows draw together marginally makes me think that she may be second-guessing herself.

"I live just around the corner, and you're nearly a half hour away from here. Just come over, and I'll make us some dinner and you can drive yourself home after you've gotten some food in your system. *Please,*" I plead with her. I see the precise moment in which her hard exterior cracks.

"I promise you, I would *never* drive if I didn't feel completely confident I was safe, and I'd never put other people at risk, but if it'll make you feel better," she sighs, relaxing back into her seat, "I'll let you make me dinner. But after that, I'm gone, you got it?" she clarifies, her words stern, but they light me up inside. *Fuck yeah!*

I nod, probably a little too over excitedly, and close her car door, running across the parking lot to my motorcycle. I pull my helmet on and drive up behind her. She pulls out and heads toward my place. In less than two minutes, we're pulling into my driveway.

Chapter Forty-Four

Samara

What has gotten into me? Why did I say yes?

Because you're hungry, obviously. That's the *only* reasonable explanation.

And since when does this man have a motorcycle? I've only ever seen him in that massive Tahoe.

The gall of this man to get on me about driving home after two beers I had over the course of two freaking hours, only for him to climb onto a motorcycle minutes later as if those things are safe!

I try to calm my temper, doing my best to remind myself that at least he's wearing a helmet and *he* hasn't had anything to drink.

I meet him at the front door, but I can't help the small step back I take when I see Cecily open it, standing with Gia in her arms.

She smiles brightly at me, the sadness in her eyes all but vanished since the last time I saw her.

"Gia, *mia bambina*," Luca calls to his daughter with outstretched arms as he goes to grab her from her mother. He presses a kiss to the top of her head and bounces on the balls of his feet, looking into her eyes as she giggles at her nickname.

"Thanks for watching her tonight, Cici. How'd it go?" he asks her as she grabs her purse from a hook by the door.

"It went really well." She draws her shoulders back and stands tall. "Thank you for trusting me with her," she adds quietly. "Would you, um..." She looks down at her feet, appearing bashful. "Would you mind if she maybe slept over next weekend? I'd like to give an overnight visit a go if you think it's safe?" she asks him, unsure of herself.

It must kill her to have to have these conversations with him, but Luca takes it in stride, reassuring her as he does. "You're doing great, Cici. I'm proud of you," he tells her, squeezing her upper arm gently.

"Of course she can stay with you next weekend. I'll make sure to be available in case you need anything. I *know* you're going to do great, but I'd rather be around in case you feel like you need something," he says, reassuring her with a smile. His eyes remain soft, and there's no hint of a lie anywhere in his features.

I feel like I'm intruding, so I slip past them, nodding at Cecily as I walk over to the kitchen counter. They finish up their conversation within seconds, and the door closes behind Luca as he heads over to me.

"Take a seat anywhere you'd like. I'll be back in a few. I'm gonna change Gia into her jammies," he tells me before heading toward his room.

I take a seat on one of the gray barstools at the kitchen island. My heart clenches in my chest at hearing Gia's cries and Luca's subsequent pleas for her to calm down.

I know he has help because his family is incredible, and I'm glad Cecily is doing better. But Luca's entire life has taken a complete one-eighty from where it was before, and I wonder if anyone's thought to see how he's *actually* doing underneath the cool composure he seems to wear so well.

A few minutes later, he comes out of the room bare-chested with a diapered Gia lying against him.

"Sorry, I know this looks ridiculous, but all of the daddy blogs talk about the importance of skin-to-skin for bonding, and it keeps her calm while I warm up her bottle. I'll just feed her and then get started on our dinner." I wave him off because the apology is entirely unnecessary.

Besides, now I get to watch his coiled muscles flex as he gets her bottle ready. *It's the little things in life.* He pulls a plastic baggy out of the fridge and places it on the counter before restocking the fridge with a frozen packet just like it.

Seeing him with her and how meticulous he is about ensuring she's well cared for has my ovaries doing a little dance.

"She doesn't drink formula?" I ask him, curiosity taking hold of me.

He shakes his head. "She did the first few days, but one of the single-dad forums on Reddit was talking about all the options for donor milk. After looking into it, I figured it would maybe be a better option for her, and if it wasn't, we'd swap back to formula. I'm doing what I can, but with no tits of my own, this is the best I've got," he says, bouncing on the balls of his feet and chuckling at his own joke.

The sound is warm and light. It sends a shiver down my spine that makes me bristle in my seat.

I don't think there's anything wrong with formula-feeding your child. Most parents are just doing their best, but I'd be lying if I said it didn't impress me that Luca is really going the extra mile for his kid.

I watch as he holds her, setting her bottle in the warmer. Standing from my chair, I walk over to them with outstretched arms. "Can I feed her?"

His eyes flicker up to mine, crinkling at the sides with his widening smile. "I'd appreciate that," he tells me, pressing a kiss to her head, grabbing a blanket off the counter and wrapping it around her. He places her gently in my arms.

I smile down at her and graze my thumb over the soft fabric of her green blanket. My heart aches in my chest, and my limbs suddenly feel heavy.

He grabs a towel from the kitchen counter and sets it on my shoulder, his fingertips trailing down my skin, leaving a blazing path in their wake.

Gia babbles happily, her tiny hands reaching out to tangle in my curls. Light laughter slips past my lips as I detach the strands from her tiny clutches and give her my finger to play with instead.

Luca comes around the kitchen island, handing me her bottle, which she takes immediately, sucking ferociously. "Don't let her fool you. Cici texted me less than two hours ago that she'd fed her," he says, rolling his eyes playfully at her. "She's just got a big appetite. She'll be big and strong like her dad." He shoots me a playful wink that settles its way into my core.

Damn him.

"Are you okay with burgers for dinner? I could also make pasta, or we could order in if neither sounds good to you," he asks me.

"Burgers sound great." *I love a good burger.*

Gia looks up at me, meeting my gaze with hers. You'd never need a paternity test to know who her father is. She's all Luca.

This kid is too damn cute; it makes my ovaries weep.

"These kids really spend nearly ten months inside their mother's wombs just to have the *audacity* to come out looking like their father," I joke, mostly to Gia.

"Arielle complains about that all the time. She said it took three tries to get one with red hair. After that, they closed up shop."

"How long have Arielle and Dante been together?" I ask, curious because they seem like they've known each other their whole lives. That's the same impression I'd had of Kat and Alessandro, but she told me they've only been together a couple of years.

Some people are just made for each other, and it's clear to everyone around them.

"Since Arielle turned eighteen. She's three years younger than Dante and me, so I guess about twelve years."

My brows pinch together at this. "You and Dante are the same age?"

He nods, continuing what he's doing at the stove. "Yeah, he's the oldest of my adopted siblings, but he and I were born the same year."

"Adopted siblings?" How come I didn't know about this?

Oh, right. *You didn't ask.*

"Yeah, my mom has multiple sclerosis, so after me, she and my dad decided to adopt. They weren't sure if it was safe for her to have more children, and they had wanted to adopt anyway. Insert the family of three children showing up on Christmas day," he says, smiling softly as he works in the kitchen.

I *did* know about her MS, as well as Alessandro's. I remembered from the media fiasco a couple of years ago that I read about while looking into Luca's past. So at least that part doesn't come as a shock, but how hadn't I known his other siblings were adopted?

"How come you all look alike?" I finally ask.

He chuckles, shaking his head. "I don't really think we do. We've all got dark hair, but that's really the only resemblance. I'm sure it helps that they're half Italian. Gianni has blue eyes that are sort of like my mom's, but Dante and Charlie are the only ones with brown eyes."

I've nearly fallen victim to those eyes of Dante's, and I certainly wouldn't call them "brown." They're like polished onyx, so dark you can see your reflection in them, and I'm sort of convinced the man is capable of hypnosis with those things.

I nod, understanding seeping in slowly. Against my better judgment, I ask, "Growing up with such a big family, did you ever want kids of your own?"

The moment the words leave my mouth, I'm annoyed that I'd even asked them. "I'm sorry, Luca. You don't need to answer that." As someone who's dealt with infertility and all of the emotions surrounding it, *I know better* than to ask questions like this.

"No, no, it's okay, really," he tells me, wiping his wet hands on a dishcloth. "I've always wanted kids but never found the right person, and truthfully, I felt undeserving of children." This makes me pause. *He's felt undeserving of something so many people consider a normal part of life?* "I was always making the wrong decisions, and when Ale was diagnosed with MS, I put a lot of that on myself. I didn't think it was my fault or anything, but I figured that if one of us should've ended up with it, it should've been me." My muscles tense, and I have difficulty swallowing my saliva. Luca casts his eyes down at the cutting board, meticulously chopping onions for the burgers he has cooking in a cast-iron skillet on the stove. "He was always the one taking care of me and my siblings, so I knew he'd be a good dad, and I didn't want his life to be harder than it needed to be. Then Gia falls into my lap. Meanwhile, Kat and Ale are struggling with adoption agencies, and it just feels"—he takes a deep breath— "wrong?" he says like he's asking a question.

"Wrong, how?" I can't seem to stop myself. The fact that he's thinking some of the same things I've been holding against him since the day I met him sours my stomach. *Guilt is a tricky bitch.*

His eyes slide to mine, and a pained expression crosses his handsome, chiseled features. "I'm able-bodied, not worried about the day that my career will end or that my body will stop working how I'd like it to, and I have this gorgeous, sweet kid who I already love so goddamn desperately; it kills me that I didn't get to be there for her from the beginning." His voice is filled with anguish at the thought of missing out on time with Gia, and it hits me like a punch to the gut. "But I make mistakes all the time, Samara. I'm constantly doing dumb shit, making impulsive decisions, and yet my brother has to bear the weight of so many obstacles. I just feel really fucking *undeserving.*"

My chest tightens, and my heart starts to pound harder against my ribcage. He's probably thought all of these things because of people like me, who've misjudged him time and time again. And now that I'm finally allowing my stubborn brain to fully recognize that, *all I want to do is comfort him.*

"You can't help the things you can't change, Luca. You aren't to blame for your brother having different struggles than you, and it doesn't mean that you *don't* have your own. Yes, you had a child literally fall into your lap, and she's adorable beyond words, but you're also having to learn how to be a father. That in itself is hard." It nearly takes my breath away as I say the words I haven't allowed myself to think until this moment. Until now, I'd genuinely been holding onto so much resentment toward Luca, partly for reasons out of his control. Some of those reasons really *aren't* his fault.

He looks over at me, sad eyes meeting mine, as he quietly says, "Thank you, Samara. I needed to hear that."

I avert my gaze to Gia, who's just finished her bottle and is looking rather milk drunk. "I think she's done," I say, chuckling and using the moment to change the subject to something not as heavy. I lift her semi-limp body onto my shoulder to burp her.

Once she's thoroughly passed out in my arms and Luca has two absolutely massive burgers plated, he comes around the counter, taking her from me and heading to the room to put her down.

"We can eat anywhere you'd like. I'll be a few minutes, and I don't want you to eat a cold burger," he tells me over his shoulder as he walks away.

Jesus Christ. I hate to see you leave, but I love to watch you go.

His ass is phenomenal, not that I expect anything less from a goalie. *Aren't those guys supposed to be the extra weird ones?*

I avert my gaze to the burgers on the counter and resist the urge to dig in, not wanting to seem rude by not waiting for him to return. *Yeah, Samara, eating the burger he told you to eat is the most rude thing you've done to this man.* I scoff at myself, and when he closes the door behind him, I'm hit with a little wave of sadness at the fact that he's now covering those tan, corded muscles with a black T-shirt. *Such a shame.*

"Oh, come on, princess, don't look so disappointed," he says with a smirk as he grabs the plates from the counter.

"I don't know what you're talking about," I retort, hoping to save myself just an ounce of my pride, but it's no use.

"Sure you don't." He winks at me as he brings the plates over to the couch and sets them down on the coffee table.

I grab some paper towels, joining him on the couch, but he stands and goes back to the kitchen. "Want anything to drink? I've got water, Gatorade, and Coke."

"Coke. You can't eat a burger with water," I tell him.

"I couldn't agree more," he says, pouring us each a glass and bringing them back to the couch.

I expect him to turn the TV on to fill the silence, but instead, he turns toward me, grabbing the plates and placing one in my lap.

The smell is delicious, and I can't help but finally dig in.

I hate eating in front of other people. I always feel like they'll think I'm a slob. I don't eat dainty meals like I'm sure women like Cecily do.

But Luca chowing down on his own burger makes me feel a little less self-conscious about myself and spurs me on to actually enjoy my meal.

Chapter Forty-Five

Luca

I *love* a woman who can eat.

Sure, food is fuel, but I'm also a firm believer that it can be fuel for your soul and not just your body. That's something my mom always ingrained into us as kids, so it's nice to see a woman who can enjoy her meals instead of eating nothing but a sad bowl of lettuce.

And that's another thing that gets me. Salads can be fucking delicious if they've got the right components. They don't *have* to be sad, but I've dated so many women who thought they needed to eat a certain way to be desirable, and it was always a turn-off for me. I realize it isn't their fault that they hold those beliefs.

They were taught these things from a young age, and the media just reinforced it, which is total shit, but *someone* has got to break that cycle. This means that this is one of many conversations Cici and I will have to have the older Gia gets. I refuse to let my daughter grow up thinking she's anything less than beautiful, strong, and capable beyond imagination just because her mother thinks those things about herself. Hell, I hope Cici can move past those beliefs for herself too.

As we sit in comfortable silence, I find myself caught on the question Samara had asked earlier.

It's hard not to wonder whether or not she wants kids too. Or even *a* kid. But I know children and fertility can be a difficult subject for some, and the way she tried to backtrack after she asked has me pushing my own questions to the sidelines.

"Alright, Samara, if we're going to be fake boyfriend and girlfriend, I've gotta know all there is to know about you." It's the perfect way to find out more about her without having to deal with her inevitable reluctance. She has a lot riding on making this believable, though I don't think there'll be any problems on my end. I already find myself wanting to be around her when I know I shouldn't because she's not reciprocating those feelings.

She swallows her bite of burger and wipes her mouth before repositioning her body on the couch to face me more easily. "What do you wanna know?"

"Everything," I tell her without hesitation.

She rolls her eyes at me, but a small smile graces her lips, and warmth spreads in my gut. "I need specific questions, Luca." She smirks. Those full, plump lips are going to be the death of me someday.

"What kind of hobbies do you enjoy?" I ask, starting off in easy territory.

"I read a lot in any free time I've got, and I enjoy sewing and cross-stitching."

"Where'd you learn to sew?" I ask, genuine curiosity wrapped around my vocal cords, begging me to keep her talking about anything and everything. For some reason, I have a difficult time picturing Samara performing something so seemingly domestic. She carries herself with an energy that I'd always believed translated to a woman who'd rather work and be out of the house than in it.

"My mom is a seamstress. When she first moved to the US, she was a teenager and worked anywhere she was hired. One of those jobs was as a seamstress in a small dry-cleaning shop. When she and my dad met, they bonded over their desire to start their own businesses."

I nod my understanding, hoping she'll continue without me having to beg her. I breathe out a small sigh when she starts speaking again. "So eventually, my dad opened up the restaurant he and my sister now run together, and Mom was able to get enough work on her own to open her little shop in their apartment. She taught my sister and me growing up, but Vea was better at cooking, so she took more to that with my dad." It's clear in every word she speaks how proud she is of her family.

"Where's your mom from?" I ask.

"My mom is originally from the Dominican Republic, and my sister was born in Jamaica. My parents had moved there for a while when Mom was pregnant with Vea. They wanted the support from my grandparents since they were first-time parents but moved back here before having me." The fact that she elaborated without me having to ask feels like a major win, but I guess everything she's said has just been for the benefit of our now blossoming, fake relationship. At least, *I hope it's blossoming.*

"And do you just have the one sister?"

"Yep, but a few of my mom's siblings moved here after her, so I grew up with a lot of cousins nearby. This can't be one-sided though. Tell me about your hobbies outside of hockey," she urges, clearly done with talking about herself for the moment.

"Well, as you've seen, I ballroom dance." I smile when she rolls her eyes at me. I wonder if she's thinking back to that first dance class before she knew about my family's history with ballroom dancing. "And I kickbox, and um"—I cough—"bake."

Her eyes light up. "You bake?" she asks, her mind getting caught on the hobby that's arguably the least likely to be a panty melter.

I nod, unwilling to give up any more detail than that.

Her mouth hangs open until she snaps it shut. A playful grin spreads across her face as she leans into me, her lips brushing against my ear the same way I've done to her time and time again, always aiming to rile her up. And when her breath skitters across my skin, my balls tighten with every word she speaks. "So Luca…" *Is it hot in here?* I have to resist the urge to wipe at the sheen of sweat now coating my forehead as heat burns through me.

"Yes, princess?" I ask, feeling out of breath with her this close to me. My tongue darts out to wet my dry lips.

"Do you…" she says before trailing the tip of her nose down my jaw, agonizingly slow. *Fuck, that's hot.*

"Know the muffin man?" she asks, leaning away from me before bursting into a fit of laughter. My mind feels like a fog has settled over my brain as I try to dissect her words, but I keep getting caught up in how goddamn gorgeous she looks when she's laughing. It takes a moment for my mind to catch up past my lust-induced haze, and when it does, laughter rips through me.

My smile is the size of Texas when I finally meet her eyes. "So, the tough-as-nails lawyer *does* have a sense of humor, huh?"

Over the next half hour, my heart rate calms down, but my feelings for Samara start to morph into something entirely different from the arousal I'm used to feeling around her. I rattle off just about every question I can think of, but my mind keeps on snagging, and with each answer she freely gives me, my confidence builds until I can't hold it in any longer.

Especially not after she's *finally* warmed up to me.

"So what you said about not wanting to go on this vacation," I say, clearing my throat. "I gathered that maybe..."

She rolls her eyes at me, but she's wearing a grin, so I don't *think* she's annoyed. "Maybe what, Luca?" she asks with a smirk, tilting her head to the side and taking another sip of her Coke.

"Maybe you've felt like you don't live up to their expectation of you no matter how hard you try?" I ask, my voice soft.

Her expression twists, and she turns her face away from me, her throat working on a swallow. I scoot closer to her, wrapping my arms around her on instinct. When she doesn't pull away, I collect her warm body into my arms and settle her in my lap.

Apparently, we're being fucking bold tonight, huh?

A tear slips down her cheek and over her clenched lips. I swipe it away with the pad of my thumb; my heart feeling strangled in my chest.

"I ask because I feel the same way." I clear my throat again, trying to dislodge the massive lump settling there. "A lot, actually. I think I do it to myself, really. Ever since I was little, I wanted to be as good as my brothers were at everything, and when I'd struggle, I'd beat myself up about it."

"Luca, I think we *all* feel that way. At least some of the time," she tells me. Her voice is the most gentle I've ever heard it.

I nod because, clearly, she doesn't want to get into any more deep conversations with me tonight.

I'm just her fake boyfriend. So, *of course,* she doesn't.

Samara scooches off my lap, and the loss of her in my arms has a chill settling over my skin.

She sits closer to me than she had been before, though, and reaches over to the coffee table, grabbing her soda and taking a sip before setting it back down.

She's got a little dribble of it on the corner of her lip. Leaning across her, I wipe it with my thumb, not even thinking about the possible repercussions until her body has gone still, and her sharp intake of breath has my cock twitching. I bring the droplet to my mouth and suck, keeping my lips just inches from hers, reveling in the way her warm breath comes more quickly the longer we make eye contact.

"I don't remember Coke tasting this sweet," I say, low and slow. "It must be *you*."

"Luca," she scoffs, but the way she's dragging the word out sounds more like a moan. *My name sounds so good on her lips.*

"Yes, princess?"

"It's literally *all* sugar." She pulls away from me, rolling her eyes and slipping back into what I've come to know is her usual defense tactic, but I don't miss the way her chest heaves. Satisfaction ripples through me each time I've caught even just a glimpse of what's hiding beneath her meticulously manicured surface.

"Maybe so, but I bet you're sweeter." I chuckle, raking my eyes over her deliberately. "You're still wearing my jersey," I observe.

"I've had no reason to change since getting here," she says, defiance thick in her tone.

I dip my head, loving that I don't have to strain my neck to coast my lips over the shell of her ear. *She's so tall, and so damn perfect.* "I could dirty you up and give you a reason," I tell her, a little *too* curious to find out just how far I can take this before she knees me in the nuts. "Though I have to say, it looks better on you than it does me."

She sucks in an audible breath, turning her face to mine. I watch with enraptured interest as her pupils dilate, and out of the corner of my eye, I see her thighs clench together.

"Oh, hell," she says before finally running her hands up my chest, gripping my shirt in her fingers, and dragging me into her for a mind-numbing kiss.

The moment her lips are on mine, it's all fire and ice, and I fucking *love* it when she finally lets go of some of that perfectly curated control.

My lips move against hers, pleading for entrance as I swipe my tongue along the seam of her pillow-soft, plump lips. She refuses me at first but leans all the way back until she's flat against the couch, dragging me over top of her.

I run my hands up her thighs, pulling them apart so I can sink between them. She hikes them up my back, locking her ankles behind me.

I can feel the heat from her core radiating off her body, and sparks erupt through each of my muscle fibers.

Her lips finally part for me, and I don't hesitate. My tongue sweeps in, tangling with hers, before I gently nibble on her bottom lip.

A moan escapes her, and I wish I could bottle it up and save it for later. *She sounds so sweet when she's needy like this.*

I work a hand under the jersey and shirt underneath, wiggling my fingers under the lacy fabric of her bra until I've got her nipple pebbled in my grasp. Trailing kisses down her neck as I rub and pull on the sensitive skin at my fingertips, her back arches into me.

"Samara," I rumble against the base of her neck, her fingers curl into my hair, tugging firmly.

"Yes?" she moans as I drag my tongue up the length of her throat.

"Do I get to have my dessert now?" I ask, nipping my way down her chest before placing open-mouth kisses on her stomach.

"That depends on what you want for dessert," she gasps out as I squeeze her nipple tightly while biting the skin just above the button of her jeans.

I move down farther, kneeling beside the couch and dragging my nose up the seam of her jeans, hovering my mouth over her cunt. "I think you know exactly what I want for dessert, *principessa*."

"It should be illegal to pull out the Italian at a time like this, but I'll allow it," she jokes, her voice husky as she lifts her ass up and unbuttons her jeans.

"Thank fuck." I groan as I pull them down along with her black lace thong, removing them both as gently as my trembling fingers will allow. *I want this woman desperately.*

"God, you're so pretty like this. I can't wait to taste this sweet pussy," I tell her, leaning over to flick on the lamp. Her hands immediately grab for a throw pillow, covering herself up as quickly as the light turned on.

"Lights off," she says adamantly, and my stomach drops to my toes. This resilient, courageous, confident woman is being reduced to covering her body because she's afraid I'll think something's wrong with it. *This* is precisely what I meant about social media.

"Samara." I say her name firmly, being sure to look her straight in those gorgeous brown eyes. "If you want to come, I'm keeping this light on. I want to see *every inch* of you as you fall apart on my tongue. Do you understand?"

She tries to sit up straighter, a familiar expression of defiance hardening her features. "This may come as a surprise to you, Luca, but I'm not a model like the other women you've been with. I don't look like them, and I'm *sorry* if me not wanting to see the look on your face when you see my tummy *offends your delicate sensibilities*," she scoffs, refusing to make eye contact with me now, but I hear the vulnerability behind her words.

The only model I've even been with was Cecily, but now probably isn't the best time to bring that up.

I grip her chin gently, dragging her eyes back to mine. "If you don't want this to go any further, that's entirely up to you. I'll stop right now." *God, I really hope she doesn't want to stop.* "But if you think for a single second that there's any piece of your body I wouldn't gladly devour, you're not as intelligent as I'd thought."

She tries to interrupt me, but I stick my index and middle fingers in her mouth and watch as her eyes widen, but when she instinctually sucks on them, I know I'm fucking done for. I hold her gaze as I speak my next words. "Size doesn't matter to me, Samara. I don't discriminate. You're gorgeous, and if you'd just shut the hell up, I could have you using that mouth for good instead of all the bitching you're choosing to do."

"Luca, I swear to god, if I weren't so turned on right now, I'd slap you," she grits out once I've removed my fingers from her mouth.

"Do it." I chuckle. "Chances are, I'll like it." I smirk, lowering my face between her legs as I pull that fucking pillow off her.

Chapter Forty-Six

Samara

My core is clenching so tightly I feel like I could combust at any moment. Luca's hair is tickling the inside of my thighs, practically begging me to squeeze them around his head.

He *finally* slides his tongue inside me, and all the air leaves my lungs in that moment. I release a strangled moan, twining my fingers in his hair and pulling him farther into me.

The need to cover myself up gnaws at my gut. It's such an ingrained part of me that I can't help it, but the way this man looks at me is like he'd rather *die* than ever have a single inch of my body covered up.

Luca's calloused hands slide up my legs, wrenching them farther apart and tossing them over his shoulders as he drags my body closer to the edge of the couch for his mouth to dive more deeply into me.

All coherent thought leaves my brain, and I find myself seeping deeper and deeper into the electric feeling zipping through my body at having this gorgeous man between my legs, savoring me, and committing every second to memory.

"Don't stop," I beg, needing the release more than he could ever know.

I've made myself come to the thought of Luca De Laurentiis's tongue every night this week, but as it turns out, there's not a single toy on the planet that could compare.

He dips his tongue inside me once more, pulling out to suck on my clit, but before I can get the friction I need, he hoists my hips up, lapping at my ass. My cheeks clench at the sensation, wanting more but being too embarrassed to ask for it.

The flat of his tongue trails up the seam of my ass. He makes the most intoxicating sounds as he sucks and slurps on my skin and *finally* pushes a finger inside my dripping center, curling it to hit my clit from the inside.

My body is on fire, heat blazing through me as I shiver under his touch. My hips buck to meet his movements, urging him on, but he pulls away, keeping his finger inside me as he meets my gaze with a sly grin.

"Who'd have thought..." He shakes his head in disbelief, his grin morphing into a smirk that makes his right dimple burst free. "The same woman who hated me not long ago"—he leans forward, kissing just above my clit—"is now on my couch, writhing against my tongue and *begging* me not to stop."

Before I can respond, he licks a path up the seam of my folds and says, "And somehow, she's the sweetest fucking thing I've ever tasted."

Jesus Christ, who even is this man? And where did he get this mouth from?

He sinks back down to the floor, slipping a second finger inside me, stretching me out as he takes my clit between his teeth, tugging gently.

"Oh, yes," I moan out. My hands grab his shoulders, trying to steady myself as he twirls that magnificent tongue around my sensitive skin, nipping and sucking as he brings me over the edge.

"Fuck, yes!" I scream.

"Say my name, *principessa*," he mumbles between tastes.

And for once, I actually do as I'm told. "Luca!" I shout, and immediately, I'm rewarded by the second wave of my orgasm that hits me as he drags my clit between his teeth. My skin is on fire as pleasure zips up my spine, dancing with the electrified feeling rushing through my blood.

"What a fucking good girl you are, princess." Just the sound of that name tightens my core even further, leaving me a trembling mess in his arms as he cleans me up with his tongue rubbing against my overly sensitive skin.

When he's done, and I'm sated, he stands up to his full height, and the rock-hard dick staring back at me through his thin gym shorts has me doing a double take.

"Jesus motherfucking Christ!" I yell at him. "Where do you hide that thing?"

He laughs, the sound reverberating throughout the room. "I swear, it's not usually this big." He winks at me. "Your perfect cunt just makes it *bigger*."

Luca saunters off to the kitchen. "Where are you going?" I ask in disbelief. Did he really just walk away from me before I could take care of him?

"I'll be right back," he tells me. I watch as he makes his way to the sink before wetting a few paper towels and returning a moment later. He falls to his knees before me for the second time tonight, spreading my thighs as he wipes me clean and blots me dry. *I've never had a man take care of this part of things afterward, especially not until he'd had his fun too.*

He leans forward, placing a tender kiss along the inside of my thigh, then looks up at me beneath his thick lashes as he kisses my tummy. Not once, not twice, but *three* times this man kisses my soft stomach, making it known that he genuinely sees no flaws there.

I'm hit with a new wave of desire.

I want that thick dick in my throat, and when I'm done, I want it buried so deep inside me that I won't even be able to *think* about anything besides Luca De Laurentiis for the next week.

"Luca," I tell him sternly. "Stand up and let me see that pretty dick," I demand, taking back some of my control.

He rewards me with a huge smile, placing his hands on either side of my hips as he leans in to capture my mouth in a kiss that leaves me dizzy. He pushes up to stand over me. "Yes, ma'am. Whatever you say, *princess.*"

I lean forward, gripping the waistband of his shorts and edging them down his thighs. His massive dick bobs out, practically looking me in the eye. It's so big, it's got a life of its own, but it isn't the length or even the girth that has my mouth gaping open.

"Is that—" I stammer, looking up into his eyes, the smirk on his face answering my unspoken question.

"A Jacob's ladder?" he asks, hiking a brow. "It absolutely is, my sweet Samara. Though I'd prefer you call it a Luca's ladder. I wouldn't want you speaking another man's name," he says, tapping his chin, "well, ever. But especially not *now*."

He takes my gaping jaw in his hand and angles my face toward his thick length, a bead of precum glistening from the top. "Now, *princess,* show me how badly you want it."

Saliva pools in my mouth, and warmth spreads throughout my aching core. Placing my hands on his thighs, I look up to meet his eyes, wanting to see the exact moment he loses himself when I touch him.

I drag my hands up his muscular legs, the dusting of hair tickling my fingers as I make my way to wrap my hands around the base. He drags in a breath, twitching in my palms and sucking his full bottom lip between his teeth to muffle his moan.

"You may not have guessed this," I say, averting my gaze and pumping his girth until more of that salty liquid is trickling out of the top, ready for me to taste. I wrap my lips around the head, and a moan travels throughout my whole body as the taste lights my senses.

"Guessed..." His voice wavers. "What?"

I lift my head, meeting his pretty, hooded eyes. "I like my men *vocal* when I'm sucking them off, so I'm going to need you to let every last sound fill this room if you want me to keep going," I tsk.

He groans loudly, gripping the base of my skull and tugging at my roots.

My tongue trails down along the underside of his dick, and I toy with the cool metal barbells, letting my saliva coat him. "Just like that. You're perfect," he moans out.

I open my mouth wide, ready to take him to the hilt and feel him as he fills my throat.

Loud screams jolt me out of my lust-filled fog, and I realize at the same moment as Luca.

"Fuck," he grits out, gently pulling me up onto the couch before wrenching his shorts back up his legs and running over to the kitchen sink. "Just one second, Gia!" he shouts to his daughter as if that'll help calm her at all.

He's frantically washing his hands, and then his entire face is in the sink before he dries off and sprints into the room for his child.

"It's okay, Gia, *mia bambina*, it's okay. Daddy's got you, baby girl."

My face and neck feel impossibly hot as embarrassment rushes through me. I push to stand, my eyes searching the room quickly for my things. I run around the couch, grabbing my bag and hoping to make it out of here before Luca can send me out, but the moment the crying stops, I know I wasn't fast enough.

He steps out of the room, shirtless again, with Gia lying against his chest, wriggling in his arms. "It's okay, honey," he coos to the little girl as he softly strokes her dark peach fuzz hair.

"I'm sorry, Samara," he tells me, his brows pinching together.

"It's fine, really. I've, um," I stammer, and my eyes bounce around the room for something to rescue me, landing on a stuffed pink kitten sitting on top of a pile of baby blankets. "I've got to feed my cat," I rush out. I'm not even totally sure why I'm so humiliated other than the fact that I came here with very different feelings toward Luca than the ones I'm leaving with.

He arches a dark brow at me. "You have…" He says the words slowly, dragging out every syllable. "A cat?"

"Yep, sure do," I confirm with one firm nod.

I definitely don't have a fucking cat.

He gently shakes his head, his lips curving in a smile as he laughs softly, peering down at the ground. "Alright then, can I at least walk you out?"

"That's really okay. Thanks though. Have a good night, Luca, and thanks for dinner," I say, trying to avoid the rest of this awkward conversation as I make my way to the front door.

"Thanks for dessert," he says with a wink that has my ears burning. "And thank you for everything else too," he tells me, walking himself and Gia over to me. He presses a kiss to each of my cheeks and unlatches the door, holding it open for me.

I give him a curt nod and hightail it out of there, resisting the urge to look back as I rush over to my car.

What was I thinking? Clearly, I *wasn't*. This is *Luca*, my *fake boyfriend*, who I absolutely should *not* be getting involved with, let alone allowing him to eat me up like a five-course meal. He has a child and a whole life that I don't fit into.

I've got to get out of here.

Chapter Forty-Seven

Samara

I really, *truly* have not a single clue what came over me tonight.

Yes, Luca is gorgeous. I'm done denying that because, frankly, it's exhausting. His eyes are stunning, and there isn't a single speck of his body that doesn't look like it was carved by the most skilled sculptor. But that doesn't mean I can go lose myself in him and give in to my body's whims.

I've already made some horrendous decisions by agreeing to let him be my fake date for this vacation, *which is apparently an even worse idea than I'd originally thought.*

I need to prioritize *myself* because the woman I once knew myself to be would have *never* lied to her mother about something like having a goddamn boyfriend. I'd have just told her straight up that it was none of her business.

Clearly, I have some things I need to work through, and Luca is the last person who needs to be there for that. He has entirely too much on his plate right now. He's navigating so much of his life changing with an infant in the mix.

Regardless of *all that*, my mind still can't seem to stop thinking about that infuriating man.

***

It's not a surprise when I can't seem to sleep despite the exhaustion weaving through my brain.

And when my phone vibrates beside me, I look at it against my better judgment.

Luca

I can't stop thinking about you, princess…

Luca

But I really hope your cat didn't go hungry for too long. Wouldn't want her to starve.

I groan, and a flush creeps over my cheeks.

My cat is a boy, and HE is doing great. Gave him a whole extra scoop of wet food tonight as an apology. Thanks for asking.

Maybe this is why people think all lawyers do all day is lie.

Luca

Lucky boy. Do I get an extra scoop of -you- as an apology for running out on me?

Nope.

Luca

Bummer.

Luca

What about if I fill you up next time? You know, as an apology for cutting things short tonight.

He's really trying his luck. And unfortunately for him, his banter has the opposite effect, acting to remind me of why we were interrupted. As sweet as his daughter is, I can only imagine how much change he's dealing with and will continue to deal with going forward. Luca seems like he's just recently decided to put his past behind him and become a grown adult, and he needs to put all of that energy into Gia. I can't act as another distraction for him, and I have entirely too much to accomplish myself.

When I meet the right person, they'll be as ready as I am to start a family and grow together, building each other up. Not that Luca would ever be a *real* option, but I can't stand the idea that we'd only act as an unnecessary anchor, keeping the other from drifting off to better opportunities.

No need to apologize. You have responsibilities.

Luca

Okay, Samara. I see that grumpy, pouty princess has entered the chat. Your cease and desist warning has been received, loud and clear.

Goodnight, Luca.

Luca

Goodnight, principessa.

Luca

And for the record, I happen to like all versions of you. The grumpy one might just be my favorite.

My eyes squeeze shut as I blow out a long, calming breath. *Everything would be so much easier if my body didn't react to him this way.* But Luca De Laurentiis is like an anthill. From the surface, there's just one small part of his persona, but the further I dig, the more there is to learn about him. He's multifaceted in a way I would've never expected, and as much as it'll pain me when I try to forget I'd ever known him after Kat's wedding, I want to carry each piece with me so I can hold onto them like little treasures.

Chapter Forty-Eight

Luca

Saturday, August 22, 2026

I haven't heard a single thing from Samara since the night she left my house. Not that I had expected to.

She's never willingly contacted me before, and she seemed embarrassed when she ran off. That's a hit to my ego, but I'm mostly just worried about her.

I dropped Gia off at Cici's house an hour ago, and while I don't want to be *that* guy, I can't stop pacing.

I trust Cici, I really do, but I know she doesn't trust herself yet, and I'm just waiting for her to call me crying at any moment, and I don't think my heart could take that.

I want to be there for her, and Gia needs her mom, but things feel like they've almost been going too well, and it's making me irrationally nervous. I've been pacing the floor of my living room for so long I feel like I'm leaving visible wear marks in the vinyl.

Between Cici, Gia, and Samara, I feel like I'm losing my mind.

I've tried texting Samara and calling her, and I've had to keep myself from sending her a damn email or, I don't know, a fucking carrier pigeon?

I'll just call her *one more time*, and if she doesn't answer, I'll let it go. *I'll have to let her go.*

Pulling out my cell, I check my messages again in case I missed anything from Cici. I haven't. I've checked my phone a hundred times.

I search for Samara's contact and hit the call button. It rings and rings and *rings* some more, and all the while, my mind is running in circles. Just as I'm about to hang up and save myself some of the humiliation of leaving her *another* voicemail, she answers.

Or at least, I think she does?

"Samara?" I ask, waiting for any kind of response to tell me she actually meant to answer her phone.

"You called me, Luca. Shouldn't *you* know who you called?" she asks me, but there's no bite to her words despite the clear annoyance she's trying to portray. I can almost picture her smirking face as she goads me, and instead of their desired effect, I'm a giddy schoolboy.

She answered! Hell yeah!

"I just couldn't be sure, you know, since you've been dodging me for over a week," I tell her, fully recovering from my mini panic attack moments before.

"I've been busy. I have a job, you know," she scoffs as if I'd really believe that's the reason she's been avoiding me.

"Well, you must not be busy *right now* since you answered the phone. Can I come over?" The words nearly fly out of my mouth.

"What? *No.* Why would you come over here?" she asks, clearly flustered. *Just the way I like her.*

"We're about to go on a vacation with your family as a couple. What if your parents say something about your place? I should at least know what it looks like," I explain, pulling that out of my ass and hoping that she still plans to go on this vacation at all.

"First of all, we aren't a couple. We're *fake* dating." It takes everything in me not to bring up the fact that we definitely *looked* like a couple while she was coming around my fingers. But that's probably just because of what my brothers refer to as me being "serial monogamous." I don't do one-night stands, but my definition of a relationship tends to be looser than most. Meaning that I'm typically only *in* a relationship for a couple of weeks. "Secondly, I can send you pictures of my place or video call you. You don't have to come over here and disturb my peace just to see what it looks like." She sounds flustered, and I love it.

Does she really not think I'll have another reason to go over there?

"Princess," I say, drawing out the name. "Are you trying to tell me you want to try phone sex with me? Because I'm totally game."

"Luca!" She huffs, and I think I hear steam billowing out of a tea kettle. On second thought, though, that's probably just the smoke from her ears. "How did your mind manage to twist my words into *that*?"

"Pure talent, baby."

"I think you need to find a dictionary."

"You know, I'm more of a table of cocktents kind of guy, but I'd be glad to take a look at your dicktionary if you'd like," I say, continuing to tease her.

"You're an idiot," is all she comes up with. I'm disappointed. I'd hoped for more bravado.

"Oh, come on, Samara. What do you think is gonna happen if I go over there?"

"Nothing good." She groans. I disagree... I think things could be *very* good, but I don't say that either.

"I dropped Gia off at Cici's an hour ago, and I'm wearing a hole in the ground with all the pacing I've been doing. Help me out and give me a distraction, *please, principessa.* I promise I'll keep my hands to myself if that's what has you worried."

Not that I *want* to keep my hands to myself when I'm around her.

I hear her smack something on a hard surface and try to picture what the hell it could've been. A book on her table, maybe? *No,* I shake my head. She wouldn't risk injuring a book like that.

"Fine. You get *one* hour and not a minute more, Luca. You see the place, and then you *leave.* Got it?"

"Yes, ma'am," I say, smiling ear to ear. "Text me your address."

The line goes dead, and my gut starts to sink, but a text with her address comes through a moment later. *Hell, yes!*

Chapter Forty-Nine

Samara

Why had I agreed to this again? Oh, right... Because I've lost my goddamn mind.

Clearly.

I'm running around my apartment, making sure I don't have anything lying around that would be easy for Luca to pick on.

I don't need him telling my parents about anything he's seen over here. Something tells me he isn't going to shy away from opening that big mouth of his, even while on *my* family vacation.

Is it a vacation though? More like hell-cation. It's about to be the longest four days of my life. My parents will be dissecting my every move, with my mom making note of every morsel of food I put into my mouth, just like she has my entire life. And now I've added the need to resist Luca to the mix—as if my resolve isn't already paper thin where he's concerned. *More like tissue paper.*

The loud rumbling of an engine from outside my door is followed immediately by an obnoxious knock done in a pattern of six beats.

I take a long breath in through my nose and slowly release it through my mouth as I make one final sweep over the living room. I'm nearly certain there's nothing here that even Luca could manage to make an inappropriate comment about.

He knocks three more times, pulling me out of my thoughts. *Well, shit.* I guess I'm really doing this then.

I'd been half hoping he'd just leave.

Unlocking the door, I yank it open, and Luca's towering frame greets me. He's wearing a snug black T-shirt that perfectly hugs his every muscle, and his dark waves are tousled and a little sweaty from his helmet.

He reaches out to my face, running the pad of his thumb across the corner of my lip, startling me. I swat his hand away. "What the hell?" I snap at him.

"Figured I'd help you out and wipe that drool from your mouth, *princess.*" He winks at me, only annoying me further.

"I wasn't drooling, you jackass. Are you coming in or not? Your hour has already started, and I'm more than happy to let you spend every moment of it out on my porch."

"Whatever you've gotta tell yourself," he says, letting himself into my space. He removes his shoes at the door and drags a hand through his dark hair, pushing it out of his face.

I shut the door behind him, relatching it. "You know, you don't have to lock me in here. I'd gladly stay," he tells me with a smirk.

My gaze swings over to the clock hanging in the entryway before meeting his eyes. "You're down to fifty-three minutes. Use them wisely," I inform him.

He chuckles. "Yes, ma'am. Do I get the official tour, or should I just show myself around?"

I let out an exasperated huff, sauntering off, assuming he'll follow after me.

When I get to the back of the apartment, I swing a door open, pointing inside. "Laundry room." He pokes his head inside to look around, and I slam the door when he straightens.

I lead him around my apartment, pointing out the main rooms and allowing him the bare minimum amount of time to visualize everything. When we make it to the guest room, he pushes past me and lifts the edge of the duvet cover, looking under the bed. *What is he on?*

I don't bother asking him because that'll only act to further delay how long he's here. When he's finished, we walk across the hall to the only thing he hasn't seen yet. *My bedroom.*

I'm feeling some rather heavy animosity toward Luca. It feels like he's doing everything in his power to make this encounter as uncomfortable for me as possible, and I have no desire to let him keep boosting his ego with his snide remarks. *Yes*, I came all over this man's face last weekend. But that doesn't give him the right to act as if it should happen again or as if I'd even *want* it to happen again.

It was a moment of weakness due to an unfortunate dry spell. I'm talking drier than the desert. Dustier than my grandma's knick-knack shelf. That's all this little fluke can be chalked up to.

I twist the knob, pushing the door open, and without a word, he looks over at me as if asking for my approval. Gone is the cocky jerk who reared his ugly head less than an hour ago, and in his place is the somewhat respectful and cautious guy I've gotten glimpses of over the last couple of months.

The moment I give him a reassuring nod, he practically runs inside, full steam ahead. He runs his fingers over the edge of my duvet, taking his time to lift and stare at each individually framed photo and trinket placed on my nightstands and dresser.

When he's made his way around my room, with me awkwardly standing in the doorway, he picks up the edge of my duvet, getting on his hands and knees to peer underneath it.

"Luca, what are you doing?" I finally ask, my temper getting the best of me after thirty *long* minutes of watching him scrutinize my home.

When he peers over his shoulder at me, his firm ass still in the air, he slowly stands, and the sly grin he's wearing is like a beacon, reminding me how much trouble this man brings everywhere he goes. Whatever he's about to say is going to ruin my whole damn night.

"Well, *principessa*, I was just looking for your cat," he tells me, prowling over to stand not even a foot in front of me. *That damn, nonexistent cat.*

I don't step away though. I hold my ground, steeling my spine for whatever bullshit is about to come flying out of that sinful mouth of his. "But it seems the only pretty pussy around here"—he leans in farther, his cool breath coasting over my heated flesh—"is yours."

My skin feels flushed, and as his words skate over me, my annoyance with him is renewed.

The fact that I've told multiple lies in the last few weeks irks me. It makes me feel slimy, and considering the negative association people often feel toward lawyers, that furthers my discomfort. But Luca's words both ignite a fire in my core and extinguish it all at once.

I can't lie about this fucking cat again. I clearly *do not* have a cat. More than that, I don't *want* a cat. I can barely take care of myself these days; how could I be trusted to care for another living being?

Maybe this is why I haven't gotten pregnant. Maybe I'm just not ready.

That familiar self-doubt wiggles its way to the surface, but Luca's fingers trail across my chin, turning my face up to look at him and bringing me back. "Hey, *princess*, where'd you just go?" he asks softly, concern lacing his words.

I draw away from his touch, refusing to let this confusing man try to comfort me. "I think it's time for you to go."

His dark brows pinch together, and I'm hit with that two-tone gaze of his. "Samara, I'm sorry if I took things too far or if I've made you uncomfortable. I know you aren't my biggest fan, but *I like you*, and when I'm nervous, I flirt. It's a really flawed defense mechanism, but it's something I've leaned on for a long time." He sucks nervously on his bottom lip, and my eyes are drawn right to it. "I don't want you to feel disrespected, ever. So I'm gonna leave now, but please tell me I'll see you at the studio tomorrow." He averts his gaze, his cheeks turning pink. "I'd really miss you if you weren't there, and I'm not just talking about getting a rise out of you. I like being around you no matter your mood," he confesses, sounding so sincere that it almost makes my heart crack in two.

Very few people have ever been that vulnerable with me *unless they wanted something from me.* The thought alone makes my hackles stand on end, but I need to take Luca at face value.

I have to recognize that I've been wired to be mistrustful of others, but that doesn't mean he actually has bad intentions. What he's shown me of himself so far, he doesn't seem all that bad, and I know I'm embarrassed by the way my body responds to him. But truthfully, I'm more upset at myself by how much of a brat I've been to this man.

I guess *that* is my defense mechanism.

Shutting my eyes tightly for a moment to calm my racing mind, I finally open them to see that Luca's still staring at me, worry written all over his handsome face.

"I'll be there," I tell him, turning around to lead him to the front door. He follows after me, and as he walks out onto the porch, he presses a chaste kiss to either of my cheeks, turning to leave. "Goodnight, Luca," I tell him in a hushed tone.

He looks over his shoulder at me with a shy smile. "Goodnight, Samara."

***

As I chew on the inside of my cheek, staring down at my phone, I finally hit send on a text I wrote nearly ten minutes ago.

Did everything with Gia go okay?

Luca

So far, so good. No calls just yet, but Cici's sent me a bunch of photos.

Three pictures of Gia download, and a smile touches my lips as I look at the pretty girl with her daddy's stunning eyes.

I'll give it to you, Luca. You made a damn cute kid.

Luca

I think you know what I want to say, but I'll be a good boy and refrain.

My brows furrow as I read his message before flitting back up to the one I'd just sent. Heat climbs my neck as I realize the joke I'd just inserted myself in.

Ha ha ha. Very funny, Luca.

Glad everything is going well. Night.

Luca

;)

Luca

Sleep well, gorgeous.

Words can't begin to describe what that last text does to me as I fight for sleep.

Chapter Fifty

Luca

Thursday, August 27, 2026

"Alright, Gia, Daddy's got you all packed and ready to stay with your mom this weekend. Are you excited?" I ask her, and she just gives me a dimpled smile, drool running down her cheek.

"I thought you'd say that," I joke. "I've gotta call the pretty lawyer now and make sure we're really doing this, but afterward, it's just you and me for the night, kid." She giggles, more drool spilling out of her mouth.

I pick her up, wiping her face with a wet wipe before pressing a kiss to her head and placing her in her kiddie corral with all of her favorite toys. She leans forward on her hands, settling herself into the mat before trying to pick up a block sitting beside her.

Right now, she's mostly working on strengthening her muscles and getting used to the kinds of movements necessary for playing. I swear, every day, she gets stronger and stronger. It's wild to see her progression over the last few months, but I'm loving every moment of it.

Sure, it's been hard, but I have the best support system and the most amazing kid.

I blow Gia a kiss, one she tries to mimic but ends up just smacking her lips with her palm.

Grabbing my phone, I search for Samara's number. She answers on the second ring, which is *fucking shocking*.

"Luca," she says, her voice panicked. My heart rate starts to skyrocket from the worry suddenly building in my chest.

"What's wrong?" I ask, my voice shaky.

"How are we gonna pull this off? My family is *never* going to believe we're actually dating!" she nearly screeches into the phone.

So that's what this is about. My heart begins to settle knowing that she just has anxiety and isn't in danger.

My voice is soothing as I say, "Samara, take a deep breath."

She does so audibly, and my chest begins to relax too. "Good, now I'm gonna need you to count on those incredible lawyer skills of yours to keep your composure and go with the flow this weekend, but I promise it'll be fine. We're gonna have a good time, and I have *no doubt* that I'll be able to convince your family," I say, chuckling.

The line goes silent for a moment until I hear Samara taking in a few more steadying breaths. "We need to set boundaries," she finally huffs out.

My brow quirks. *This'll be good.* "Okay, what *boundaries* would you like to set, Samara?"

"First off, we're definitely not sharing a bed."

"That's already been established. Our room has two queens in it," I remind her, settling into the couch cushions as I put the speaker on and set my phone down.

"And no holding hands." She says this next request as if she's checking off a list.

"You have clammy hands around me, *principessa*?" I joke, trying to clear some of the tension encasing us from her worry.

I scrub at the little milk stain on the cushion beside me, squinting my eyes at it. *It sort of looks like Samara.* My chest vibrates. No, it fucking doesn't. That's the dumbest shit I've thought in a long time, and it's clear as day that I'm starting to develop some sort of dependence on her.

"Luca," she says sternly.

"Yes, ma'am, no hand-holding," I agree, doing my best to keep the laugh inside that's threatening its way out of my throat.

"*No kissing*," she stresses over the line.

A breath of air whooshes out of my mouth. "Now come on, *princess.*" I drop the rag I'd been using to clean the stain. "Have you seen yourself? Do you *really* think your family will believe I'm able to keep my hands and *lips* off you?"

"Stop being a flirt," she huffs out.

"Samara," I say, dragging her name out. "You've got to try and relax. I'm not delusional enough to think this is real, so whatever we have to do to convince your family and get them off your back within your boundaries is what we'll do. But if we want this to be believable, you're gonna have to rethink some of the lines you've drawn in the proverbial sand. Okay?"

"Okay," she finally agrees, but I can still tell she's reluctant. "But definitely *no* sex, got it?"

"I wouldn't dream of it, princess." *That's a lie, but it's one that'll hopefully ease her racing mind.*

"Be ready by six," she says before hanging up.

I peer down at Gia. "You heard the lady; we've gotta be ready by six." Gia's wide eyes shine brightly up at me, totally unaware that I'm about to leave her with her mom for an entire weekend. Meanwhile, I'll be pretending to date a woman I can't stop thinking about, even though I know damn well I should.

Chapter Fifty-One

Samara

Friday, August 28, 2026

I can't believe we're really doing this. Our flight leaves in three hours, and Luca will be here any minute to pick me up. I still have not a single clue as to why he even agreed to this in the first place.

No, not *agreed* but *suggested* this horrendous idea.

A knock at my door pulls me out of my spiraling thoughts. "Shit," I whisper-yell to myself, grabbing my bags and heading for the door. When I answer it, Luca's standing in a thin white button-down with tan linen shorts, looking absolutely delectable, and it sends a damn shiver racing down my spine.

"You know we aren't actually in DR yet, right? It's sixty degrees outside right now," I inform him as if he doesn't already know that.

"Muscle keeps the body warm, and clearly," he says, gesturing to his lean physique, "I'm not lacking in that department." He shoots me an arrogant wink, grabs my bags from me, and heads toward his SUV.

The eye roll that takes over my face can probably be seen from space as I watch Luca carry my heavy bags to his trunk. His muscles bulge as he lifts them in as if they weigh nothing at all. The ease with which he seems to do just about everything annoys me to my core, but I have to remind myself that *he's* doing *me* a favor by even going on this trip. I need to play nice. *Just this once.*

***

"Okay, so your mom is Camila,and your dad is Kemar, your sister is Vea, and she's the oldest, right?" he asks me. We just spent the entire drive to the airport going over my family tree.

"Yep, now park over there." I point to the long-term parking lot ahead.

"Yes, ma'am." He chuckles, pulling in just as I'd asked.

Once we're parked, he runs around to my side of the SUV, holding my door open for me. I roll my eyes at him. "You can save that for when my family is actually around to see you, Luca."

Apparently, it's his turn to roll *his* eyes at *me.* "Princess, I'd hold your door for you whether we were fake dating or not."

I ignore him, moving out of the seat and around to the back to grab my bags. He takes most of them from me, wheeling his things along with my own and I don't have the energy to argue with him about it.

Accept the help, Samara. I have to remind myself of that when the need to always be completely independent tries to take over.

I've got to let my fake boyfriend do *real* boyfriend things for me if anyone is going to believe this ruse.

"Come on, *principessa*," he calls over his shoulder, "we don't want to miss our plane!"

"We're nearly two hours early," I grumble under my breath, trekking across the steaming-hot parking lot after him. It's warmed up a lot in the last hour, but I'm certainly not going to admit that to him.

***

"I swear to god, if you don't move your arm, I'm gonna chew it off."

Luca peers up at me through one eye, keeping the other closed, as if I'd believe for a single second that he was *actually* sleeping.

"We're in first class, Luca. There's no reason for you to practically be in my lap right now."

Both of his eyes are open now, and a wide grin spreads across his face. "But," he says, leaning farther into my lap, "you're just *so* comfy."

Just when I was almost worried that I may *actually* like Luca De Laurentiis's company, he goes and reminds me exactly why I don't.

"You're a child. Now get out of my damn lap." I push his thick arm off me and drop it over the side of my armrest.

He chuckles, leaning back into his seat and pulling his blanket up under his chin before closing his eyes. "You're grouchy; take a nap." Before I can respond, he presses his index finger against his full lips and says, "Shh, I'm trying to sleep, princess."

I want to bite that finger right off, but I do my best to suppress my annoyance and relax back into my seat. I stuff my headphones in my ears and search for a movie to watch for the next few hours.

***

Luca is still fast asleep, and unlike him, I've never been able to rest on planes. I don't trust being asleep with strangers around me, and even in first class, these seats aren't *that* comfortable. The flight attendant dropped off complimentary snacks an hour ago, and despite having eaten mine already, my stomach is still growling.

I'm a "three meals a day with snacks in between" kind of gal, and today, I was too anxious to eat before we left.

Luca shifts in his seat, but his eyes remain closed, and I swear I hear his pack of pretzels call to me from his tray.

I don't even *like* pretzels, but if Luca thinks I'm cranky now, wait until I haven't eaten all day.

Actually, screw Luca. I deserve those pretzels for having to put up with his antics all the time.

I blow in his face a few times, double-checking that he's really asleep, and when he doesn't so much as twitch, I lean across him, grabbing his pretzels and chocolate chip cookie from his tray.

Sitting back, a small smile forms on my lips as I open the little bag of goodies and pop one crunchy, salty bite into my mouth.

"Fuck you, Luca," I whisper happily, fighting the urge to kick my feet like a child.

As I bring another pretzel up to my mouth, he strikes. Luca is suddenly in my face, his teeth biting gently into the pretzel I'm holding between my fingers. He snakes his tongue out to pull it into his mouth, chewing before sitting back in his seat with a smug smile.

My stomach drops with the realization that I've been caught, but also, something about that whole exchange was so hot, it has my blood singing in the most delicious way.

"You didn't have to steal from me, Samara. I'm more than happy to share with you," he says, wearing a grin that makes me want to slap it right off his face. *Or kiss it off. Undecided.*

"Flight attendants, prepare for landing," the pilot says over the intercom, the seatbelt signs glowing and my frustrations subsiding. *I can't wait to get off this plane.*

Chapter Fifty-Two

Luca

As much as I miss my kid, I'm finding it surprisingly easy to cope just by annoying Samara. It gives me a sense of ease I never knew possible.

And as soon as we landed in Santiago, I switched my phone out of airplane mode. It's taken a few minutes to fully load everything, but now that it has, I'm breathing more easily. Cici sent close to thirty pictures of Gia doing absolutely nothing, but I love them all the same. Dante texted that he spoke with her on the phone to check in, and she was doing well.

"Gia doing okay?" I hear Samara's voice trickle in through my thoughts.

Lifting my gaze from the pictures on my screen, I meet her pretty brown eyes, they're a mixture of espresso and caramel, two of my favorite things. I smile gently at her. "Yeah, she seems to be doing really well, and judging by all the pictures I've gotten of her doing literally nothing, Cecily is just about as obsessed with her as I am."

For the first time in forever, Samara actually *smiles* at something I've said. "Good, every little girl deserves to be loved by parents who are obsessed with her very existence. Little boys too," she says, nodding as if to confirm her own statement. *I couldn't agree more.*

The flight attendant opens the door to let us out, and immediately, everyone starts standing to rush out. Luckily, sitting in first class means we get to get out of this tin can first.

Once we've exited and are heading toward baggage claim, I finally ask, "Okay, so if your family lives in Philly, why didn't we all fly together?"

She shakes her head. "I love my family, but they're overwhelming in large doses, especially to travel with. So, as soon as I turned eighteen, I set a firm boundary of not using any form of public transportation with them. My parents thought I'd lost my mind and assumed I was just going through a phase, but it's been over a decade, and I haven't flown with them or so much as ridden a bus with them since high school."

I smirk at that. "I like that. You know exactly what you want, and you've paved a path to getting it. I can respect that."

"Well, Luca, I'm *so* glad you can respect something about me." She rolls her eyes and trudges forward to wait in the crowd of people surrounding baggage claim.

Does she really not think I respect her? I hope she was being playful, but I'm never certain with her.

I sidle up to her and have to stop myself from laughing when I see her glare up at me from the corner of her eye. "Come on, princess, do you actually think I don't respect you?"

"To tell you the truth, Luca, I'm not sure. Sometimes, you're super sweet and seemingly understanding of my boundaries, and other times, you do everything in your power to stampede right over them." She says this without even looking at me, keeping her eyes glued to the conveyor belt of luggage.

"I'm sorry I've ever made you feel disrespected, Samara, truly. I know my personality can sometimes be a lot, but I promise to do my best to tone it down for you." I keep my tone soft as I tell her this, hoping she'll believe my words.

She assesses me, her dark brows pinching together and her lips pursing. "*Never* dull your shine for someone else's comfort," she says, shaking her head. "Those of us with big personalities are taught to do so at a young age, but it isn't us that's the problem, Luca." She reaches out, rubbing the pad of her thumb over the space between my thumb and forefinger before she draws back, straightening and looking over at the black belt carrying our luggage. "It's their fault for trying to adjust our expectations to make themselves seem more interesting," she says, her words almost a whisper.

Warmth spreads through me, my limbs tingling, and my chest expands. She may never know it, but her words settle something inside me that has never felt like anything less than a beast trying to break free of a cage.

Our luggage comes zooming by, and Samara leans over, wrapping her manicured fingers around the handle, and tries to pull hers off the belt, but the strap gets stuck.

This cute little crease forms between her brows, and I just wanna kiss it right off, but I assume *that* would be crossing some lines, so instead, I lean over her, dislodging the strap and yanking it off.

"Thanks," she mumbles reluctantly, and that same laugh is climbing up my throat. By the will of god, I keep it tucked away this time too.

Once all of our bags are accounted for, I extend my arm toward the exit. "Where are we off to now?" I truly have no clue because she booked everything, and I just gave her my card to cover it. I told her to pay for her portion, too, as my treat, but of course, she refused. *Always so stubborn.*

"We have a town car waiting for us outside. It's an hour and a half drive from here to our resort in Punta Rucia."

"Ooh, a resort. *Fancy*," I murmur. Truth be told, I'm stoked about this trip. I haven't gone on a real vacation since my senior trip in high school.

I've had the money to do it, just never the time with my hockey schedule, and when the season was over, I didn't have anyone to go with. Most of my friends are married or just have their own lives with such little time for anything else, so it hasn't happened.

It's another part of the reason I suggested this wacky-ass idea in the first place. Even if Samara can't stand me, I'll have a little time to enjoy a few good naps and some sun while I'm here.

Chapter Fifty-Three

Samara

We're finally here, and as nerve-wracking as this whole vacation is, I'm actually kind of excited now that it's really happening.

My hope is to slip away for a few massages, wake up early to read with the sunrise, and maybe even run off to one of the nearby beaches so I can relax by the water without being seen by my family sans Luca.

"Alright, princess, here we are," Luca says, dragging me out of my thoughts as he rounds the side of the town car and holds my door open for me.

His bright eyes are striking in the sun, and his lightly bronzed skin is a glowing contrast to his thin white shirt. Luca De Laurentiis is *stunning*, and as hard as it is to admit to myself, I don't think I'll be able to keep my eyes off him.

"You ready?" he asks, worry lacing his tone.

I clear my throat, taking his hand to help me out. "Yeah, I'm ready."

Once we've tipped the driver, we head into the resort and get blasted with the cool AC. It's such a stark contrast to the humid warmth outside. Goosebumps break out over my skin, and a chill shivers through me.

"Cold?" Luca asks quietly as we approach the front desk.

I shake my head, turning my attention to the woman seated behind the counter. "Checking in?"

I nod. "Yes, for Luca De Laurentiis and Samara Perez-Allen."

She turns her gaze toward the computer, typing in the information, and when she gets to it, her eyes light up. She smiles brightly at me as she grabs key cards and pamphlets, getting them all together for us, and slides them across the counter. "You're all set. Enjoy your upgraded suite—on the house—thanks to a last-minute cancellation," she tells me with dimpled cheeks. "Enjoy your stay at La Rucia, and if you need anything, don't hesitate to let us know."

"Will do, thank you," I say, turning to hand Luca a key. He takes it in his large hand before heading down a hallway toward the back of the resort. I follow after him, walking for what feels like forever until we're standing in front of a massive double-paned wooden door with a fresh floral wreath hanging on it in the shape of a heart.

My stomach drops to my toes.

An upgraded suite.

Luca swipes the key card, pushes the door open, and steps into the beautiful oasis. Or it *would* be an oasis if we were actually a couple. But as it stands, I'm now looking at the next several days of torture.

In the middle of the room is a massive canopy bed with white linens and a palm-tree-printed duvet. The entire back wall is one mega-size window with sliding doors that lead straight out to a private hot tub, and I can see a path down to the beach from here.

It's breathtakingly gorgeous, and while I still have a little piece of my sanity screaming at me to be upset, I'm not. That bed is more than big enough, and we can just create a divide with pillows down the center. *Problem solved.*

He turns around to face me. "Don't worry, Samara. I can make a bed for myself on the couch. Don't let this freak you out," he assures me.

That was oddly... *considerate.* No. Sweet?

I shake my head. "It's fine. The bed is massive. Just stay on your side," I tell him with a pointed stare.

Luca wears a playful grin that toys with my emotions as he says, "Which side am I on, princess?"

"The one closest to the windows." I groan, resigning as I dump my belongings at the end of the bed.

"Oh, come on, snookums. I know we were waiting till marriage, but this could be a good little test run," he says playfully, winking when my eyes meet his.

"Just stay on your side, and I'll stay on mine," I remind him.

"Yes, ma'am." He laughs with his whole body, setting his suitcase on the luggage rack provided by the hotel. He unzips it and meticulously starts putting all of his clothing away in drawers and on hangers.

Something about that just seems so strange and not what I had expected of Luca for the first day of vacation. I'd truthfully expected him to already be at the pool with a drink in each hand.

Our hotel phone starts ringing just as he finishes putting his things away, and he answers on the second ring. "This is Luca."

A broad smile stretches across his face as he listens to the person on the other end of the line. "I'm looking forward to meeting you too, Mrs. Perez," he says and a beat later, "Sorry, sorry, *Camila*."

My brows shoot up my forehead as I register the interaction. *He's on the phone with my mom!*

"Hey, *principessa,* after we get settled, would you want to meet your family by the pool for an early lunch?" *Wow,* he's already laying it on thick.

"That sounds great," I tell him. My stomach feels like it's eating itself; I'm so damn hungry.

"She says she can't wait. See you in a half hour, Camila." He beams at me before hanging up.

"Alright, princess, get on your skimpiest bikini, and let's get to the pool."

I try to play it off, but can't help the pang of anxiety that bobs around in my stomach. I bought a dozen bathing suits for this vacation and only felt semi-decent in three of them. None of which are a freaking bikini.

Reluctantly, I grab the cherry-red one-piece with the cut-out sides and my white cover-up and head to the bathroom to get changed.

I wash my hands, staring at my reflection in the mirror, and it all hits me at once. I'm really on a vacation with my family for the first time in *years*, and I'm lying to them about having a boyfriend. I'm a grown-ass woman, and I'm lying to my parents as if they can ground me or something, but the fact of the matter is that I *wish* it were that simple. Because being grounded is so much easier than seeing the disappointment on my parents' faces every time I tell them I *still* don't have anyone to bring on these vacations with me or even just to bring home for family dinner.

I wet my hands one last time, using the water to smooth my curls up into a ponytail before giving myself one last once-over in the mirror and heading back into the room.

Luca is sitting on the end of the bed, scrolling through his phone when I enter. His eyes lazily lift to look me over but quickly turn into something else entirely.

His smoldering gaze sends heat pooling in my core, and my thighs clench together on instinct.

He runs a ragged hand over his face and cups his jaw. "Jesus Christ, this is gonna be harder than I'd thought."

I know I shouldn't, but I ask, "What is?"

He shakes his head with a humorless laugh. "Keeping my hands off you when you're within arms reach, *looking like that*," he says, dragging a hand through the air for emphasis.

The hungry look in his eyes nearly brings me to my knees. I feel unsteady on my limbs from his admission, but it's best that I ignore it. "Well, it sounds like you'll just have to practice some self-control," I say, hoping he doesn't notice the way I gulp for air. "Are you almost ready? Because I'm starving."

"So am I," he says under his breath, standing immediately, putting his cell back in his pocket, and heads to the door. He looks me over with a soft expression and asks quietly, "Are you ready for this?"

I blow out a long breath before nodding, and we make our way out into the hallway.

Chapter Fifty-Four

Luca

We make our way out to the pool, where there's a restaurant attached, and I see a family that rivals my own in size and know it must be Samara's. I recognize their faces from our little family lesson, and several of the women have her same beautiful curls too. *I couldn't miss those anywhere.*

When one of the older women sees us heading in their direction, she throws her hands up. "Mara! My baby girl and her man are here!"

Samara tucks her chin, looking a little embarrassed by the faces we're getting from those hanging around the pool.

When we reach her mom, she throws her arms around me immediately, squeezing the life out of me before grabbing my cheeks for a big kiss on either side. *Damn, she's stronger than she looks.* I return the gesture, familiar with this type of greeting from my own family. "You must be Luca. We've been dying to meet you!"

I give her a wide smile. "And you must be the beautiful Camila."

She pretends to fan herself with a playful smile and says, "Such a charmer," before looking to Samara and adding, "You've got your hands full with this one."

She winks at me, and I hear Samara say, "You could say that again," just loud enough for me to hear. I pinch her on the back of the arm, pulling her out of her doom spiral. Blazing eyes sear up at me. "What was that for?" she whisper-screams.

I smirk at her, heading to greet the rest of her family. They each take turns hugging us and introducing themselves. If I hadn't spent a solid three hours the other day going through Samara's social media accounts so I could match faces to names, I'd be unbelievably lost.

This must be how everyone feels meeting my family.

"Come on, come sit down." Her sister, Vea, instructs us to sit beside her, her husband, and their children.

Shortly after, the waitress brings out menus for everyone.

Samara bites her lip as she looks over the menu, her eyes flickering back and forth between her mom and sister.

I lean into her, keeping my voice low as I speak. "Having trouble deciding?"

Her eyes flit up to mine. "I want the coconut shrimp, but the grilled mahi-mahi with tostones sounds good too."

My brows pinch as I tilt my head. "Just get both."

She shakes her head. Those pretty curls framing her face fly around, and I catch a whiff of her signature scent. I fight the groan working up my throat at what it does to me.

"That's too much food," she tells me quickly, straightening in her seat.

"Fine, I'll order the coconut shrimp and the hot honey and pepperoni flatbread, and you can have as many of my shrimp as you want. Sound good?" I don't really get what the big deal is. We're on vacation, and coconut shrimp are basically an appetizer, but the panic written across her face when she looks to where her mother sits makes something very clear to me.

She's uncomfortable.

I've genuinely never seen this side of Samara in the months that I've known her. She's been nothing but headstrong, self-assured, confident, and sassy, uncomfortable on occasion but never like this. Ever since we landed here, she's been the opposite. She's acting all timid and looks like at any moment she might shatter, and it fucking breaks my heart to see.

I settle my hand on her thigh, giving it a reassuring squeeze, and revel in the fact that she can't push me away with her family watching. It's a serious misuse of my newly found powers, but I think I just love having my hands on her.

After the waitress takes everyone's orders and collects our menus, the string of excited questions begins.

"Suh, Luca, wah yuh do fah a living?" her dad asks.

"I'm a goalie for the Philly Scarlets hockey team, sir," I tell him from across the table.

"So wah mek yuh choose hockey?" he asks.

A small smile turns my lips. "To tell you the truth, I just wanted to do whatever my older brother was doing when I was a kid but ended up really loving hockey and stuck with it."

"Do you have any kids?" Camila asks me, and I see Samara tense up from my periphery.

"Yeah, I have a daughter. Her name is Giavanna." I smile, pulling my phone out of my back pocket to show everyone photos of her.

They smile and tell me how cute she is, but her father's brows are pulled taut as he eyes me quizzically. "Shi nuh fayvah yuh, shi a even six months hul yet. How lang ave yuh an har madda bin separated?"[1]

I go to open my mouth, but Samara stops me, squeezing my hand on her thigh. "Dad, that's not a conversation for now, and it isn't any of your business. They're co-parenting beautifully, and it's really wonderful to see, especially in my line of work." Her approval, even if disingenuous, warms me to my core. I'm always so worried that I'm messing everything up with Gia because I have no idea what I'm doing.

He puts his hands up in surrender, smiling brightly at me. "Aright, aright. Eff yuh get di stamp ah approval fram mi hard-ass dawta, mi will mind mi owna biznizz."

Camila cuts in before I can say anything. "How'd you two meet?"

Samara groans beside me. "He was my client."

That's all she says. Nothing more. No further explanation.

Her family all look at her expectantly, so I wrap an arm around her, pulling her close. "I was her client, and as much as she tried to deny our chemistry..." I pause, pressing a kiss to her temple. "I fought tooth and nail for her attention, and finally, I won," I tell them with a wink at Samara.

---

1. Jamaican Patois: "She don't look like she's even six months old yet, how long have you and her mother been separated?"

"Mi dawta let yuh win something?" Her dad laughs. "Dat nuh soun like ar at alla."[2]

Samara rolls her eyes. "Maybe I *wanted* him to win," she says. *If only that were true.*

The waitress came by and took our orders, and I couldn't help but notice that Samara was staring at her mother the entire time she ordered. Her shoulders relaxed when the server finally left.

Overall, lunch went pretty well, but I'm excited to get back to our room for a little downtime. I can absolutely understand what she'd been talking about with her family being a little exhausting in large doses.

As we're all standing to leave, everyone starts chattering about what they plan to do with the rest of the day. Camila turns to Samara and me, asking, "You two going to join us at the main pool?"

I immediately cut in, hoping to give Samara an out if she wants it. "I was actually going to get my daughter on a video call for a little while, and I know Samara loves seeing Gia, so I was hoping she'd join me," I say, turning my full attention to Samara.

She gives me a warm smile, and her eyes crinkle in the corners. "That sounds great," she tells me before turning back to her mom. "You okay if we go out on our own for a while and meet you all for dinner later?"

Camila's eyes bounce back and forth between us but finally settle on Samara. "Not at all. You two have fun. I look forward to

---

2. Jamaican Patois: "My daughter let you win something? That doesn't sound like her at all."

seeing more pictures of your daughter at dinner tonight," she tells me with a bright smile before heading back into the crowd of her family.

Samara and I walk in the opposite direction as her family, and I can't help but slip my hand into hers. It isn't too dainty, so it doesn't feel like I'll break her. She fits just right in the palm of my hand, my fingers entwined with hers as she surprisingly lets me lead her back toward our room.

The moment we're inside, she pulls out of my grip. "Thanks for that," she says, and her eyes look a little glassy.

"Anytime, princess. What would you like to do now that we've gotten away from your family?"

She flops down on the bed, tossing her forearm over her face. "I just want to read and lie by the pool." She groans.

"Well then, let's do that," I say, confused as to what all the groaning is about.

"If I go outside, they'll find me," she says, sounding so damn dramatic it makes a laugh burst out of me.

She squints at me, trying to hold onto her frustration, but when her eyes meet mine, I swear I see her soften.

I look over to the private pool on our patio, and unfortunately, she's right. It's fucking gorgeous, but the gate surrounding us doesn't provide a lot of privacy, and it's overlooking one of the main pools.

She deserves to enjoy this vacation. As much as I know she's going to have to balance being around her family with having time to herself, I don't want her to have to spend it hiding inside this room, no matter how gorgeous it is in here. I'll figure it out just as soon as I check in on baby Gi. *I'm trying out new nicknames, so sue me.*

"Alrighty then, I'm gonna call Cici and see if she and Gia are free to chat for a bit."

She nods, so I pull out my cell and try for Cici, who finally answers after several rings. Her pink cheeks and blonde bun fill the screen, the sun shining overheard making it difficult to make out where she is. "Luca, hey! Do you mind if we call you back in a bit? We just got to the park by my house, and I don't want to take my eyes off her."

"That's totally okay. Call me when you can," I assure her, and she smiles before hanging up.

I'm surprised she felt comfortable taking her out of the house, but I'm glad she did. I'm even more pleased that it's the park inside her community.

As my eyes skim over Samara, an idea hits me for how to salvage her plans for the day without having to worry about her going to a beach by herself because she absolutely would leave me here if given the option.

"Do you need anything from the front, princess? I'm gonna go grab something real quick."

She shakes her head. "No, thanks. I think I'm actually going to take a shower or maybe a nap."

"Okay, I'll be right back."

I make my way toward the front desk, careful to check every hallway I pass for any signs of her family. I wouldn't want to lead them back to her.

When I get to the desk, I'm greeted by two smiling faces whose eagerness to help me sends unease sinking into my gut.

"What can we help you with?" one of the women asks, leaning across the desk, clearly using her arms to push her breasts forward.

In another life, I'd not only look but flirt and probably wind up with her in my bed later. Maybe even both of them. But now? All I can think about is getting back to my room and making sure Samara actually enjoys this vacation.

These women do nothing for me. Hell, no one has since I met Samara, and I'm not ready to think about that too hard.

"Could I get a bunch of flat sheets for the bed?"

"A bunch?" she asks, tilting her head to the side.

I nod. "Yeah, like ten of them."

Her brows lift as she rises to her feet, but luckily, she doesn't ask any follow-up questions. "Sure, one moment."

She heads to the supply closet and comes back with an arm full of white flat sheets. "Thanks," I tell her, heading quickly to my room with the sheets in my arms.

Samara isn't in bed, but I hear the water running in the bathroom, so I get to work.

I step out onto the patio and start lining the gate with the sheets, tying them at the top and bottom to keep them from blowing away. When I'm all done, I set up the chairs, laying out towels on each of them.

There's a small sign on one of the tables with a QR code for the hotel's room service, so I sort through it and order a bunch of random snacks and drinks.

When I get back into the room, my heart is racing, and my eyes are wide. "Fuck," I say, but it comes out sounding more like a prayer.

Samara is standing in the middle of our room, wrapped in nothing but a towel. Her long curls are soaking wet, hanging down her back, and her gorgeous almond-colored skin is still damp and glistening.

I watch as a bead of water trails down her neck and between her breasts. The urge to lick it off her skin is overwhelming.

She stands, staring at me, unmoving. Her plump lips are parted in surprise.

A knock at the door drags us both out of our thoughts, and our eyes snap to the door. "Shit, they found me," she groans out.

I chuckle. "No, they didn't. I got us room service. Go get your bathing suit back on, please. You're too damn distracting in that towel," I tell her as I head to the door. *Not that her in a bathing suit is any less distracting.*

To my utter shock, she actually does as I ask.

I wait until she slips back into the bathroom before opening the door for room service. A man dressed in a palm-tree-print button-down and khakis greets me. "Hello, sir. You ordered room service?"

"Yes, thank you. Would you mind setting it up by the pool?"

"Of course, sir."

A few minutes later, he has me sign the bill and heads out. I knock on the bathroom door. "The coast is clear, princess."

I hear it unlatch, and she steps out, this time wearing a black one-piece with a deep V-cut that has my mouth fucking watering.

"Jesus Christ." I shake my head, squeezing my eyes shut, and rub my hand over my face. She ignores me, heading into the closet to grab her bag. I watch her as she sorts through it, and finally, she grabs a book out.

"Wanna join me out by the pool?" I ask.

She shakes her head. "I'm thinking about taking a taxi to a nearby beach so I don't risk running into my family."

Standing in front of the sliding glass doors, I grab hold of the curtains. "Why would you do that when we have this?" I ask as I pull the curtains back, revealing the pool outside our door with the makeshift privacy fence.

Her mouth hangs open as she takes in the sheets neatly tied to the fence before her eyes meet mine. "You did all this? For me?"

"You should enjoy your vacation, princess. Join me outside?"

She nods slowly and follows me out to the pool with her book in hand.

Chapter Fifty-Five

Samara

He really set all of this up. *For me.*

Luca De Laurentiis surprises me at every turn, and it annoys me to no end. I almost wish I could forget his past, but unfortunately, ignorance is only bliss to those who are ignorant themselves. Though, I also think there's something to be said about growing and maturing. He's shown me in the last few months that he's done a lot of that. *Maybe it's my turn to do the same.*

I settle in on the cushioned lounge chair. As the sun heats my skin and the light breeze whisks by, I finally feel myself start to genuinely relax for the first time since we arrived.

I open my book to where I had left off, but I can't seem to focus. Doing my best to ignore the feeling of being watched, I finally give up, glancing in Luca's direction. He's lounging in one of the chairs opposite me, but with his sunglasses on, it's difficult to tell if he's actually looking at me or not.

Hopefully, the same can be said for my sunglasses because I can't seem to look away. Luca appears like he was carved from marble. Every tan abdominal muscle chiseled out, one by one with extreme care. He looks damn near radiant and entirely relaxed as he rests with his arms behind his head, showing off his impressive biceps.

I avert my gaze back to my book, mortification seeping in. *God, I need to get laid.*

Doing my best to keep my mind focused on the book in front of me, I pay extra close attention to each word, and it does nothing to settle me.

Regrettably, I left off at the scene where the enemies just became lovers. The tension has been building this entire book, and finally, they've given in to their desires.

The FMC has a strong personality, and she's confident, which is definitely why I like her so much. Throughout the entirety of this book, they've been battling for dominance, and the words written across the page now are no different.

Even during the spicy scenes, she's demanding, and for once, he gives in rather than talking back or doing the opposite of what she wants.

I glance back over the top of my book, and even with sunglasses on, I can feel the heat from his gaze crawling over my skin, leaving goosebumps in their wake.

I start reading again, hoping to get sucked in and away from my current reality, but with every turn of the page, it's becoming more and more unbearable to lie here.

"Always so demanding," he tsks, but for once, he does as I say. He's on his knees, crawling to me, and goddamn,

is it a fucking turn-on. Heat sears through me, zipping down my spine as it pools in my core. I clench around nothing as I wait with anticipation for his body to finally be on mine."

My thighs squeeze tightly together, my core pulsating with need the further I read. *This is torture.*

I can feel the wetness between my legs, and I'm praying that Luca can't see it. But when I look up over the book again, I know he does. He's got his bottom lip clamped so tightly between his teeth that it must be on the verge of drawing blood, and when my eyes skate down his torso, his massive erection gives him away. He's been watching my every move and my perusal of his incredible body.

Fuck.

"Wanna go for a swim, princess? Maybe cool off a bit?" he asks, calling over to me.

This is a bad idea. Regardless, I slam my book shut, tossing it onto the table beside me as I stand, removing my sheer cover-up and descending the steps into the pool.

As expected, Luca jumps in with no preparation. Water sloshes along the sides of the small pool, jostling me.

When he emerges from under the water, he's just a few feet from me, dripping as he brushes his hair back away from his face.

He gives me a knowing, cocky smile as he stands in front of me.

"How's your book?" he asks.

"It's good," I start, clearing my throat. "Very, uh, enlightening," I finish.

"Enlightening, you say?" he asks mockingly. "Maybe I'll have to borrow it sometime then." He winks, further invading my space.

Backing myself up against the wall of the pool, I think of a response, but nothing believable comes to me, so instead, I own up to it. "Enlightening wasn't the right word," I tell him as he further encroaches on my space, and I have nowhere to go this time.

The smooth pool tiles behind my back act as a reminder of that.

"It wasn't, huh? Then what is the right word, Samara?" he asks, testing me.

I've dug my own grave. Time to lie in it. "It was *hot.*"

He quirks a dark brow at me, and a teasing smirk coasts his lips. "Hot?" He places either hand on the edge of the pool behind me, boxing me in. My chest is heaving with the effort it takes to focus, not wanting to fully give away how goddamn turned on I am.

My pulse is at a sprint, nearly singing beneath my skin the closer he leans in.

"I'd love to know what's making you so hot, *principessa,* "he says, his lips merely an inch from mine as he bends to meet my height.

My core is clenching, and I must've officially lost my mind because I'm the one who set boundaries, and here I am, ready to break them all because I'm turned on *by a book.*

Yeah, Samara. *A book.* Even *I* know I'm lying.

"Come on, *enlighten* me. I'm sure whatever's in that book, I could make come true and do it a thousand times better than your imagination," he taunts.

I'm sure he could. *That's the problem.*

His lips are a millimeter from mine now. I can feel his warm breath and practically taste him. My body reacts to him as if my brain has no say in the matter. I tilt my head back, finally ready to give in. *One good orgasm, and we can pretend this never happened at all.*

His hands slip into the pool and drag down my sides, pulling me against him. I feel his heavy length slip between my legs, pressing against my clit. My head tilts farther back, and a whimper pushes through my lips. Rocking my hips into him, I release a long sigh, ready for the pleasure I know only he would ever be able to give me.

I slide my hands over his shoulders and wind my legs around his waist, further rubbing my center along him. He lets out a moan that has my whole body coiled so tightly I'm ready to burst.

Luca grips my ass, crushing me to his solid body, and just as our lips are about to meet, music blares from behind us, jolting me back into reality.[1] My eyes are wide with shock as I realize what we were just about to do. *What I was just about to let happen.*

"Shit," Luca says, climbing out of the pool, not even using the steps as he gets out in two seconds flat.

He towels off his hands quickly and grabs for the phone, bringing it to his face. As soon as the music stops, a brilliant smile spreads across his lips.

"Hi, Gia, *mia bambina*," he coos into the phone. "Did you enjoy the park?" he asks her, but Cecily answers.

"We didn't do much, obviously, but she seemed to enjoy being outside at least," she tells him, and it feels like I'm intruding again.

I get out of the pool quickly, rushing to grab my towel and dry off before taking myself and my book back inside.

---

1. **Cut the Cord — Shinedown**

"One second," I hear Luca say, and a moment later, his hand is at the base of my spine. "You stay and read. I'll talk with Gia inside so you can enjoy the pool," he tells me, redirecting me to my seat.

Kind and considerate Luca is a dangerous drug.

Chapter Fifty-Six

Luca

It's both a blessing and a curse that Samara is seated beside me and not in front of me. A blessing because while she's letting me keep my hand in her lap, at least I don't have to keep staring at her gorgeous curves and stunning face while I try to eat my meal. In reality, I just want to eat *her.*

It's also a curse for those exact same reasons.

"Suh, Luca, do yuh ave anyting fun planned fi yuh an Samara tomorrow? We love tuh spen di whole day wid both of uno, but Camila an mi ago pan a romantic excursion," her dad tells me, looking down at his wife lovingly.

"I actually do have a little something planned for her, but it's a surprise, so we'll have to tell you about it afterward." I wink at him. Little does Samara know that I'm not just covering for us. I really do have a surprise planned for her. I rented a cabana at a beach just outside of the city so we could be completely away from the prying eyes of her family.

"Oh really, a surprise," Vea says, her chestnut eyes glimmering. "I'm all for it, but this one," she says, bumping her shoulder against Samara's, "ain't havin' it."

A surge of protectiveness possesses me. I don't like the way her family sometimes speaks about her. In fact, it drives me up a goddamn wall, and as much as I'd like to believe that this is a part of their normal banter, I've gotten to know Samara well enough to realize it affects her, even if her family doesn't seem to recognize that.

"I don't know, Vea. It seems to me you must just have crappy surprises." I wink at her, hoping to cut the edge from my words.

"You got jokes, huh?" She chuckles again, laughing at her sister's expense.

Mercifully, the waitress comes out with dessert menus. "Does anyone want something for dessert?"

I certainly know what I'd like to be having, but it doesn't sound like she's on the menu for tonight.

Samara and I immediately shake our heads in unison. I'm stuffed to the brim. "I'm so full I could burst," I joke. "Thank you though." I smile at her.

"Same here, thank you," Samara tells her with a friendly smile.

"Oh, come on, Luca, you can't come to the Dominican and not have pudin de pan!" Camila argues. It doesn't go unnoticed to me that Samara stiffens at her mom's choice of words, only addressing me and not her daughter.

"I promise, I'll save room for it tomorrow night." As an Italian American, I know how important food can be culturally, but I don't make a habit of overeating. It makes me feel like shit, and ultimately, I wouldn't enjoy it anyway.

She rolls her eyes. "Fine, but I'm holding you to that. You're missing out," she assures me.

After they've had their dessert, we all say our goodbyes and go our separate ways.

Thank fuck because I'm exhausted.

Chapter Fifty-Seven

Samara

We've been lying on our individual sides of the pillow divide for what feels like hours but has probably only been thirty minutes. I'm unconvinced that Luca is asleep either if the way he's tossing and turning is any indication.

My mind is reeling and refuses to turn off.

"Samara," Luca whispers into the dark room.

"Yes?" I ask, almost relieved by the break in the silence.

"You can't sleep?" He sounds a little concerned.

I huff out a laugh. "Clearly, you can't either."

"Fair. I can't stop thinking about Gia. I know she's fine. Cici's sent me hundreds of photos of her, and Dante even stopped over to check on them with Arielle, but it's almost impossible not to worry," he confesses.

Warmth spreads through my chest. "I imagine that's normal, Luca," I tell him, rolling over on my side to face him in the dark. "She's your first child, and not only that, but this is the first time you've left her for more than a night or two, and you aren't just down the road anymore. You're in a whole other country." I feel my face soften, and an overwhelming sense of pride for how far he's come in the few short months that I've known him fills me. "But you have the best family, and they'll drop everything to be there if something happened." If I were in his position, I have no doubt my family would do the same. Hell, even Luca's family would probably do the same for me. *Because, to their core, they are good people.* It's going to be impossible to try and distance myself from them.

I hear him blow out a long sigh and feel the bed shift as he turns over to face me. The blackout curtains are working so well that I can barely make him out, but I feel his gaze on me.

"What you're saying is probably true and definitely the more rational version of my own thoughts," he agrees but releases an exhausted sigh that I feel deep in my bones. "Unfortunately, anxiety doesn't seem to be very rational."

"No, no, it doesn't," I agree, resisting the urge to reach out and take his hand.

"Why are you having trouble sleeping?" he asks me.

I take a moment to consider this and decide just how much of my thoughts I care to divulge to him. "I'm feeling a little overwhelmed. I see my family in small doses a couple of times a month, but now that includes my cousins and aunts, uncles, and everyone's kids. It just has me thinking about things I don't really want to, and sometimes, the things my family says make me feel like shit." The admission has a boulder settling in my stomach. I feel terrible for admitting that to someone. I feel horrendous for even *feeling* that way, but it's true. "I know they don't mean anything by it, or they have this false belief that they're helping me in some way, but I can only take so much before I can't stop going down the path my mind is taking me on." That was vague but still more than I was planning to share.

It's Luca who reaches out like I had wanted to but wouldn't allow myself to. His pinky grazes the back of my arm before he rests his hand on my wrist, rubbing soothing circles along the thin skin. "I can't know how you're feeling or what kinds of things bother you most, but I can sort of relate. I've obviously got a massive family, and even though no one has ever intentionally made me feel shitty about myself, sometimes, one of my siblings or even my mom will make a joke about how many women I've slept with, and I know that if I'd ever shown any kind of discomfort, it would stop. But I haven't because until recently, they weren't wrong. I played into the playboy stereotype the media has labeled me with. The jokes still hurt though." His admission makes my prior guilt surrounding his sexual prowess hammer even deeper into my heart and mind.

"It's awful when we *know* they mean nothing by it because I think that almost makes it harder to deal with. For me, at least, it feels like I have no right to get upset with them."

"Same here, and then I just feel even guiltier because my family has given me everything. They've supported me relentlessly, no matter what a little shit I'd been growing up, or even as an adult," he admits with a tired sigh.

I can hear just how much of a burden he's felt. "Do you ever feel like your parents treat your siblings differently than you because you're single?"

He chuckles. "I'm not single, Samara. I'm your boyfriend," he jokes. He goes silent for a moment, and I don't respond, hoping he'll take my question seriously. "Honestly though? Never. They've treated every one of us equally my entire life."

We say nothing for a short stretch of time, but then he breaks the silence. "Are you asking because you feel like your parents treat you and Vea differently?"

My voice gets stuck in my throat, but after a pause, I decide to answer. "They didn't use to, or at least it wasn't that noticeable. Now that she has a husband and kids, they've made me feel like I'm doing something wrong with my life, even though I've literally put every ounce of myself into making them proud. They didn't have it easy when they moved to the States, and I just want to make their sacrifices worth the struggle, but it doesn't seem like I can truly make them proud unless I'm married or pregnant. Preferably both."

"I can't say for certain, but I'd really like to believe that isn't true. You're fucking incredible, Samara." Butterflies swarm around inside me, and heat creeps up my neck. "There's not a chance they aren't extraordinarily proud of everything you've accomplished. I think they love you an immeasurable amount, but I also think that maybe they haven't loved you the way you needed to be loved." He squeezes my wrist before resuming those soothing circles, and the spot where his hand is feels tingly and heated. "Some people only know one way of showing it, and maybe that's worked for your sister, but it hasn't for you, and that's okay to recognize. If you think it'll serve you to speak up about it and try to teach them how to love you the way you need, then do that. And if not, I strongly believe that someday, you'll find someone who loves you exactly the way you need and deserve." He sounds so sure of himself, but I can't seem to say anything to him just yet because he somehow summed up every thought I've always lived with and made it feel almost... normal?

"Is that what you want?" he asks, his voice quiet. Except I have no idea what he's referring to.

"Is 'what' what I want?" I ask, confusion lacing my words.

"A spouse... kids..." he answers.

"I..." I can't answer that without baring my soul to this man. I thought that would be something I'd fear, but I feel safe and comfortable with Luca.

"It's okay, princess," he whispers. "You don't have to answer that. I shouldn't have asked."

His words only act to spur me on. I don't share this side of myself with almost anyone, and something tells me that the last person on the planet who would judge me for this is Luca.

"It's okay. It just took me off guard," I say, shaking my head. "I'm not used to talking about what I want. I do a lot of family planning with my clients, but the questions aren't steered in my direction." I take a deep breath before answering. "I want it all. I want a daughter I can raise to love herself the way no one ever taught me to. I want to show her that Black women *are* worthy of love and that we can have absolutely everything that everyone else can, just like my parents always drilled into me and Vea. I want a son who can learn to love and be loved the way I hope my husband will someday. I want a husband who adores me and a freaking cat too. Everything short of a picket fence."

Luca's arms wrap around me; his crisp scent and intense body heat envelop me as he tugs me to his chest over the pillow divide.

"Someday, Samara," he says, and I swear I feel him kiss the top of my head. My cheeks heat, and my throat feels like it's closing, hot tears welling behind my eyes. "Someday, you'll find someone worthy of your love who knows exactly how to love you the way you deserve, and the kids will follow," he assures me.

"Someday," I agree, but the word feels foreign in my mouth. Like I'm holding onto hope for something I've stopped allowing myself to truly wish for. But it's easier than telling him the truth. That I'll never be able to carry my own children and that I'm not even sure *how* I need to be loved. How could someone else?

"Goodnight, Luca," I tell him, rolling to face away from him. I think I've taken all that I can of this conversation, and my lids feel so heavy.

"Goodnight, princess."

Chapter Fifty-Eight

Luca

Saturday, August 29, 2026

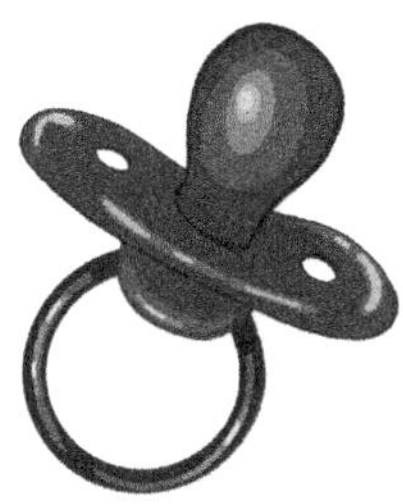

My senses all liven up, one at a time, as I start to wake. The warm smell of Samara fills my lungs, and a soft tickle flits over my chest. I feel something across my legs, but it's too heavy to be a blanket.

Forcing my eyes open, I blink rapidly, but there's no light in here for my pupils to adjust to. Instead, I pat myself down, and realization dawns on me the moment I feel the satin bonnet on my chest... Which must mean that my legs are being pinned down by *Samara.*

As luck would have it, my dick is so hard I could probably chop wood with it.

I will it to go away, but unsurprisingly, it won't. Especially not with Samara lying on top of me, making me delirious with her sweet scent. *Fuck*, why is she so damn perfect?

If this relationship were real, I'd already have her on her back, screaming my name.

My dick twitches. Well, *that* thought certainly didn't help my current situation either. Goddamnit.

Donald Trump naked. Dead puppies. A baseball bat pummeling my dick. Maggots crawling out of my dick.

I reach down, gripping my shaft and hoping like hell that it worked, but as it appears, I'm still as hard as ever. Even the most disgusting shit I can think of isn't working to soften this thing up.

Samara shifts, further gliding her body onto mine. I hold completely still, hoping there's still a shot I might be able to slide out from underneath her, but when I hear her sharp inhale and feel her hands roaming over me, I know I'm not that lucky.

I hold my breath as she pats me down, trying to get her bearings, and when her hand lands on my dick, I can't help the groan that slips past my lips. "Oh fuck." I moan, leaning into her touch.

Just as quickly as it came, it disappears. Samara shoots up, pushing away from me. "What the hell, Luca? I said to stay on your side!" she shrieks at me.

I reach over to the lamp beside me and turn it on. The room is suddenly much easier to visualize, and when my eyes meet Samara's, hers are wide with shock.

I hike a brow at her, smirking as I say, "Well, princess, it appears *you* are on *my* side. Just couldn't keep your hands off me, could you?" I tease her, hoping she takes the bait so we can end this awkward stare-down.

Just as I'd hoped, she huffs before rolling out of the bed and snatching her bag from the closet, dragging it into the bathroom with her.

"It's okay, princess!" I call after her, "I love cuddles."

"Fuck off, Luca!" she shouts back, but I swear I hear her laugh the moment the bathroom door closes behind her.

It looks like I *will* be sleeping on the couch tonight.

***

"Do you have any plans for what we should do after breakfast?" I ask her, hopeful that she'll include me in them.

"Yep, I'm going to drag my ass to the nearest beach that isn't within walking distance of my parents, read for hours, and then have a relaxing massage," she tells me, sounding excited. Her words hit me like a ton of bricks, though, as I realize not only am I not included in those plans, but it actually *hurts* that I'm not. *What the fuck?*

I put on my best smile and tell her, "Sounds great. Mind if I call Gia real quick, and then we can get out of here?" I guess my plans to take her away for the day are a wash if she'd rather be alone.

"Not at all," she says just as the room is filled with the sound of our ringing phone. "You call Gia and Cecily, and I'll take care of this."

I nod, grabbing my phone and dialing Cici. She answers quickly. "Good morning, Luca! Gia, your daddy's on the phone. Do you wanna talk to him?" she coos, her voice high-pitched and filled with joy.

I chuckle. "Sounds like you're having a good time."

"We are." She sighs dreamily. "It's really"—the line goes quiet for a moment before she finishes—"just really nice. Having her with me, knowing I have support, knowing that it's *okay* to not be perfect, and finally feeling like I have a way to cope with the impending thoughts of imposter syndrome."

My heart clenches, and I'm overwhelmed with joy at that. *Maybe someday I'll figure that out too.* "That's incredible, Cici. I'm so proud of you," I tell her, and out of my periphery, I see Samara hang up the phone, her dark brows pulled together.

"I'm proud of both of us," she whispers, clearing her throat. "Okay, here's Gia," she quickly tells me.

"Gia, *mia bambina*! Daddy misses you," I tell her, and she babbles at the sound of my voice. "Your mom has sent me so many pictures of you. I bet you're having so much fun with her." More incoherent babbles come over the line.

Samara sits on the edge of the bed, clasps her hands over her knees, and a thread of worry spirals through me. "Hey, Gia, Cici, I'm gonna have to go, but do you mind if we do a video call tonight?"

"Of course not," Cici assures me. "Just send me a text when you're ready, and I'll keep flooding your inbox with pictures and updates."

"You're the best! Talk soon," I tell her and then say, "Gia, Daddy loves you. You're my whole heart, okay? I'll be home soon."

Of course, she doesn't answer, but Cici does. "Have fun today, Luca," she says before hanging up. A couple of photos roll in the moment the call ends, and Gia is wearing a pink-and-white dress with ruffles and the cutest little matching bow, looking just like Pebbles from *The Flintstones*. I'd expect nothing less from Cici.

"Everything okay, princess?" I ask tentatively as I approach her side of the bed. I crouch down in front of her when she doesn't immediately respond, and I can feel my heart pounding in my throat the longer it takes her to answer me.

"Yeah, it's just..." She swallows.

"Just what?" I ask, my brow arched in question.

"Apparently, everyone who ate dessert last night got sick, so they won't be able to join us for breakfast today," she tells me hesitantly.

"I'm not seeing the problem, princess. You're gonna have to spell it out for me because we didn't have dessert, and I thought time away from your family was a *good* thing."

"It is, but my parents had some romantic excursion booked for this afternoon, and it's non-refundable, so they begged us to go in their place, and I said yes."

My heart rate starts to slow. "That doesn't sound so bad. I'm sure we can have fun together," I tell her with a wink, hoping to, at the very least, help her mood change from sad to annoyed. Annoyance I can handle. I'm used to her being annoyed with me. Sad? Not so much.

"I mean, I guess not. But I had my massage planned, and now I can't do that, so I'm just a little bummed," she explains.

Understanding dawns on me. *If my girl wants a massage, she's getting a massage.*

"Let's just make the most of it, okay?"

She nods, standing. "Ready for breakfast?"

"Always," I answer, following her to the door. I make a mental note to call the spa as soon as we're done eating.

***

"I'm gonna go make a call. I'll be ready in a few minutes, and then we can head out," I tell Samara, closing the sliding door behind me.

The phone rings a few times as I wait for the hotel spa to answer. "La Rucia Spa, how can I help you?"

"Hi, my girlfriend had a massage booked for today and had to cancel due to some last-minute changes in our itinerary. I was wondering if you have any open availability?" I ask, making sure there's a smile in my tone.

"I'm so sorry, sir, but we're booked out until next March," she informs me. *Shit.*

"Could you check to see what kind of massage Samara Perez-Allen in the honeymoon suite had booked for today?"

"Yes, sir," she answers, and I hear her typing and clicking. "She had a ninety-minute full-body deep-tissue massage with hot stones added."

"Great, and how much does that usually cost?"

"Twenty-two hundred Dominican pesos, which is about three hundred and seventy USD," she informs me.

"Great, how does two thousand USD for all of that, plus a facial and body scrub done in our hotel room, sound?"

She sputters on the other end of the line. "Sir, I, we... We don't have any availability."

I feel horrible for putting her on the spot, but money talks, and I'm willing to pay if it means Samara gets the vacation she *wants.*

I'm not okay with using money or influence to get what *I* want, but this feels a lot more like a necessity. Samara's been known to make me do and think differently than I typically would, even if she has no idea she's doing it.

"Is there anyone..." I clear my throat. "Any *female* massage therapists willing to stay after normal working hours? I'll pay whatever their price is. Hell, I'll double it," I tell her.

"One moment, sir," she says, and I hear her speaking Spanish with a few people in the background. I can make out some of what they're saying, thanks to Gianni's language proficiency, but I'm not great at speaking anything aside from English and some really shitty Italian.

She gets back on the phone, releasing a long sigh. "We can make that work. Two thousand USD at six tonight."

"Sounds great," I tell her. "Thank you so much."

"The pleasure is mine, sir," she says before hanging up.

I smile to myself, heading back inside to meet Samara for our *romantic* excursion.

Chapter Fifty-Nine

Samara

I pull off my flip-flops, tossing them in my backpack as we step out onto the sand, not wanting to kick any up onto my legs.

A short man with dark hair is wearing a cowboy hat, standing by the edge of the water with two huge brown horses.

I hear a sharp intake of breath and turn to see Luca staring at the horses, eyes wide and jaw clenched.

"Everything okay?" I ask him, stopping about thirty feet away from the man.

"No"—he shakes his head adamantly—"I am *not* okay, Samara," he tells me, his chest heaving.

"What's going on with you?" I ask him, confused.

"Horses. No one said shit about horses!" He sounds near hysterics.

"What's wrong with horses?"

"They're terrifying. That's what!" he tells me, his voice thin. "They're these giant, omnivorous beasts, and everyone tells you they're sweet as can be, but what's to stop them from knocking us off and kicking our skulls in? Not to mention how goddamn high off the ground we are! And the shit! They take massive shits, Samara! How is this supposed to be *romantic*? Why would anyone choose this for a day away on vacation?!" His arms are flailing in front of his face the same way his mom's do when she's passionate about something.

I can no longer contain my laughter. It bubbles out of me, spilling over as I lean forward, grabbing my thighs to keep myself upright. *Luca De Laurentiis, six-foot-four hockey god, is afraid of horses.*

By the time I catch my breath, my cheeks are burning from smiling, and Luca is shooting daggers at me with his arms crossed over his chest.

"What's so funny, princess?" he asks, his tone sounding so grumbly, it's *almost* cute.

"Come on, Luca. It'll be fine," I assure him, stifling another laugh.

His eyes narrow at me. "You're right, princess. It *will* be fine. Because we'll be sharing one of those beasts since you know so much about them. You'll keep me safe." He smirks.

"Absolutely not," I tell him, my tone firm.

"It's that or nothing."

I look over my shoulder to the man waiting by his horses, feeding them each a carrot.

Releasing a quick breath through my nose, I reluctantly agree. "Fine," I say before stomping off toward the horses. The sand slows me down, and I lose some of the dramatic impact. *I'll never admit this, but I'm actually glad we're sharing a horse because I'm a little afraid of them too.* I'm not a fan of relying on another being for my safety.

The man introduces himself as Yandel and then the horses. The larger one is named Nitro, and the smaller one is Poppy.

He hands us carrots and apple slices, instructing us on how to hold our palms open to feed them. Luca refuses, standing behind me and using my body as a shield. My smile refuses to fade. I love knowing this about him.

"Alright, give me one of those carrots." He huffs, grabbing one from the bucket on the ground.

He stands with his spine ramrod straight, arm extended out and palm up with the carrot, but when I look at his face, his eyes are clenched shut, and his head is turned away. "Luca, look." I point to the horse as she gingerly takes the carrot from his palm. His eyes burst open just in time, and a grin spreads across his lips into the most breathtaking smile.

"I guess that wasn't so bad," he says, his voice quiet.

"We'll be riding the same horse. Is that okay?" I ask our guide.

He nods. "I'll follow behind then."

I stick my foot in the stirrup and feel Luca's warm hands squeeze my hips as he hoists me up onto the horse's back. Once I'm sufficiently settled, he follows suit, groaning as he does. A cool, salty breeze wraps around us. "This was a horrible idea. Your parents have atrocious taste," he murmurs as he settles in behind me.

Another giggle slips past my lips, and I take the reins, just how Yandel had shown me. I see him mount the horse beside us, and we take off at a slow trot.

"I think I'm gonna be sick." Luca groans behind me. He's got a death grip on my hips, and I feel his words vibrate through my spine, his chest pressed firmly into me.

"You'll be fine, and if you puke, you better do it over the side, or I'll kick your ass," I nearly hiss at him.

"Noted," he says, trying and failing to hide his chuckle.

We maintain a slow, steady pace, and the sun's rays heat me all over. The sounds of the waves crashing against the sand are so soothing that I barely even realize it when Luca starts to relax behind me, loosening his grip.

I look over my shoulder for a moment, noting that Yandel has started to trail farther behind us. "Eyes on the road, Samara," Luca growls behind me.

"Sand, eyes on the *sand*," I correct him.

"Yeah, yeah, yeah, whatever. Eyes forward, *principessa*." He drags his hands down my waist, settling them on the tops of my bare thighs. A shiver wracks through me, and goosebumps line my skin all over.

"It's a hundred degrees out here; how do you have a chill?" he whispers against the shell of my ear. I suppress the shudder that threatens its way through me.

I'm realizing just how romantic this excursion could be. With the right person that is.

I do my best to ignore him, focusing instead on the palm trees dancing in the wind, the sounds of children laughing as they play with their families in the water, and the music surrounding us each time we pass a cabana or a bar.

We stroll by a couple lying on their sides, facing one another under their rented cabana. I try to pull my eyes away when I realize that the man is fondling her topless breasts, squeezing her nipples tightly in his grip, but I can't peel my eyes away. Luca's hot breath coasts over the side of my neck, and I feel his hard length press into my spine. "We could be doing that right now if you didn't have me sitting on the back of this vegetarian monster."

I shake my head. "No, we couldn't. Remember, Luca, this is a *fake* relationship," I tell him, but my thighs still clench from the feeling of his growing erection trying to burrow itself into me.

"The relationship might be, but that doesn't mean we can't still work out our frustrations together," he says, groaning as I involuntarily wiggle my ass farther into his embrace.

His hands trail up my thighs, one settling on my hip and the other slipping under my bathing suit cover-up. The closer his fingers trail near my core, the harder it is to protest. I lean forward, hoping the separation between us will clear my head, but the new position has my clit pressed firmly into the saddle. My breath is knocked out of me, and my fingers grip the reins more tightly.

The hand on my hip trails toward my navel, lying flat on my stomach and pressing me back into Luca. His dick is hard as ever, straining against me through the thin fabric of his swim trunks. "Just this once, *principessa.* Let me make you feel good. No one's looking," he whispers, dipping his head to tug on my earlobe.

My limbs tingle, and as much as I try to convince myself that it's just from my legs dangling, I know it isn't true.

I can't take it anymore. My eyes scan our surroundings, and as luck would have it, we've reached an alcove with no one besides Yandel around. He's trailed so far behind us, I'm sure he couldn't see *or hear* anything. My resolve shatters.

I nod, giving in to Luca's request to make me feel good. "No can do, princess. I need your words. If you want me to finger-fuck your soaking cunt, you're going to have to open that pretty mouth of yours and tell me."

A moan slips past my lips, and he sucks on the side of my neck in response, nipping the skin and releasing me. A finger trails up the side of my bathing suit, slipping under the strip that's covering my center. "You say you don't like me," he whispers, "but your pussy has other ideas. You're absolutely drenched, and it's all for *me*, isn't it?"

Damn this man and his delicious, sinful mouth.

"Yes." I groan.

"Yes, what? Yes, you're drenched for me, or yes, you want me to make you come? Or... both." He chuckles, already knowing the answer.

"Luca," I grit out. "Shut up and make me come." Annoyance and desire tingle through me in equal measure.

"Yes, ma'am," he says, sliding one thick finger into me. I cry out, clenching around his finger. I slump forward, but Luca's hand on my abdomen keeps me straight, pressing me into his chest. "God damn, princess, you're so tight." He pumps that finger in and out of me.

We're now traveling so slowly we may as well be at a complete stop. He slips another finger inside, separating them once inside me and stretching me out around him. It sends pain and pleasure spearing through me, and my chest heaves with the effort to sit still.

"Look at you, soaking my fingers and practically begging for me. I bet if you got that stick out of your ass, we could have a *fantastic* fucking time with that too," he purrs.

"Fuck you," I grit out, but his words have me reluctantly spasming around his fingers.

He trails his nose up my neck, breathing me in, and whispers, "That can be your job." My skin is on fire, and I know it's not just from the sun. A gentle gust of wind breezes by, pulling tendrils of my hair into my face. Luca gently tucks the errant hairs behind my ear with his free hand before returning it to my waist.

He pumps his fingers, changing his tempo and, finally, speeding up as my moans become louder and more uncontained. "Yes, just like that," I tell him, pleading for my release.

His thumb grazes my clit, and he presses himself farther into me, holding me up as he brings me to the edge. My vision starts to narrow, my breath coming out in pants. He whispers as he ruthlessly drags me toward my orgasm, "I'll always give you *exactly* what you need, *principessa*," as his hand trails from my waist to my breast. His fingers graze over the pebbled bud, and I'm a goner.

My pussy clenches around his fingers, my orgasm sucking the air out of my lungs as I pulsate around him, stars littering my vision. And just when I've had enough, maybe even too much, my skin searing with heat, Luca pinches my nipple. He does it the same way the man on the beach had his partner, and a second wave of euphoria hits me, rearing through me until I'm a puddle. I fear Luca De Laurentiis has ruined me for every man after him.

"You're so pretty when you come undone for me," he whispers, licking a heated trail up my neck and extracting his fingers. He brings them to his lips, and I turn my head, watching as he sucks them into his mouth, effectively cleaning them of any trace of me. "And delicious too," he says, moaning. He gives me a small smile, straightening me and grabbing the reins for himself, steering us the rest of the way around the alcove and back the way we came. When my breath has returned to normal, I take them from him, eager to busy myself with anything but the concern rearing through me at the realization of what we'd just done.

"This needs to stop," I whisper to myself, but he hears me.

"I disagree." He chuckles, wrapping his arms back around my waist.

This is bad. *Really fucking bad.*

***

After our excursion, we have a quick lunch and head back to the room.

I make it out onto the deck to lie by the pool and read, and Luca decides to go to the gym. I guess a body like his doesn't make itself.

My book is good, fantastic even, but it's hard to focus when I'm still wound up from earlier.

And this book has so much sexual tension in it that it's almost painful to read right now. I've never been someone who was overly sexual. I enjoy it, usually, and really enjoy reading it, but I haven't been with someone who left me feeling simultaneously fulfilled and perpetually unsatiated.

Until Luca, that is, and we haven't even had sex.

Nor will we ever.

That was the last time I let myself get carried away.

The last time, Samara. Even just telling myself this, it feels like a lie.

My entire life, I've never struggled to make a decision. Hell, I'm *usually* the most decisive person in any room, but that changed when Luca De Laurentiis entered my life.

I shake my head, and once inside, I drop the book and climb into bed. I turn off the lamp, allowing the light seeping in from the sheer curtains to illuminate the space to be comfortable.

Grabbing for the remote, I turn the TV on, flipping through channel after channel and not finding anything that catches my attention.

"Okay, maybe a nap then," I say to myself, turning off the TV and rolling over onto my side.

I close my eyes, but my mind wanders all over. I can't stop Luca from popping into those thoughts over and over. His pretty eyes, that damn dimpled cheek, and his pretty, pierced dick all swarm my mind.

My core floods, clenching as images of Luca's fingers delving inside me race through my brain.

My hand snakes down between my thighs, and my eyes snap open. "Shit," I groan out.

Awareness of what I was about to do hits me like a horse's hoof to the face, and I'm catapulting out of the bed. "I need to get out of this room."

I grab a pair of leggings, sliding them up my hips and grabbing the room key before making my way down the endless halls of the resort. I know I'm risking running into my family, but at least with them around, I wouldn't be thinking about Luca.

It's our second day here, and I haven't had a chance to explore, so I wander aimlessly, passing conference rooms, the spa I so badly wish I were at right now, and an infinite number of rooms.

When I pass the gym, I stop in my tracks.

Luca is facing his phone, which is propped up on a piece of equipment. I watch through the wall of windows, staring as his impressive muscles glide with ease through the air, his fist repeatedly making contact with a punching bag. He turns to face the camera again, saying something I can't make out, but he's smiling.

I hedge closer, and my hand wraps around the door handle. I look around, ensuring no one is here to see me standing outside the door like a total creep.

When I've confirmed the coast is clear, I crack the door open, just enough that a rush of cool air shocks me for a second until I hear Luca speaking.

"Alright, ladies, you try next. I probably won't be able to fix your form too much since I'm having to do this on my phone and can't see you all very well, but just have some fun with it. We'll make corrections next week when I'm back," he assures his viewers.

What the hell is going on?

"Hell yeah, just like that, Charice!" he cheers. "You've got this, girlfriend!"

He's clapping excitedly, nearly bouncing on the balls of his feet as he cheers for the "ladies" on the other end of his phone.

I continue to watch, maintaining the death grip I have on the door handle, afraid to let it slip and risk making my presence known.

I'm utterly stunned as he continues teaching what appears to be a self-defense class. What bothers me is the familiarity I notice.

There's something that's not sitting with me, and I can't figure it out.

Luca claps once more, beaming at his phone. "Alright, ladies, you all did an incredible job. I'm sorry for the lack of a live class today, but we made it work. Everyone, give a huge round of applause to Brandi. Not only does she flawlessly execute every job she's given, but today, that includes camerawoman too."

They all cheer, clapping enthusiastically, and it clicks.

Charice.

Brandi.

Luca is the one teaching the women at the shelter self-defense lessons. And according to Brandi, he has been for *years.*

Shock continues to ripple through me, but I have to get out of here before I'm caught.

Releasing the handle, I spin toward the direction of our room and haul ass out of here, my mind left reeling with this new information.

I'm the worst person ever because Luca is clearly the best.

Chapter Sixty

Luca

Class went better than I'd anticipated with the tiny screen on my phone, but Samara showing up was quite the surprise.

She clearly hadn't wanted to get caught, and I had no desire to embarrass her, especially not in front of the women at the shelter.

Women she knows, I remind myself, thinking about what Brandi had told me about her good deeds.

If only her family knew about that side of her, maybe they'd be less likely to make her feel like shit for not having a partner and children yet. She already sacrifices so much of herself for others to have the opportunities that they make her feel horrible for not having. And from what she's told me, she definitely *does* want those things.

Regardless of whether they know or not, there's zero excuse for the way they make her feel, and if they aren't careful, I'll be letting them know *exactly* how I feel about it.

As I head back to our room, I make sure to walk slowly, allowing Samara time to get herself together and pretend she hadn't just spent the last half hour eavesdropping on my class.

Little does she know, I always know when she's around. I can *feel* her presence the moment she enters a room. And when her eyes are on me? It nearly burns me alive.

CHAPTER SIXTY-ONE

Samara

It takes Luca a lot longer to get back to the room than I'd expected, but I'm thankful for that.

The extra time allowed me the space I needed to calm my heart rate and drop my ass onto one of these lounge chairs by our private pool so I could pretend to have been out here this whole time.

Luca slides the door open, poking his head out. His eyes dance with mischief, and his smirk sends my gut into a tailspin. "You enjoying your book, princess?" he asks.

"Yep, it's really great."

His hand slips out from behind his back, holding onto the book in question as he wags it around, taunting me.

He stalks toward me, and I'm stunned.

Goddamnit.

Luca lowers, his lips ghosting over mine. "Looks like you forgot this," he says, his minty breath coasting my lips and sending a chill down my spine despite the lack of wind out here.

He presses the book to my lap and straightens. "I'm gonna get washed up. Your surprise will be here soon," he tells me, winking over his shoulder before heading back inside.

Surprise?

Twenty minutes later, Luca still hasn't left the bathroom, and I'm starting to get anxious. The phone rings in the room, and when I answer, it's my mom's voice that sounds through the line. "Mara, how was your excursion today?" she asks, sounding ten times better than she had this morning.

"It was good, really fun actually. We had a great time," I tell her, chuckling. "And I discovered that Luca is terrified of horses."

"Oh my god, I'm so sorry!" she says, not sounding all that sorry the moment her voice breaks on a laugh.

"Well, I have a favor to ask," she tells me, and my stomach drops. "I wanted to call and ask since we're still not feeling great and won't make it to dinner tonight. But Yera visited us today at the resort and wanted to see if you'd still be willing to have a little date with her son."

I'm about to protest when she cuts in. "You and Luca said your relationship is new and still a bit casual, right? So what would it hurt to just grab brunch with her son? Maybe you'll really like him."

Suddenly, it doesn't feel like there's anything particularly casual about my fake relationship with Luca. *And that terrifies me.*

"Mom, this is completely inappropriate. I'm here on *vacation* with my *boyfriend*," I tell her, allowing the full weight of my frustration to seep into my voice.

"I know, Mara, but it's just an hour. Come on. Absence makes the heart grow fonder," she tells me. *That's exactly what I'm afraid of.*

"Fine, one hour. That's *all*,"I concede.

"Incredible! You're going to have such a good time. I'll go tell Yera!" she shouts enthusiastically.

"Great." I groan, hanging my head. "Text me the details," I tell her before hanging up.

Luca comes out of the bathroom, freshly shaven and prettied up. "Who called?" he asks, tossing his dirty gym clothes in the laundry bag hanging in the closet.

"My mom." I groan involuntarily.

He lifts a brow at me. "What's she up to now?" he asks, taking a seat on his side of the bed.

"She set me up on a date with one of her friend's sons. Which is exactly the reason *you* are here in the first place."

His eyes sharpen, cheeks hollowing and nostrils flaring for a split second before he cools his expression. "That's absolutely fucked," he tells me. "And not happening."

I shake my head. "I already agreed to it. Only an hour. We're having brunch."

Before he can say anything else, there's a knock at the door. My brows pinch in confusion. "Did you order room service or something?"

His easy smile returns. "Nope, that's your surprise," he tells me as his long legs hitch over the mattress, climbing off and heading toward the door.

A woman dressed in an all-white uniform smiles at me as she brings in a folded table, and someone behind her is carrying a box loaded with items.

"Hello, I'm Valentina. I'll be your massage therapist," she informs me, setting up the table. Luca helps her, opening it with ease.

He sees me gaping at them and leaves her to stand in front of me. He grips my shoulder and looks down at me, our eyes only a few inches apart. "You deserve to relax, Samara. This is your vacation, too, not just your family's. Go get changed into the robe I left in the bathroom for you and get your ass back in here for the massage of a lifetime. I'll be just outside, waiting to hear all about it when it's over," he says, winking and spinning me toward the bathroom before giving me a light smack on the ass to urge me toward it.

I walk there like a zombie, too dazed to even threaten to bite his hand off for smacking my butt.

My heart constricts painfully in my chest. *This man is both an angel and a devil.* His sweet words and actions, combined with his sinful mouth and body, have me tripping all over myself. It's certainly not something I'm accustomed to.

***

That was not only the most incredible massage I've ever had, but Luca also added on a facial and body scrub. It was amazing, and I feel so blissed out. My bones are made of jelly, and when Luca offered to order room service for dinner, I didn't hesitate to take him up on it. There's nowhere I'd rather be than in this feather-soft bed, lying beside Luca, watching whatever dumb movie he put on ten minutes ago. I have no idea what it's about, but that's only because I can't seem to take my eyes off *him.*

Chapter Sixty-Two

Luca

I guess the massage was good because Samara didn't kick me out of the bed tonight like I'd been anticipating.

And just like last night, I can't get my brain to shut off.

I can't stop thinking about her with another man tomorrow, and my inner child keeps throwing ideas into my mind of ways to sabotage their date.

This isn't a scene from The Parent Trap, *Luca.*

I've been grumpy all night, and not even my call with Gia fixed it.

I mean, it definitely helped. I've got the cutest kid on the planet; how could it not? But the moment I got off the phone with her and Cici, I was immediately back to the grumpy little shit I'd transformed into the moment Samara told me about her mom's scheming.

And yes, I'm fully aware that we're *fake dating*, but shit, sometimes, it feels pretty goddamn real. Yes, Samara is also a brat. Yes, she can be snarky. *Yes*, she still seems to get fed up with my crap, but I think those may be the things I like most about her.

It makes me feel like a good boy. Like I've managed to earn every smile, every laugh, and *every breathy moan.*

I love how fiery she is and that she doesn't hesitate to put me in my place. I can't see myself with someone who doesn't do exactly that.

But she's made it immensely clear that we will never *really* be together, so instead, I'll just enjoy my time with her while I have it.

Or at least, I'll *try* to enjoy my time with her when her mom isn't setting her up with other men, that is.

"Luca, if you don't stop huffing and puffing over there, I'm going to suffocate you with my pillow and drag your body into the ocean," Samara complains.

That makes me laugh because I think she might *actually* do it, and it only makes me like her more.

Fuck me.

Chapter Sixty-Three

Samara

Sunday, August 30, 2026

The hostess leads me to the outdoor patio to seat me at a table for brunch. My palms feel a little sweaty. I haven't been on a date, a *real* date, in so long.

And the way Luca looked like he hadn't slept a single second last night made it even more difficult to leave him for this. Truthfully, I crave his company more than I've ever craved anyone's, and it's nerve-wracking to think about.

I take a seat, sipping my water and hoping I don't fuck this up, or I'll be hearing about it till the end of time. My mom would never let it go.

A tall, handsome man with kind eyes approaches my table, extending his hand for me. "You must be the lovely Samara. I'm Jasiel. It's a pleasure to meet you," he tells me, taking my hand in his and grazing the back of my knuckles with his full lips.

Alright, Jasiel's got game.

"It's nice to meet you, Jasiel. I'm sorry our moms pushed you into this." I chuckle, trying to laugh off my discomfort.

"It's really not a problem. Sometimes, I think my mom wakes up in the middle of the night just scheming over how she'll find me a wife," he says with a laugh. It's a deep sound that has my ears tingling.

"I know the feeling." I smile, picking up my menu and taking a look so I can stop staring at his handsome face.

As I look over the options, I can't help but think about how nice it's been to have Luca around for meals. He's taken on the role of sharing entrées with me, so I always get what I want in the end, without compromise. And the moment the thought passes, my eyes snap up to meet Jasiel's kind hazel eyes, making me feel guilty for even thinking about Luca in the first place.

***

Jasiel walks with me all the way back to the resort and stops at the front doors. "I had a really great time, Samara. Thank you for going out of your way for this. I'm sure our moms will both be happy to know that at least I had fun."

"I had a great time, so thanks for that," I say, smiling.

He drags a hand through his soft brown curls and closes the distance between us. My mind short-circuits, realizing too late that he's about to kiss me. The moment his mouth descends upon mine, it's like my body decides on its own. I turn my head, and his lips land safely on my cheek for a chaste kiss. His cheeks start to turn pink when he straightens. "Have a great rest of your day, Samara," he tells me before hurrying out of here.

When he's out of earshot, I blow out a long breath and turn to head inside.

The doors open, and I'm blasted with cool air from the lobby. Luca's arrogant smirk greets me as soon as I step inside.

"Hey there, princess. Looks like the sparks weren't flying after all, huh?" he asks, sarcasm dripping from his tone.

I muster up the best eye roll I can manage as we head down the hall toward our room, but before we get there, Luca's large hand wraps around mine, pulling me into his chest. A breath gets knocked out of my lungs as I steady a palm on his hard chest to balance myself.

He brings his lips an inch from mine, his warm, minty breath coasting over my lips and sending a chill through me. The tip of his nose drags slowly down the bridge of mine, and I see his eyes dilate when I peer up into them, unable to step out of this trance.

Luca closes the distance, and just as our lips are about to meet, he pulls away entirely, dragging me along behind him as he chuckles. Poorly contained anger trickles through me. *I just got played.*

"Don't be angry, Samara," he chides softly. "I just had to prove to you that you want me as badly as I want you, but I'm not going to be the one to make the next move. You're the only one hung up here, so *you* have to be the one to make the decision. I won't make it for you," he explains, gently squeezing my hand.

What the hell? When exactly had Luca decided he wanted something other than sex with me?

It appears I fully dropped the ball on this one.

Chapter Sixty-Four

Luca

I can't help the smug grin plastered across my face right now. I've been stewing all morning over Samara being on this date. While I had absolutely started to come to terms with the fact that I no longer wanted this relationship to be fake, I hadn't anticipated just how fucking jealous I'd be when I watched her leave this morning for brunch with another man.

And when I saw him coming in for a kiss, I wanted to body-slam the fucker, but seeing her turn her face away made lightning strike right through the center of my goddamn heart. I'm *happy* that he just wasn't doing it for her. And even more than that, I'm *elated* that apparently, *I do.*

That simple fact *almost* washes away the last bit of contempt I'm still holding onto that his lips got to touch a single part of her.

"Come on, princess, let's get changed. We're meeting your family." I smirk.

She looks at me warily, releasing a groan. "For what?"

"It's a surprise," I tell her, grinning.

"Luca, I thought we'd already established that I don't like surprises."

I tap my chin, pretending to mull this over. "Yeah, ya know, I really don't think we ever *did* establish that. And too bad because we're going. Besides, it seemed you *really* enjoyed yesterday's surprise."

She flips me off, stomping into the room the moment we get to our door. *God, I love it when she's cranky.* It just means I get to watch her perfect ass as she leaves.

***

We spend the day enjoying the sun with Samara's parents, Vea, and her family.

The weather's been gorgeous, but despite everything I could be looking at right now, considering this *is* a glass-bottom boat tour, I still can't keep my eyes off Samara.

Her deep chestnut coils are blowing in the wind, and with my sunglasses on, I get to outright stare at her. I take in her every feature. The way the sun highlights her high cheekbones and how her denim shorts hug her thighs.

She's been doing a good job at ignoring her family's comments while we've been out here, and I imagine it must be the only way she can truly enjoy her vacation. Just ignoring them and letting them roll off her.

Unfortunately, I don't find it that easy.

Even if I don't show it, I've always been someone who internalizes every comment made about me. And right now, I'm holding onto every ill word her family speaks of her.

Chapter Sixty-Five

Samara

A note from the author: Please click the hyperlink at the end of this message. It contains a Spotify link for all four songs included in this chapter, in the order they should be played. I've done this so you're able to play the music and fully immerse yourselves without leaving to click on each hyperlink. These were written with the average reading rate and the distraction the music would cause in mind. Readers are intended to listen to the music in the background as they imagine this scene. I hope you enjoy reading it! <3[1]

---

1. **Chapter 65 Playlist**

This day has been a complete whirlwind. I'm not sure what to make of it, and while I was expecting to be ready to get home by now, I'm not.

We are having a fairly late dinner, and by the time we finish up, it's already getting dark out.

There's a band setting up under the large wooden pergola, and the palm trees are all lit with warm, twinkling lights.

"Ooh, we should join the party for our last night!" my mom tells us, and I'm not sure what's shifted, but I actually want to.

Luca leans in closer to me, bringing his lips to my ear, and whispers, "Come on, princess. Let's show them our new moves. It *is* Sunday." He presses a kiss to the skin just below my ear, and a shiver races through me.

I nod. "Sure."

His hand settles on my thigh. "Really?"

"Mhmm."

He squeezes my leg, and my thighs clench, accidentally trapping his hand there. He chuckles against my ear. "That's okay, princess. You can keep my hand. I didn't need it for anything but you anyway."

I grab his wrist, moving it back to my thigh as my family starts to get up, making their way over to the dance floor in front of the band.

Luca pushes out of his chair, the metal feet scraping across the ground, but his hand never leaves my lap. As he hovers over me, he drags his hand up my body from my thigh to my soft tummy and over the side of my breast before making his descent down my arm to grasp my hand.

He helps me out of my chair, gathering me into his strong arms and warm embrace. I tell myself this is all for show. That we're just giving my family the final push to really sell this fake relationship, but somewhere buried deep inside, I know that's not true.

I like Luca.

I like Luca a lot.

And it might be the scariest thing I'll ever do.

He nuzzles his face into my neck, not having to bend much thanks to my nearly six-foot height and the added boost from my heels. I slide my hands up his firm chest and feel the heat radiating off him through his thin light-blue shirt. He looks insanely good in linen fabric, and I'm a little jealous that he can pull off white shorts.

"You smell so damn good, baby." He moans, and the sound goes straight to my clit.

I nip the side of his neck, and I'm rewarded with a low rumble that vibrates through his chest and into my own.

He unwraps himself from me but maintains his hold on my hand, walking me over to the dance floor.

We catch the end of a song, and my parents finish in the center of the floor, with my dad spinning my mom dramatically before pulling her back into him.

Everyone cheers, and the huge smile lighting her face brings one to mine too. "Alright, princess, I'll follow your lead," Luca says to me, keeping his voice low. A giggle slips from my lips, and I smack my hand over my mouth, my eyes wide from the sound coming from my own mouth.

"Did you just—" Luca lifts a hand to my forehead. "You don't *feel* like you have a fever, but..."—he checks my cheeks too, and I squirm under him—"you just *giggled*."

I roll my eyes playfully, dropping my hand back to my side.

He gathers my hands in his, dragging me to the center of the dance floor. "Have you ever danced bachata?" I ask him, and he nods.

"I have, but not often or recently."

"Just let the music take you where you wanna go," I tell him as the band starts playing a new song.[2]

The beat is slow, and the male lead begins singing as Luca pulls our arms to our sides. His molten gaze singes me as our feet mingle together, and he slides his hand behind my back, maintaining his grip on my right hand.

The song has a fast buildup, but it's long enough to allow us the time we need to adjust to one another's movements.

The singer's voice has trailed off, but returns quickly, the man's deep baritone fills the space around us. The song hits a peak, and that's the moment I realize what I'm *really* in for tonight.

What started as quick foot movements and swaying hips has very quickly turned into so much *more.*

Luca slides his hand down to the base of my spine, keeping our hips tucked together as my hand travels up his arm and around his neck. I grip the hair at the base of his skull, doing my best to stay in his grasp. Though something tells me, *he'd never let me go.*

---

2. **Yo No Sé Mañana – Luis Enrique**

"Yo no sé mañana," the man sings, and as if the moment couldn't be any more telling, it's a song about not knowing what tomorrow holds.

There's a push and pull in the song, so that's exactly what our bodies do. My hand trails down to his chest, and he maneuvers his body so our legs are staggered. I push off his chest as he maintains his grip on me, pulling himself into me. Our pelvises line up with one another, but I push off him as he drags me back in.

The song talks about living in the moment and not waiting for tomorrow to show affection to the people you love.

I turn my face away from his as he twirls me out before winding me back up into his arms. My low back extends, and he plants his hands firmly above my ass, providing the stability I need to dip backward. My gaze lands on the smiling faces of my family, and my chest fills with warmth.

My tense muscles relax, and I feel myself finally ready to let go. *Just for tonight.*

Luca spins us so our backs are pressed to one another, and we sway our hips, our asses touching as we do, and our hands are intertwined overhead.

He twirls us back together, and this time, his hands are covering my ass, grinding me into him. There's a feral glint in his eyes, and my breaths become shallow.

God, he's gorgeous.

"You're fucking stunning, princess," he mutters, twining one of his hands into my hair, pulling my face into his shoulder as we dance in place, our hips continuing to sway with the beat, but we're both working to catch our breath.

"We can't let your parents show us up, sweetheart." He breathes into my ear before pushing me away from him, only to draw me back in. We maintain about a foot of space between us as he holds one of my hands and presses his other to my lower belly. Luca leans his top half forward, and I mirror him, shimmying our shoulders and pressing our foreheads together for a beat before he spins me so my back is pressed to his front.

We press ourselves tightly together, grinding against each other as we sway our hips, and I slide down his body and back up. Luca drags his hands up my sides and pulls my arms up and over our heads, as he rests his cheek against the side of my head.

My pulse is racing, and my thighs burn with the effort it takes to stay upright while this gorgeous man has me in his arms, and I feel like I could shatter in his embrace.

When the song begins to speed up for the last time, Luca must be able to tell because he widens his stance, lowering himself into a squat, and positions me over his right leg, settling me down onto him. I jump off his leg, smiling brightly as he pulls me back onto his thigh, my legs swinging backward and then to the front to straddle him as I grind against his knee. He bucks his leg up, pulling me into him, and as the song comes to a close, he twirls me out, my left arm and his right fully extended before he rolls me back into his chest, tugging me tightly to him. Everyone claps loudly, whistling at the couples still left on the dance floor, and of course, my parents are included.

They have such wide smiles as they look dreamily into each other's eyes, and I can't help the pang I feel in my chest.

I want that.

The next song is "Mi Corazoncito."[3] Frustration flares through me at just how annoyingly perfect these songs are for describing the feelings even I don't fully understand. It's a song about heartache, regret, desire for reconciliation, and the rollercoaster of emotions that can be felt during the back and forth of a relationship you aren't sure is meant to be but can't seem to keep fighting.

Luca and I maintain eye contact as he walks backward, very dramatically might I add. He keeps about two yards between us, and as the music speeds up, he starts to mirror my movements, bending his elbows and shifting his weight from one foot to the next.

We close the distance between us, and he reaches out for my hands, drawing them into his chest and holding them there as we bounce around one another with quick steps. Luca's smoldering gaze shifts to a small grin, making that dimple I hate to love pop out from the corner of his mouth. "How do you do that with your hips?" he asks.

I look down between us, trying to figure out what he means because he looked like he was doing fine all on his own.

I drag my hands down his chest, reveling in the way his muscles ripple under my touch, before removing them and taking a step back, standing in front of his on flat feet. "I think the heels help a bit because it has the balls of my feet already in the right position for it, but"—I point to either side of my hips—"you kind of shift your weight between one foot to the next, moving your hips like a washing machine."

---

3. **Mi Corazoncito – Aventura**

He smirks. "A washing machine?"

A loud laugh escapes me, but I rest my hands on his hips. "Mirror my movements, hip up, roll your abdomen into the movement, and bend this knee"—I point to the opposite one—"and end on the ball of this foot."

He does as I say, and no surprise to anyone, he executes it perfectly. "Yep, just like that. Now do it again but on the other side."

"Like this?" he asks, snaking his hands out to grab my hands, twining his fingers through them.

I nod, my breath caught in my throat as he runs his lips over my knuckles. "Thanks, *principessa,*" he murmurs, dragging my body back into his.

Something tells me this man knew exactly what he was doing the whole time.

He moves us around the center of the dance floor, spinning me out and twirling me back into his body. When the song hits a high point, we pull away from one another, our hands still interlocked as I twist, and we drop to the floor with my legs straight and core tight like a plank. Luca keeps me hovering a foot off the ground before dragging me back up against his hard chest. My hands rest on his chest, and he runs a thumb over my cheek, tucking my hair back behind my ear.

He pulls me in close, rolling his hips against mine. He groans low in my ear, his warm breath tickling my skin. "Fuck, princess. This wasn't supposed to get me so hard, especially not in public," he whines.

I love the sound of this man, desperate and always so needy. He makes sure I know exactly what he's thinking all the time, and I appreciate it as someone who has to rely on my own perception of a situation all the time. Sometimes it's nice just to have someone tell me what they're thinking instead of making me guess. It gets exhausting.

"Sounds like a personal problem," I whisper, not bothering to hide the laughter from my voice.

"We *are* a couple, Samara. We could tackle it together," he says, sliding his hands down my sides and cupping my ass so my front is pressed against him.

By divine intervention, the song changes again.[4] It gives me the opportunity to swing out of his grasp, a playful smile turning my lips as I dance around him. I don't miss the loud groan he releases before shaking his limbs out and positioning himself in front of me.

I *also* don't miss the massive bulge in his dress slacks that he's got tucked into the waistband.

Damn this man and his perfect dick.

Luca places his hands on my hips, dropping down low and spinning me around before he pops back up, taking my hands in his and staggering us so my knee is between his.

This song is a lot more upbeat; our movements are faster, and when he spins me out, he winks over at my dad, who swaps with him. Suddenly, my dad and I are dancing, and my mom is in Luca's arms. She has her head thrown back, laughing loudly at something he's said.

---

4. **Tengo Un Amor – Toby Love**

"Cyaan kip yuh yeye dem offa 'im cyaah you?"[5] my dad asks, smirking at me.

A small grin forms on my lips, and I shake my head, turning my attention fully on him.

"Hard not to," I admit.

"Yuh difrent wid 'im. Mi hav neva si yuh like dis bifuor wid nobady else. Mi like ih," he says.[6]

Heat creeps over my cheeks, and I avert my gaze, but Dad swings me out, and he and Luca execute a perfect swap. I'm now back in Luca's arms, and his warmth is radiating into me like a furnace.

"Your mom wants us to get married and have your babies. She recognizes the error of her ways and now sees that Jasiel isn't the better man," he tells me with a confident smile.

"Mhmm, I'm sure. And what'd you tell her?" I ask, curiosity getting the better of me.

He pulls me into his chest, winding an arm up and twining his fingers through my hair as his other hand rests just above my ass over the bare skin of my backless dress. "I gave her the PG version of what I'm really thinking," he murmurs.

"And what's the R-rated version?"

"I'll give you anything you want, princess. I'd gladly fill you up and leave you begging for more of me."

---

5. Jamaican Patois: "Can't keep your eyes off of him, can you?"

6. Jamaican Patois: "You're different with him. I've never seen you like this before with anyone else. I like it."

My thighs clench, and I can't muster up any words for him because right now, *I couldn't think of a better idea.*

We continue dancing for the next hour, the sun setting on the horizon, lighting the sky up with beautiful shades of pink and purple. Luca takes turns dancing with Mom, Vea, and even my dad. When I'm beyond exhausted, and my feet are swollen, he sets me up with a chair to rest my feet on before going back out on the dance floor for one last dance with my nieces and nephews after the previous thirty minutes of them begging for a dance with him.

It's adorable, and I sincerely hate to admit that.

The palms of my hands sting from clapping so much by the time he's done, and the band announces they've got one more song for the night.

Luca approaches me with his arm extended. "May I have this dance, princess?" he asks, and Vea whistles at us, shooting me a suggestive wink.

Reluctantly, I stand, taking his hand in mine as the band finishes getting ready for the last song of the night.

"You ready to do it up big?" Luca asks me with a sly grin.

I shake my head, but my smile gives me away. "Only because it's the last one," I tell him.

"Yes, ma'am," he says, smirking.

His multicolored eyes glitter under the soft lights around us, and my heart tightens in my chest, my pulse speeding up as the band begins to play the last song.[7]

---

7. **Corazón Sin Cara – Prince Royce**

This band and their impeccable music selection is gonna do me in. This is my all-time favorite bachata song. It's about love, vulnerability, and *self-acceptance.*

By this point, Luca has totally mastered this dance style. We start off easy, working around one another, shifting to stay in-line with each other while staying as close as possible.

He's not only rolling his hips but his shoulders now too. He drags the back of his knuckles over my cheek and runs his palm over my side. A shiver runs down my spine from where his fingertips settle over the exposed flesh along my back.

We pull away from one another, but he grips my hands, and I roll my neck into the movement, my hair cascading in an arch around me.

When I right myself, Luca's lips are parted slightly and his eyes are glassy. He blinks rapidly, swallowing hard and sucking in a strained breath through his nose.

He snaps out of his daze, bringing my back to his front and winding our right arms over my head and our left arms in front of my abdomen. He turns me again to face him, breaking the connection between our hands but dragging his over my hair and down my body.

Our bodies move in sync as if perfectly created for one another.

My mind feels foggy as I take in this perfect moment.

This man is more than I could've ever anticipated, and the way my body lights up for him leaves me in a daze. I don't feel like myself at all, and I'm not even sure I don't like it. What disturbs me most is that I think I *do.*

He makes me feel alive and wanted. My body is on fire, and my heart is about to explode as my pulse skyrockets. Luca drags me into him, winding his arms tightly around my midsection and upper back as he extends his back, dragging our bodies in a circle. He swings me out, pulling me back into his firm grip before spinning me with an arm over my head. As the end of the song approaches, he rolls his hips into mine again, matching my steps and stepping farther into my space.

He runs the tip of his nose along the side of my neck, nipping at the skin. He whispers huskily, "Ready, *principessa?*"

I nod stupidly because I don't have a clue for what.

Next thing I know, I'm being spun out, twirled back into his arms and dipped so low I feel my hair graze the floor before he pulls me back up and wraps his arms around me in a tight hug, swaying us side to side. My heartbeat hammers violently against my chest.

We're panting, and everyone is cheering loudly. My whole family is clapping and whistling at us, and as much as Luca's stolen the breath straight from my lungs, I'm not sure I've ever felt better.

Fireworks crackle through the sky, turning everyone's attention away from us and back to the bright colors erupting over the glass-like water. It's beautiful, but nothing could be as stunning as the look on Luca's face as he smiles down at me.

Chapter Sixty-Six

Luca

I'm glad we decided not to call it an early night because as exhausted as I am, I wouldn't change a single thing about the way we just spent our last night here.

I'd never admit this to anyone because I'd run the risk of sounding like Alessandro's sappy ass, but tonight was... magical.

I had a great time today and really loved getting to know Samara's family, but they're just as tiring as she'd said they were. Which happens to be very similar to my experience with my own family, though I think my family fuels me more than drains me, most days anyway.

I lie in bed, pulling out my phone to call Cici, but before I do, I watch as Samara grabs her clothes out of her bag and heads to the bathroom. "You need help in the shower, sweetheart?" I call out like the cheeky ass that I am.

"Screw you, Luca," she says, rolling her eyes at me, but I don't miss the little grin she's wearing.

I don't even get Cici's contact up before Samara's backpedaling out of the bathroom wearing a completely different expression.

"Something wrong, princess?" I ask, nerves settling into my gut.

"I just realized," she says, biting her bottom lip. *Fuck, I wish it were my teeth sunken into that plump flesh.*

"Realized what, sweetheart?"

"We never used the hot tub." She juts her chin out to the patio.

My eyes widen, and I swear to god, my dick salutes this woman on the spot. He's a soldier, ready and waiting for her command.

Samara saunters past me, her ass swishing as she does, and the movement drives me wild.

I practically catapult out of the bed to follow after her, and when she gets to the sliding glass doors, drawing back the curtains, she undoes the zipper on her dress, looks over her shoulder at me with a sly smirk, and drops it to the floor. The fabric pools around her feet, and I know I'm a fucking goner.

Next thing I know, I'm sprinting out of here, tearing my clothes off like a madman, tossing them over my shoulder, and leaving a mess in my wake. Samara has the hot tub bubbling already as she sits on the ledge, dangling her feet inside. She gathers her hair into a bun on the top of her head. Stray strands fall around her beautiful face, framing her high cheekbones.

God bless her genetics because Kemar and Camila created a fucking angel.

I've never in my life met a woman as flawless as she is.

"If you're done drooling over there, feel free to pick your jaw up off the floor and climb in. The water's heating up quickly," she says with a grin.

I climb in, taking a seat beside where her legs are dangling in the water.

My breaths come in quick spurts, and I work to calm my racing heart down. Samara gives me a small, content smile before closing her eyes and leaning back slightly onto her palms.

I tentatively stroke the side of her calf with my thumb, trailing it down her ankle. She sucks in a breath but doesn't complain.

Her feet and ankles are swollen from dancing and those sexy heels she's always wearing.

It's a love-hate relationship for me.

They accentuate her impossibly long legs, making her look even more delectable, but they also look so painful that I resent them for causing her any discomfort at all.

I have a visceral reaction to the idea of that and have to remind myself I'm talking about a pair of *shoes* right now.

My hands wrap around one of her feet, dragging it into my lap, which makes her pretty thighs part, and I consider begging her to let me put my face between them for just a minute. I dig my thumb into the heel of her foot, and her eyes burst open, her lips parting as she sucks in a breath.

"Too much?" I ask, relaxing my hands and applying less pressure.

She shakes her head. "No, it's perfect." Her voice is practically a whisper.

The cool air and dark sky surrounding us make this feel like the most intimate moment we've shared, and we've been sleeping in the same bed all weekend.

I continue rubbing her feet, working my hands up and down her strong calves, and revel in every moan and hitch in her breathing.

My lids feel heavier with each passing minute, and when she seems totally blissed out and ready for bed, I press a kiss to the inside of her knee before picking her up and taking her back to our room.

She winds her arms around my neck, sleepily shaking her head at me with a small smile on her lips. “Thank you,” she whispers.

I dip my head, pressing a light kiss to her temple and setting her back on her feet.

“Anytime, princess.”

“I’m gonna take that shower now. You calling Cici before bed?”

I nod. “I’ll text first since it’s late. If she’s already asleep, I can wait for her call in the morning.”

She reaches out and squeezes my hand before gathering her things and heading to the bathroom.

***

“Gia doing okay?” Samara asks me as she sits on the edge of the bed, detangling her curls and getting ready to put them up in a protective style, just like she does every night. I like that I get to see her like this. Just doing mundane, everyday things that show me little bits of herself.

An easy smile crosses my face. “Yeah, it looks that way. Cici’s doing a really great job with her, but fuck, I miss her,” I admit.

I see Samara’s expression twist in the closet mirror. “Cecily or Gia?” she asks.

“Princess, are you *jealous*?” I ask, a slow smirk stretching my lips.

"Don't be ridiculous. Of course not." She waves a hand through the air. "I'm just trying to gauge how quickly I'll have to tell my parents we split up," she says matter-of-factly. Unfortunately for her, I see right through her, and not only that, but my ego's big enough to withstand her bullshit.

"Keep telling yourself that." I chuckle, lying back with my arms tucked under my head. "And for the record, I have no interest in Cici. I'm thankful to have her support and want nothing more than for us to effectively co-parent for our daughter, but that's all there is to it."

Our eyes lock in the mirror, but neither of us speaks another word. I can tell she's fighting herself right now. Hell, probably biting her tongue so she doesn't have to deny how she feels about me and subsequently lying all in the same breath.

What she may not realize is that everything about tonight showed me how she really feels, and there's no going back now. Not for me, at least.

***

Samara's lying beside me, reading her book. I keep stressing about Gia, and my thoughts are racing as I worry about all the things I could've done *already* that might've messed her up for the future.

It's annoying how tired we'd both been, but sometimes when I reach that point of sheer exhaustion and don't go to sleep right away, it messes with me. I have trouble falling asleep, and my mind doesn't seem to want to shut off.

I roll over to face Samara, and she immediately rests her book on her stomach. She rolls over to me, and her eyes are glancing at me like I'm about to start talking when she doesn't want me to. It's an expression I've become incredibly familiar with.

"What is it?" she grumbles.

"When you agreed to work with me, I know that was only as a favor to Rome. But with your other clients..." I trail off, unsure of how to phrase this.

"With my other clients, what, Luca?" She sounds wary.

"How do you know if they'll be good enough?"

She narrows her eyes at me, closing her book and setting it on the nightstand before propping herself up on an elbow to face me. "Good enough for what?" she asks, tilting her head.

"To be a parent, I guess. I'm wondering how you decide the parent is worth your time, and if they're actually going to be worthy of that child."

Her expression softens a fraction as she considers my words. "Luca, I'm not God," she says, her voice soft. "I don't know, hell, I don't think *anyone* knows who's fit to be a parent or even what that constitutes. I do the best I can to make an informed decision about who I want to work with, but that's the best I *can* do."

"Do you research your clients before you work with them?"

"Of course I do. I research all of my clients because, unfortunately, I can't trust them to tell me every bit of the truth. That doesn't make them a bad person either. We all have things we're embarrassed by and wouldn't want to openly admit to someone, including things we'd done so long ago we may not even remember doing them. That's part of my job. To make sure that if it can be found by someone else, I find it first, so I know how to handle it when in court," she explains, lying on her side, facing me in the dimly lit room.

Something about the way she says this doesn't sit right with me. There's something missing. "Samara," I tread lightly.

"Mhmm?" she mumbles, yawning.

"Is that the reason you had such a problem with me when we first met?" She quirks a brow, so I elaborate. "When you looked into me, did you find something you didn't like? Is that why you hated me?"

Her expression is inscrutable as she shifts uncomfortably. "I did," is all she says.

"And what was it?" I ask, prying the information out of her because there are about a million things she could've found that would have left her with a bad taste in her mouth, and I wouldn't even fault her for it.

She stares at me for an uncomfortable amount of time, chewing on her bottom lip as she decides what to say, if anything. By the time she finally answers, I'm nearly convinced she was going to just roll over and ignore me, but what she says next knocks the fucking wind out of my lungs.

"I came across an article that showed a picture of you heading into a non-profit reproductive care clinic with an unidentified woman." The moment the words are spoken, I feel my stomach plummet. I know exactly which article she's referring to, and not a single thing in it is true.

"Samara, I know the article. And I can assure you that not only is none of it true, but that I'd never do any of the things I was accused of," I tell her, keeping my voice firm.

Her eyes look sad as she meets mine. "Explain it to me then, please." Her voice breaks on the last word.

I shake my head. "I can't."

Her brows pinch together in confusion. "Why not?"

I take a chance, moving to the center of the bed to pull her against me. And to my immense surprise, she doesn't pull away or give me shit for it. "Because, sweetheart," I whisper into her hair, "*It isn't my story to tell.*"

Chapter Sixty-Seven

Samara

It isn't my story to tell.

As much as it annoys me to not know the full story, especially because I'm now really starting to believe I have it all wrong, I respect him for not telling me.

And as for the cuddling situation, I have little fight left in me when it comes to him. It's been so long since I've trusted someone just to hold me, let alone get any comfort from doing so.

It feels *nice* to be held. So, just for tonight, I allow myself this seemingly simple pleasure as I melt against his hard chest and nestle my face in closer to him. I take a deep breath, filling my lungs with the intoxicating scent of citrus, leather, and amber.

Luca rolls onto his back, dragging me on top of him as he keeps one arm secured around my waist.

I feel him reach over for the lamp, and a moment later, the room is filled with a calm darkness. His calloused fingers rake over the skin of my lower back, pressing soothing circles just above the waistband of my sleep shorts.

He cups my jaw, gently angling my face toward his, and still, I make no move to pull away.

His warm breath and sweet words are like a caress over my lips. "Thank you, princess."

"What for?" I ask, confused.

"*For this.* For not pushing me to tell you more, even though I know the wheels are turning and you really want answers." My heart cracks open wide, the contents spilling free. "For just being here, holding me and letting me hold you," he whispers, his voice sounding broken. Luca presses a gentle kiss to my forehead before moving his hand from my jaw to wrap it around my ribs.

I close my eyes, unable to formulate a response, and allow my actions to speak louder than words ever could.

It doesn't take long before I'm drifting off to sleep.

Chapter Sixty-Eight

Luca

Monday, August 31, 2026

Soft moans are the first thing I notice as I start to wake up. My name, spoken in a desperate cry, is the next.

I open my eyes, adjusting to the lack of light, and goddamn do I wish I had good lighting right now.

Samara is still on top of me, similar to how she had been when we fell asleep last night, but now, her hands are gripping the sheets beside my waist as she rolls her hips against my thigh, seeking the friction she's apparently desperate for.

My dick is already rock hard, pulsing with need for her.

I run my fingertips up her arm, trying to get her attention, but the more I take her in, the more I realize *she isn't awake.*

Fucking hell. What are the rules of consent for something like this? Do I wake her up? Do I let her ride it out... literally?

I shake my head, clearing my thoughts and the cobwebs still residing from the last few hours of sleep.

"Samara," I say, trying to speak clearly despite the arousal sinking into my bones. She continues with her soft cries, completely unaware.

Bringing my hand to the base of her neck, I tug on the roots of her thick hair. "Samara, wake up."

Her body loosens, the noises stop, and finally, her eyelids burst open, frantically meeting my eyes. "Hey there, princess, don't let me stop you," I tell her, trying to break the tension.

Her bottom lip juts out before she drags it through her teeth. Her dark brows pinch together.

We stare at each other for an agonizingly long moment before she says, "*Please*."

The word comes out like a puff of air. Her voice filled with need.

"Please?" I question.

"I'm..." She casts her eyes away from me, refusing to meet my gaze. "God, I'm so fucking horny."

Excitement flutters through me. "Like I said, *don't let me stop you*."

Her eyes shoot up to mine, and she sharpens her gaze before saying, "No sex. That's the rule."

"You have lots of rules, sweetheart," I joke. "But okay, no sex. Just use my body and get yourself off. I'll just enjoy the show." I smirk, removing my hands from her and resting my head on my forearms.

She eyes me tentatively but ultimately decides to take what she wants.

I watch intensely as she shifts her weight, bringing the leg from between mine to the outside of my thigh. She straddles me, hovering over my cock before lowering herself down.

"Oh fuck." I groan, squeezing my eyes tightly shut to clear my thoughts. But when she rests her hands on my chest and starts to grind her hips onto me, I can't stop the sounds that rip from my throat.

Samara throws her head back, her full breasts straining against her white T-shirt as she takes her pleasure. "Yes," she cries. "You feel so good, and you're not even inside me."

The retort is on the tip of my tongue, but I bite down, restraining myself.

My fists clench under my head. The desire to reach out and touch her, to drag my thumbs over her nipples or sink my fingers into her luscious hips, is overwhelming. My dick is pulsating, twitching with excitement as heat sears through my every cell.

"That's it, *principessa.* Take what you want, sweetheart," I beg. I want her release just as bad as she does.

Her pussy lips hug my shaft through her thin pajama shorts, her wet heat seeping through the thin fabric.

"Oh god." She moans loudly, her movements speeding up, becoming more erratic as she meets her release. "Yes!" she cries. Her hips continue moving frantically in an attempt to continue the pleasure rolling through her. My hands jut forward, gripping her hips as I take over for her, allowing her to just relax into me, taking what she wants and feeling the ache in her core subside.

When she goes quiet and her body slumps against mine, I have to Kegel a handful of times to will the blood from my cock back into my body. Of course, it barely works with her still lying on top of me.

Samara rolls off, lying beside me. "Thanks," is all she says, her voice uncharacteristically small.

"Anytime, princess." I chuckle. And I do mean that. *Anytime* she needs me, for an orgasm or anything else for that matter, I'll be here at her disposal.

***

I came harder than I ever had in my life in the shower after Samara got dressed and started packing.

We'll have breakfast with her family, and then we'll say our goodbyes and head to the airport.

"You almost ready to go?"

"Yep," I tell her, grabbing my phone off the nightstand as it begins to ring. "*Arielle*" flashes across the screen, and my heart jumps to my throat. "Hey, I've gotta take this. I'll be ready in a few," I say, heading outside.

"Hey, Arielle, everything okay?"

"Of course it is, silly." She laughs. "I just figured I'd call and let you know your kid is doing great."

My thoughts derail. "Wait, she's with you?"

"Yeah, Cici has her private therapy session and an hour-long group session this morning, so she asked me to come over and hang out with Gia until she's done."

Every muscle in my body begins to loosen. I blow out a deep breath. "Oh, thanks, *sorellina.*[1] I hope Gia isn't giving you a hard time."

---

1. Italian: "Little sister."

"Not at all! She's much sweeter than her father." She laughs. "Now, tell me how your trip is going! Has Samara finally caught up and decided to allow herself to fall in love with you?"

Shaking my head, I laugh and tell her, "Nobody is falling in love with anyone here."

That's dead wrong, and the words feel sour on my tongue. There's silence for a moment before Arielle says, "You already know you have feelings for her, right?"

There's no point in denying it, especially when my family is all up in each other's business. "Yes." I groan, not loving where this conversation is headed.

"Great, now have you figured out what's holding *her* back?"

"Yeah, actually." I tread lightly.

"Go on now, tell me," Arielle prods.

"Last night, she admitted that she looked into me before we started working together and..." I clear my throat.

"Jesus Christ, just spit it out, *stronzetto.*"

"She found that article from when I brought you to the clinic." It takes a moment to finally get the words out, but when I do, it feels like I'm choking on them. I do my best to never make her relive that day, so it's hard to utter a single word about it now.

"And she believes the reporter's lies?" she guesses.

"I think she's starting to question the legitimacy of it, but when she asked me about it last night, I probably didn't do myself any favors by telling her I couldn't explain what really happened."

"And why on earth would you do that?" she asks, raising her voice.

"Arielle, just like I told Samara last night, *that is not my story to tell.*"

She says nothing for several beats of silence. "Then I'll tell her."

Shaking my head, I say, "No, Arielle, you don't have to do that. She's just got to learn to trust me, and if I said it isn't what she thinks, then she needs to believe that if there's a chance of anything working between us anyway."

"Luca, you don't know what that woman has been through, and neither do I. But if I've learned anything in my life, it's that women like Samara aren't guarded without reason. Just consider that she may not be capable of blindly trusting, and that might not be her fault either. It isn't usually something we choose," she reminds me.

"Hopefully, I can earn her trust another way, but sharing that day with her won't be how I do it. Please, don't worry about it, okay, Arielle? I promise that if things between us are meant to work, they will. I've gotta go. We need to meet her family for breakfast and head to the airport. Thanks for watching Gia; give her hugs and kisses for me."

Shockingly, she drops the previous conversation. "Of course I will. I'll send you a bunch of pictures soon. Have a safe flight home," she tells me before hanging up.

Chapter Sixty-Nine

Samara

"Wasn't this so great, Samara?" my mom prods, wanting recognition for her idea.

"Yep, it was a lot of fun. I'm glad we could make it," I tell her with a small smile, hoping she'll stop now that she's gotten what she wanted.

"You know, if you quit being a workaholic, you could settle down, start a family, and really begin to enjoy all of that money you've been working so hard for." And just like that, all hopes of a peaceful last day of vacation are shattered.

"I *enjoy* my job. Have you ever considered that?" I ask, unable to keep the misery out of my voice.

I feel Luca's large hand settle on my thigh, gripping me gently, but he says nothing.

"Of course you enjoy it. I never said you had to quit!" Mom tosses her hands in the air, exasperated, as if she isn't the exhausting one. "But children are just so much fun, and having a partner to come home to every day is a different kind of joy!" She turns her attention to my side, settling her gaze on Luca. His hand tightens around my thigh, and I place my hand on top of his. "Don't you agree, Luca?"

She stares at him expectantly, but he doesn't answer for a long moment. The whole table goes quiet as they wait for him to reply. To say *anything*.

His bright eyes meet mine, and he dips his head, bringing his lips a hair's width from my ear. "Do you want to go cool off for a minute inside, and I'll thank your family so we can get out of here without starting a war?"

My shoulders slump at his words. My family may not have heard him but thank god I did because I want nothing more than to get out of here. I give him a small nod and pry his hand from my lap before pushing out of my chair to stand. "It was great seeing you all, and thank you for inviting me," I tell my family, smiling tightly.

I head inside to use the restroom and hope that Luca is ready to go by the time I get out.

Chapter Seventy

Luca

The moment Samara is inside, my eyes are pinning her mother to her seat.

"I appreciate you all welcoming me on your family vacation. For the most part, I had an incredible time, and I really hope you all did too. But I can't leave without saying this one thing." I shake my head, sincerely disappointed that they don't see it—they don't see *her* or what their words do to her.

"I genuinely don't think the way you speak to her is intentionally malicious," I say, but Camila tries to cut me off.

Kemar shakes his head, taking her hand in his, and presses a kiss to the back of it, urging her to let me speak.

I nod, silently thanking him before continuing. "You've raised an incredible woman. I mean, really, you should all be so unbelievably proud of her. She's feisty and compassionate and so damn smart." I'm baffled that it isn't obvious. "And I'm sure you all already know that about her because you'd have to be blind not to. But despite her composure, your words cut her. It's clear as day to me that the reason she works her ass off in the first place is to make you all proud. It's her way of thanking you for the sacrifices you made for her and Vea."

"There were no sacrifices," Camila tries to argue, but Vea shuts her down this time.

"Ma, let him finish," she says.

I nod at her in silent thanks. "From what I've seen, you're a kind and loving family, and I don't think you even realize you're doing it. Genuinely, I don't," I tell them as they stare at me in confusion, unsure of what I mean by "it."

"From the first day we arrived, it was obvious to me that you all love Samara, but the way you speak to her and *about* her is not okay. In the beginning, it just pissed me off." Her mom's eyes widen a fraction as I admit this. "But now? I realize you think you're helping her or, at the very least, making sure she knows you're concerned for her well-being. But that isn't how she sees it, and truthfully, from an outside perspective, it isn't how it comes across at all. Even though she won't admit it, all the time she spends working is to prove herself to you guys. She wants to make you proud, and having to hear your comments about how she needs to stop working so much to make a man happy or how she needs to prioritize herself if she ever wants a family doesn't help her. It just makes her feel more and more like she isn't good enough and doesn't fit in with her own family."

"And she's told you this?" Camila asks.

I shake my head. "No, she hasn't. And I should know by now not to put words in that woman's mouth," I admit with a humorless chuckle. "But it's exactly how I sometimes feel when my family jokes around with me. I know they don't mean to make me feel the way they do, but that doesn't mean it doesn't happen on occasion."

Camila reaches out the hand that Kemar isn't holding, and I meet her in the middle, squeezing gently. My eyes soften as I meet hers. "Maybe try to see things from her point of view and take a step back before you lose her for good. People can only take so much before they shut down, and I can see it. She's teetering over that line."

I give her hand another squeeze before I stand from my seat, taking in their pinched expressions before I turn to leave. I see Samara heading toward the door from inside, and just as I'm making my way to her, I hear Camila's soft voice behind me. "Thank you," she whispers, her voice sounding watery.

I make it to the door just in time. Wrapping my arm around Samara's waist, I revel in the feel of her against me.

I know this vacation is almost over, and that means our fake relationship is, too, but it doesn't feel like this is the end for us. My chest feels tight as I realize just *how real* this whole thing has become for me.

This isn't fake anymore, at least *not for me.*

"You ready, princess?"

She nods. "More than you know."

Chapter Seventy-One

Samara

We're waiting at baggage claim, so I turn airplane mode off, staring at my screen as all of my missed messages come rolling in.

One in particular catches my eye.

Arielle

I hope you guys had a great vacation! Any chance you have a free moment to grab lunch with me tomorrow?

My fingers flit over the buttons, ready to tell her that I could make time for her, but something catches me off guard.

Luca is suddenly surrounded by a crowd of gorgeous women, all fawning over him as they flirt. A tall brunette trails her fingers down his bicep, and he steps out of her grasp. His uncomfortable smile stays plastered in place as he searches the area for me, and when his eyes land on me, he lets out a long breath. He excuses himself from the women, shaking his head as he stands by my side.

"Sorry, princess. They swarmed me," he says with a laugh.

I nod and turn my attention back to my phone screen, erasing the message I'd typed out.

Sorry, first day back at work. No time. Rain check?

There's no point in getting even more attached to Luca's family when I won't be sticking around after the wedding anyway. Even if Luca and I could manage to make things work between us, there's not a chance in hell I could deal with the constant attention he gets.

Nausea roils through me, and I suddenly can't wait to be home.

Chapter Seventy-Two

Luca

Tuesday, September 1, 2026

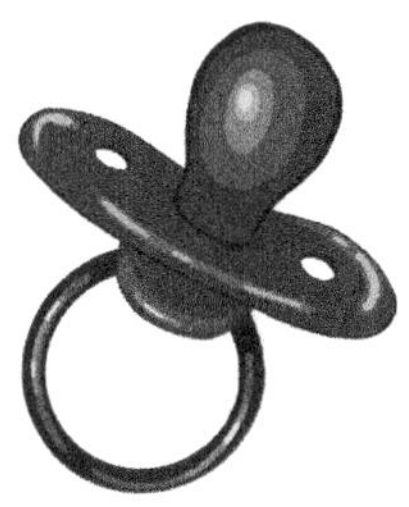

I'm already dragging ass, and for once, it isn't Gia's fault. No, *she* slept great, actually. I, on the other hand, cannot say the same. I was up all night watching her sleep, terrified that if I took my eyes off her, she'd disappear. And when I finally let myself relax, Samara's expression when those women were surrounding me at the airport haunted me all night long.

She barely spoke to me on the ride home, and when I texted her before bed, I never got a response.

Being away from Gia this weekend was harder on my mental health than I'd realized, and being *with* Samara makes it even more difficult to not have her around when I'm home. But I'm still glad I went. I had a great time, and Cici proved to herself that she could be responsible for Gia without anything bad happening.

We agreed to start rotating weekends going forward, and once the hockey season starts up, she'll take Gia the day before, during, and after my away games. That way, I don't have to worry about getting a sitter for her, and Cici gets about half the week with her at a time.

"Come on, Gia, let's get you off to Uncle Mateo's," I say, lifting her onto my thigh.

***

"Hey, man. Thanks for letting me mooch off your babysitter," I tell him.

"It's not a problem. Thanks for the ride," Mateo says as he dumps his gear into my trunk. "This week is about to be brutal. I've been slacking on my workouts," he tells me, climbing into the passenger seat.

"I feel that. I worked out once the entire weekend I was away, and I couldn't sleep for shit last night."

He closes his eyes, resting his head on the headrest.

"Just one day at a time. That's all we can do. We do this every year, and we're still around." He chuckles quietly.

***

"Come on, Luca! You're slow as shit! We're never gonna win a game if you don't actually block the goddamn pucks!" Coach hollers at me, exasperated with my piss-poor performance today.

"Sorry, Coach." I groan, knowing damn well there isn't a response in the world that'll save me from the absolute lashing I'm going to receive from him after training camp is over for the day.

He shakes his head, disappointment written blatantly on his face. Coach Allister turns his attention to the center of the room, pinning each of us with a withering glare. "Have any of you bothered to actually do your goddamn job and train *properly* in the offseason?"

Half of the team is standing here with our tails tucked between our legs. *That would be a no.*

"Figure it out!" he yells, stomping off toward the locker room.

An eerie quiet takes over the rink. We're all on edge, out of practice, and out of shape. But no one is as terrified to fuck up as I am.

My brother may be the assistant coach now, but even he won't save me if I mess this up. I'm only here because I proved I'm a good enough goaltender to make myself worth all the bullshit that follows me in the media. If I can't even keep a puck out of our net, I'm a goner.

And I can tell everyone in the room sees that based on the way they're all staring at me.

It won't take long. I'll get it together. I just need to stop the racing thoughts from distracting me.

***

"Goodnight, Gia, *mia bambina*," I coo, pressing a kiss to her forehead. Her eyes are closed, and her breathing has slowed as she sleeps peacefully.

I've got another long day ahead of me tomorrow, but I can't go to sleep without trying Samara one more time.

I send her a text.

Hey, princess. I hope you don't miss me too much.

Who am I kidding? *I'm the one who misses her.* Not the other way around, but fuck, I wish the feeling were mutual.

Chapter Seventy-Three

Samara

Luca's text strikes a nerve. Because, regretfully, I *do* miss him. And I hate that because it's the first time in years that I've allowed myself to have feelings for a man, and it *had* to be Luca De Laurentiis, heartbreaker extraordinaire. He may not intentionally do it, but having hordes of women trailing after him will inevitably weigh on me.

So, for that reason, I delete our message thread and try to get some sleep.

Chapter Seventy-Four

Luca

Sunday, September 6, 2026

This week, we don't have dance lessons because the studio is observing Labor Day today, and as much as my sore muscles need the break after the week I've endured, I miss the excuse to see Samara. Though I'm not sure she'd come anyway if how aloof she's been this past week is anything to judge that assumption by.

I've texted her a few times and even called her once. She did eventually respond and chalked it up to being busy with work after the weekend away, but I don't buy it. Samara's the kind of person who makes time for the things that matter to her, and I don't appear to be among them.

Despite the canceled dance lessons, Sunday dinner is still in full swing.

Chapter Seventy-Five

Samara

Wednesday, September 16, 2026

Arielle reached out again about grabbing lunch, and again, I declined. I'm hoping she takes the hint and doesn't ask again because I wouldn't be able to say no. Not three times in a row. Especially not since I actually *like* her.

But her brother-in-law has become a much larger part of my world than I'd ever imagined, and I have a feeling she knows that.

***

I hear a loud knock on my door, one I know belongs to my sister. "Come in!" I shout from the kitchen.

A moment later, I hear the click of the lock as she opens the door, letting herself in.

"Smells good, sis. What're you cookin'?"

"I need comfort food, so I'm making beans and rice, plantains, oxtail, and I made beef patty that I just need to warm up," I tell her, rummaging through a drawer for a spatula.

"Really digging into your roots tonight, huh, Mara?" she asks, pulling a blue velvet barstool up to the kitchen island.

"Guess so," I say, stirring the rice and beans. It's almost ready, and I'm starving.

"Why the need for comfort? Doesn't your man comfort you enough?" she asks, a dark brow arched, but I can read it in her expression. *She knows.*

I roll my eyes, focusing on the task at hand. "Don't try to bait me. Just say what's on your mind," I chide.

She leans forward on the counter, staring me down with her dark-brown eyes. "You and that man aren't together, but you wish you were," she muses.

"And I'm sure you have a lot of thoughts on that," I say, leaning back against the counter.

"Of course I do." She laughs. "But I think they might surprise you."

Well, there goes that. Consider me officially baited.

"Go on."

"Did you know he told off our entire family?"

That catches me off guard. My head whips in her direction, eyes locked on hers. The little smirk grazing her lips makes my stomach twist in knots.

"Yep. You got up to cool off, and he sat there, telling us all off about how much we underappreciate you, how incredible you are, and that while he knows we have good intentions, we don't show you love in the way you need it. You could say that I may have judged the book by its cover with him, but I'm finding that I like what's written on those pages." Her smirk remains in place as she twists her curls up in a pile on her head.

He defended me to my family?

The knots release, and in their place, a swarm of butterflies takes flight. Though it doesn't take long for me to swat them all down, doing my best to protect myself. I feel my meticulously spackled walls rebuilding around me.

"Mara, he's a good man, and he was respectful even while handing us our own asses. Besides," she says, glancing over at me again. "That man is nineties fine."

A full-bodied laugh spills out of me. "He absolutely is. He's sexy beyond reason," I agree, still unsure of what to say about the rest of what she just said.

Unfortunately, I don't have the time to dwell on that either because there's a knock at the door.

Vea scoots out of her chair, heading to answer the door for me. "Now, don't be mad, okay? You can kick them out at any point."

My stomach does another flip, and bile creeps up my throat. My appetite is suddenly gone.

***

My family's seated around my small, glass dining room table. Mom reaches out a hand for mine. It's an unfamiliar gesture, but I accept it, my muscles tense with anxiety.

"We don't want you to feel cornered, so please tell us to leave if you want to. We can have this conversation another time if that's what you need, but it's important that we *do* have this conversation at some point," Mom says.

I nod slowly, still in a daze.

"I'm sure Vea has already told you about our conversation with Luca, but we want to make a few things clear."

My stomach continues to churn, and my pulse is hammering behind my temples.

"You and Vea are the biggest blessings we could have ever hoped for, and we couldn't be more proud of either of you."

My muscles begin to relax, warmth seeping into my chest.

This may not seem like a lot, but they're the words of affirmation I'm realizing I've needed to hear for so long.

"Baby." She squeezes my hand. "I'm so sorry that I never realized we were hurting you. It doesn't make up for it, but I want you to know that the reason I talk about you settling down and having kids so much is because you and your sister are the best thing to have ever happened to me," she says, looking over at Dad.

"Tuh wi," he corrects. *To us.*

"We just want you to get to experience that, but we realize now that you'll do everything in your own time," she adds.

The next several minutes are spent like this. My family apologizes for things they've said that have hurt me, and it feels good to hear my thoughts validated. Now that they're aware of how they've impacted me, they understand it and feel bad about it. It's why I go on to apologize for the way I've sometimes spoken to them out of anger, feeling like a caged animal.

By the time they leave for the night, there's an overwhelming sense of relief that's settled into my being, and I'm even more grateful for my time with Luca than I had been before. Without him, we may have never gotten here.

Chapter Seventy-Six

Luca

Friday, September 25, 2026

I can't even express how excited I am for the wedding tomorrow, and despite Samara being distant tonight, I had a great time.

"Gia, *mia bambina*, come on, little girl. Let's head to your mommy's house."

Alessandro squeezes my shoulder, a big, dopey smile on his face. "Hey, you heading out?"

"Yeah, I've got to get Gia over to Cici's. She's gonna spend the weekend with her and head back over after the wedding, but I didn't want her to miss one of her days, so I told her I'd bring her over tonight."

"You guys are really doing this co-parenting thing, huh? I'm proud of you," he tells me. I hadn't realized how much my brother's approval would mean to me, but now that I have it, my heart feels like it's bursting wide open.

"Yeah." I smile at him. "I guess we are."

He gives me a hug, nearly crushing Gia between us as he does, and presses a kiss to her chubby cheek.

"What? No kiss for me?" I joke, but he leans in and makes a big show out of the fat, slobbery kiss he leaves on my forehead.

I wipe it off with the back of my hand, shaking my head as I head out to my car with a wide smile on my face.

Chapter Seventy-Seven

Samara

I've never been to a wedding where I felt so many emotions, and it isn't even the actual wedding day yet. I think I've fallen in love with this entire family, so much more than I'd ever intended to, and I can already feel the crushing weight on my shoulders at the idea of never seeing them again after this.

They've made me feel like I was a part of every detail, always remaining considerate of my wants and needs and never compromising them. It's been an honor to get to know these people.

Arielle's red hair swishes by as she joins me in the back of the dining hall, her bright-white smile plastered across her face. "Hey, mind if I pull you away for a few minutes? There's something I've been meaning to talk to you about, but I have a sneaking suspicion you've been avoiding me." She smirks.

I don't bother backpedaling; the lie would be evident. "Sure," I tell her, following after her as she leads us down a paved, tree-lined path.

"Luca told me you found the article," she says, surprising me because this is not where I'd expected the conversation to go.

"I did." I tread lightly.

"He also said that he told you it wasn't his story to tell."

I nod, agreeing. He definitely had said that.

"That's because it's mine," she says, stopping in the middle of the trail to face me.

What is that supposed to mean?

Before I can even ask her, she starts speaking, and I have a feeling my world is about to be tipped upside down.

"When I was sixteen, I ran away from home," she says, a pink blotchy flush starting to spread over her chest. "My father was abusive, my mom was nowhere to be found, and I figured I'd be better off on my own. And I was," she says with total certainty. "Until I met Jackson. He was charming and seemingly sweet, and of course, he let me move in with him. He made sure I had what I needed when I was with him, making it easy to strip me of everything I had for myself so I couldn't leave him." Her eyes turn glassy, and my throat feels tight. "Not easily anyway." She pauses, assessing me before going on. "By the time I was seventeen, he'd let his mask dissolve entirely. He'd beat me and spit in my face. And one night, when I refused him, he beat me until I was nearly unconscious and forced himself on me." She shakes her head, the memory of that night seeping into the forefront of her mind. I can tell it's something she doesn't think about often.

Unease spreads through me, hot tears pooling behind my eyes. An image of Cora flashes in my mind, and my heart wrenches with the thought.

I remain silent, allowing her the space she needs to tell her story or to stop if she no longer feels comfortable.

"He left me like that. Discarded by a dumpster, like trash." Her voice wobbles, and it sucks the last remnants of air from my lungs. "Dante found me when he was on his way home from a class at the university. He'd taken some late classes so he could be home during the day to help take care of things for Gloria, take her to appointments, and bring Gianni and Charlie to school, after-school clubs, and sports," she explains, a small, sad smile turning her lips. "When he found me, he tried to call the police, but I lost it on him." She shakes her head. "I refused to let law enforcement get involved. I was less than two weeks away from turning eighteen, and if the police found out, I'd have been returned to my father. One abuser to the next and back. I wasn't having it.

"He took me to his apartment, let me get cleaned up, gave me some of his sister's clothes, and tried like hell to get me to report it, but I wouldn't." Her voice is smaller than I've ever heard it. I don't like that this is so painful for her. "My only compromise was that I let him take me to the women's shelter."

I reach out for her hand, and she gives it a gentle tug. "You really don't have to tell me all this. Luca was right; it wasn't his story to tell, and I don't need you to relive your trauma to get your point across," I tell her.

My stomach is churning with bile. This story sounds so familiar.

My heart aches at the thought of Cora. She never got to see what life free of abuse could look like. Not like Arielle has. And this incredible life Arielle has with Dante and their kids—it's everything I could've wanted for Cora.

"I want you to hear this, Samara. I promise," she says, her voice cracking again. When I don't try to interrupt her, she continues.

"A few weeks later, things were better. I was able to stay at the shelter, and they helped me figure out a plan for getting my GED and finding a job so I could get out of there. Then my period never came, and I hoped and prayed like hell that it was just the stress."

"But it wasn't." I breathe, already knowing the answer.

She shakes her head, the loose red curls dancing in the setting sun. "It wasn't," she confirms. "I took a pregnancy test, and another, and probably five or six more after that. Every one of them told me a truth I had no interest in believing. And when I didn't know what to do, I tried to find Dante again. He'd made me feel safe." She averts her gaze for a moment before finding mine again, her wide blue eyes acting like a window to her soul. "Safer than anyone ever had in my life, and he'd only known me for a few short hours. But when I got to his place, it wasn't him who opened the door."

A slight smile grazes her lips. "A tall, lanky Luca had answered the door, and when he saw me sobbing, he tried to make a joke about how out of all his brothers, Dante wasn't usually the one who left the ladies crying on his doorstep. And, of course, that made me cry more because my brain was fried. I was just so tired. I couldn't even explain who I was, and when I tried to leave, he convinced me to come inside. And again, I felt so safe with him. It was different with Luca. Like my soul had already known that Dante was the one for me, but that Luca was an extension of that, and that I'd be safe with him too." *God, I hate how I know that feeling too.* "I shouldn't have felt safe with anyone after what I'd gone through, but there's just something about those damn De Laurentiis boys," she says, the corner of her lips curving in a smirk.

Don't I know it?

"Luca brought me in, explained who he was, and told me that Dante was away for the week taking Gloria for a clinical trial for her MS." Her eyes soften at the memory. "Unfortunately, nothing ever came of the trial, but regardless, Luca was apartment-sitting for him while he was gone and taking care of Dante's cat. I poured my heart out to him, blubbering all over his chest, and he just held me." *That damn firm chest of his really is calming.*

"He let me get it all out, and when I was less of a mess, he asked me what I wanted to do, and when I didn't know, he started looking into options. He sat with me for hours, searching through images and websites to explain what each procedure would be like, how they would feel, and what I could do if I wanted to keep it or put it up for adoption."

This doesn't surprise me at all. After getting to know Luca better, I have no doubt that's exactly what he'd have done.

"I was a scared seventeen-year-old with no money, no home, and barely a future if you'd have asked me back then. And more than that, I didn't want to carry a child who would remind me every day of the abuse they'd been brought into this world as a result of. So when I decided I wanted an abortion, he made me promise to sleep on it. He brought me back to the shelter and swore he'd pick me up the next morning to take me to a clinic if I still wanted it. And the next day, *he saved my life.*"

Tears are freely streaming down my cheeks now. I swipe at them with the back of my hands, my eyes burning.

"I hadn't realized it then"—she breathes, her voice wavering—"but I know now that if Luca hadn't done what he had, I wouldn't be here. I'd have done anything to end the cycle of abuse for myself, and I was in such a dark place, I would have ended it all if it weren't for him."

She smiles down at her feet, a sad smile that has my heart clenching in my chest. When her baby-blue eyes meet mine, unshed tears are rimming them. "Luca thinks the women's shelter is what saved me." Her voice cracks. "But that's just not the truth. It was him. He may think he's undeserving of love or that he'll never be enough, but he's so wrong, Samara. That man has so much love to give, it's bursting at the seams. Did you know that he's been teaching self-defense to the women at the shelter for over a decade?"

My eyes widen. I'd put pieces of that together but had no idea it had been going on that long.

"Yeah." She nods. "After Dante and I finally got together, Luca had decided he wanted to give back to the shelter and ensure none of those women ever felt defenseless again. Then, when he got drafted to play for the New York Monsters, he continued teaching those classes every week on Wednesdays over video call, like clockwork."

"I had no idea," I answer honestly.

Her eyes soften as she assesses me. "There's a lot to Luca that doesn't meet the eye, Samara. I've seen the way you look at him, and I've had long conversations with that man about his feelings for you, and believe me, you two are it for each other. I think you'd just be prolonging the inevitable if you didn't go after that man and make him yours. The invisible string tethering you together will always win in the end; it's better not to fight it. Trust me, I'd know better than anyone," she says with a wink.

She extends her hand for me to take. "Now come on, let's get back before they send out a search party for us." She giggles, but the sound isn't the same as it usually is, but she clasps her hand around mine and gives me no time to recover.

She's right. There's so much I don't know about Luca, but I think I'm finally coming to terms with the fact that I want to. *I want to know everything about him, and it's time I finally tell him that.*

***

I looked all over for Luca, but by the time I made it in, he had left with Gia. Alessandro mentioned that he was dropping Gia off at Cici's so she wouldn't miss out on her Friday with her daughter.

He really is doing an impressive job with co-parenting Gia, but I can't help but feel like I missed my shot.

Though, I guess having the night to fully think through what I want to say to him wouldn't be a bad thing either.

Chapter Seventy-Eight

Luca

Saturday, September 26, 2026

The sun is starting to rise, and the shit-eating grin spread across my face is growing with every step we take toward Kat's room in the cabin.

As Italian Americans, we have a lot of traditions we follow, especially on wedding days. We wouldn't want to fuck up the good luck.

We crouch down outside Kat's window, with Ale holding the ancient boom box we've used for every family wedding since I was a kid.

"You ready?" I ask him.

Ale nods emphatically, excited to get the day started, I'm sure.

Seconds later, music is blaring from the speaker and straight into Kat's room.

I see her head pop up first, followed by Aiyana's, who looks more pissed than I've ever seen her.

She practically climbs over Kat as we continue singing along to the obnoxious music, serenading the bride on her big day.

Aiyana finally figures out the lock on the windows, pushing it open and sticking her head outside. "You have exactly five seconds to turn that shit off before I make you!" she screeches.

Kas is cackling behind me, keeled over where he stands, using his hands on his knees to support himself.

"Sounds like your girl isn't much of a morning person, huh?" I joke.

"Like you wouldn't believe," he manages to get out. His eyes go wide, and he takes off in a sprint.

Aiyana's tiny body practically flies out the window, heading directly for Kas.

Poor fucker, this wasn't even his family tradition.

Dante, Gianni, Ale, and I can't contain the laughter that spills out of us, and when Kat sticks her head back out the window, her cheeks are pink. "You may have just gotten my brother killed on my wedding day, you know that?" she asks us, shaking her head, but her smile stays put.

"He'll be okay. Aiyana loves him too much to kill him," Gianni notes, but I'm not so sure. Gi bounces on the balls of his feet with a hand cupped to the back of Jer Bear's head, where he sleeps peacefully in his carrier.

Ale finally turns the music off and we see Kas making his way back over to us, now with Aiyana draped over his shoulder, thrashing and smacking his ass.

"You're gonna pay for this," she grumbles.

"Yeah, yeah, yeah. I'm sure I will," he tells her, all smiles as he tips his chin at us with a wink.

"You guys better get out of here before he sets her down," Kat urges, leaning farther out the window to give Ale a kiss.

"Good morning, groom," she tells him quietly.

"Good morning, bride," he says.

They sound so deliriously in love, and I couldn't be happier for them.

***

Despite the fact that Samara showed up to the rehearsal dinner last night, I still have doubts about whether or not she'll actually make it today. The girls are getting ready in the bridal suite, and I'm compelled to wonder whether or not Samara actually made it here or not.

I shouldn't care as much as I do, especially because I'm so excited for Kat and Ale to finally get married and be one step closer to closing on that adoption. But Samara has infiltrated my brain, and I'm unable to stop thinking about her.

"Hey, you good?" Rome asks, leaning up against the side of one of the few trees that aren't wrapped in twinkling warm white lights.

"Yeah, just a little nervous," I answer honestly.

"She's here," he says, a slow smirk creeping across his face.

I lift a brow at him, wondering how he knows.

"Perks of being engaged to the wedding planner." He grins. "I was volunteered to bring the non-alcoholic limoncello for their good-luck shots before the ceremony. I saw Samara getting her makeup done when I dropped it off," he tells me.

"There's clearly something on your mind—get it out, or it'll ruin your night."

I shake my head, trying to clear my thoughts, but ultimately sink to the ground beside him with my back up against the tree.

"I keep thinking that with the way she's been keeping her distance from me, tonight's the last time I'll see her." The moment the words leave my mouth, it feels like a tight vice is wrapped around my heart.

"If it's meant to be, it will be. And if not, then at least make tonight the absolute best that you can," he tells me as he stares out into the dense woods surrounding us.

"Like a goodbye?"

"Yep. Exactly like a goodbye. One last night together. Make the memories so you have something to hold onto when she's gone."

I can't say that's the best idea I've ever heard, but it's all I've got.

"Come on, assholes! It's time to get dressed. If we're late, Arielle and Aiyana will cut our nuts off!" Kas shouts to Rome and me, ushering us toward the groom's dressing suite.

***

The instant Samara makes it outside with the rest of the bridal party, my eyes are glued to her.

Mateo nudges my shoulder, and I take it as my cue to peel my jaw up off the floor before they make their way over to us.

Samara looks like a fucking goddess. Her bronze skin is luminous, her cheekbones dusted in a light golden shimmer, and her lips painted in a brown gloss that makes them look like something I could eat. As does the rest of her.

She's wearing a floor-length satin gown that matches the rest of the bridal party in cabernet. I called it "wine" the other day and nearly got my head bitten off, so I'm well-versed in this particular color now.

As she approaches me, a smile turns the corners of her lips, and my heart takes off at a sprint.

"Samara," I say, at a loss for words. "You look— You look *stunning*."

"You clean up pretty well yourself," she tells me, winding her arm through mine and leading us toward where the rest of the wedding party is waiting for Kat and Ale to have their first look.

"Hey, Luca," Samara whispers beside me.

"Yeah, princess?" I ask.

"Can we talk later?"

That has my ears perking up and my stomach dropping to my toes.

This is it. *This* is how she's decided to do it. She's going to cut me off entirely, and when she's gone, I'm not sure how I'll live without her, but I will.

People always leave; she's no different, and if I'm not what she wants, I'm not going to push the subject.

I clear my throat and finally answer her. "Yeah, princess. We can talk later."

Chapter Seventy-Nine

Samara

Arlo trails down the aisle with her baby cousin in tow, haphazardly tossing flower petals all around as she tries to balance the two of them. It's simultaneously the scariest and most adorable thing I've ever seen, but it's clear that growing up in an athletic family has helped her out. She's got Gia clutched against her like a running back with a football.

When she makes it to the end of the aisle, we all release a relieved breath, and Cecily takes Gia, settling her onto her lap. Arlo runs to stand between her moms, who are standing next to me as we watch Kat make her way down the aisle.

She looks flawless. Her gown is a lace, sleeveless sheath with a V-neckline that's modest but still makes her breasts look phenomenal.

Truly, she's gorgeous, and it's no surprise to me when I look across the aisle to find not just Ale but the entire row of De Laurentiis men with tears in their eyes and Kas outright blowing his nose between sobs.

I want to laugh so badly, but the moment is too sweet for me to risk ruining. I've never been a part of a family like this, but the feeling of having so much love and support is a little intoxicating, and I can't bring myself to laugh at these men.

Even Angelo, the quiet, dutiful father and co-leader of the family, is misty-eyed.

When Kat makes it to Ale, they embrace and take their places on two small stools placed in front of Gloria. She's seated in her wheelchair, ready to officiate this wedding.

The next twenty minutes are filled with tears, swoon-worthy moments thanks to Alessandro, who I'm realizing has the tendency to be a walking green flag in every aspect of his life, and of course, a few laughs along the way, mostly courtesy of Gloria.

"I pronounce you husband and wife! You may now kiss the bride!" Gloria shouts excitedly at the couple.

Alessandro grips Kat's waist, dragging her to him as he dips her low in his seat and gives her a kiss that has me blushing.

When they finally come up for air, they stand and dance down the aisle toward the reception area. Each pair from the wedding party heads out after them, and when it's Luca's and my turn, butterflies swarm in my stomach.

He wraps his arm around my waist, and the feel of it sears my skin.

"We'll get you a glass of water soon, big guy," I joke.

His brows pinch in confusion, so I say, "You must be dehydrated from all that crying you did."

"Real men cry, Samara." He winks at me. His grin turns to a smirk, and a moment later, he says, "You think I'm big."

I roll my eyes playfully. "You've got a big head, that's for sure."

"Keep telling yourself that, princess. What you don't know is just how fragile my ego can be." I know we're joking with one another, but the way he says those words feels like a heavy blow to my chest, and it leaves me wondering just how true they are.

***

The reception hall is decorated in various shades of red and white carnations and peonies, gold accents, and loads of brass candelabras that line the tables. It's elegant, unique, and everything I'd imagine Kat's wedding would be like, even after just getting to know her these last few months.

After cocktail hour, dinner and more photos than I can count, it's time for the first dances.

Alessandro takes a seat in the center of the room, and Luca follows behind Gloria, kneeling between the two of them.

My chest feels tight as I see what's unfolding.

Luca meticulously straps his mother's legs to his brothers. He helps stand them up and ties the last set of straps around them with Gloria's feet settled over the top of Alessandro's. Luca and Dante pull their chairs away and clear the floor for their mother-son dance.

The lights around us dim, and the ones on the dance floor grow brighter.

There are already tears brimming in my eyes before the music even starts, but the moment Gianni starts playing "You Are The Reason" by Calum Scott, the floodgates are officially open.[1]

He masterfully plays the piano, even with a baby on his chest and Lark seated beside him with her head on his shoulder. We all watch in awe as Ale and Gloria share this dance together, swaying on the dancefloor.

When their song is finished, there isn't a dry eye in the room.

Luca takes his time undoing the straps, and Ale helps set his mother back in her wheelchair, pressing a kiss to each of her cheeks and following her off to the side.

Just when I thought this family might stop making me tear up, Angelo heads in Kat's direction, her brows climbing her forehead when she sees him extend his hand for her to take.

"It was a surprise since her parents aren't around," Luca whispers into my ear as he takes his place seated beside me.

"That's really sweet," I say, my words sounding watery.

Kat takes Angelo's hand in hers and follows him to the center of the floor.

They sway back and forth, and at the halfway point in the song, Angelo twirls Kat. She's less than graceful as she follows through with the movement to the best of her ability and lands straight in her brother's arms.

Kas smiles down at his sister, helping her straighten before they begin to sway together. "They wanted it to be as special for her as possible. What better way than with her brother and

---

1. **You Are The Reason — Calum Scott**

father-in-law?" Luca whispers to me, his breath coasting over my ear.

When the song ends, there's just one more dance that we have to get through. The one I've personally been waiting months for.

As Ale steps onto the dance floor, taking Kas's place, he settles his hands around Kat's waist and picks her up, placing her gently on his shoes.

He whispers something in Kat's ear that makes her smile brightly, and they start their dance to "Conversations in the Dark" by John Legend.[2]

Luca chuckles beside me. "Months of ballroom classes, and Kat was still dancing around like a drunk baby elephant."

My cheeks burn from smiling so much, and at the end of their dance, when Ale lifts Kat off his shoes and twirls her out, she manages to stay upright as Arlo, Benny, and Sammy shoot gold confetti cannons at them. Everyone claps and cheers as Kat and Ale take their seats again, preparing for the speeches.

Luca stands, grabs the mic, and makes his way to the center of the floor. "We promised Kat to limit the number of speeches because they give her anxiety and, apparently, bore her," Luca tells the room filled with their closest family and friends, which equates to roughly fifty people.

Everyone laughs, their attention focused on Luca, but I see Kat's cheeks flush from her seat beside where he's standing.

The more he speaks, the more my palms start to sweat.

---

2. **Conversations In The Dark — John Legend**

"I think we'd all agree that I've never known two more deserving people in my life. I'm surrounded by so much support, love, and truly just the greatest people, so it's with a lot of experience that I feel I can say that." He chuckles, and everyone follows suit.

"Ale has always been the best example for my siblings and me. He's kind, compassionate, and patient beyond measure. I mean, he sort of had to be growing up with me," Luca says, shooting Ale an exaggerated wink. "He's been the perfect example of the kind of man I want to be, and I didn't think the day would come that he'd meet someone who matches him in every way. Truthfully, I never thought he'd find anyone deserving of him, but in walked Kat. Or, how did the story go? Oh, right!" Luca says, snapping his fingers as if he actually just remembered how they met. "Ale *literally* stumbled upon Kat, sleeping in the hallway of his apartment building." The room is filled with laughter, clearly knowing the story too.

"I won't take up too much time here for Kat's sake. But I wanted to say what a blessing you've been, Kat," he says, turning his attention to her. "Not everyone is lucky enough to experience the kind of love you two have, and I can say without a doubt that anyone who finds that..." His eyes lock on mine now. My breath gets caught in my throat as he finishes his sentence. "Well, they better not screw it up because it's a once-in-a-lifetime sort of thing." Luca lifts his glass, and everyone takes their cue. "To Kat and Ale, the most incredibly deserving people I know. May you live long, happy, healthy, and fulfilling lives, side by side in this lifetime and the next."

"To Kat and Ale!" everyone shouts, clinking glasses with one another.

I bring my glass of champagne to my lips, my eyes still locked on Luca's as he does the same, his eyes never leaving mine, even as he drags a long swig into his mouth.

The bubbles tingle on my tongue, and the warmth from the alcohol slides down my throat.

I know I'd already wanted to confirm how he felt about me, but now more than ever, that's true. I'm realizing that my fear of getting hurt by Luca has never really been about him or how the media portrayed him but about my own insecurities.

Even at the airport, when those women were all over him, he didn't return the flirtation at all.

And that makes me think, just how long has it been since Luca De Laurentiis has been seen with a woman who wasn't me or someone in his family?

As Luca takes his seat beside me, I work to keep the questions from boiling over when Ale and Kat stand.

"Thank you, Luca, that was, well, that was really sweet," Kat says, her cheeks flaming with a blush. That's kind of her trademark.

"Since it's our perfect night, a night we've been waiting for what feels like forever, we thought it would be the best occasion to share something equally, if not even more important to us."

A woman dressed in a black pantsuit enters the room with a manilla envelope in hand. Kat addresses her. "This is Sarah Thompson. She's been working with us for the last several months, and today, in front of all of our friends and family," she says, her cheeks tightening as she holds back tears, "we get to sign the adoption papers for our son, Oliver. He'll be joining our little family really soon, and we wanted you all to be here for this moment."

"Fucking hell," Luca says, choking back tears. "I swear to god, I've never cried this much in my life, and believe me, I cried a whole lot when Gia first got here."

I place my hand on his knee, squeezing gently and trying to hold back my own tears as Kat and Ale sign the adoption papers.

Kat looks around the room again and says, "I'm not really a speech kind of person, as I'm sure you all know, but I just wanted to thank you all for welcoming me and Kas into your family. It's been the most extraordinary and unexpected blessing of my life." Her eyes meet Gloria's, and a tear slips down each of their faces, as if in sync with one another. Ale wraps his arm around his wife, squeezing her tightly to his side and pressing a kiss to the top of her head. "Kas and I have only ever had Aiyana and her family for most of our lives, and our Lola, for not nearly long enough. So I know I can say with absolute certainty that while raising a child may take a village, I'm glad that you all are mine."

A sob threatens to break free of my lips, but I suck it back in and focus on the place where Luca's hand and mine meet.

When they're done signing, Ale crushes his mouth to Kat's, overwhelmed by the moment.

An ugly sob leaves me as everyone jumps up, clapping, crying, and smiling.

***

The last couple of hours have been filled with so much dancing and karaoke, I feel like my feet could fall off, and my throat has been rubbed raw. After the kids were all brought to one of the cabins to get settled in for the night, the adults all reconvened by the firepit.

As things start winding down, I'm feeling the opposite. The longer this night has gone on, the more desperate I am for a free minute with Luca so I can finally tell him all the things I'm thinking and to clear the air before it's too late.

I get up to use the restroom and manage to make it the thirty feet away and down the gravel-laden path without breaking an ankle in these heels. I don't regret wearing them because they're stunning, but the terrain here was a little more than I'd been anticipating.

I make it to the bathroom, locking myself inside. I spend an eternity staring back at my own reflection.

My skin is dewy, and my eyes are somehow both wild and, well, wildly exhausted. I've dedicated so much time to pushing Luca away that now that I've finally started to come to terms with these feelings, every suppressed emotion is weighing me down.

I wet a few paper towels with cold water, blotting the back of my neck to cool my overheated skin.

There's a light knock at the door.

"One second," I call.

The knocking doesn't stop though; it only gets louder. "Samara, let me in."

My head snaps to the door.

"Luca?" I whisper in disbelief.

I pull the door open, and he doesn't even wait for me to let him in before he barrels inside.

His large hands cover my cheeks, and before I know it, his lips are crashing into mine.

The kiss is frantic and full of passion, sending zings of electricity through me.

I melt against him, allowing him to snake his arms around me. He seats my ass on the edge of the bathroom sink, holding me close to him as our tongues tangle.

I feel like I'm being *devoured.*

My whole world is spinning, and if I'm going to fall off the edge of the earth, *I want it to be with Luca.*

He finally loosens his grip on me, pressing his forehead against mine as our lips separate. We stay here, panting and breathing each other in.

Luca's bright eyes lock onto mine, and I'm a puddle in his arms.

"Hey, princess," he says, sounding as out of breath as I feel.

"Hi." I'm barely able to get the word out of my mouth.

"Does this mean you're officially ready to stop fighting me and let me take you home?" he asks, and his swollen red lips turn up in a smirk.

I roll my eyes, feigning disinterest, but my hand snaps forward, gripping his burgundy dress shirt between my fingers and pulling him back into me.

This time, it's me who takes the lead. My lips meet Luca's, and sparks climb up the base of my spine. I nip his bottom lip, and when his mouth opens on a surprised inhale, my tongue dances with his.

His large hands grip my hips firmly, pulling me farther toward him. My thighs fall to the sides, allowing him to slip between them. His rough fingers snake down my legs, and I feel the satin gown slipping across my skin as he glides it up to my hips.

Luca's lips remain on mine, but his thumb coasts over my center, pressing firmly on my clit over my lace thong.

A loud moan slips out, and I'm forced to separate my lips from his. He continues rubbing firm circles along my seam.

My head hangs back as my fingers dig into the porcelain sink. His hot breath skims over my neck and stops at my ear. "Does my princess want to come?"

"Yes." I moan, pushing my center farther into his thumb.

"So needy all of a sudden," he says with a chuckle. "All this from a woman who's made it infinitely clear that she doesn't need me... or anyone else for that matter."

Unfortunately, I haven't exactly had the time to tell him that I may have been wrong about that.

"Come on, princess, you're gonna have to beg for it like I've been begging you for months."

My eyes snap open, meeting his as I grit out my next words. "Please, Luca, make me come."

His eyes dance as he smiles, pulling my panties down my legs and stuffing them in his back pocket. "That wasn't so hard, was it? All you had to do was ask nicely."

Instead of fingering me like I expect him to, given the current circumstances, he unbuckles his belt, which may be just about the sexiest thing I've ever seen in my life. Luca undoes his zipper and drops his black dress pants to his ankles. He reaches for me next. "Arms around my neck, *principessa*."

Without a second thought, I do as I'm told, and he grips my thighs, pulling them around him. He hoists me up his body, and my legs wind tightly around him. Luca's hands are firmly planted on my ass, supporting most of my weight, and when he slowly lowers me down his body, I feel his massive erection settling between my pussy lips.

"I think—" I huff out, my mind in a frenzy. "I think you forgot something," I finally manage.

"The first time I fuck you won't be in a public restroom at my brother's wedding. Sorry to disappoint, princess." My retort gets caught in my throat as he bounces me up and over him, the head of his dick creating the most delicious friction. He's simultaneously thrusting into me from below, making sure not to enter me, but he maintains the perfect amount of pressure with just the head of his dick. I'm already so close to coming that when he adjusts his hands more inward, spreading me farther open to slip a finger inside me from behind, I'm barely able to hold onto him as I ride the wave.

"Yes, god, yes!" I shout.

"So gorgeous, Samara."

"Luca," I pant.

"Eyes on me, princess. Let me watch you," he says as I continue to spasm.

Tingles ripple down my thighs, and when the tides have washed away the last of my orgasm, I can finally start to think straight.

"Alright, princess. Let's get you back home so I can finish what we started," he tells me, lowering me to the ground on unsteady legs.

Luca pulls my panties from his pocket, lifting my legs one by one and sliding them up my thighs and in place. He then takes the bottom hem of my dress, pulling it down and smoothing it against my thighs before fixing his pants and buckle, tucking his shirt back in.

He extends his hand for mine. I willingly take it.

He unlatches the bathroom door, and when we exit, there are about twenty of his closest friends and family seated around the bonfire, smiling gleefully at us.

Embarrassment sears through me, and my cheeks heat instantly. I feel like I'm on fire.

Suddenly, they all break out into a fit of excitement, clapping and whistling at us. "Finally!" Arielle shouts, and Dante just shakes his head beside his wife, wearing a small grin.

His entire family, save for Gloria and Angelo, just heard that, and they're *clapping.*

"Don't worry, Mom and Dad said, and I quote, 'I'm glad they're finally getting their heads out of their asses, but I have no desire to hear my son do the hanky panky,'" Charlie informs us, grinning ear to ear.

Luca wraps his arm around my waist, tugging me into his side, and presses a kiss to the top of my head. His warmth seeps into me, ridding the chill from my bones.

"Sorry, princess. Looks like I wasn't the only one who'd been waiting for you to finally let me have you, *even if just for one night.*" The last part of his sentence rings in the back of my head like alarm bells, but I'm determined to get out of here so we can finally have the conversation I should've had with him the moment these feelings started to brew.

Chapter Eighty

Samara

As we approach his bike, apprehension starts to settle into my gut.

He sees the look written plainly across my features, and his brows pull together. "I thought you were over hating me," he says, sounding so defeated it nearly cracks my heart in two.

"I never hated you, Luca. I've never been on a motorcycle."

He starts to relax, his shoulders dropping from their place by his ears as the meaning of my words settles in. "Don't be scared, princess. I'll take good care of you," he tells me, lifting a compartment under the seat and pulling out a spare helmet.

He places it on my head, being careful not to mess up my curls too much as he secures it in place. He then gets his on and settles onto the bike, looking over his shoulder at me, wearing an easy smile.

"Climb on, Samara." I do, but I have no idea where to put my feet or my hands. Luca grips each of my legs firmly in his massive hands and settles my feet safely out of the way. "Wrap your arms around my waist and hold on tight," he tells me.

I have a death grip on him by the time he has the kickstand up, and we're pulling onto the dirt road.

He speeds up, and my grip only tightens as he does. The wind whips around us, and my heart is pounding rapidly against my chest as we take off toward my place.

My chin is resting on his shoulder, and I can feel Luca's chuckle reverberate through his chest. "Don't worry, I've got you, princess," he shouts so I can hear him.

This time, though, I'm not afraid of being *with* Luca De Laurentiis. I'm afraid of being without him, and that alone is ten times scarier than this donor cycle could ever be.

My limbs feel rigid as I nearly strangle him to death, praying my big ass doesn't somehow fly off this thing, and I'm thankful there doesn't seem to be anyone else on the road out here.

My anxiety is ricocheting through me at every twist and turn we make, and I know he can feel it.

Luca skids to a stop along the side of the road and pulls us over off the edge.

"What are you doing? Why did we stop?" I ask him, sounding just as frantic as I feel.

"We're only halfway home, Samara. You've got to calm down, or you're gonna have a heart attack before we ever get there," he tells me, maneuvering himself so he can see more of me. He stands from the bike, ensuring it's secure, before taking a step closer to me. "I plan to make sure you're *very* relaxed." He chuckles deeply.

I can already feel the pool of warmth in my panties, and if this wasn't both terrifying and so goddamn sexy, I'd be embarrassed by it.

My dress has ridden up so high on my thighs from the way I've had to straddle this thing that I'm leaving nothing to the imagination as he lifts one of my legs up high to further expose me to him.

His smirk says it all as his eyes stay trained on mine. I feel his thick fingers slide along my seam, but I refuse to break eye contact.

Luca settles my leg onto his shoulder, causing me to fall backward a bit. I settle my hands behind me, leaning back, trying to keep myself up despite the way my legs are starting to shake with need.

His finger slips under the silk material of my thong, and he tugs on it hard, causing it to snap back against my sensitive skin. The sting sends a jolt of electricity through me, and I arch into him, releasing a moan. "I can't say I'm surprised by how wet I make you, *principessa,*" he taunts. "But god, it's still such a treat to see you like this. Splayed open and absolutely soaked, just for me." He tugs on my panties one more time, snapping the thin material and pulling the shreds from my body. He smiles wickedly, maintaining eye contact as he sucks my juices off them before stuffing them into his back pocket. "Just as sweet as I remember," he confirms.

The fact that it's even possible for me to be "soaked" is a miracle. Before Luca, PCOS had taken even that small luxury from me. I was just about as dry as the Sahara Desert with every other man I've been with, but maybe that's because he's practically been edging me for weeks.

It takes a lot for me to get this turned on, but thankfully, Luca does it for me.

He presses two thick fingers into me, distracting me from my thoughts. He's stretching me so deliciously I almost forget where we are.

His fingers are buried inside me, relentlessly diving into me as I keen against him. "Yes." I moan. "*Please*, Luca, don't stop," I beg.

"Well, you asked so nicely. How could I?" he says, adding a third finger and pressing his thumb to my clit. My body lights up under his touch, coming alive for him as sparks surge up my spine. My core clenches around him, pulling him farther into me. "Holy shit, Samara," he says, shaking his head, his face a mask of pure agony. "I can't wait to drag you home, devour your gorgeous cunt, and have you absolutely strangling my cock until the sun rises," he pants out. He splays his fingers inside of me, stretching me farther, almost to the point of pain, and I'd be lying if I said it wasn't incredible.

This man, he can do no wrong. He laughs darkly as I move my hips to meet his hand. "Should I add another finger, Samara? Would you like that?"

"No," I grit out, not wanting to keep agreeing with him. Four fingers would probably split me in two. "You'll split me in half." I groan, but his hand stops abruptly.

My eyes widen in shock. *This jackass!*

"It's four fingers or none, Samara. If we have any chance of fitting my massive cock inside you tonight, you'll need to be stretched out a bit," he says, moving his hand downward to tease my other hole.

Goosebumps litter my skin, and I wish he weren't right. Now that I've seen that thing, I know he's not even joking. He has all the reason in the world to walk around like a big dick slinger because his dick really is huge, *and god, is it pretty.*

"Fine," I tell him, defeated by my needy pussy. "But if you try to fist me, I'll return the favor." I scowl at him, and his eyes widen before he releases a deep chuckle.

He removes his hand entirely and then pushes his four thick fingers into me, stretching me out even farther. He leans into me, my leg over his shoulder, adjusting with him to split me even wider.

His deft fingers dive in and out of me as he changes rhythms against my clit, applying more and then less pressure. Finally, when I can't take any more and my body is practically levitating off the seat of this bike, he pinches my clit, dragging it between his fingers, and sends me spiraling over the edge. "That's right, *principessa,* just like that, baby," he encourages.

I'm spasming around his fingers, my core tightening and my breathing ragged. I feel his lips and wet tongue graze over the thin satin of my dress, sucking my pebbled nipple into his mouth, and the sensation has me soaring.

I slump back against the seat, panting and shivering as he removes his hands from my body, sucking me off each of his fingers before pressing a kiss to the side of my neck.

My body is like jelly as he stands from the bike, putting his helmet back on and sliding back onto his seat in front of me again. I do my best to hold onto him, but this time, I'm barely hanging on as he drives us home.

Chapter Eighty-One

Luca

The moment I pull into a parking space in front of Samara's condo, my body floods with adrenaline.

I've been thinking about dead puppies, and every old, decrepit political candidate I could think of on this drive just to keep from blowing my load in my pants from the thought of being inside her.

I practically throw my body off my bike, unbuckling the strap of her helmet and tossing it back under the seat before taking mine off and hauling her over my shoulder.

"Luca, what the hell?" she shouts at me.

"Keys, Samara, I need your keys," I plead.

I hear her rustling around in her purse before she says, "Catch."

The keys are flying over my face, but I grab them just in time, smacking my free hand over Samara's ass and fumbling with the door to yank it open.

I kick the door shut and toss her keys on the gold mirrored entryway table, carrying her into the room I now know is hers after my first and last trip over here.

Swinging her over my shoulder and into the center of the bed, she hits it with a thud, and I can see the annoyance in her eyes.

"Sorry, sweetheart, gotta nut," I joke.

She rolls her eyes, sitting up to start taking the pins out of her hair.

Jesus Christ, I'm an asshole.

I take a deep, calming breath in through my nose, hold it for a few beats, and push it out through my mouth.

Once I've managed to settle the horny beast that's running rampant inside of me, and apparently, causing me to lose all manners, I take her foot into my palm.

"I'm sorry, Samara. I've just been wound so tightly after what feels like the edging of a lifetime that all I could think about was burying myself inside you. That's no excuse though," I say, unbuckling the straps of her golden heels. I set the shoe down beside the bed and work my thumb into her heel, then along the arch of her foot, and finally, along her sole.

I repeat that process with the other foot, watching contentedly as her expression softens and her body starts to melt into her bed.

Her ankles are swollen, and the straps look like they were digging into her, so I glide my hands up to them, massaging where the straps were.

When I'm done, I move to sit behind her and start to gently work the pins out of her curls.

Once I'm convinced they're all out, *all two hundred of them*, I press a soft kiss along the side of her neck and blow gently on her skin. "Would a scalp massage feel good?" I ask.

"Mhmm," she replies, leaning farther into my touch as I scoot up the bed to allow her to lie back with her head in my lap.

We stay like this, with my fingers massaging her roots, doing my best not to cause any frizz.

"Hey, princess," I whisper, fully expecting her to be asleep with how firmly shut her eyes are.

But she responds, "Yeah?" Her sleepy voice is damn cute, I'll admit. It makes me fucking sick to think that after tonight, I'll never hear it again.

"Do you want me to leave?" I ask, making sure I'm not forcing myself into her life or her home any more than I already have.

"No," she says, shaking her head.

Samara rolls out of my lap, pushing up onto her hands, and stretches her neck from side to side before standing. She looks back at me as her hands slip into the satin of her dress, winding around her back to unzip it. She tugs the straps over her shoulders and down her arms, letting the silky fabric pool around her feet.

My cock is no match for how sexy this woman is.

It springs to life despite my earlier efforts to contain it.

I have to tuck my hands under my ass to keep from prowling across this bed and mauling her like an animal.

Her glowy brown skin is on full display from the back. The round globes of her ass are practically begging me to bite them, but I stay as still as can be, enraptured as she unclasps her bra, letting it fall down her arms and at her feet.

When she turns around, her warm eyes look heated, and my breath catches in my throat. “Fucking hell, Samara.” I groan, shutting my eyes for a moment, but it’s physically painful not to look at her. Especially when she looks like *that.*

Her dark nipples are pointed directly at me, and those gorgeous breasts need to be in my mouth. Is there a single part of her that isn’t fucking perfect?

The answer is simple. *No.*

She laughs lightly, crawling onto the bed toward me. “Can’t trust yourself?” she asks, tilting her head to the side in question as her eyes flick to my hands, still planted under my ass.

“Not around you.”

“Good thing you don’t have to restrain yourself with me,” she taunts.

She presses a hand to the center of my chest, dropping her mouth to my ear and sucking on my lobe. “You talk a big game, Luca. Are you ready to play ball?” she asks, and the moment the words leave her mouth, I’m on her.

I have her pinned under me, chest heaving, and those sweet brown nipples are inches from my face. I pluck one into my mouth, sucking on it fervently as she cries out, gripping her fingers in my roots.

Releasing her nipple, I bring my mouth to the edge of hers and whisper, “I’m more than ready, princess. But I don’t play with balls, so I hope you’re ready to get pucked.”

Her head falls back in a fit of laughter, and the sound is glorious.

I nuzzle my face into her neck, littering her skin with kisses. She runs her fingers through my hair, and suddenly, I’m on my back.

Rolling my eyes at her, I grip her hips as she rotates them over my erection. "You just can't help yourself, can you? Always need to be in control," I tsk. "Good thing I'm happy to bow down to you, princess."

She sucks her bottom lip between her teeth, gripping my shoulders for purchase as she continues to glide over me.

I can feel her slick heat through my slacks, and if I don't get them off me immediately, they'll tear at the seams.

My fingers trail down her thighs and stop at my belt buckle. I undo it, trying to work my zipper down in between her movements, but she readjusts to sit between my thighs.

Her hand cups my balls through my pants before she finally undoes my zipper, and my cock springs free. Her fingers dig into my hips as she grabs hold of my pants and briefs, working them down my legs until she drops them to the ground at the end of the bed.

She settles between my thighs, wrapping those pretty fingers around my base. The pad of her thumb rubs along the shiny silver metal barbells. I'm holding my breath with every move she makes, and when she finally directs my tip into her hot mouth, my eyes roll to the back of my head.

Chapter Eighty-Two

Samara

Sunday, September 27, 2026

"Oh, *fuck*." He moans loudly, his head tossed back in ecstasy. *I've barely even touched him.*

The head of Luca's dick is quite literally dripping in precum. The salty flavor glides over my tongue as I run it along his engorged length, paying special attention to the metal piercing his skin.

My skin feels feverish as I work to suppress the thoughts creeping in. *God, I can't wait to know how these feel inside me.*

I take as much of him into my mouth as I can, but I'm already choking, and I'm just over halfway. My eyes are brimming with tears. I look up to meet Luca's gaze, and it's practically boring holes into me.

"God, you're so fucking perfect, *principessa.* That sweet, glossy mouth of yours wrapped around my cock is the prettiest sight I've ever seen."

His words spur me forward despite how full my throat feels. I adjust my angle, taking him another inch and pumping my hand along the base to make up for whatever I can't reach. My throat stretches to accommodate him, but it isn't enough. "Fuck, yes, princess, *just like that*," he groans out.

I continue with the same pace, trying like hell to breathe through my nose as I do. "Samara…" He moans. Luca's thumb slides into the corner of my mouth, unlatching my hollowed-out cheeks from his shaft. He removes himself from my mouth, replacing it with that thumb.

I look up at him, stunned.

"Lie on your back, Samara," he instructs.

"Don't you want me to—" But he cuts me off when I don't move as quickly as he'd like.

He has me sprawled out on my back in the center of my bed. I watch as he crawls down my body, nestling himself between my legs.

Luca slides his hands beneath my thighs and pulls them up, placing my legs on his shoulders as he wrenches my body closer to his mouth. "I'm starving, princess. Aren't you gonna feed me?" he asks, a devious smile playing across his lips.

When I don't answer, too busy staring at him in shock, he rolls his eyes playfully, taking a chapter out of my own handbook. "Fine, if you don't intend to feed me, I can do it myself, but what I can't do is warm my ears while I eat. So, princess, will you be my earmuffs tonight?" A cheesy grin plays across his plump lips, and I can't help but relax a fraction.

This sexy, hard-headed, absolute brute of a man is also a giant goofball, *and I absolutely adore him.*

I squeeze the sides of his head with my thighs, and he shakes with laughter. "Such a good, *obedient* girl," he jokes.

"I've never been accused of being obedient in my whole damn life," I tell him.

"Don't I fucking know it," he grumbles. Within seconds, his mouth is on me, licking a hot trail up my seam.

Tingles shoot up my spine, and everything tightens as he flicks his tongue over my clit, swirling, then sucking it between his lips.

"It should be illegal to taste this good and look just as magnificent." His tongue darts inside me, and my back is arching off the bed, driving me closer to his face. My thighs relax around his head as pleasure courses more freely through me. "How is anyone supposed to think straight after having you like this?"

I'm nearly certain I haven't had a coherent thought since meeting Luca, and right now is certainly not the moment things are about to start clearing up.

He nips along my lips and positions his thumb just right so it settles over my clit. He applies the perfect pressure before going to town, slurping and sucking on my sensitive flesh.

"Don't stop, please!"

He continues his onslaught, moaning and grunting with every spasm and each squirm of my legs around his head. "Oh god, I'm so close." I moan.

He tugs on my thighs, loosening them from his head, and rolls us awkwardly so I'm half seated on his chest and confused as fuck. "What the hell?" I ask, annoyed and frustrated.

"Come on, *principessa.* Sit on my face and take what we both want. I've been dreaming about this for months."

Apprehension starts to bubble in my gut, but he shakes his head. "Absolutely not, Samara. I can already see the gears turning in your head. *Sit on my goddamn face.*"

Damn him and his all-knowing ways.

"I want all of you tonight. Give me what I want, just this once," he begs.

And just like that, I'm climbing on top of him, settling myself over his mouth and coming undone for the third time tonight at the hands, or rather, mouth, of Luca De Laurentiis.

Chapter Eighty-Three

Samara

Luca saunters back into my room, bare-ass naked and carrying two glasses of water.

He hands me one, which I gulp down before collapsing back into the bed. I feel boneless.

"Not a chance, princess. The night isn't over yet."

Why is he acting as if the moment this night is over, I'm going to turn into a pumpkin?

He finishes his water, taking my glass and setting both on the nightstand before grabbing his wallet out of his pants.

My heart rate starts to speed up when I see the condom between his fingers as he crawls up the bed and between my legs. He hasn't put the condom on yet, but he sets it beside my head.

His hand trails down my abdomen and dips between our bodies. He cups me, sliding his middle finger into me at the same time. My mouth pops open on a sigh. I'm sore, but I want this. *I want him.*

He dips his head, flicking his tongue over each of my nipples, which leaves me reeling. I'm aching with the repressed need I've felt since meeting him. Our vacation only heightened all of those feelings and so much more.

Luca presses the flat of his tongue against the top of my breast and licks a long, slow trail up the length of my neck. My fingers wind into his hair. My breaths quicken, and my body heats as tingles flutter through me.

He nips the base of my neck next and sucks on my collarbone, lavishing my skin.

"Samara," he breathes out. "Do I *finally* get to fuck this sweet cunt?" he asks, rubbing his palm against my clit.

"Only if you stop saying 'cunt.' I don't know how many Black women you've been with, but the ones I know don't use cunt or cock. It's just—" I wrinkle my nose. "Harsh."

He makes a face of recognition and gives me a small nod. His lips curve into a smirk that tells me exactly what kind of night I'm about to have.

"Anything you want, *principessa,*" he whispers, his hot breath over my nipple has goosebumps erupting on my chest. "Let's try that again, then. Shall we?" He sucks a path to my jaw, his stubble scraping the sensitive skin. "Do I finally get to fuck this beautiful *pussy?*"

I nearly jolt out of the bed, my core clenching around his finger as he adds another, and my body is already begging for more.

A whimper skates past my lips. "Please."

"Please, what?" he asks, hovering his lips over mine.

"Please fuck me, Luca."

"That's a good girl who gets prizes," he says, removing his fingers from me. We maintain eye contact as he sucks them deep into his mouth, his eyes only closing briefly as he releases a moan.

He shifts his weight off me, kneeling back onto his calves as he grips the condom, tearing it off with his teeth and rolling it onto him.

"If they make condoms big enough to fit *you*, there's not a man on this earth who should be using that as an excuse not to use one." The accidental compliment slips right out as I shake my head, taking in the beauty of a fully naked and erect Luca.

"I am pretty..."—he strokes himself—"impressive," he says with a wink. "Aren't I, princess?"

"I don't need to stroke your ego, Luca. It looks like you're doing a fantastic job of that all on your own."

"I don't know, I think you could do it better. Why don't you lie back, and let's give it a whirl?" he asks, wagging his dark brows.

He lines himself up with my center, pushing in slowly. My world stops spinning as he pumps inside me, inch by blissful fucking inch.

"God, this is better than I'd imagined," he groans out. "And believe me, I've been doing a whole lot of dreaming about this moment."

You and me both, Luca.

My bones are jelly, and my blood is molten lava. Delicious heat licks up my spine, through my core, and down to my toes.

There's an ache in my center as I accommodate his size, but he takes his time, allowing me to stretch to him.

Once he's seated inside me, he doesn't take his lips off mine.

He devours my every gasp with his mouth as he pumps into me. His piercings create a unique friction that fulfills something I hadn't even known I was missing. They rub against my walls, stroking me with each of his thrusts.

His hot mouth tangles with mine, his full lips searing into me, and it feels like literal sparks are flying between us.

I've never experienced anything like this in my life.

His movements become less smooth as he fights to restrain himself. "So gorgeous," he whispers to me, and the way he says it cracks my soul open.

We both near the peak of our pleasure, and as we do, our cries intermingle as we come apart together. And when he holds my cheeks in his strong hands, gazing down at me like I'm a figment of his imagination that could disappear at any moment, a single tear slips down his cheek, and the alarm bells from earlier ring loudly in my mind.

My heart seizes in my chest, constricting as my gut wrenches wildly.

This isn't "we're finally doing this" sex.

No. He thinks it's *goodbye sex.*

Chapter Eighty-Four

Luca

Samara's expression turns to confusion. My hands are gripping her cheeks as I take her in. Her every feature, making a mental note of each of them for every time I wish she were with me, but she won't be.

She covers my hands with hers and holds them steady as they begin to shake.

"Luca," she says softly.

I clear my throat before daring to speak again. "Yes, princess?"

"What exactly do you think is going on here?" she asks, her voice still quiet.

I can't even answer her, knowing that I have no right to feel as torn up about this as I do. She was clear from the start, and I'm the one who went and became emotionally invested.

I knew this would break me.

But I did it anyway.

At least I know she was worth it. *Because every moment spent with Samara has been worth the inevitable soul-shattering heartache I'm about to experience for the first time in my life.*

"Luca, you've gotta talk to me here because I think there might be a misunderstanding, and there's nothing I hate more than miscommunication when it could be easily solved by both people opening their damn mouths," she tells me, her voice now a more familiar volume.

I work my jaw, trying to unlatch it from its hinges so I can finally speak, but my tongue is glued to the roof of my mouth.

When I manage to speak, my voice sounds as choked up as I feel. "I figured if I only got one more night with you, we may as well make it a good one. Go out with a bang, ya know?"

I try to lighten the mood with a chuckle, but the sound never makes it out of my throat.

She squeezes her eyes closed, dropping her hands from mine and rolling out from under me. Samara sits up, staring me down as she shakes her head, seemingly in disappointment. "Luca, you stupid, *stupid* boy."

"I know," I agree. "It was stupid. You told me from the beginning that we weren't ever going to be anything, and here I am," I say, smacking my forehead with my palm, feeling even more like an idiot now that I've spoken the words out in the open.

I feel her wrench my hand away from my face as she clutches the fine layer of hair in the center of my chest. "No! God, Luca. This isn't goodbye sex!" she shouts.

"This is 'hello' sex!" she says, her voice an octave higher.

"'See you in the morning' sex!" Her voice continues to climb. "'Let's do this again' sex! 'Cuddle me after this' sex! 'Let's go another round' sex!"

I stare at her, stunned, my mouth agape. "I'm sorry, what?" I ask, tilting my head, hoping the confusion I'm feeling will lift enough for me to fully grasp her words.

She grabs my cheeks between her palms and pierces me with her gaze. "You, Luca De Laurentiis, are a fucking *prize.* And I'm a fool for taking this long to realize it. And no, before you do that dumb shit your brain is probably formulating up there," she says, tapping on my forehead with her index finger, "I don't mean that I suddenly found clarity after having sex with you. I like *you*, Luca. Not just your dick. *You*, the sweet, funny, kind, compassionate man who drives me up a goddamn wall and simultaneously keeps me from jumping off the top of that same wall when my family is driving me nuts. *You,* the man who had a literal child thrown into his life with absolutely no warning, and still managed to do the right thing, pick up the pieces, and then shock me in my own courtroom by still finding that compassion woven so thoroughly into you that you can find empathy for just about anyone, even the woman who didn't tell you about that child. *You*, Luca, the man who I've been fighting so damn hard not to fall for, and yet, somehow, you've made that feel impossible." When she's finished, she's panting with the effort it took to shout directly into my face that long.

The understanding that Samara is falling for me, though definitely not as hard as I've fallen for her, knocks me flat on my ass, but the weight I've been carrying around, waiting for an entirely different outcome to this night, leaves me immediately. The corners of my mouth turn up, and finally, I can speak. "You like me?" I tease.

There's that eye roll I love so damn much. "You're insufferable." She huffs. "But yes," she confirms, her voice softening. "Very much."

I meld my lips against hers and pull her body down beside me in bed.

"Too much, I think," she whispers softly.

My lips brush over her hair, and I just hold her.

My heart squeezes tightly in my chest, an unfamiliar serenity enveloping me as I dig through the pieces of tonight and list out the most important ones.

Kat and Alessandro are finally married, and the wedding was beautiful.

They're adopting a little boy named Oliver, who I'm bound to love more than life itself, just like I do all of my nieces and nephews. I love being an uncle.

The next one makes me feel every bit like the idiot that Samara told me I am. *I thought this was our last night together.*

And the last thought makes my heart pound so hard and fast it might just explode out of my chest. I was wrong, and more than that, *she wants to be with me.*

Minutes that feel like hours pass by, and when she rolls over, still facing me, I have another question on the tip of my tongue.

My brows pinch slightly as I look down into those warm-brown eyes I adore. "Call me apprehensive, sweetheart, but I can't just accept that you're falling for me because I'm simply the best," I start, making sure I'm being open and honest to avoid any further miscommunication between us. "We need to have a real conversation about this. I want to know the real reason, *every* reason that you ever felt you couldn't trust me or that things between us wouldn't work. Because as much as I want them to, they won't if we aren't honest from the jump."

She nods, taking a moment to gather her thoughts.

"When I first met you, I was jealous and pissed off." My head rears back as surprise clutches at my neck. *What was there to be jealous of?* I was a wreck when we met. Hell, I still sort of am. "I had recently finished a round of IVF that I decided was going to be my last, and with no baby in sight despite years of trying, here you were, asking for my help after a perfect, healthy little girl fell right into your arms."

A gnawing feeling eats away at my sternum. I rub my hand over the spot, trying to soothe the ache as if it were physical. "I may not be able to understand your personal experience with infertility, but I can imagine that that would be really upsetting. Especially working with parents every day who actually do know their children and need to fight to keep them."

"That definitely didn't help," she agrees, but her lips pinch and her glossy eyes only add to the soreness I feel. "But then when I looked into you and found that article, coupled with the endless stream of beautiful women you were photographed with, it made me feel even more like you weren't deserving." The look on her face is so pained I want to do anything in my power to wipe it right off.

"To tell you the truth, every day that I get to see my gorgeous little girl, I feel undeserving. Imposter syndrome has threatened to strangle me practically my entire life, and it's no different with Gia." I shake my head, squeezing the bridge of my nose as the burning in my nostrils subsides. "Just like when I blame myself for every loss in the rink and hold myself personally responsible even though I know it's a team sport, I do the same with Gia. And when I realize something isn't working or I'm not at my best, I work for it. I strive to be the father she deserves, and I'll work toward being the partner you deserve too."

She bites the corner of her lip before she says, "I see that now, Luca. And I'm not just saying that. I've seen you grow as a father and a prospective partner every day. You always put the needs of others ahead of your own, but you aren't too caught up to forget to ask for help when it's what's best for both you and Gia." Her words are like a warm, tight hug, and my heart sings with her praise. "I'm proud of you and the way you and Cici have managed to co-parent so beautifully," she admits. Tears stream down her cheeks, and I kiss them away, clutching her to my chest.

"Thank you, princess. That means more than you know," I say into her hair. "Now lay it on me. What else do we need to cover before we agree to really be together? Why did you pull back from me after we got back from our vacation?" I feel my muscles tense. I know I'm the one asking for this, but it's a unique kind of self-inflicted torture as if I'm reminding her of all the reasons she may still choose to leave me.

But I'd rather know now.

Her sniffles quiet. "I was jealous," she whispers, and the embarrassed way she says it has me coughing to cover up my laughter.

"Sorry, sweetheart. What was that? You were what?"

Her dark eyes shoot up to pin me with a glare. "I said," she answers dramatically, "I was fucking jealous." She swats at my chest, and the fiery look in her eyes sends tingles through me. I love it when she gets all riled up like this. "I was jealous of the women flirting with you at baggage claim."

I snort, and it's loud and obnoxious, but she doesn't bother trying to hide her amusement. "You know, I don't think you ever mentioned them, but I had barely noticed them. Unfortunately, it comes with being a professional athlete. I'm so used to brushing people like that off that I rarely pay attention anymore. But I want you to trust me when I say that I will continue to fend them off, and I'll even wear a giant sign telling everyone that my body and my heart belong to Samara Perez-Allen, and anyone who dares to try you will suffer a great deal."

"You're absurd," she says with a laugh.

I reach over to the nightstand and grab my phone, typing my name into the search bar.

"What are you doing?" she asks, confused.

I move the phone in front of her face and watch as it registers for her. I slowly begin scrolling through the images. "I know you wouldn't ask me to do this, but I just wanted to make absolutely certain that you knew. I haven't so much as looked at another woman since Gia arrived at my home and haven't wanted to since meeting you."

Her eyes begin to well with tears. "Arielle explained what really happened in that photo," she tells me.

I smile at her. "I know, princess," I say, kissing the top of her head. "There's nothing that happens in my family that we don't all know about. You better get used to it." I smirk.

"But I need you to understand why it upset me so much," she says.

"You can tell me anything, Samara," I answer, though I'm not sure I'll be able to handle it if she's dealt with even half as much as Arielle has firsthand. It'll crush my heart, and I can't be held liable for the things I'd do to whoever hurt her.

She peers up at me with glossy eyes pooling with tears. "When I was in law school, my best friend, Cora, still lived here. She had gotten married at the courthouse after her boyfriend got her pregnant," she says, her voice cracking.

I lean into her, kissing a fallen tear off her cheek.

"I didn't even know what was going on with her until it was too late," she says, her words breaking on a sob. Guilt flows freely through her voice, and the familiar constricting feeling of my throat closing and eyes burning with unshed tears hits me like a tidal wave.

I continue rubbing soothing circles along her back, allowing her the time she needs to find her words. "Her daughter was only two at the time, and when she finally got up the courage to leave him, he used it against her. She made it to the shelter and was *so damn close*, but then he convinced her that if she didn't come back, he'd take her to court. And as a Black woman with no job, she was too terrified to take the chance."

She blows out a breath, shaking her arms out to recenter herself before continuing. "When she returned, he killed them both and then himself."

Her words leave me stunned, and rage rips through me. I wrap my arms around her, clutching her to my chest as she continues to sob.

"I can't even begin to imagine how difficult that must have been for you," I whisper. "But I'm so goddamn proud of you for everything you do for the women at the shelter and just for being you."

"I'm sorry, Luca," she says once her cries have stopped. "I misjudged you so much, and I shouldn't have put all of that on you." Her voice is strained and quiet.

Kissing the top of her head, I roll her on top of me so I can hold all of her. "I'm not sure what you're apologizing for, but there's no need. I've been reckless in how I've let the media portray me, and that's no one's fault but my own."

I press another kiss to the top of her head.

She brings her lips to mine, kissing me slowly. Every emotion she's felt in the last twenty-four hours sinks into my skin as she does.

"There are things I don't know how to do. Things I'm not very good at yet. I've never felt this way about anyone else in my life and that means something to me. I *want* to put in the effort, for you, and for *us*. I might need a little direction sometimes, but I'm good at making corrections. My career depends on it."

"What are you saying, Luca?" she asks, always so blunt. Yet another thing I love about her.

"I'm saying that I recognize that I'll never truly understand the intricacies of the struggles you face on a daily basis, but I want to learn. I want to bear some of that weight with you, and learn what *you* need from me as a friend and as a partner."

She peers up at me with her big, soulful eyes. "Luca, as a woman, I have to work twice as hard, and as a Black woman, three times as hard to be afforded the same respect as my colleagues. That extends outside of the workplace. My Blackness is a part of who I am, and I *love* my culture and am honored by the strength of the people who've laid the groundwork for all that I've accomplished, but make no mistake that there will be things you'll have to endure too. Interracial couples experience racism every day, and the fact that you're a white hockey player doesn't change that."

My heart clenches tightly, thumping painfully against my ribcage. "I'm not worried about me, Samara. I'd walk through fire to get to you, sweetheart. I just need to know that I'm what you want, and that *you* are willing to deal with even more societal pressure and stigma by being with me. I'll understand if you're not." *It would break my heart, but I would understand and respect her decision.* "Anything you need to feel comfortable and safe, I'm willing to do or learn how to."

She reaches her hand up to cup my cheek, her eyes glittering with unshed tears. "For you, Luca, I'm willing to try."

That's all the confirmation I need.

I take her hand, turning my cheek to press a kiss to her palm. "Thank you," I whisper, folding my body around hers, tugging the covers up under her chin.

She lets me hold her the entire night, and it's easily the most restful sleep I've ever gotten in my life.

When I wake up with this stunning, capable, strong, and fearless woman in my arms, I know without a shadow of a doubt...

She's the one.

Epilogue Part One: Samara

Tuesday, December 22, 2026

I'm in the stands, surrounded by Luca's family and an arena filled with thousands of his fan base. We're all jumping, shouting at the top of our lungs, and it's all for *my man.*

I've got Gia latched onto my hip, and luckily, she's in her element when it's chaotic like this. I guess that comes along with having such a loud-ass family.

A loud-ass family that I adore, but loud, no less.

I point to the center of the ice where Luca is doing his celly. "Look, baby girl, there's your daddy! He won the game!"

She babbles excitedly but, obviously, has no idea what's going on.

Despite that, my eyes still widen in shock each time I see him reach this part of his signature celly. I clamp my hand over her eyes. "You *definitely* don't need to see that," I tell her.

"She better pray that man is retired before she starts school, or she's going to have a lot of embarrassment to combat," Arielle says.

"That's one way to grow a thick skin," Charlie adds with a snicker.

When the game is officially over, we meet the guys in the tunnel, ready to head home for dinner.

Luca makes it out into the hall, and his eyes lock on mine. The reporters trying to get his attention are no match for his long strides.

He beelines over to me, blowing a kiss at Gia, who's now latched onto Arielle's hip, giving my back a much-needed break. Luca's arms wrap around me, and he lifts me off the ground, spinning me in circles with reckless abandon. I giggle as he does this but shout playfully at him, "One of these days, you're going to knock me right into someone."

He smashes his lips to mine for a chaste kiss and smiles widely, that damned dimple shining back at me. "Well then, they better stay the hell out of our way." He places me gently back on the ground and reaches for Gia. "Isn't that right, Gia, *mia bambina*? They better stay out of our way," he reiterates, pressing a kiss to the top of her head.

A few female fans try to interject as we head out of the building. I've gotten over my jealousy. Luca has proven himself loyal, time and time again, sometimes even to a fault.

Like right now as these women shout for him, one of them gripping his bicep to get his attention. His eyes widen with annoyance, and his gaze swings to hers. He gently plucks her hand off him and drops it as if it were a piece of trash. "Ew," is all he says, and Arielle, Kat, and I have to cover our mouths to contain our laughter.

"Ruthless," Ale says, chuckling as he joins our group, heading toward the parking lot.

"What?" Luca asks, not the least bit apologetic for his actions. "Firstly, you don't put your hands on other people without their permission." He looks down at Gia. "Take notes, kid. You don't do a great job of that, considering I keep waking up with your slobbery fist in my mouth when I try to take a nap." He goes on, addressing the rest of us again. "Second, how fucking—" His eyes widen as he clamps a hand down on Gia's ear. "Oops, sorry." He snickers. "As I was saying, how stupid can you be? My woman is right beside me, wearing *my* jersey with *my* number on her back. Freaking rude," he finishes.

"And what a stupid number it is." I nearly cackle.

He wags his dark brows at me. "That's not what you were saying last night." His smirk tells me just how proud of himself he is, and I can't bring myself to crush it.

"And if you're good, maybe I'll let you try it out again," I say with a wink.

His brows climb his forehead, and his light eyes shoot to Alessandro. "Practice makes perfect, right, Coach?"

"Jesus Christ," Ale says, winding his arm around Kat's waist and pressing a kiss to Oliver's head. "Come on, let's get out of here. Your Uncle Luca is creeping me out."

Epilogue Part Two: Luca

TUESDAY, JULY 10, 2029

"Just a few more pushes and they'll be out of there! Come on, you've got this!" Giuliana, the physician assistant, chants, encouraging her the entire way through.

"You're doing incredible; you've got this!" I tell her. *I'm so damn proud.*

"Get them out of me!" she screeches through the pain.

"Baby A's head is out! Give me another strong push. Come on!" the PA says. The RNs gathered in the room are waiting to collect the babies one by one, ensuring their safety with each step.

She takes a deep, steadying breath and shoots me a death glare as she starts the last push. "Fuck yes, you've got this! Almost there!" I'm yelling, cheering her on the way I would someone on my hockey team. I feel like a douche, but it seems to be working.

Their whole body nearly flies out, and that's the moment the waterworks hit me.

"Dad, do you wanna do the honors?" the PA asks excitedly, nodding down to our son or daughter. We waited till this very moment to find out the sexes, and I couldn't be more happy we did.

Emotion wells in my chest. "It's a boy," I say, my voice cracking. I turn away, clutching my heart as a sob wracks through me. My cheeks tighten, and I can't help the tears that spill over uncontrollably. My eyes burn, but Samara's steady hand brings me back to reality.

She's sitting beside Arielle in her own hospital gown, waiting to do skin-to-skin.

"It's a boy," she says to me in a small voice, her eyes brimming with tears. She's wearing a smile that has me bursting with joy.

"It's a boy," I whisper back to her. "One more to go." *God, I hope it's a girl.* I won't hear the end of it from Gia if we don't manage at least one girl, and frankly, raising her has been the most incredible experience of my life. I'd be more than happy to do it all over again.

The nurse brings our son over to us and places him directly on Samara's waiting chest for skin-to-skin.

"This is so surreal," she says, holding him tightly against her.

The nurse looks to me and asks, "Do you want to do skin-to-skin for baby B?"

My eyes immediately swing to Samara. She's waited countless years for this moment. I would never want to take it from her, but I'd give nearly anything to get to hold our next baby in my arms for a moment like this.

"Would that be okay?" I ask my gorgeous wife. Somehow, she's even more stunning with our handsome little guy perched on her chest, nuzzling himself further into her.

"Of course, baby. This is as much your moment as it is mine." She smiles at me, and it strangles my heart.

"Then fuck yeah, I'd love that!" I tell the nurse excitedly, pulling my shirt off over my head immediately.

Samara releases a loud cackle. "I don't think you need to get shirtless just yet."

"Am I distracting you?" I wink at her, and I earn one of her signature eye rolls.

"Always," she says with a smirk.

I turn my attention back to Arielle, who's lying in a position I was certain I'd never see, nor had I wanted to, but fuck, am I grateful for her.

"I get that these are your kids, but if you could stop staring at my wife's pussy, I'd appreciate it," Dante grits out as he catches me staring. Though there's absolutely nothing sexual about this. I'm just fucking amazed at what the human body can do, and getting to see my children born is astonishing. It's something I missed with Gia and I'm so thankful I get to experience this time.

I chuckle at his brashness. "I'm not looking at her *vagina*; I'm just checking to see if the next one's ready to make their appearance."

"Giuliana will tell you when they are, so stop fucking looking," he tells me, and immediately, I avert my gaze back to Samara, who's sucking her cheeks in, holding back her laughter.

"Will you two just shut the fuck up?" Arielle grits out, and when I look back over my shoulder at her, I swear I see steam pluming out of her ears.

"Giuliana, please don't let me miss anything, okay?"

She nods, and I crouch down in front of Samara and our son. I rest my hand on the back of his head, his soft brown curls tickling my fingertips.

"What should we name him?" I ask her, my eyes welling with more tears.

She may not have gotten to grow these little guys in her belly, but she's finally able to have this moment.

I'd have done *anything* to give her this.

I know she adores Gia, and they share the most special bond that will never cease to amaze me, but this part is just so freaking cool. It's a first for us both.

"Ajani. It means 'noble birth' and is a traditional Jamaican boy's name," she tells me.

"Ajani," I repeat, letting the letters roll around in my mouth. We've written a very long list of names but couldn't settle on anything until we actually met them. Plus, not knowing if we were having two boys, two girls, or one of each made it even more difficult. "Something tells me you'd already decided on this name a while ago," I tell her, my lips curving in a lopsided grin. "Ajani it is," I say.

She smiles at me before looking down at him. "Happy birthday, Ajani," she whispers to our son.

"I should've had another fucking water birth," Arielle screams beside us. She had one with a doula and midwife for all of her other pregnancies, which we were totally on board for, but with the increased risk of complications and there being two of them, she said she wanted the epidural. Ultimately, it was her decision to make, as it's her birthing experience, not ours.

"You're almost there, Arielle. You're so close; their head is *right there*, just give me another big push!"

I stand to let her squeeze my hand, and the RN comes around to take Ajani from us so the neonatologist can check him out under the warmer. Samara stands beside me, placing a cool cloth on Arielle's forehead. "Come on, Arielle, you've got this. Get them out of there, and I swear to god, I'll send you and D on the cruise of a lifetime," Samara tells her.

Arielle's eyes cut straight to her. "As soon as my coochie is back in working order, *you* are watching *all* of the children so I can get dicked down by my husband," she growls.

I can tell Giuliana is doing her best to hide her laugh but is failing miserably. Her face contorts, and her shoulders are shaking with the repressed laughter.

I look down and see the head poking through. My eyes are wide as realization cuts through me. "So much hair!" I practically screech, and Samara smacks the back of my head. Then Arielle grabs my hand and squeezes it so tightly I think she might have actually fractured something as pain sears up my arm, but I ignore it. She's doing the hard part here. A few broken fingers are a small price to pay.

She screams as everyone in the room is cheering her on, and finally, the head is out. "Arielle, don't push. We've got a nuchal cord," Giuliana announces to the RN, who starts typing in the chart.

"What's that?" I ask, feeling frantic, my heart rate bounding.

"Calm down, it's alright. The cord is just wrapped around their neck. It happens all the time," Samara assures me.

Giuliana nods her head, keeping her eyes trained on our kid. "Babies have a tendency to get a little tangled in there, but like Momma said, it's completely fine."

I watch as Giuliana skillfully slips her finger under the cord and reduces it before repositioning, placing her hands on either side of their head and curling her fingers under their jaw. "Alright, Arielle, one last big push and you're all done!"

Arielle's face turns bright red as she pushes our baby out, and the moment they burst through, the waterworks are back. "It's a girl!" Samara shouts, turning her wide eyes on mine.

"Either of you wanna cut the cord?"

I press a kiss to Samara's cheek. "Your turn, princess," I tell her, and she gladly does after we wait for the delayed cord clamping—the same as we had with Ajani moments ago.

Once our little girl is all cleaned off, she's in my arms and on my chest. I hold her snug to me as she wriggles around.

"Welcome to the world, Chiara," I whisper to her and realize my mistake immediately.

"Chiara, huh?" Samara asks, a brow quirked at me, but there's no bite to her tone. She's fully smirking. "When did you plan to tell me you'd officially decided on a name?"

"Uh, right now?" I ask, giving her an apologetic smile as my cheeks burn.

"You're lucky I'd decided on Chiara already too." She laughs, and the sound fills my chest with those familiar butterflies I've grown accustomed to.

Samara wraps her arms around me from behind, resting her chin on my shoulder.

"I love you, Luca," she whispers into my ear.

"I love you more, *principessa*."

And I mean it. There's not a chance in hell that this woman could love me more than what I feel for her. Some days, it feels like I'm overflowing with affection for her, and it threatens to choke the life out of me when I imagine a world without her in it.

That's a world I never want to be a part of.

Because, for me, *this* is my world. Samara, Gia, and now Chiara and Ajani too. Just like Chiara's name suggests, they're the light of my life.

And what an incredible life it is.

Epilogue Part Two: Samara

My heart has never been so full as it is at this moment. I never thought this day would come. I'd completely given up hope that I'd get this chance, and frankly, once Gia had embedded herself into my very being, that didn't bother me quite as much.

I love her as if she were my own flesh and blood because, as far as I'm concerned, she may as well be.

That kid has brightened even the worst days for me, just like her daddy. I guess it runs in the family.

And right now, as my back aches from this blow-up mattress that Luca demanded we bring to the hospital, saying, "My wife isn't sleeping on one of those glorified plastic tables the hospitals call a pull-out bed," I couldn't care less. My cheeks ache from smiling so much, and even though I know last night will have been the last full night of sleep I'll be getting for a while, *this* is more than I could've ever hoped for.

Arielle is fast asleep, snoring loudly in the postpartum hospital bed they swapped her to after cleaning her up. Dante's squished in beside her with an arm slung over her deflating belly.

Luca is sprawled out on the tiny pull-out seat, his long limbs spilling over the edge and his cheek pressed into the dark-blue plastic, his mouth hanging open and drool pooling out.

Ajani and Chiara are swaddled in their bassinets just feet from me.

And tomorrow morning, Cici and Paul will bring Gia to meet her siblings, and Gloria, Angelo, and my parents will get to meet their newest grandchildren.

I know without a shadow of a doubt that there's no better feeling than this.

This is where I'm meant to be.

I couldn't have dreamed of a better life, and I just know, deep in my soul, that Cora's here somehow, acting to *stabilize* me. I can feel her presence like a familiar squeeze of my hand or a hug when I've had a rough day. She's ever-present, and more than anything, *she's proud.*

And so am I.

The end.

Bonus Epilogue: Luca

Saturday, October 23, 2032

"What are the chances your mom doesn't do something that'll scar our kid for life?" Cici asks Samara and me.

"I'm not a gambler, but I'd bet that our chances of that are extremely low," Samara says with a chuckle.

"Alright, Paul, you're the math whiz. What are our odds?" I direct the question at Paul, Cici's husband, the accountant.

He looks up into the corner of the room, wiggling his pointer finger in the air, pretending to do the math. Hell, maybe he really *is* doing the math. Very little would surprise me at this point.

"I'm going with a solid 0.03 percent," he finally answers with a snort.

"Better than I thought," I remark. Samara grins at me, wrapping her arms around my bicep and leaning her head on my shoulder.

I'm about to kiss the top of her head when our kids come zooming toward us like three little tornados.

"Moms! Dads!" Gia shouts at the four of us. "Did you see Nonna's cake? It's huge!" she says excitedly, waving her little arms in the air to indicate just how *huge.*

"Yeah, baby girl, it's her sixtieth birthday. She's gotta make the most of it," Samara tells her before sitting Gia on her lap.

Ajani and Chiara are bouncing with excitement as the lights start to dim, and the band begins a literal drum roll.

All three kids start tapping their fingers on the edge of the table along with the sound. The absolutely massive cake in question gets wheeled out into the center of the room by my dad, who's dressed like an overly extravagant magician and is wearing an extremely weary look on his face. Every adult in the room has the same reaction.

Gianni's sitting at a piano pushed off to the side, his guitar lying over the top. Lark is sitting beside him, holding a tambourine, which is still the only instrument she's really learned to play despite Gi's lessons.

When Dad looks back at him, Gi scrubs a hand down his face, and his pinched lips have my gut twisting.

A chorus of "Oh no" and "She didn't" erupts in the room seconds before my mom does. *Literally.*

She pops out of the cake wearing a red vintage tassel dress and a glittery headpiece to match. Gianni swaps from the piano to the guitar, the pained expression still prevalent on his face as Lark taps her tambourine on the palm of her hand, her smile wide as she works to contain her laughter.

Kat is clutching at her roots, looking as stressed as ever. I swear, even in the dark room, I can see her cheeks flaming bright pink.

Ale wraps his arms around her, a wide smile plastered on his face as he laughs into her hair.

Their oldest, Nataly, turned twenty this year, and she's turned into the coolest adult. I see her seated at their table, keeping Oliver occupied as they color together. Nat glances up, smirking and shaking her head at my mom, who's apparently trying to get herself killed.

Mom grabs for Dad's hand, and he shakes his head in embarrassment but grips her hand tightly, supporting her as she climbs out of the fucking cake, looking like a newborn baby giraffe.

And for all intents and purposes, *she may as well be.*

"I didn't know she was cleared to walk yet," Samara whispers to me, her mouth agape.

"She wasn't," I grit out.

When I retired, I was bored half to death. I needed something to do, and when Mom was approved for a new clinical trial that gave us hope that she might be able to walk again, I knew exactly what I wanted to spend my time doing.

I went back to school and got a degree in physiotherapy, and when the medication started working, I got to be there, every step of the way, for my mom, just like she's been for me all these years.

Helping her gain her strength back and relearn how to walk has been every bit as incredible as raising my kids and being there for their first steps.

But this woman has officially lost it.

"I'll be right back," I tell Samara, standing to rush over to my parents.

"What's Nonna doing?" Ajani asks his momma in a hushed whisper as I rush toward the stage.

"Mom," I groan out. "We talked about this. No walking without your rollator until the doctor can evaluate you and clear you!" I whisper-yell at her.

"Don't take that tone with me, Luca. It's my sixtieth birthday, and I intend to do it up big. So you'll either help me get my ass back over to my damn chair because my legs fucking hurt, or you'll just have to watch as your father and I do it alone."

"Please, help. My back hurts." Dad groans from the other side of Mom.

I roll my eyes at her. "You're becoming even more stubborn in your old age."

Her head veers back as if I'd just slapped her. "Did you—" Her mouth hangs unhinged. "Did you just cuss at your mother?"

"Oh, now you've really done it," Dad says, shaking his head but letting me take on Mom's weight as I lead her back to her chair.

"You stop it." I laugh. Once she's seated, I squat down beside her and look into her big blue eyes. "I love you, Mom, and I'm unbelievably proud of you. Now, for the love of god, please use your walker."

She gently taps my cheek with her hand and smiles down at me. "Fine, but only because you asked nicely."

I press a kiss to her cheek and stand, heading back toward our table. I faintly hear Mom start blabbering into the microphone about something, but I can't seem to pay attention because at that table are all of my wildest dreams come true. Between Samara and our three kids, my heart feels like it could explode with love, and yet, growing up the way I did helped me learn that there's always room for more love in your life.

Bonus Epilogue: Samara

Luca and I stumble into the house, his hands gripping my ass as we make our way over the threshold with our mouths still connected.

"Thank fuck for Paul and Cici," he grunts as he sets me down to lock the door.

Even though Ajani and Chiara aren't theirs in any way, they've been a huge help in watching them a couple of nights a month when they have Gia.

Mr. Whiskers sits still as an old, grumpy-ass gargoyle on the entryway table, pointing daggers at Luca and me. The damn cat hates everyone besides the kids. Luca blows him a kiss. "Sorry, little guy, no time for all the cuddles I just *know* you're desperate for. I've gotta take care of *my wife*."

When his eyes meet mine, a wide smile spreads across his face. "I'm glad we actually *have* a cat now. Doesn't it feel good to not have to lie about that?" he asks me with a wink.

"*Dickhead*," I say, rolling my eyes, but I feel heat climb up my neck in response to the memory.

The moment the word leaves my mouth, Luca has a glint in his gorgeous eyes and a wicked grin that settles deep into my core.

"Samara," he says, gripping my hips and dragging my body against his. He runs the tip of his nose up the length of my neck, breathing me in and nipping the sensitive skin behind my ear. "Is my wife ready to have all her holes filled tonight?"

"Yes," I whisper, my breath caught in my throat.

Luca cups my ass, spreading my cheeks and slipping over my tight hole.

"How did I get so lucky?" he asks, thrusting his hips into mine so I know just how lucky he thinks he is.

His dick is so hard, it's a miracle his pants haven't split at the seams. My body tingles with need as he walks us backward until we're in the kitchen with my ass pressed firmly against the cold granite countertop.

A chill wracks through my body, and goosebumps erupt all over.

Luca effortlessly lifts me onto the counter, slipping his hands back under my dress and running them along my thighs before pushing the fabric up my body to expose me to him. He takes a step back, his hands never leaving me.

He shakes his head slowly in that way he always does when he's contemplating something. "You get more and more gorgeous every goddamn day, and I think if you don't cut it out, I'm gonna die of a heart attack one day. My heart can only take so much, *principessa.*"

I feel my cheeks heat, but he doesn't allow me time to respond. His hands are back on me, pulling my dress up and over my head.

My heavy breasts bounce on my chest from the lack of support from the tight fabric that had been holding them in all night.

He dips his head, capturing one of my nipples in his mouth, and a lock of his dark hair tickles my chest as he sucks.

Heat pools in my core, and tingles erupt throughout my chest. Luca nips and sucks, prying my thighs apart as he moves down my body, goosebumps following the path of his fingers on me. I feel my muscles strung so tight I might break, but he finally drops to his knees, pulling me toward him.

"You're not allowed to finish like this, okay? I just want a little taste before we really get started," he tells me, pushing my legs even wider to accommodate his massive shoulders.

"Fine," I agree reluctantly.

He chuckles, and his tongue darts out, skimming up my seam.

I fall back against the counter, holding myself up on my fore-arms.

A shiver rolls through me, and my clit throbs with every swipe of his tongue. He's moaning as he laps me up, and it's my favorite sound in the world.

"Luca, yes!" I cry, pushing my hips further into his face.

"So fucking good," he mumbles between licks.

My back arches into his touch, and my chest heaves as tingles spread from my core down my legs.

An aching need consumes me, and as I feel my core spasm, he pulls away, his lips glistening with my arousal.

A garbled whine slips past my clenched teeth, and it only makes Luca laugh as I clench my fists at my sides.

He shakes his head at me, that godforsaken dimpled smirk undoing my frustrations as he wraps his hands around my hips and hauls me over his shoulder.

If you had asked me prior to meeting this brute of a man if I ever thought my life would entail being tossed around by some caveman who thinks he's Tarzan, I'd have assumed you were on something, but here I am.

Stranger shit has happened, though, I guess.

"Come on, princess, your throne awaits you," he murmurs, cupping my ass cheek. My core tightens as he swipes a finger through my slickness and then between my cheeks, circling the rim of my ass.

"My throne?" I choke out.

"Mhmm, 'throne,' 'my dick,' same thing. 'Toe-may-toe,' 'toe-mah-toe,'" he says.

A loud laugh jolts out of me before he tosses me into the center of the bed, crawling over top of me.

He bends his head, nipping at the corner of my lip and scraping my jaw with his stubble.

"I love you so much, princess," he whispers. "I'm fucking obsessed with you."

Warmth floods my chest. "Right back at ya, baby. I love you more than I'd ever imagined possible."

A low rumble of approval leaves his chest, and he bites out the words, "*Then show me just how much.*"

If you'd like to read the rest of this fun-filled night for Luca and Samara, join my Patreon to be the first to see it. You never know when it'll arrive in your account.[1]

1. Patreon:

Afterword

I felt it was necessary for me to end this series on a high note because it didn't feel right not including a win for Gloria and of course, my first love, Alessandro. I wanted to give all of my readers who are either living with multiple sclerosis or who love someone who is a glimpse into the future that I envision for these strong, badass individuals. As someone with not one, but two people in my life who live with MS, this was always the ending I had thought they deserved.

So no, there is not currently a cure for MS. But it's my hope that one day, very soon, there will be. And when that day comes, I hope you'll all take that for the miracle it is and live every day like you have a new lease on life.

I'll always be here, rooting for you all in your successes, especially on the low days that leave you wanting to give up.

You never know when a cure will be found, so don't give up hope. Live every day to the absolute fullest, and if you're struggling with your mental health either as a result of this god-fucking-awful disease or just because life is really fucking hard sometimes, reach out. Reach out to me. Reach out to a friend. To a counselor, a teacher, a parent, or a family member. Just please, say something.

You are worthy of joy.

All my love,

Giuliana Victoria <3

Please continue to the next page for an important message from the author about domestic violence.

The following information may be triggering to some readers. Content warnings include explicit discussion of domestic violence. Please do not turn the page if this may be harmful to your emotional well-being or if you are not in a safe space to be reading this.

***

Message From The Author

On average, it takes a victim of domestic violence seven tries before they actually leave their abuser. So, in case you know someone who you feel is a lost cause and you're tired of pleading with them to leave, *do not give up.* They need your encouragement and strength to lean on.

"Why does this matter? It'll never happen to me, right?" Think again.

1 in 3 women, 1 in 4 men, 1 in 2 trans or non-binary people, and 1 in 3 teens in the US have experienced physical violence, sexual assault, and/or stalking by an intimate partner in their lifetime.

Domestic violence is a universal community issue. It occurs in relationships regardless of race or ethnicity, socioeconomic status, sexual orientation, religious background, age, geographic location, etc.

Do you know when the most dangerous time is for a person experiencing DV? *It's after they've left their abuser.*

Seventy-five percent of all domestic violence homicides occurred while either attempting to leave or after having left the relationship.

This should not deter you from seeking help. It's to inform you so you can make the best, most informed decisions for yourself based on a plan that ensures your safety.

If you or someone you know needs help, please find a safe time to call one of the hotlines below. Aid with childcare, housing, job searches, legal fees, and emergency restraining orders are just a few of the services available to you.

Please reach out to someone.

There is no excuse for violence in any form. No amount of alcohol, recreational drug use, no "bad day," or anything you've done is an excuse for abuse.

You are strong, capable, and unbelievably deserving of a happy, safe, and fulfilling life, and no one has the right to make you feel otherwise.

The information below is available if you ever need it, and I sincerely hope you never do.

United States: https://www.thehotline.org/

International: https://nomoredirectory.org/

For the international hotline, simply select your continent followed by your country to receive a list of toll-free hotlines in your area.

For more statistics on DV:

https://domesticviolenceresearch.org/domestic-violence-facts-and-statistics-at-a-glance/

Acknowledgements

I'm seriously in awe every single day that these books even exist in the world. I mean that wholeheartedly. So when I say that this world that I've created would not exist without each and every single one of you absolutely incredible, gorgeous, intelligent, and all-around wonderful people, I MEAN EXACTLY THAT!

You've supported me and managed to help me make all of my dreams a reality, which is truly wild, considering my day to day is spent fighting the whims of ADHD and the several really extravagant dreams I have as a result of it.

So, thank you to each of you for making all of this possible. And a big cheers to the end of an era for the Philia Players series!

A massive thank you to Kai @_robyn.reads and Savannah (and her amazing mom) for aiding me with writing the Jamaican Patois used by Samara's father. To Shay, Chez, Kristin, Tiah, Essence, Sasha, Tiffany, Jessica, Nirvana, Kenya, Tati and Justine for sensitivity reading and for providing incredible feedback. To Evelyn Leigh, thank you for answering all of my questions and offering insight that was imperative in maintaining Samara's voice throughout this story. I love you immensely <3

And to each of my now over one hundred sensitivity readers who have thrown themselves into helping me write diverse stories while limiting potential harm to my equally diverse readers, you have all my love. I'm unbelievably grateful for your help!

PS. If you loved ***Shiver***, please consider leaving a review on Amazon, Goodreads, B&N, and anywhere else you review your books. As an indie author with no money, it seriously makes a world of difference in helping get my books out to the masses!

About the author

Giuliana Victoria is an author based in Pennsylvania who shares her readers' deep love of all things romance. She's a full-time physician assistant, whose passion lies in being there for her patients during their most vulnerable moments.

When Giuliana isn't writing swoon-worthy book boyfriends, she can be found yelling about human rights on Threads, hiking with her three large breed rescue dogs, and, of course, curled up with a good book beside her husband, the best "book boyfriend" there is.

She hopes you'll love ***Shiver*** as much as she enjoyed writing it, and she looks forward to sharing all of her future works with her incredible readers.

Some BIPOC Authors I Adore

& You Should Check Out!

Evelyn Leigh
Cynthia A. Rodriguez
Ruby Rana
Vai Denton
Kennedy Ryan
Nisha Sharma
Talia Hibbert
Shilo Kino
N.M. Patel
Natasha Bishop
Janisha Boswell
Deanna Grey
J.S. Jasper
Kristina Forest
A.E. Valdez
Miah Onsha
Anna P.
Varsha Chitnis
Amy Oliviera
Siren Crow

Mikayla Hornedo

Layna James

I.B. Solís

Britney S. Lewis

Danielle Brooks

Danica Nava

Ambar Cordova

Natalie Caña

Riss M. Neilson

Georgia K. Boone

MK Owens

Leigh Carron

AJ Alexander

Janiah Benitez

Nelle Nikole

Nouha Jullienne

H.M. Wolfe

Amber V. Nicole

Allie Shante

Santana Knox

Goddess A. Brouette

Ziye' Taylor

Tember Sapphire

Sophie Thomas

J.J. Greenaway

Ophelia Reign

L.M. Ramirez

Oona Arlo

Printed in Great Britain
by Amazon

60389489R00282